About the author

Chrissie Manby is the author of twenty romantic comedy novels and a guide for aspiring writers, *Writing for Love*. She was nominated for the Melissa Nathan Award for Comedy Romance in 2011 for *Getting Over Mr Right*.
Raised in Gloucester, Chrissie now lives in London.

You can follow her on Twitter @chrissiemanby or visit her website to find out more.
www.chrissiemanby.com

a Fairy Tale for Christmas

CHRISSIE MANBY

HODDER

First published in Great Britain in 2016 by Hodder & Stoughton
An Hachette UK company

5

A CIP catalogue record for this title is available
from the British Library

Paperback ISBN 978 1 473 63974 4
Ebook ISBN 978 1 473 63975 1

Typeset in Sabon MT by Palimpsest Book Production Ltd,
Falkirk, Stirlingshire

Printed and bound by Clays Ltd, St Ives plc

Hodder & Stoughton policy is to use papers that are natural,
renewable and recyclable products and made from wood
grown in sustainable forests. The logging and manufacturing
processes are expected to conform to the environmental
regulations of the country of origin.

Hodder & Stoughton Ltd
Carmelite House
50 Victoria Embankment
London EC4Y 0DZ

www.hodder.co.uk

To George Arthur Hazel

Chapter One

'Cinderella? I ask you? With feet the size of hers? Have you ever heard anything so ridiculous?' Jon leaned back in his seat and waved his fork in Kirsty's direction. 'We'll have to get a body double for the glass slipper scene.'

'Well, sweetheart,' said Kirsty. 'It was you who cast me as Cinders in the first place.'

'Would have been hell to pay if I hadn't,' Jon said with a knowing wink to one of the other guys at the dining table that night.

Kirsty smiled sweetly at her boyfriend of almost a year. Jon was usually very funny. He liked a joke. Kirsty told herself it wasn't *always* at her expense. Still, she tucked her feet a little further beneath her chair as he continued to tease her for the entertainment of their friends. She had thought her feet looked pretty in her new red leather ballet flats. Until Jon called them 'boat shoes' because 'they're the size of small canoes'.

'Tell me more about it,' said Jane, Kirsty's best friend, who was among their dinner guests that evening. 'I mean the pantomime, not your feet. I'm just glad you're going to be in the UK over Christmas. I've missed you so much.'

Kirsty had recently returned from a season spent working as a singer on a cruise ship. It was thanks to being on that ship – *The European Countess* – that she'd met Jon. He stage-managed one of the on-board shows in which Kirsty starred. In the first flush of romance Kirsty felt like a goddess every time she stepped out into the lights, knowing that Jon was watching from the wings. He had so many good ideas about improving her performance and he was always full of praise. He made her feel like a proper star. Now they were an official double act and it seemed she was playing the straight guy. Ah well.

'You'll make a fantastic Cinderella,' Jane continued. 'Your voice is so good. You'll carry the show.'

'Thank you,' said Kirsty.

'She will carry the show,' Jon agreed. 'Newbay won't know what's hit it when Kirsty lets rip with that incredible voice. But we'll have to get the shoes made at one of those transvestite outfitters,' he continued, oblivious to the fact that Kirsty's smile was slipping. 'I'm sure both the blokes playing the Ugly Sisters wear a smaller size.'

'We get the idea, Jon,' said Kirsty. 'My feet aren't exactly petite. But then I am five foot ten and if my feet were any smaller, I'd topple over. Now, does anyone want second helpings?'

All six dinner party guests were enthusiastic and not just because they too wanted Jon to change the subject. Kirsty was a very good cook. She was looking forward to having some more food herself.

Jon followed Kirsty to the kitchen and put his hands on her waist as she fetched the remains of the lamb casserole out of the oven. He leaned his chin on her shoulder. 'Thank you for cooking tonight,' he said. 'I can tell everyone is really enjoying themselves. How lucky am I to have a leading lady who's also a domestic goddess?'

Kirsty melted into him, forgetting for a moment all those bad jokes about her feet. Jon nuzzled the side of her neck and she felt her insides fizzing. The chemistry that had brought them together on the ship was still amazing. But then he gave her muffin top an absent-minded squeeze as he planted a kiss on the side of her face.

Jon probably wasn't even conscious of what he'd done but Kirsty felt her cheeks redden. She'd actually lost a few pounds recently, having put on half a stone while they were at sea, but Jon's squeeze brought back the awful memory of having her costumes let out halfway through the summer season. It wasn't unusual, apparently, for first-time cruise entertainers to put on a few pounds in the face of so much excess at the twenty-four-hour buffet, but Kirsty was still embarrassed.

Unlike Kirsty, Jon had incredible discipline around food. He was the kind of person who could eat half a Twix. If Kirsty ever ate just half a Twix, the other half would call to her from inside the fridge. She would hear nothing but its chocolatey voice crooning 'eat me, eat me, eat me' until she caved in.

However, she did her best to find some of Jon's will-power that evening. While Jon went back to the dining table with no idea of the thoughts he'd triggered in Kirsty's head, she served everyone but herself a second helping of the casserole. What remained went into the fridge before she could be tempted to pick at it.

Later, she allowed herself just a couple of small spoonfuls of the tiramisu she had made with so much love that afternoon. Her tummy rumbled miserably as her friends praised her cooking to the stars and clamoured for seconds and thirds and even tossed a coin to determine who would be allowed to scrape the serving bowl clean. In that moment, Kirsty felt like she needed tiramisu as much as she needed oxygen. But since Jon had unwittingly drawn her attention to her fluctuating waistline, there was no way she could indulge. Everyone who ever dreamed of a career in the spotlight knew that sacrifice was part of the deal. That famous speech at the beginning of *Fame* – the series Kirsty had devoured as a child – just about nailed it. 'Fame costs . . .' Well, Kirsty was paying in calories.

'I think that was a very successful dinner party,' said Jon as the last of their guests left around midnight. Kirsty was relieved to hear him say so. It had been important to her to impress his best friends from his school days, whom she met for the first time that night. They were nice people and thankfully they seemed to like her too. They left promising they would all get together again soon.

'Definitely before Christmas,' said Jon.

Likewise, because Jon and Kirsty had been on a cruise ship for most of their relationship so far, the dinner party was Kirsty's first chance to introduce him to Jane.

Jane and Kirsty had been best friends for decades and were as close as any sisters. They'd shared ups and downs. They'd bonded over boy bands and beauty tips. But Jane had also seen Kirsty through the loss of her mother when they were in the middle of their GCSEs. Fifteen years later, Kirsty had done her best to pull Jane out of her seemingly bottomless grief after the sudden death of her fiancé Greg.

It was Kirsty who persuaded Jane that she shouldn't

give up on love after Greg's death. It was Jane who convinced Kirsty that she really *should* give up her safe job as an office manager for an accountancy firm and try to make a living from her voice at the impossibly ancient age – in showbiz terms at least – of thirty-two. For all those reasons and more, it was important to Kirsty that Jane approved of Jon. Just as Jane had been keen for Kirsty to like her new boyfriend, Rob.

Kirsty had no trouble assuring Jane that Rob was great because he was. He was funny and kind and wonderfully attentive. Most importantly, he was clearly head over heels for Jane. She hoped Jane felt the same way about Jon.

Getting ready for bed in the little flat she and Jon were renting pending any wonderful job offers elsewhere, Kirsty paused to examine herself in the full-length mirror on the back of the wardrobe door. She stood sideways on, pulled her shoulders back and her stomach in to give herself the best possible profile. She even sucked in her cheeks. Then she slowly turned around, watching the curves of her body reassert themselves until she finally faced the mirror full frontal and beheld herself at her widest. Jon came out of the bathroom and caught her mid-appraisal. He gave his verdict.

'Nothing a few weeks on the 5:2 wouldn't put right.'

He also gave her what was probably supposed to be a reassuring pat on the bottom.

'I'll do it with you if you like,' he continued. 'Could lose a couple of pounds myself.'

He patted his own non-existent belly. Then he got into bed and was asleep within minutes, while Kirsty tossed and turned until three, tormented by thoughts of too-tight jeans and tiramisu.

She knew she wasn't Disney Princess perfect but isn't every woman worthy of a fairytale ending?

Chapter Two

'More tiramisu?' Judy Teesdale nudged the bowl towards her son Ben.

'No, thanks, Mum,' Ben patted his stomach. 'I've had plenty. I always overdo it.'

Judy didn't agree. 'You don't eat enough. You're looking gaunt,' she told her beloved only child. 'It doesn't suit you.'

'I'm trying to stay fit,' he countered.

'You're working too hard.'

'I'm running my own business now. I have to.'

'You've got to look after yourself at the same time. Thea needs her father to be healthy. And happy,' she added.

'I *am* happy, Mum.'

Judy merely raised her eyebrows at that.

'Come on,' she said, as she gathered up the empty bowls. 'If you're going to refuse any more of my legendary pudding, you can help me with the washing up.'

Moments later, Judy and Ben stood side by side at the kitchen sink, looking out onto the garden where Ben's eight-year-old daughter Althea – Thea for short – was playing with Buster, Judy's Border Terrier. Thea was throwing a tennis ball for the little dog. Most of the time, Buster plucked the ball from the sky before it had time to bounce. But when the ball hit the shed and bounced back in Thea's direction while Buster was still haring down the garden, Thea tried to catch it herself. She had no chance. As she made her valiant attempt, her glasses, with the thick lenses that made her eyes look enormous, slipped off her nose. Suddenly half-blind, she stumbled over her own feet. She missed the ball and somehow ended up tripping over the dog, who'd turned on a sixpence when he realised the ball had rebounded. Judy and Ben sighed as Thea completely lost her balance and sat down heavily on the muddy grass. Buster, realising that something wasn't right, quickly dropped the ball and returned to lick Thea's knees.

'She's just like you were at that age,' Judy observed. 'All legs. Thank god she got Jo's brains.'

At the mention of Thea's mother, Ben's face fell. Judy put her arm around her son's waist and gave him a squeeze.

'Jo would have known how to help her,' said Ben.

Judy knew at once to what Ben was referring. They'd talked about it as soon as Thea left the table. Thea was being picked on at school. Her myopia and the enormous glasses that went with it had marked her out as a target from the start. She was sweet and bookish and trusting that people were essentially as good-hearted as she was. That made her gullible. At parents' evening earlier that week, Thea's teacher Mrs Griffiths had expressed her concerns to Ben.

'How are things at home?' Mrs Griffiths asked as though that might provide an explanation for Thea's unpopularity in the classroom.

'Fine,' Ben had said. 'We're getting on OK.'

The truth was that things at home were sad and strange. Ben was doing his best but since Jo died of breast cancer, just over three years ago, he felt as though he had been living underwater. Everything was still muted. Numbed. It seemed to be getting worse with Christmas looming on the horizon. The world was getting ready to celebrate. Ben wasn't. He knew he needed to make more effort.

It didn't help poor Thea that they'd moved right after Jo died. They'd been living in London but with Jo gone, Ben felt he couldn't cope in the city on his own. He wanted to be near what little family he had. That was why he and Thea had moved back to Newbay to stay with Judy in the house where Ben grew up. It was meant to be a temporary move but, after a year, Ben admitted he was never going back to the job his employers had held open. He took another six months to figure out what to do before Judy came home one day with details of the empty shop that was now Ben's PC repair business.

'Perhaps we should look into more after-school activities,' Judy suggested, breaking into Ben's reflection. 'Broaden Thea's circle. I know how it can be at school. You get on the wrong side of one horrible ringleader and suddenly the whole class is ganging up on you. A different group of children could boost her confidence and help her push back in the classroom. How about the Brownies? There's a troop at the community centre. I loved Brownies when I was a child.'

'And I hated Cubs,' Ben reminded her. 'Isn't Brownies all campfires and hiking? That isn't Thea's style.'

'Then how about cooking? There's a children's cooking class at one of the hotels. They do adult classes too. They've got a special on making the perfect Christmas dinner. I thought I might do that one myself.'

Newbay's hotels were all diversifying and offering

cooking classes and workshops in a desperate attempt to keep their kitchens busy through the off-season.

'We could do it together. All three of us. Then you and Thea can be in charge of the turkey.'

'I'll look into it, Mum, I promise.'

Though how Ben would find the time to work on improving Thea's social life, he didn't know. His business seemed to require his attention almost as much as a second child. He was in the shop nearly all the time. When Thea should have been having swimming lessons or learning to play the euphonium, she could be found sitting at the back of the store, reading or drawing. She said that's what she liked to do and Ben believed her – as a child, he'd loved nothing more than reading – but perhaps Judy was right. Thea needed to be encouraged to move outside her comfort zone. Meet other children outside school. Make some real friends. She couldn't go through her childhood sharing her secrets only with her grandmother's dog.

As Ben watched, Thea got up and brushed herself off. Buster, who seemed reassured by this that Thea had not been too badly hurt by her fall, retrieved the ball. He dropped it at her feet and assumed the position that told her he was ready to play. Head low to the ground. Bottom high. Much wagging.

Thea pulled her arm back as far as it would go, ready to hurl the ball right out of the garden. Her eyes were narrowed in concentration.

'Ready, Buster?' she asked the dog. 'A-one, a-two, a-three . . .'

Thea almost left the ground with the effort of that throw and yet somehow the ball still fell straight down and landed between her muddy trainers. Even Buster looked disappointed.

'Oh, Thea,' Ben thought to himself. 'What am I going to do with you?'

Just then, she turned towards the kitchen window. She pushed her glasses back up her nose and beamed a huge smile. Ben couldn't help grinning right back at her.

Chapter Three

The Newbay Theatre Society – NEWTS for short – had been around for far longer than any of its members. That said, Trevor Fernlea, the committee chairman, was rumoured to be knocking on a hundred, though he still insisted he could play 'thirty to sixty' and, indeed, had just wowed the local critics with his portrayal of that hunky young thruster Mercutio in the society's production of *Romeo and Juliet*. And not only because his trousers split during a sword fight.

The society was especially blessed in that it had its very own theatre, created in the shell of an old Methodist hall, thanks to a bequest from one of its early members, the sainted Miss Chorley (the NEWTS' first Juliet). The conversion, which had taken place in the mid nineteen-eighties, was innovative and creative, turning the disused and almost derelict chapel into a two hundred and fifty-seat raked auditorium with a storage area for props, two rehearsal rooms, two dressing rooms, an enormous wardrobe, a box office and a tea-room/fully licensed bar. It greatly amused the players and their audience to treat themselves to an after-show tipple beneath a Victorian painting extolling the virtues of temperance. John Wesley would have turned in his grave.

Thirty years after the conversion, the theatre was looking a little shabby but goodness only knew when there would be time for a proper renovation beyond the annual dab of paint on the damp spots. The details of the bequest that allowed for the creation of the theatre in the first place stipulated that the NEWTS perform a programme of at least six shows a year. Thus the little theatre was always busy.

Every single night of the week, something was happening somewhere in the building. There were performances, rehearsals, costume fittings, dance classes, committee meetings. Not to mention the Thursday Club – the group of pensioners who met in the theatre bar every Tuesday afternoon to discuss the arts. They originally met on a Thursday – hence the name – but in recent years the day had been changed because it clashed with the local cinema's special senior citizen matinees. Trevor Fernlea's lectures couldn't compete with £2.99 for tea, a Penguin *and* Tom Hiddleston as Loki. Or Tom Hiddleston as just about anything. The Thursday Club was all a-flutter about his full-frontal nudity in *High Rise* for months.

The NEWTS drew its membership from a diverse section of Newbay society. The Thursday Club was at one end of the spectrum. At the other end, the children's drama group was always busy. On a Saturday morning, the theatre was more like a crèche as forty or fifty under-twelves were put through their theatrical paces and the auditorium rang with their laughter and shouts. There was fierce competition for places in the children's group because it was considerably cheaper than the local childminders' services. Strangely, the parents' enthusiasm for the group did not translate into enthusiasm for letting their children take part in any actual shows that might mean turning out of an evening when *Strictly* was on.

The youth group, which met on Thursday nights, was

renowned throughout the county as a hotbed of impressive talent. Several former NEWTS had gone on to drama school. One was a regular on *EastEnders*. News of her success had spread throughout Devon and made NEWTS' youth group the place to be for aspiring actors from every corner of the county. If you were casting a show that needed actors between the ages of twelve and eighteen, the NEWTS provided a very rich seam of potential.

Unfortunately, what generally happened was that when they hit eighteen, the youth group members drifted off to other towns for college or university. A few might show up again at the end of their degrees, when fruitless job searches and shaky finances forced them back to the family nest, but it was a matter of time before they would find jobs and boyfriends and girlfriends and go travelling and get mortgages and be swept up by marriage and children. As a result, there was a dearth of NEWTS between the ages of twenty-five and forty-five. No matter how much effort the NEWTS put into recruitment, it was an age group that simply didn't have the time.

After that, it was a different story. Membership picked up again considerably for the forty-five plus group. People joined the society as something to do once their children left home. Or their spouses left home . . . NEWTS had an unfounded reputation as being a cosy alternative to Tinder. And once you were past retirement age, membership numbers absolutely rocketed. Especially among the women. If you were casting an all-female stage version of *Cocoon* – that film set in an old people's home – you were in luck. If you weren't . . .

The society's demographics meant for some extremely interesting casting. Trevor Fernlea's turn as swashbuckling young tyke Mercutio was far from unusual. In the

NEWTS' performance of *The Graduate*, the actress playing Mrs Robinson was younger than her supposed student swain by ten years. So Jon had his work cut out when it came to casting *Cinderella*. Especially since all the elderly regulars wanted to be in the Christmas show. It was always the biggest, brightest and most-fun-to-be-in performance of the year.

Thank goodness it wasn't quite so important to be realistic in a pantomime. There was comedy value in casting someone whose physical attributes were at glaring odds with the part. However, Jon was determined to assemble a cast with whom he could work in exactly the way he wanted. He didn't want anyone too set in his or her ways. For that, read anyone in their eighties.

But needs must. The NEWTS was no Club 18-30. In late October, Trevor Fernlea popped a couple of extra statins and auditioned to play Prince Charming.

Chapter Four

Kirsty was mightily relieved when Jon let Trevor Fernlea down by telling him that while it was no longer fashionable to have a girl play the pantomime's 'principal boy', Jon had decided to draw heavily on tradition for his production and would thus be casting a woman as the prince.

This was a political move on Jon's part. As expected, far more women than men turned up to the auditions and Jon had to offer the ladies at least some possibility they would find a part in a play that was surprisingly low on female roles. The reality was, however, that the prince had been cast in Jon's mind from the moment he arrived back in Devon.

Choosing Kirsty for Cinderella was not without controversy. Though no one could doubt her abilities – on her first visit to the NEWTS' theatre, she raised the old church roof with her rendition of 'I Dreamed a Dream' from Les Mis – the fact was, Kirsty was a newcomer. Naturally, people were going to be a little put out when she waltzed in and took the plum role, no matter how good she was.

It was for that reason Jon had really decided to reinstate the tradition of having a female principal boy. It meant he could give a substantial part to the player who would almost certainly have been Cinderella had Kirsty not appeared. Lauren Whitwell.

Lauren was the darling of the NEWTS. Nine times out of ten, Lauren got the female lead in any NEWTS production. She was Alice in *Alice in Wonderland*, Dorothy in *The Wizard Of Oz*. She was Snow White. She was Sleeping Beauty. She was Titania in *A Midsummer Night's Dream* (though that was a disaster. Never had a prompt been so busy). Cinderella should have been hers. She was a panto princess incarnate.

It helped that Lauren was a quasi-celebrity. She was a weather girl on local television, bringing news of sunshine or showers to the whole of Devon every weekday morning at nine. At twenty-eight, she was still the ideal 'girl next door', with her big brown eyes, dazzling white smile and swishy chestnut ponytail. Think Cheryl Tweedy before that awful incident in the night-club loos.

But Jon did not rate Lauren's talent for musical theatre. He never had, he told Kirsty. Jon and Lauren had shared a stage back when they were both members of the NEWTS' youth group. She hadn't been able to hold a tune then and, despite numerous singing lessons, she still struggled. Lauren had risen through the ranks at NEWTS by virtue of three things: the general attrition of good actresses as the youth group aged, her looks (which, Jon admitted, were especially good for Newbay) and the fact she could be seen on television five days a week.

There was no doubt Lauren's fame was a tremendous draw for NEWTS' target audience, who liked nothing better than to sit in the front row with their hearing aids turned too low, speculating loudly, 'Isn't she that one off the telly?' Singing and acting talent didn't come into it with Lauren. They didn't have to.

So Lauren was to play Prince Charming. When Jon

telephoned to let her know, she was unimpressed. But he soon managed to convince her that the prince was the role she was born for.

'Everyone knows you can play a princess, Lauren. This is your opportunity to show you have *range*. All the best actresses embrace the chance to play across the genders. When I think of you as Prince Charming, I'm envisaging you as Newbay's answer to Tilda Swinton, bringing an ethereal androgyny to the piece. You will transcend the usual parameters of pantomime to bring true art to your role . . .'

'Well, I did like Tilda Swinton in *Lord of the Rings*,' said Lauren. 'I'll do it.'

Jon didn't bother to point out that Lauren had mixed up Tilda with Cate Blanchett. Lauren wouldn't get within a barn door of either actress's talent. He was just relieved she hadn't cried.

Kirsty, who was listening when Jon made the call, shook her head at the power of Jon's terrible charm. He really could talk anyone into anything. When Kirsty saw, or heard, him turn on the charm for someone else, she guiltily admitted to herself that it made her fancy him even more.

'But Tilda Swinton?' she said to him. 'It's a pantomime, Jon.'

'It's *my* pantomime,' he reminded her. 'It's going to be the best panto ever.'

Kirsty didn't doubt it. Self-confidence was another one of Jon's super-powers.

Once Lauren had been dealt with, the rest of the casting was not so fraught with risk. The Ugly Sisters were to be played by two brothers who had been with the NEWTS since they were teens.

The brothers – George and Andrew Farmer – actually had show business day jobs. After a fashion. Under the stage name *The Giggle Twins*, they appeared all over the county at children's parties, performing a hybrid clowning/magic act. With their signature yellow bowl-cut wigs and their 'hilarious' clown-style wide trousers, they made *The Chuckle Brothers* seem almost normal. When they were in costume, you'd be hard-pressed to choose two people you'd be less keen to sit between at a dinner party. But they were well-versed in the sort of clowning the role of a dame required. They were perfect for playing the Uglies.

The part of the Ugly Sisters' mother, Cinderella's stepmother the Baroness Hardup, was given to Annette Sweeting.

Annette was a woman of a certain age – indeterminate thanks to the judicious use of Botox – known to most of the NEWTS as 'the Black Widow' on account of her having had three husbands. The husbands, all sadly deceased, had left Annette with a fabulous collection of engagement rings, a Bentley and the biggest house in Newbay – a double-fronted Georgian number with fabulous sea-views.

The house, the car and Annette's Joanna Lumley-esque air of glamour did not win her many female friends. She was the subject of much gossip. It was a popular pastime of some of the less-generous ladies of the society to speculate as to whom Annette might be lining up as husband number four. Though they would never admit it, most of the male NEWTS secretly hoped they were in the running.

For the purposes of the pantomime, Vince Churchill would play Annette's husband.

Vince was a real kingpin in the local social scene. He was big chap full of bonhomie, who was a regular volunteer in the NEWTS' theatre bar (drinking twice as much as he sold). He was a dentist by profession and almost all the NEWTS had been in his chair at one point or another. Rumour was he often went to his surgery smelling of booze, with hands shaking like a Chihuahua left out in the rain, but since he still did NHS work, his patients were prepared to overlook the possibility of the odd slip with a drill.

Vince's real wife Bernadette Churchill – Bernie for short – was everyone's favourite for Fairy Godmother. Though she and Vince had no children of their own, Bernie had a maternal warmth that drew everybody to her. She had one of those faces that always seems on the edge of a smile. Bernie was an accountant and, as well as acting in many of the NEWTS' productions over the years, she oversaw the company's financial affairs and made sure everyone paid their dues. Of all the NEWTS Kirsty met in her first few weeks in Newbay, Bernie was the warmest and the easiest to see as a potential friend.

Last but not least, Trevor Fernlea, who had been so cruelly disappointed in his bid to play Prince Charming, was cast as Cinders' beloved sidekick Buttons. Kirsty grimaced when Jon told her about that.

'But Buttons is meant to be Cinderella's *childhood* friend,' she pointed out. 'Trevor is at least three times my age.'

'And he's the chair of the committee,' Jon reminded her. 'And he has his own costume.'

Kirsty was learning that in the amateur-dramatic world being able to dress the part went a long way towards actually *getting* the part. The Giggle Twins had their own comedy wigs. Annette had a collection of thigh-high boots that would be perfect for the domina-trix look Jon envisaged for her part. And after half a century as a NEWT, Trevor Fernlea's personal wardrobe contained just as many military uniforms, Elizabethan collars and space helmets as ordinary suits. Naturally he had the perfect outfit for Buttons. He told Jon he would be repurposing the costume he'd had made for playing the butler to the Von Trapp family for the NEWTS' performance of *The Sound of Music*. In 1984.

'It still fits,' he said proudly. 'I work hard on keeping trim. Do you think I should grow a moustache for this production?' he asked then. 'Might be a nice touch.'

'Promise me there is no point in the script at which I have to kiss him,' said Kirsty.

So that was it. The players were assembled. A cast list was pinned to the noticeboard in the main rehearsal room, where it soon gained some unflattering annotations.

'Take no notice,' Jon said, when Kirsty noted that someone had altered her surname, which was Watson, to 'Fatson'. 'It's just one of the kids.'

But *Fat*son? How could Kirsty *not* take that as a slight?

'Seriously, don't worry about it,' said Jon. 'They've changed my surname from Manley to Womanley. They're just writing the first thing that comes into their heads.'

Kirsty nodded but she couldn't help wishing Jon had said something slightly different. Something along the lines of, 'Well, you're not fat, darling, so obviously the *Fatson* thing is totally random.'

When the cast met in the bar to toast the fun ahead – courtesy of Vince, who bought champagne – Bernie was a little better at assuring Kirsty that it really wasn't worth getting upset about.

'It happens every time,' she said. 'I almost look forward to seeing what they'll come up with next. You wait until the posters go up. Then you'll see some proper creative vandalism. How do you look with a Hitler moustache?'

'I can't wait to find out,' said Kirsty.

'Good girl,' said Bernie. 'That's the spirit. Welcome to the NEWTS.'

Chapter Five

Rehearsals began in earnest on the first Saturday of November, the obscenely early opening day of Newbay's 'German' Christmas fayre (the town's Guy Fawkes' celebrations took place on the very same day). Jon had wanted to start prepping the panto in the morning but Lauren, as a local celebrity, was required to cut the ribbon on the town's biggest shopping event of the year. There was no point beginning without her.

The Christmas fayre kicked off at ten. Kirsty and Jon stopped by on their way to the theatre to watch Lauren do her bit. She arrived on the back of a sleigh pulled by a bored-looking horse. The sleigh was sponsored by Chillings, the local department store. Lauren wore a Santa red dress edged with white faux fur, and tinsel in her hair. A team of mortified local teenagers – Saturday boys and girls from Chillings, dressed as elves – helped Lauren from the sleigh to the podium loaded with local dignitaries from which she would make her speech.

Jon was delighted when Lauren managed to get in a plug for the panto though Kirsty wasn't sure she was so pleased when Lauren began by saying, 'I know you'll all be disappointed I'm not playing Cinderella herself but . . .'

'She means *she's* disappointed,' Kirsty translated.

'She'll get over it,' said Jon.

Kirsty nodded. 'I hope so.' But it was hard not to feel offended by the disappointed groans from certain sections of the audience when Lauren announced she wouldn't be playing the princess. Lauren's fan club was out in force. Kirsty could barely see her rival through the forest of arms brandishing smartphones trying to get a snap of Lauren's knickers as she bent to pick up a dropped microphone.

'And the weather forecast for the opening day of the annual Newbay Christmas Fayre is . . . snow!' Lauren concluded her speech and cut the red ribbon as a bubble machine spewed white foam.

As the children in the audience shrieked with delight at the bubbles, Kirsty and Jon moved away through the stalls selling mulled wine, mince pies and Christmas baubles made by 'artisans' in factories on the other side of the world. A local school band played a medley of Christmas tunes including a version of *Away in a Manger* that sounded more like *Strangled Cat in a Stable*. Still, Kirsty enjoyed the festive atmosphere and the joy on the faces of the children she hoped would be in the NEWTS' audience at the end of the year. She tucked her arm through Jon's and looked forward to the festive fun ahead.

The rest of the cast met Kirsty and Jon at the theatre at two. There was no doubt Trevor was taking his part seriously. He turned up with his script fully learned and annotated, and while the rest of the cast were busy swapping gossip, he practised his voice exercises. Lauren turned up at quarter past. 'Photo call with Santa.'

Eventually, when everyone was assembled in the

rehearsal room for the first read-through, they would all be made to do voice exercises. Jon insisted on that. Kirsty understood their purpose. The muscles that controlled the voice, like any other muscles, could be strained. Particularly if you were an amateur and overdid it with the *projection*. In any case, Kirsty rather enjoyed doing her scales. She was slightly less keen on the physical warm-up, which always seemed to involve having to move around the room like a chimp. But Kirsty threw herself into that too. She knew that as a newcomer she had a lot to prove to the people she would be working alongside for the next couple of months. She needed to make them warm to her quickly. If that meant hooting with delight over an imaginary banana, so be it.

When the warm-ups were over, the cast made a circle of chairs. The seats in the large rehearsal room were diverse in style but uniformly uncomfortable. For the most part, they were props left over from plays long since forgotten. Kirsty noticed with amusement that Jon, as director, chose the highest seat he could find. It looked like a throne but was actually a nineteenth-century commode, complete with porcelain chamber pot concealed beneath the lid. Kirsty settled herself into a vinyl-covered tub chair from the 1960s. It wasn't long before she discovered why they'd gone out of fashion. It was pretty much impossible to find a way to sit in the chair that didn't involve putting your back out.

When everyone was seated, Jon gave them a pep talk. He explained that he intended to create a production of *Cinderella* that would go down in NEWTS history.

'It's going to be more than a pantomime.'

He'd written the script himself and he had a clear vision for every single scene. The assembled NEWTS nodded along reverently as Jon referenced several plays and films they'd never heard of.

'So,' he concluded. 'If you don't think you're ready to make this *Cinderella* the best thing in theatre since Euripides staged *The Bacchae*, you know where to find the door.'

Jon eyeballed each of his players in turn. They all looked dutifully serious. They were all wondering who Euripides was. Did he work with Andrew Lloyd Webber?

'Right,' said Jon. 'We're ready. Let's begin.'

Bernie, as the fairy godmother, opened the show. She admitted she had not had a chance to learn her lines since she got Jon's phone call confirming her part – she'd been on a VAT course – but even reading from the book, she delivered a performance that immediately put everyone at ease.

She began.

'*Welcome to our humble play. Set long ago and far away. Where the goodies were good and the baddies were bad. And the meanies were mean and nice people were sad. Look, here's Cinderella. A lov-er-ly girl. But the way she's been treated will make your hair curl.*'

That was Kirsty's cue. She got to her feet and moved to the middle of the circle, sweeping the floor ahead of her with an imaginary broom.

'*Oh me,*' she sighed. '*Oh my . . .*'

She swept an extravagant figure of eight, twirled and went straight into her first song, called 'Beyond the Dusty Hearth'. It was loosely based on 'Beyond The Sea'. The words had been changed to protect the NEWTS from a lawsuit.

'*Beyond the dusty hearth,*' she sang. '*Is a world of true delight, but if I can't take a bath, it will never reach my sight . . .*'

Kirsty was gratified and relieved when her fellow cast members clapped her first attempt at the song. It was always tough to sing without musical accompaniment. Glynis, the company pianist, was absent from the rehearsal that day. Something about 'community service'. Everyone assumed she meant charity work.

'Brava!' said Trevor Fernlea.

'That was great,' Jon winked. Kirsty felt a little shiver of delight whenever she saw that wink. 'Ugly Sisters. You're up next.'

The Giggle Twins got up and bustled into the centre of the room, bickering and ad-libbing as they went. They had the body language of two dames off-pat. Andrew hoiked an enormous imaginary bosom. George patted an invisible curl of hair.

'So, I said to Buttons,' George began. 'Is that a Christmas tree in your pocket or are you pleased to see me?'

'Cut,' Jon shouted. 'This is a family show. Please stick to the script.'

'Whatever you say, *Euripides* . . .' said George.

Once ticked off, the Giggle Twins were thankfully very professional. Kirsty was surprised that without their yellow wigs, they were two reasonably good-looking men. Indeed, Andrew Giggle later revealed that the brothers had been child models. They'd made enough from campaigns for John Lewis and Marks & Spencer to buy the first two flats in what was now a sizeable buy-to-let empire.

Meanwhile Jon and Annette soon showed themselves to be on the same wavelength. Annette was all about proper direction even if she was playing a wicked step-mother rather than Blanche Dubois. At one point, she even asked Jon – to his delight – 'But what is my motivation?'

Bernie was peerless. She read her part beautifully and was tactful and helpful with suggestions to her scene-mates when they were needed. Vince took a lot of fag breaks but when he was in the room, he gave it his all. He delivered his jokes like an old school comic from a working men's club. His gravelly laugh reminded Kirsty of Sid James in the old Carry On films that had been her gran's delight.

Even Lauren had learned her lines, though she spoke them all with the same tone and rhythm as she delivered the weather report.

'Think Tilda Swinton,' Jon reminded her.

'She talks exactly like this in *Lord of the Rings*,' Lauren replied.

The rest of the cast stifled a giggle.

The only painful moment of the first day came when Kirsty had her first scene with Trevor Fernlea as Buttons. It took place after the scene in which the Hardup house-hold received invitations to the Prince's ball. The invite was addressed to 'all' of Baron Hardup's daughters, which meant that Cinders was included.

'*Oh no no no,*' said Andrew Giggle, wagging his finger in Kirsty's face. '*Not you, my dear. You're not invited. You're just a servant.*'

'*Who will make sure our supper's on the table when we get back if not you?*' George Giggle asked.

Then they swept out – or rather sat back down on their matching 1970s armchairs – leaving Kirsty in the middle of the circle with the ripped halves of her invite. That was Trevor's cue.

Trevor knew his part. He stood up and jumped into the circle, where he gave Kirsty/Cinderella a low bow. It was a *very* low bow and it slightly unsteadied him. Kirsty grabbed his elbow as he straightened up to make sure he didn't topple over. He rearranged his bifocals and began.

'*Why so sad, Cinderella?*'

Kirsty showed him the two halves of the invitation – which was actually a flyer for a curry house.

'*Two for one on biryani?*' said Trevor.

An excellent ad-lib, Kirsty thought.

'*It's an invitation to the prince's Christmas ball,*' said Kirsty. '*Everybody's going except for me.*'

'*Or me,*' said Trevor, suddenly googly-eyed.

The script then had Buttons and Cinderella duet to the tune of 'Sixteen going on Seventeen', the classic song from *The Sound of Music*, in which teenage sweethearts Rolf and Liesl declare their love. Though once again the lyrics had been slightly altered to fit the panto (and avoid those pesky copyright issues), the moment the music started up and Trevor let out his first wavering note, the Giggle Twins gave a simultaneous derisory snort and Vince slapped his thighs with amusement.

'Sixty going on seventy, more like,' said George Giggle.

'And the rest,' said Andrew.

When Trevor accidently slipped into the original words of the song and warbled, '*I-I'm in love with you,*' Annette spluttered. After that, no one held back. It was unintentionally hilarious.

Jon turned off the tape.

'Yep. Fine. Maybe we should consider using another song at that point.'

Trevor looked crestfallen. 'But I've practised this one,' he said.

'And because you're such an old pro, I've no doubt you'll pick up something new just as quickly.'

Kirsty smiled sympathetically. 'It's not one of my

favourite songs,' she said. 'I'm sure something else would do more justice to your voice.'

She was just glad they hadn't had time to get to the bit where Cinders and Buttons dance around the kitchen table. That horror was for another time.

Chapter Six

The first read-through took almost three hours. It was dark by the time the players emerged from the theatre and headed in their separate directions. Early Bonfire Night fireworks dotted the sky.

'I thought that went OK,' said Kirsty as she and Jon drove back to their flat.

Jon was less optimistic. 'This is going to be a shambles. Why on earth did I come back to Newbay?'

'Oh, come on,' said Kirsty. 'We're going to have a laugh.'

Kirsty needed Jon to be happy. They had both come back to Newbay because at moments like that one, stepping out of the theatre into the cold damp embrace of a November night, when she could have been in the Caribbean, the question 'why on earth am I here?' was definitely on her lips as well.

'It's going to be great fun,' she said firmly.

Jon snorted.

'And I'm really glad to be in the UK for Christmas. I feel a bit Christmassy already, what with the Christmas fayre this morning and this afternoon spent singing carols.'

Many of the songs in Jon's script were based on well-known Christmas tunes.

'Shall we get a Chinese?' Kirsty suggested in an

attempt to cheer him up. 'I really fancy one after all that acting and singing.'

'I thought we were doing a fast day today,' was Jon's response.

It was not exactly a fairytale moment.

'Salad it is then,' said Kirsty.

'I'm sorry,' said Jon. 'It's just this play is so important to me.'

'I know,' Kirsty reached across the gear stick and squeezed Jon's thigh.

Kirsty had come to find work on a cruise ship in a perfectly fairytale fashion.

She'd been holidaying in the Med with Jane, accompanying her best friend on the cruise that would have been her honeymoon had Jane's fiancé Greg not died in a car accident the previous December. It was an odd sort of holiday. It was Kirsty's idea that Jane should still take the cruise but a couple of days in she began to wonder if she had made a mistake. Jane was so very unhappy. Understandably, she could not do anything on board ship without imagining how it might have been with Greg by her side. Jane barely left their state room. Not even to eat. When she wasn't sitting on the balcony eating room service sandwiches with Jane, Kirsty roamed the enormous ship alone.

One evening, making another tour of the ship's entertainments by herself, Kirsty happened upon some karaoke. Karaoke had always been her thing. It was ng too, before Greg died. They used to spend lnesday evening singing at their local pub, The rp. It was the best night of the week for Kirsty.

She loved seeing all the familiar faces, going through their familiar routines. It was the same singers and the same songs every week, but it was never dull. Most of all, Kirsty loved to belt out her own old favourites and revel in the applause of her friends.

At first, she just snuck into the back of the room where the ship's karaoke was held and watched as other people took the floor. But it didn't take long for the performing bug to bite again and Kirsty soon found herself requesting 'It's Raining Men'. The moment she opened her mouth, she had the audience on their feet and the compère insisted she take part in the karaoke competition that would begin the following night.

The contest took place over several evenings. Jane made it out of their room to see the final and watched and cheered as Kirsty won the competition by a landslide. Afterwards, while Kirsty and Jane were celebrating her success, they were approached by a woman who worked for the cruise line – one of the people responsible for on-board entertainment. She gave Kirsty her card and suggested she get in touch.

In that moment, Kirsty was thrilled by the idea of working as a singer on board a cruise ship but by the time she and Jane got back home, it started to seem utterly daft. Kirsty worked as an office manager. She was nearly thirty-two. It was way too late for her to start a career on the stage. She was practically retirement age in musical theatre terms. Wasn't she?

'No!' said Jane. 'This is your chance to change your life. You can live your dream.'

'Or find out it's a nightmare.'

'Maybe, but isn't it better to find that out than go to your grave with a head full of *shouldas*?'

Jane knew what she was talking about on that score.

She'd had so many plans for life with Greg. After the cruise, which seemed to mark the rock-bottom point of Jane's grief, she was a making serious effort to get back up and out there. The least Kirsty could do was email the cruise director and ask exactly how one went about applying for a job at sea.

The cruise director responded so quickly and so warmly that it would have been rude not to go to the cruise line's auditions in London. And when Kirsty aced her audition and was invited to a presentation regarding careers with Countess Cruises, it seemed a shame not to find out more. And by that point, even Kirsty's boss at the accountancy firm was telling her she should give it a try. He revealed he too once harboured the dream of a life on stage but marriage and children had forced him into accountancy. A steady job. A steady life.

'There are so many people out there not living their dreams. Just sleepwalking through their days,' he said.

'And which of us knows how many days we've got?' Jane reminded her. 'Do it for me *and* for Greg. You know he would have told you to go for it.'

So Kirsty went for it. A month after the audition, she was in Los Angeles, at the cruise line's state-of-the-art rehearsal facility. It was the first time she had been in the United States (another tick on her bucket list). And a very long way from Essex.

Chapter Seven

Strictly speaking, it was in Los Angeles, not on board *The European Countess*, that Kirsty met Jon for the first time. It was in the canteen. He was sitting at a table of young dancers – male and female. They were hanging on his every word, marvelling at his charming accent. He didn't have to say anything particularly witty. To them, by sheer virtue of his voice, he was as gorgeous as a cross between Hugh Grant in his prime and James Bond.

'Thank goodness,' he said, when Kirsty joined the table at the behest of the dancer with whom she was sharing a room. 'Another Brit. We can have a conversation without you going into meltdown over my Hugh Grant accent.'

'You don't sound anything like Hugh Grant.'

'Exactly. But try telling this lot.'

Kirsty smiled. Jon didn't look like Hugh Grant either. He was more like Daniel Craig. Which suited Kirsty fine.

'I'm Kirsty . . .'

'I know,' said Jon.

Kirsty felt a frisson of pleasure. He had noticed her.

'I've seen you rehearsing. Your voice is something really special,' he added. She could tell he was sincere.

'Thank you.'

'Is this your first season?'

'It is.'

'Me too. Where were you working before?'

'In an accountancy office,' she told him.

'No way,' said Jon. 'What a waste. Thank goodness you made your escape.'

'How about you?'

'Drama school. MFA in directing. Then various jobs in the West End. Thought I would give this a whirl. Good experience. Good money. Get to see the world in style.'

After that first meeting, Jon seemed to seek Kirsty out whenever there was a break in rehearsals. A little voice inside Kirsty's head kept asking why he was so keen to spend time with her when they were surrounded by beautiful, skinny dancers who could wrap their legs around their necks. Kirsty was all too conscious that she couldn't match up to their physical perfection. Because of that she told herself she mustn't read too much into Jon's attentions.

The long weeks of flirtation came to a head at a crew party during their week on board the old decommissioned ship the cruise line used for crew training. They spent a week sailing back and forth from Fort Lauderdale to the Bahamas, spending their days practising safety drills and muster procedures and listening to lectures about the proliferation of e-coli. They got their afternoons off on incredible beaches. The food was amazing. The drinks were free. The whole experience reminded Kirsty of that old Wham 'Club Tropicana' video. The crew worked hard but they played even harder.

On the very last night of the training cruise, a few of the musicians on board grabbed their instruments and formed an instant band, playing the sort of tunes that everyone had to get up for. It was hot. Tropically so. Kirsty and Jon were dancing on different sides of the dance floor. Jon got closer and closer until he was by her side. They danced an approximation of the salsa, with his leg between hers. Kirsty felt herself growing hotter and hotter as they swayed together. She fancied him so much. Jon rested his forehead against hers and stared deep into her eyes. Kirsty tried to stare back but she was a little bit dizzy from all the free alcohol and Jon was too close for her to be able to focus.

Then Jon kissed her. And that was that. There were fireworks. Quite literally. On shore someone was having a party. It seemed like an excellent omen that, as their lips touched, a rocket flew into the sky.

Two weeks after their kiss on the training cruise, Jon and Kirsty flew back to the United Kingdom to join *The European Countess* in Southampton. Kirsty was especially delighted she would be working on the cruise ship where the magic had started – where she had sung 'It's Raining Men' in the karaoke competition and changed her life's direction.

Of course, this time her experience wouldn't be quite so luxurious as sharing the honeymoon suite with Jane. But Kirsty was pleased with her room. It was, at least, above the waterline. Kirsty knew from her training that the men and women who worked in the ship's kitchens, restaurants and as housekeepers would not be so lucky.

And having Jon around made the cruise perfect. Even if he did spend much of his time moaning about seasickness. He had a terrible time with it. Couldn't even raise his head from the pillow in the morning without first popping a pill. But apart from that he was the funniest, sexiest man she'd ever had the pleasure to be with. She liked to listen to him talk about his dreams. Unlike her, Jon had never deviated from his career path. He had always wanted a career in the theatre and he had never done anything but work in the field he intended to dominate.

'You've got to keep your dreams firmly in focus,' he told Kirsty. 'I can't believe you ever worked at an accountancy firm.'

'It certainly seems like a very long way away,' thought Kirsty as they disembarked in Barcelona, with a free day ahead of them. What other job gave you the opportunity to spend your time off in such fantastic places? It was heaven.

The summer season went by in a flash. Kirsty made some good friends. She got the sort of suntan she'd always dreamed of. She saw the great cities of the Mediterranean. She became more confident in her skills as a performer. And, of course, she was head over heels for Jon.

But what would happen next?

Chapter Eight

Kirsty had already been asked if she would like to continue to work for the cruise line, taking *The European Countess* across the Atlantic and staying on-board for her winter season in the Caribbean. Kirsty was delighted by the prospect. But Jon, who also had the chance to stay, was not so happy.

'I can't keep taking tablets every day,' he complained. 'I'm sure they're messing with my mind. They're squashing my creativity.'

Jon was very protective of his creativity.

'And crossing the Atlantic? Have you got any idea how rough that can get?'

Kirsty hadn't really thought about it, though she'd heard plenty of horror stories from the old hands. Hundred-foot-high waves. Windows blown out and cabins full of seawater. Days spent confined to the very bowels of the ship because the upper decks were too dangerous. Kirsty just focussed on the balmy weather on the other side.

'You could fly across and join in Fort Lauderdale,' she suggested.

'The Caribbean will be no better for me. The Med is a millpond and I've still been sick as a dog. Besides, aren't you getting just a little bit tired of seeing the same old faces day after day? Don't you find living on ship claustrophobic? Everybody knowing your business the whole time?'

'I like it,' said Kirsty. 'It feels a bit like family.'

Unlike Jon, whose parents were still together, Kirsty, a child of divorce with only one much younger half-sibling, yearned for that sort of closeness.

'Well, I don't. The minute this stretch on board comes to an end, I'm off. I'm going to look for something in London.'

Kirsty's heart sank. What chance did she have of maintaining her relationship with Jon if she was at sea but he was back in England? There would be days without a mobile signal. Incredibly expensive Internet that was slower than in the good old days of dial-up connections. She would have no real time off for at least three months. Her fellow performers had warned her that on-board relationships rarely survived the real world. Why should she and Jon be any different?

Of course, in the end, Jon didn't find a job in London. He found a job – well, a sort of job – in Newbay.

Kirsty tried to hide her astonishment as Jon told her his new plan.

'It's an amateur company,' he said. 'But they have their own theatre and it's my chance to write and direct a production according to my own vision. It will give me the opportunity to create something which really showcases my talents.'

'You're going to turn down another cruise to go back to Devon to direct an am-dram panto . . .' Kirsty said slowly.

Jon nodded.

'Will you come with me? Will you be my Cinderella?'

'What?'

'Play Cinderella for me. You'd be perfect. You've got

all the right skills for panto. You sing like an angel. You know how to get a laugh. It could be a good platform for you too.'

Kirsty wasn't sure she could see it. However, Jon continued and what he said next had her wondering if she did want to go to the Caribbean after all. He took her hands in both of his and looked deep into her eyes.

'And I want you to be there with me. I can't imagine spending Christmas without you.'

It was the most romantic thing she had ever heard. Until he capped it with, 'I love you.'

Jon went on to describe how it could be if they spent the Christmas season together back in the UK. The wild majesty of the Devon coast in winter, contrasting with cosy nights cuddled up indoors by the fire. By the time he had finished, Kirsty could almost smell the mulled wine in Jon's favourite Devon pub.

The following morning, Kirsty regretfully informed the entertainment director that she would not be taking up the offer of a Caribbean tour that winter. She made the excuse that she wanted to be back in the UK for 'family reasons'.

'You mean you're going to do a *pantomime*,' said the director. 'In Devon.'

Of course the director had heard about Jon's scheme. News travelled fast on board ship.

Kirsty admitted that was the truth of her sudden decision.

'Jon's writing the show around me,' she explained. 'We could take it on the road next year. Touring panto's really lucrative.'

Jon had told Kirsty about an old friend of his who made a small fortune putting on mini-pantos in fancy hotels. Not that Kirsty needed a financial incentive to follow Jon back to England. It was those three little words that had swung it. Kirsty was sure she felt the same way. Before meeting him, she had almost given up on finding love. There was no way she was going to risk losing it now.

The director nodded. 'Well, I know how important it is to be happy in your personal life.'

'Thank you for understanding.'

'But if it doesn't work out, then of course you must let me know.'

Kirsty was sure it would work out.

Walking off the ship at Southampton for the last time, Kirsty couldn't help feeling a pang of sadness but she looked towards the future with great optimism. It was working in entertainment that had always been her dream, not necessarily being at sea. She would still have that – the working in entertainment bit – and she would have Jon. And she would even have the sea. She'd just be *beside* it instead of on it. It wasn't what she had planned but it could still be fabulous.

That was why she needed Jon to be excited about being back. That was why she felt a little annoyed with him when he complained about the NEWTS. He'd given up the seasick tablets. She'd given up a great deal more.

Chapter Nine

The day after the first read-through, a Sunday, Jon woke up on the wrong side of the bed. He grumbled and growled his way through breakfast. Overnight, he'd received a text from Lauren saying that she'd Googled Tilda Swinton and now she knew Tilda was the 'blokey-looking one with the weird neck' she wasn't sure if she wanted to be Newbay's answer to the beautiful world-famous gender-bending actress after all. She wanted to be Cinderella or nothing else. Jon had to spend half an hour talking her round.

When Jon had finished, Kirsty suggested a walk. Jon didn't want to join her. He always ran on a Sunday morning (even on the ship, he would jog around the top deck) and he claimed that after a run he had no more energy for the rest of the day. Kirsty had asked him if he wouldn't prefer to save his energy to do something with her instead, but Jon said that he had *always* run on a Sunday. The implication was that he *always* would.

So Kirsty went for her walk alone. It was no big deal. At least she could do it at her own pace which was always slightly more leisurely.

* * *

There were two beaches within twenty minutes' walking distance of the flat they'd rented for the winter. The first – the main beach – was a two-mile stretch of pristine yellow sand dominated by a grand old Victorian pier. That was Newbay's showstopper, the one everybody thought of when they talked about the town. But if you turned right instead of left at the bottom of the road where Kirsty and Jon were living and went up and over the headland, you came to a smaller bay edged by rocks. It was known as Duckpool Bay because a family of mallards frequented the shallows there.

Kirsty was intrigued to see the ducks when Jon took her to Duckpool as part of the obligatory tour of the area when they first moved in. She'd always thought of ducks as freshwater creatures.

'They are,' Jon told her. 'But that lot hang around for the ice cream cones and chips people drop on the beach. It's why they're so fat. They're no better than rats.'

Not quite so romantic.

The beach at Duckpool Bay was not so picture perfect as Newbay's main beach either. The sand was darker in colour and there were slick wet patches that Jon explained were quicksand. The very idea that quicksand really existed outside the sort of adventure stories she read as a child made city girl Kirsty's heart beat a little faster. When Jon told her, she clung tight to his arm as though it might ooze up to get her where she stood on the concrete terrace that had been built for the cafe and ice cream hut.

'It's not deadly,' said Jon. 'Though I've seen a few people lose their shoes. And their dogs.'

'You're joking.'

'OK. Maybe I was joking about the dogs.'

Kirsty wasn't comforted. When she visited Duckpool Bay from then on, she stuck to the bits of sand that were obviously dry. Better safe than sorry.

As she walked across the headland to Duckpool Bay that Sunday morning, Kirsty was practising her lines. Jon had written the play but it was obvious at the read-through that he'd never read the script out loud. There was plenty to stumble over. Lots of inadvertent tongue twisters. Kirsty hoped Jon wouldn't be too precious to let her make a few edits. She segued into imagining how that conversation might go. How could she put her concerns tactfully?

She'd seen a slightly different side to Jon in the time they'd been back in the UK. He wasn't quite so laidback as he had been on board ship. Maybe it was just that now they knew each other better, he felt he could be honest about his frustrations as well as his ambitions. Let her see him for worse as well as better. Kirsty knew it was all part of being in a proper relationship, feeling comfortable with showing *all* aspects of your personality to the one you loved.

When Kirsty reached the beach, it was quieter than she had ever seen it. A combination of the hour – still relatively early – and the weather – overcast with a definite autumnal chill in the air. There was a single dog walker on the sand. Steering clear of the dodgy sinky bits, Kirsty hoped.

The tide was half-in but Kirsty was ashamed to say she couldn't tell whether it was coming in or going out. The tide table on the side of the cafe hadn't been amended since the cafe closed at the end of October, officially marking the end of the season.

The cafe, when it was open, was a good one. It didn't just serve coffee and tea. It served delicious panini and fresh pasta dishes. And it was decorated in proper hipster seaside style with lots of the old machines from the pier that couldn't compete with the type of high-tech games that kids demanded now. Among them was an automatic 'fortune-teller', a glass booth containing a spooky-looking mannequin, dressed in early twentieth century exotic, with a turban and a neatly pointed beard. You could buy tokens to use the machine along with your cappuccino.

The first time Jon brought Kirsty to Duckpool Bay, the cafe was open and Kirsty bought a token to go with Jon's espresso and her tea. She was embarrassed by the racket the machine made when you dropped the token in – there was no way of pretending you hadn't just handed over a quid to have your 'fortune told', as the mannequin's eyes dropped open and it swayed and shuddered to the accompaniment of mysterious music and flashing lights. But Kirsty was delighted with the fortune it spat out. Just a single line on a piece of stiff cardboard.

'*You are where love is,*' was what it said. Kirsty took that to mean that her having followed Jon back to the UK was the right decision. She was where her love was. She showed Jon the card when she joined him at the table.

'What's that supposed to mean?' he asked.

'I suppose it's an old-fashioned way of saying "love is all around",' said Kirsty, feeling too shy to tell Jon her real interpretation.

'Don't say that,' said Jon.

'Why not?' Kirsty was taken aback.

'Because you'll give me a Wet Wet Wet earworm . . .

Too late,' he groaned. 'I am going to be thinking of that song all day.' He mimed shooting himself in the head.

The fortune card lay on the middle of the table. They finished their drinks. It was a good morning. The sun was shining. The sea was sparkling. Jon was full of enthusiasm for the project ahead. He had Kirsty in stitches as he described the NEWTS. She still had yet to meet them at that point. Then he told her how glad he was she had chosen to come back to the UK with him. He promised it would be worth it. He took her hands across the table and pulled her closer for a kiss.

While Jon took their empty cups back to the counter, Kirsty surreptitiously pocketed the little piece of cardboard. She tucked it inside her purse.

'I *am* where love is,' she thought as she and Jon walked back home. He slung his arm around her shoulders and held her tight and she felt as though she could be happy in Newbay for ever.

On that Sunday morning almost six weeks later, the ducks that gave Duckpool its name were sitting on the sand rather than floating on the waves. The water must be as cold as it looked, thought Kirsty. The sun was barely making an effort. Kirsty wished she'd brought the ducks some crusts of bread to eat. But then, Kirsty was no longer in the habit of leaving bread crusts uneaten. Now that Jon was helping her keep a closer eye on her weight, Kirsty allowed herself just two pieces of toast for breakfast. And if she was only having two pieces of toast, she was going to make sure she ate every last mouthful.

Oh, no. Thinking about food made Kirsty feel hungry

again. That was the problem with diets. The moment you start to restrict what you eat, you become obsessed with the things you can't have. The extra toast. The pain au chocolat. The warm bread roll with your salad. Kirsty was glad that the beach cafe was shut.

She must be more disciplined. Part of her new regime was that she was supposed to be walking ten thousand steps a day on top of cutting back on the calories. Walking the length of the beach would go some way to reaching that total. But it had to be brisk. That's what Jon kept saying. No point pottering along.

Arms pumping, Kirsty marched to the far end of the sand and back again. She checked the step counter on her iPhone. How was it possible that all that energy only accounted for eight hundred steps, she wondered? She marched back and forth again. She shook her phone to see if it was actually working. It was.

Another two beach circuits later, she sat down on a rock and looked out over the water. In the distance, she could see a ship. It was hard to tell from so far away whether it was a cargo ship or a cruise liner. Kirsty wondered where it was going. Who was on it? Who had taken her part in the show she'd left behind on *The European Countess* to follow Jon back to the UK?

As if Jon could read her thoughts, at that very moment, he sent her a message. Kirsty opened it eagerly, hoping for a little love note like the ones he used to send when they were first together. Something to remind her why love had won out over clear blue skies and azure seas.

'We're out of milk,' it said.

Chapter Ten

Duckpool Beach was Ben's favourite. Always had been. When he was a little boy, Judy used to take him there to feed the ducks. Until one of the ducks got a bit too brave and took an ice cream cone straight out of his hand. There were tears that day. After that, Ben refused to go anywhere near the famous waterfowl.

Ben never trusted ducks again – still didn't, if he was honest – but as a teenager, Ben came back to the beach with his friends. They would skive school to spend sunny afternoons sitting on the rocks, secretly drinking cider and complaining about the out-of-towners who thronged the main beach in the summer.

Later, when he was at university, Ben would come to the beach during the holidays to be moody and intellectual, imagining himself to be especially enigmatic as he gazed out to sea while listening to emo music on his headphones. Then, in his twenties, he met Jo and brought her to see his childhood haunt. He was pleased when she told him she loved it too and took off her trainers to paddle in the waves. He had feared she might be too sophisticated for British beach life. Showing Jo Duckpool was like showing her another piece of his heart.

Then they got married and they came to the beach together with Thea. They had Thea christened in the church that overlooked the bay one beautiful Sunday in June but it felt like her proper baptism happened afterwards when they carried her down to the water's edge and dipped her toes in the surf. Thea squealed but she loved it at once. When she was a toddler, she would cry when it was time to go home after a day of paddling and building wonky sandcastles.

Thea still loved Duckpool Bay and, since it was the closest beach to Grandma Judy's house, they would often bring Buster down there. Out of season, they could let him off the lead. Buster liked nothing better than to race across the sand after a ball. Though Thea always had to be reminded not to throw the ball in the direction of the 'sinky bits'. Or the stinky bits. Buster loved a quick roll in rotten seaweed. Or worse.

Six years after Thea's first dip, Ben walked to Duckpool Bay alone to cast Jo's ashes onto the waves, just as he had promised when they talked about funeral arrangements in the weeks before her death. Though she had grown up in London – and that was where she and Ben and Thea lived until she became ill – Jo had come to love Newbay perhaps more than her own hometown. She claimed she must have been a Devon woman in a previous life. Perhaps a fisherman's wife.

'You mean a *fishwife*?' Ben suggested as a tease.

Before she got ill, Jo and Ben had often discussed how they were going to retire to Newbay and watch their grandchildren throw bread for a new generation of ducks. With that version of the future no longer possible, Ben made sure the ducks were out of the way when he committed Jo to the sea.

And since Jo's death, Duckpool Bay was the place Ben came when he wanted to be close to her. His memories of her first visit to the beach were so clear. She sat on a rock and turned her face to the sun, while her feet were in the surf. That was the moment when Ben knew he really loved her. That was the photograph he wished he had taken. Moments before she turned and smiled at him and told him she loved him too.

Seeing the woman gave Ben a start. She was sitting on the rock. Jo's rock, as he had come to think of it. She had her head tipped back to face the sun just like Jo used to, though Jo would have complained that the weather was much too cold to be hanging around by the sea that day. There wasn't much sun to be had.

Ben studied the woman for a moment. She was taller than Jo had been. She had blonde hair, curly, piled up in a messy bun, where Jo's hair was dark. Her bright-yellow mac seemed to mark her out as a visitor but it was the wrong time of year for tourists. She must be local, though Ben hadn't ever seen her before, he was sure.

Thea drew Ben's attention to the fact that now they were at the beach, Buster could be allowed off his lead. The terrier was full of tense energy as he waited to be set free. The second his lead was off, Buster was away at sixty miles a minute.

'Come on, Buster!' Thea called though it was she who was following him. She threw Buster's ball.

'Watch the quicksand,' Ben reminded her. That seemed to be where she was inadvertently aiming. Ben needn't have worried. If Thea ever managed to throw a ball more than six feet, she would throw it in a completely different direction to the one she was aiming for. This time, the ball flew out of her hand backwards. Ben had no idea how she managed it. The second time, she did a little better but her aim was still hopeless and Buster was soon haring in the direction of the woman on the rocks.

Excited to be out in the open air and off his lead, Buster was going so fast that even once he had the ball in his mouth, he couldn't stop. He ended up skidding to a halt about half a metre from the stranger, kicking up wet sand and surf as he did so. He made a spectacular mess, as though he were a jeep rather than a small mutt.

'Hey!' the woman cried out as she bore the brunt of a fan of salty, sandy filth.

'Sugar,' Ben muttered.

'Language, Daddy,' said Thea automatically.

'I said *sugar*,' he pointed out. 'Sorry!' He shouted to Buster's victim. 'Buster, come back. Come back here right now!'

But Buster was intent on making matters worse. He refused to return to his owners. Instead, he decided he was going to make the woman his new friend and was making extremely enthusiastic overtures. Wet sandy paws all over her pale-blue jeans. Slobbering over her hands as he tried to persuade her to throw the ball for him.

'I'm so sorry,' said Ben, racing over to put Buster on his lead.

'It's OK,' said the woman, who was holding Buster's tennis ball gingerly between her thumb and forefinger. 'Really. I love dogs. Wish I had one.'

'But he's jumping up and making a mess.'

'Doesn't matter. Honestly. These jeans are old.'

They weren't. Clearly they weren't.

Ben went to brush the sand off the woman's legs before realising that could only make things even more awkward. Now Buster was on the lead again, Ben pulled him out of the way and apologised some more from a distance.

'He's not normally so unbiddable. He's ruined your trousers.'

'It really doesn't matter. They'll wash.'

'Well, if they don't wash, you must send me the bill. I'll buy you some new ones.'

'Really, they will be fine. It's a wet and windy day on a wet and windy beach. You've got to expect to get a bit mucky, haven't you?'

'We're still sorry. Aren't we, Buster?'

Buster just grinned, with his pink tongue lolling from the side of his mouth.

'He's very cute,' the woman said.

Ben wasn't sure why that made him blush.

'What breed is he?'

'Border Terrier.'

Thea took Buster's lead from her father and attempted her own version of disciplining the pooch.

'You're a very bad dog,' she told him. 'You've got to come when we tell you.'

Buster's response was to set off in pursuit of an interesting smell with such speed that he pulled Thea to her knees.

'Now he's got your jeans dirty too,' the woman observed.

'He won't be trained. Grandma says he's half-wolf,' said Thea, brushing sand from her hands as Buster raced away. His lead dragged behind him gathering up seaweed and other beach detritus.

'He's just got spirit,' said the woman.

'That's very generous,' said Ben. 'I think he's a little—'

'Language!' said Thea before Ben could use any.

'Monster . . . But you were having a quiet moment,' Ben continued. 'We should leave you in peace. Though . . . if the jeans are spoiled.'

Ben fished out a business card from his wallet. As he did so, it struck him that while he had yet to use one in an actual business context, he had handed out at least eight to people who might be seeking damages thanks to his mother's crazy pooch.

'Thanks,' said the woman. 'Ben Teesdale.' She read his name from the card. 'I'm Kirsty Watson.'

Ben put out his hand to shake but Kirsty was still holding the tennis ball. He relieved her of the horrible, slobber-covered thing.

'This is—' Ben turned to introduce his daughter but she was already pursuing Buster who was in a stand-off with an angry-looking gull over god-only-knew-what.

'Probably the remains of someone's fried chicken,' Ben sighed. 'I'd better go and sort this out before Thea gets pecked. Thanks for being so understanding. You must let me know about the jeans.'

'I won't,' said Kirsty. 'They'll be fine.'

'Dad!' Thea shouted. 'Dad! Buster's eating a bone! Quick! Hurry! He might get it stuck in his throat.'

'I'd better go,' he said to Kirsty. 'Bye.'

'Bye.'

Ben sprinted in the direction of his embarrassing pet.

Kirsty watched him for a while then turned her face back to the watery sun.

Chapter Eleven

On Tuesday, two days later, Ben was deep in concentration when the shop doorbell rang. He was trying to restore the data on a hard drive that had fallen foul of a stray cup of tea. He didn't notice the sound of the bell at all. It was Thea who drew his attention to the fact that somebody had come in and was standing right in front of him, waiting to be noticed.

Ben started a little as he realised who it was. It was Kirsty. The woman from the beach. She was taller than he remembered but maybe that was just because her big blonde hair was now piled right up on top of her head like a pineapple. She was wearing the bright-yellow raincoat again. It had been raining non-stop since Sunday afternoon. The residents of Newbay were used to seeing a lot of wet weather between September and April. Hell, it rained more often than not in May, June, July and August as well. Around her neck Kirsty wore a blue spotted scarf. Her Technicolor outfit made it look as though she had stepped from a cartoon frame into an old black and white movie. Ben's shop seemed suddenly very dark and grey by comparison.

'The jeans were ruined, weren't they?' said Ben.

'No. It all washed out. Look. I've got them on.'

In which case, why was she there?

'Do you do printing?' Kirsty asked.

'Of course. It says so . . .'

'On your card. I know.'

For the moment, Ben's PC business was doing whatever it took to generate income.

'That's why I'm here.'

Kirsty dug around in her handbag for a computer USB stick. 'It needs to be done in a hurry, I'm afraid. I was going to do it at home but the printer's run out of ink and I can't find anywhere that stocks the cartridges. It's only black and white.' She continued, 'Just a flyer. Though if you could do it on coloured paper . . .'

'Which colour?' Ben asked. 'Blue? Pink? Yellow?'

'It needs to be Christmassy. Any ideas?'

'Green?' Ben suggested.

'Perfect.'

Ben plugged the USB stick into the side of his desktop PC and brought up the list of files.

'Which file is it?'

He let Kirsty come round the desk to find what she needed and pretended not to notice when she accidentally clicked on a jpg which showed her in a bikini on a bright sunny beach that definitely wasn't in Newbay.

'This one,' she said. 'I need a couple of hundred. A5.'

She opened the file. It was an advertisement.

Do you love to sing and dance?
The NEWTS are looking for children
between eight and sixteen to join the chorus
for their Christmas Panto, Cinderella.

'The auditions are this coming Saturday,' Kirsty said as Ben read that exact information and corrected a small typo. 'We're not sure we'll get much of a turn-out so I'm doing one last push, leaving leaflets in all the local cafes and restaurants.'

'So you're a NEWT,' Ben observed.

'I am indeed. Do you know them?'

'I've been to some of their shows.'

'It's my first season with them. First season in Newbay as it happens. I just moved here. Though I think I might have been here once or twice as a child. Did there used to be donkeys on the beach?'

'There did,' said Ben. 'But health and safety . . .' He shrugged.

'Ah well,' said Kirsty. 'I always felt guilty about riding them. They always looked pretty fed-up to me.'

'Like Eeyore,' said Thea.

She'd been so quiet, Ben hadn't noticed that Thea hadn't gone back into the storeroom.

'Exactly! A.A. Milne had it right. Donkeys have *such* miserable faces.'

'*House at Pooh Corner* is one of my favourite books,' Thea continued.

'Mine too,' said Kirsty. 'Though my absolute favourites are the Moomins.'

'I like them as well!' said Thea. 'And the Harry Potters.'

'I haven't read those.'

'You should,' said Thea. 'They're the best of all.'

Ben wondered when he had last heard Thea say so much to someone she wasn't related to.

The printer whirred into action. As she waited for the leaflets, Kirsty made a little circuit of Ben's tiny shop. There wasn't much to look at – unless you were genuinely interested in hard drives – but there was a noticeboard, onto which Ben had tacked a list of prices for various PC-related services. Thea had added a drawing of the shop with her father standing on the doorstep. She'd written 'Good luck, Daddy' above his head in bright-pink bubble letters.

'Did you draw this?' Kirsty asked Thea.

Thea blushed to the roots of her hair. She hung onto the edge of the counter, swinging backwards and forwards. Finally she admitted it. 'Yes.'

'It's very good. Is drawing your hobby?'

Thea nodded. 'One of them.'

'What other things have you drawn?'

'I'm designing a Christmas card,' Thea said. She darted into the storeroom and came back with the picture of a reindeer with a big red nose she had been working on that morning.

'That's excellent,' said Kirsty. 'Rudolph, I presume?'

'It is. I did this one as well.'

Thea pulled another picture out of the drawer in her father's desk to show to her new friend. It was a house. Pretty as a cottage on a biscuit tin. On the doorstep were three figures. A little girl between two adults. Her mother and father, obviously.

'Oh, that's really lovely,' said Kirsty. 'You should put that one up too.'

Ben winced. Kirsty didn't know what was written on the back of that drawing in the faintest pencil, as though the fading grey represented fading hope.

'Get well soon, Mummy,' was what it said.

'Well, you are a very talented artist,' said Kirsty. 'What's your name again?'

'Thea.'

'Hello, Thea. I'm Kirsty.'

'My daddy is called Ben,' Thea added helpfully.

'I know. I've got his card.'

Kirsty smiled at him again. Ben suddenly felt quite warm.

The flyers were soon finished.

'Could I leave a few here?' Kirsty asked.

'Of course.'

'Perhaps you could mention it to your friends at school, Thea.'

'I haven't really got any,' said Thea. She was heart-breakingly matter of fact.

'Oh. I'm sure that's not true,' said Kirsty. 'But if it really is true, then maybe you should come to the auditions yourself. You can make lots of new friends at the NEWTS. That's what I've been finding out.'

Ben expected Thea to pull a face at that, just as she had been visibly horrified by the thought of the Brownies when Judy suggested joining them. Instead, to his surprise, Thea nodded. Something about this Kirsty person seemed to have charmed her.

'I do quite like singing,' Thea said.

'And I just know you can dance,' said Kirsty. 'It's settled then. We'll see you on Saturday. And dads are very welcome too. We're always looking for fresh blood at the NEWTS.'

Kirsty picked up her flyers and headed out into the rain.

Seconds later she was back.

'I can't believe I did that,' she said. 'I just walked out without paying.'

'Don't worry about it,' said Ben.

'But the cost of the ink and the paper . . . I've got to pay you.'

'I still owe you for the jeans.'

'The jeans are fine. I told you. Just tell me how much you want for the printing.'

'Think of it as my contribution to the NEWTS. And maybe you can buy me a drink one day,' he added.

Kirsty cocked her head to one side. 'OK,' she said. 'Thank you.'

Then she left again, leaving Thea full of excitement and Ben suddenly cringing. Where had that come from? Why on earth had he mentioned a drink? She'd looked surprised.

Moments later, it dawned on him. Of course she was surprised. As far as she knew – thanks to Thea's drawing – Ben had a wife waiting at home. Ben pinched the bridge of his nose. Well, he hadn't ever seen her before except for the one time in Duckpool Bay. With luck he wouldn't see her again. Except that . . .

'Can we do it, Dad? Can we go to the auditions? Look. They need eight to sixteen year olds. I'm eight. I could be in *Cinderella*.'

Ben knew exactly where he was going to be on Saturday morning.

Chapter Twelve

The second rehearsal for *Cinderella*'s main cast took place on Wednesday evening. Everyone turned up and everyone was on time but not everyone was absolutely engaged with the business at hand.

Whenever she wasn't actually in a scene, Jon's Prince Charming, Lauren, slouched back in her chair and took selfies. Having made Lauren's acquaintance, Kirsty was now following her on Facebook, Twitter and Instagram. It was astonishing how many of the photographs Lauren posted were of her own face. She had almost exactly the same expression in each one. Her chin tilted down. Eyes up to the camera. Always from her left side and never her right. She had obviously worked hard to know her best possible angle and now she had found it, she wasn't going to be tempted into any other pose.

'I mean,' said Jon, during a tea break. 'You expect celebs to be a bit self-obsessed but Lauren makes the Kardashians look positively modest.'

'It's not all her own face. Sometimes she takes a picture of avocado on toast. And I suppose it will be good for the show,' said Kirsty. 'She's got a lot of followers.'

It was quite extraordinary, the reach of Lauren's celebrity. Who knew that twenty-five thousand people watched the local weather news? If even one per cent of those people wanted to see Lauren in the flesh and bought tickets to the show as a result, the NEWTS would be laughing.

But Lauren didn't have much of a sense of humour. Though they were only two rehearsals in, she was proving to be more difficult to handle than her carefully curated girl-next-door persona had suggested. Any hint of disagreement or disapproval from Jon and Lauren's lip would start trembling. She would have to be allowed to sit in a corner, checking her Twitter and Instagram accounts for praise until she felt better again. Her posts at this time would be outrageous bids for public sympathy, scattered with hashtags such as *#actingmyheartout* and *#sohard*.

Apparently Lauren was always like this when she was taking part in a show. Annette, who had worked with Lauren on *A Midsummer Night's Dream* earlier that year, and had little patience for Lauren's obsession with social media, took to ending her every scene by shouting out a hashtag parodying Lauren's Twitter posts.

'Hashtag *nailed it*.'

'Hashtag *professional actress*.'

At least it made the Giggle Twins laugh.

Bernie would just shake her head. As she said to Kirsty over one break, in-jokes of that nature, which definitely came under the category of 'laughing *at*' rather than 'laughing *with*', were bad news.

'These things always blow up right at the worst possible moment,' Bernie said.

At least Trevor Fernlea was concentrating on his part. He seemed oblivious to any sniggering from his cast-mates and was always keen to hear what Jon had to say about his performance, even when it wasn't praise.

Cinders and Buttons' first song was no longer to 'Sixteen Going On Seventeen'. Instead, Jon had reset his lyrics to the tune of 'You Say Tomato', which was much less controversial. Trevor soon 'hashtag *nailed it*', as Annette would say. It was unfortunate the same could not be said for his dancing. Trevor seemed incapable of waltzing without stepping on Kirsty's feet. When Kirsty squeaked in indignation as he caught her toes yet again, Jon said, 'Perhaps if your feet weren't so long.'

'I'll have a couple of inches cut off, shall I?' asked Kirsty. 'It will help with my weight loss too.'

Which made everybody laugh, at least.

'You don't need to lose weight,' Trevor told her as they made a cup of tea in rehearsal room two while the Ugly Sisters and Baroness Hardup went over one of their dances.

'Thanks, Trevor,' said Kirsty.

'I'm serious,' he said. 'You're lovely just as you are. And that's not Buttons talking,' he added.

'Thank you, Trevor. I appreciate it,' Kirsty assured him.

'If I were ten years younger . . .'

'Try fifty,' said Vince, who had been listening in with great amusement. 'Hey, Jon!' he shouted. 'You wanna watch it. You've got competition! From Buttons!'

Jon puffed out his chest and pantomimed the part of a jealous boyfriend, grasping Kirsty round the waist.

'Watch yourself, Fernlea,' he joked. 'Everyone knows Buttons doesn't get the girl.'

* * *

Saturday soon rolled around: the day of the auditions for the pantomime's chorus. The children's call was in the morning. Adults in the afternoon.

Though she wouldn't have much say in who was chosen – that was down to Jon and his assistant Elaine, the production's stage manager – Kirsty agreed with Elaine, who would also be in charge of the children, that it would be nice if she came along to meet the kids who turned up. Many of them would have to go home disappointed that they weren't up to scratch. Having a chance to meet Cinderella might soften the blow.

Elaine asked the Giggle Twins, as local celebs, if they would show up too. They declined. They were going clubbing on Friday night and had no intention of being fit for human company before Sunday afternoon's rehearsal. Meanwhile, Lauren had to be in Exeter for a personal appearance at a charity fashion show raising funds for a local Alzheimer's support group.

'Lauren does quite a bit of fundraising work,' Elaine explained. 'She actually auctioned off half her wardrobe on eBay for Alzheimer's research last year.'

So, Kirsty would be the only 'star' there. It was a pity the costumes weren't yet ready. In lieu of a princess frock, Kirsty pulled out one of her glitziest dresses. It was a rose-gold sequinned number she'd bought for formal nights at sea. As she held it up to herself in front of the mirror, she smiled at the memory of the times she had worn it to dinner and of dancing with happy cruise passengers who showered her with compliments for the dress and her singing.

As she stepped into it, however, she realised it was not going to go on as easily as it once had. She frowned with disgust as she saw how the material creased across the front of her thighs. She thought she had been eating carefully. She'd certainly been doing plenty of racing around. How was it possible that she had put on even more weight?

Jon came into the bedroom as Kirsty was standing there.

'Need a hand with that zip?' he asked.

Kirsty told him no. The last thing she needed was to see the look on his face when the zip wouldn't close as it should.

'No,' she said brightly. 'I was going to wear this for the auditions but maybe it's a bit over the top. Don't want to intimidate any of the little ones by turning up looking like I'm off to the BAFTAs.'

Jon didn't question Kirsty's excuse. She had the feeling he would be happier if she wore something more low-key anyway. Though he never usually failed to compliment her when she dressed up, the previous day he had complained about her habit of leaving clothes draped across a chair in the bedroom.

'And everything you wear is so bright. It looks like an explosion in the staff changing room at Disneyland.'

Kirsty waited until he had gone back out of the room before she wriggled out of the dress that now seemed as appealing as a sausage skin. She got back into her jeans. Her 'fat day' jeans and a pale-pink sweatshirt that wasn't quite as clean as it might have been. Of course, she didn't notice the stain on the front until they were at the theatre and she couldn't come back home and change.

Chapter Thirteen

As was the case for so many children who would be at the audition, Kirsty's own first experience of the theatre came with seeing a Christmas pantomime.

She was five years old. It was New Year's Day and a cold snap had covered much of the country with snow. Kirsty remembered sitting at the kitchen table with her mother, listening anxiously as the local radio news presenter read out a list of events that had been cancelled due to the adverse weather conditions. How her mother Nicole had beamed when the newsreader announced, 'The matinee performance of *Cinderella* at the Sarajevo Theatre in the town centre will be going ahead.'

'We're on,' she said. She pinched Kirsty's cheeks. 'Kirsty Watson, you will go to the ball.'

'But how are we going to get there?' her father Stu asked. 'They might be opening the theatre, but the roads between here and there are all six inches deep. We can't take the car out in that.'

'Then we'll walk,' said Kirsty's mother.

'What?'

'People have been walking in the snow for centuries, Stu. So can we.'

And that's exactly what they did. The three of them, all wrapped up in their new Christmas jumpers and scarves and hats and wearing wellies like they were off on a Polar expedition. They walked from their house to the theatre through the deserted snow-bound town. Kirsty managed very well, only asking to be carried for the last quarter mile.

Oh, but it was worth it. The theatre was warm and welcoming. The glow of the lobby, decorated with a real Christmas tree that nearly touched the ceiling, seemed especially magical after the walk through the largely empty streets. Those audience members who had made it greeted and congratulated each other on their endeavours. There was none of the usual reserve between strangers that afternoon. It was replaced by the laughter and camaraderie that comes of a shared experience.

'Can't let the children down,' said Kirsty's dad, drawing a wry smile from Nicole.

Once they were into the auditorium itself, however, it became clear how few audience members had made the effort to get there. Back in November, when she booked the treat, Kirsty's mother had bought the best seats she could afford, but they were still a long way from the stage. And though Kirsty was tall for her age, she couldn't easily see over the seat in front, even when sitting on a pile of coats and her mother's handbag. So they were delighted when the assistant stage manager came out in front of the curtains – which Kirsty now knew were called 'tabs' – and said, 'If you see an empty seat you fancy more than the one you're in, please feel free to move into it.'

Kirsty's mother took her by the hand and led her

straight to the front row to bag three prime new places, leaving her dad to deal with their belongings.

Before the performance began, Kirsty had been given strict instructions not to fidget or talk once the lights were dimmed and the curtain went up, but her parents need not have worried. Though she was still very young, Kirsty's behaviour was exemplary due to the simple fact she was transfixed.

From the moment Cinderella walked on from stage right, sweeping the floor ahead of her, Kirsty was lost in the fairytale world. It was so much more wonderful than she had ever imagined. The dresses, the scenery, the shimmering lights. The fairy godmother's glittering wand. The glass slipper. The handsome prince. The music from a proper orchestra (albeit missing the horn section thanks to the snow). The dry ice and the indoor fireworks to mark the coming of midnight. Everything was perfect.

When Buttons asked for volunteers to help with the 'song-sheet' – that part of the panto where the kids are asked to join in with singing an old classic – Kirsty was on her feet so fast it took the people on stage aback.

'A little more enthusiasm, please,' said Buttons as Kirsty clambered up the steps as fast as her short legs would allow. The adults in the audience laughed indulgently. Kirsty was joined by just one other child – a boy two years older and a whole head taller than her. But though the other child was older, there was no doubting which of the two was more confident. When Buttons passed Kirsty the mic, so she could tell the audience who she was and where she had come from, her voice was loud and clear.

'I'm Kirsty Watson from Greenwood,' she said. Buttons went to take the microphone to hand it to the other child but Kirsty hung onto it and brought it back to her mouth to add with pride. 'And I'm five. And a half.'

The audience gave her an 'aaaahhhh'.

'And I'm forty-five,' said Buttons. 'But I think I can pass for twenty in the dark.'

The audience laughed along.

The song-sheet that year was 'Old MacDonald'. The children were given animals to interpret. Because the audience was so small and the volunteers so few, Kirsty was given pig, sheep *and* cat. Her companion was dog, cow and horse. Kirsty played her part with huge gusto. She didn't just make the sounds, she pulled faces and made up her own animal actions (though no one knew why Kirsty's sheep flapped its wings). She had the audience in the palm of her hand.

At the end of the song, Buttons asked for a round of applause. And that was it. Kirsty was hooked. She was still taking bow after bow, mixed with the occasional curtsey, when Buttons offered her a bag of sweets and a little teddy bear as a reward for her participation. She took another four bows and would have kept going for as long as the audience were happy to clap. In the end, Stu had to go on stage to fetch her down so the show could carry on.

Returning to her seat, Kirsty was glowing with pride and happiness.

'You're a natural,' her mother told her.

'She doesn't get it from me,' said her dad.

* * *

69

Kirsty kept that panto teddy bear for years. Whenever she held it, she felt a little bit of the magic she'd experienced that night. After the performance, the cast came on stage for photographs, to show their gratitude to the people who had made it through the snow. Having been full of confidence for the song-sheet, Kirsty was surprisingly shy when she was introduced to Cinderella herself. Up close, the princess seemed even more wonderful. Her jewels were as big as Christmas baubles. Her glittering shoes were the stuff of every small girl's dreams.

'Would you like to try one on?' Cinders asked.

Kirsty sat down on the boards to struggle out of one wellie. Even with her thick winter socks on, Kirsty's foot was tiny in the glass slipper (which was a Dolcis pump with sequins glued on). She was delighted.

'It fits you better than me,' Cinders exclaimed. 'I'd better tell the prince.'

Kirsty wondered what had happened to that Cinderella. She wished she'd kept a programme from the night so she could look the actress up. She'd have liked to tell her how she'd been inspired by her magical performance. Even now, knowing what it took to put on a show and how dusty and dirty a business it was to produce such sparkle, when Kirsty remembered her very first panto the memory shone like the stolen gold in a pirate's chest, or the treasure in Aladdin's cave, like Cinderella's tiny glass slipper . . .

Chapter Fourteen

If he was honest, Ben was astonished that a whole four days after Kirsty came into the shop to get her flyers printed Thea was still keen to audition for a part in *Cinderella*. Judy thought it was an excellent idea and reminded Ben that he too had been interested in the theatre as a child.

'It's the perfect activity for Thea,' said Judy. 'I don't know why we didn't think of it before.'

Still Ben had assumed she would go off the idea. But no, every single night that week, Thea had insisted on watching YouTube clips of dozens of different versions of the classic fairytale. From cartoons to ballets to obscure opera productions. She sang along (or rather hummed) in English, French and Japanese. She speculated on what the actual parts available to an eight year old might be. Mouse? Sparrow? Dancing Tea Pot?

She worried about the plot.

'Dad,' she said. 'I don't understand why the prince had to go round the whole country with the shoe. Couldn't he tell as soon as he looked at the Ugly Sisters they weren't the one he was looking for? Why couldn't he recognise Cinderella by her face?'

'Good point,' said Ben.

'And the coach turned back into a pumpkin and the horses turned back into mice and her dress turned back into rags. So why didn't the glass shoe turn back into one of her tatty old slippers? And how come she had *both* her old slippers on when the prince came round?'

'All excellent questions,' said Ben. 'And I can't answer a single one.'

Jo would have known the answers. Or at least had a good stab at making some up. What's more, she would have agreed that Thea was right to be worried about the prince. In the weeks before she died, Jo insisted she and Ben talk at length about how he would parent Thea as she grew and changed. Jo thought of everything. She even ordered a book on puberty from Amazon. Ben had it tucked away in a drawer, with a postcard from Jo inside the front cover that reminded him not to expect Thea to want to read it *with* him. He should just hand it over and let her read it at her own pace. She could ask questions later if she wanted to. He hoped he wouldn't have to think about that particular parenting hurdle for quite a few years yet.

Jo had also made him promise that he would talk to Thea about love and relationships and make sure that she never ever gave away her power to someone who didn't love and cherish her. Just because Thea was female, she should not sit around waiting to be chosen. She should remember her equal right to choose, Jo said. She should make sure that any person she became involved with – of course it didn't have to be a man – was worthy of her time and attention. That her beloved had more going for him or her than material things. That they weren't the kind of person whose head could be turned by a pair of fancy shoes.

'Oh, Dad,' said Thea, when he failed to give her a satisfactory answer as to why the single glass slipper hadn't lost its magic at midnight like all the other Fairy Godmother charms. 'You are rubbish sometimes.'

'I'm sorry I'm rubbish but I'm glad you're asking these questions. Because I would be very worried indeed if one day you decided to marry a man who could only recognise you by your footwear. Even if he did own the whole kingdom.'

'Maybe he just needed glasses like I've got,' Thea suggested.

'Perhaps you should write the sequel, in which Cinders uses her new-found riches to buy Prince Charming some specs.'

'Or contact lenses,' said Thea.

'Glasses are better,' said Ben.

'Nice big glittery ones,' Thea agreed. She was sporting a sparkling sticker of a holly leaf on the side of her own specs. Judy had bought Thea a sheet of Christmas stickers from the corner shop as an end-of-the-week treat. Ben had agreed to have a snowman stuck to the cover of his phone.

But despite the silliness of the story, Thea was still determined that she wanted to be a part of it. Liking fairytales doesn't mean you have to buy into them, Ben supposed.

The night before the auditions, Thea set the alarm clock for seven and placed it on Ben's bedside table.

'In case you forget to do it yourself. And because Grandma's not here to remind you.'

Judy was visiting friends that weekend.

'Set your phone alarm as well,' she instructed him. And she watched to make sure he'd got it right.

As it happened, Ben didn't need an alarm clock to wake him the following morning. Thea was awake at five. She stayed in her bedroom watching YouTube clips on her tablet until six, when she decided it was surely late enough to rouse her father too. Today was important after all.

Ben was barely conscious as he followed Thea downstairs and prepared her some breakfast. Thea explained that she needed to have a particularly hearty breakfast that morning because auditioning would require stamina and focus and it was difficult to focus if you hadn't been allowed to have a scoop of mint-choc ice cream with your Coco-pops. Ben was still too bleary-eyed to disagree.

After breakfast, Thea dressed in the clothes Ben had laid out the previous evening. Thea had chosen the ensemble herself. It comprised the dress she had worn to her aunt's wedding two years earlier. It was much too big at the time. Jo bought it to last, which meant that the sleeves had to be rolled up three times when Thea first wore it to the register office. Now, it was almost a little too small. But Thea still wanted to wear it. She wanted to look smart. Her school sweatshirt wouldn't cut it.

She made Ben polish her shoes as well.

'Make them shine, Dad.'

When Ben had done that, he suggested that he and Thea practise Cinderella's big moment. Thea sat down on the bottom stair, while Ben knelt in front of her with the newly polished ballet pump.

'*Whomsoever this shoe shall fit*,' said Ben, '*shall become my new queen.*'

'And get half the kingdom?' Thea bargained.

'We'll have to consult a solicitor,' said Ben.

Thea delicately stretched out her leg so that Ben could fit the shoe to her foot.

'It fits! It fits!' Thea cried. 'Bring me my crown. And the money.'

'Actually,' said Ben, 'it looks a wee bit tight. Have you been growing again? We'll have to go shopping for a new pair.'

'More expense!' Thea echoed her grandmother.

Helen, who lived next door, knew all about the auditions. She was coming out of her house just as Thea and Ben were getting into their car.

'All right, my little superstar!' she shouted to Thea. 'Big day today.'

'Yes it is,' Thea confirmed. 'I'm off to the auditions.'

'Knock 'em dead,' said Helen. 'And while you're at it, break a leg!'

Thea was perturbed.

'What did she tell me to break a leg for?' she asked her father once Helen had gone.

'It's just a saying,' said Ben. 'It's what people say to each other in the theatre instead of "good luck" when they're going on stage. For some reason, it's bad luck to say "good luck" or something like that.'

'That doesn't make any sense,' said Thea.

'There's lots of things that don't make any sense in this world,' said Ben. 'Like me being up at this time on a Saturday morning.'

'But why don't they say something nice? Why can't you say "good luck"?'

'I don't know. But you can't say Macbeth either.'

'Macbeth? What's that?'

'It's the name of a play about a Scottish king and his murderous missus. But don't say it!' Ben made a hammy show of his distress. 'You must never say Macbeth.'

'Oh, no,' said Thea. 'What's going to happen?'

Thea looked so worried that Ben relented.

'Nothing's going to happen. Theatre people are just weird, that's all. And they don't like you mentioning Mac-anything. I don't know why. Something to do with witches in the play, I think. Now let's get this over and done with.'

'Can I say MacDonald's in the theatre?' Thea asked as they cruised through Newbay's quiet streets. 'What if someone asks where we had our dinner last night?'

'You must never let on that we had our dinner at MacDonald's,' Ben said. 'Just say we went to Nando's.'

Chapter Fifteen

It was a long time since Ben had been to an audition – he hadn't set foot on a stage since performing in a few pretentious productions at university – and as soon as he and Thea turned into the theatre car park, Ben knew he was woefully underprepared. The professional stage mothers were out in force. They came carrying more bags than a newly minted lottery winner on the way home from Selfridges. They had garment bags, vanity cases, huge heavy freezer totes stuffed with healthy picnics . . . Did that mean they expected to still be in the theatre at lunchtime, Ben wondered. He had hoped he would be able to open the shop that afternoon.

'Name?' asked the young NEWTS volunteer in the theatre lobby.

'Althea Penelope Teesdale,' Thea announced.

The girl looked for Thea on her list. Ben had applied for a slot via email.

'Here you are. Age?'

'Eight. And five months.'

'Eight. Excellent. Music?'

Thea looked at her father. Ben's confused face offered no reassurance.

'Your music?' said the girl. 'Have you got your music with you?'

'We haven't got any music,' said Ben.

One of the stage mothers tutted and shook her head. 'Were we supposed to bring some?'

'Er, yes,' said the girl. 'But it's OK. What is Althea planning to sing? I'm sure we can improvise.'

'Thea?' Ben looked to his daughter to provide the answer.

The realisation that she and her father were somehow upsetting audition protocol was making Thea anxious.

'Look,' the girl tried to be kind. 'Just tell me your favourite song. I'm sure Glynis the pianist will know how to play it.'

Thea was blanking. Her favourite song? She looked at her dad. Ben was blanking too. Eventually, he pulled it back from the brink.

'She's going to sing "Somewhere Over the Rainbow",' said Ben. 'That do for you, Thea?'

Thea beamed. That was one of her favourites.

'"Somewhere Over the Rainbow",' said the girl with the clipboard.

'Does Glynis know that one?' Ben asked.

'Er, *duh*?' said the girl.

The stage mother standing behind them in the queue let out a derisive laugh that was almost a bark. Ben turned and gave her a look. It shut her up.

'OK. Another "Rainbow". Right.' The girl gave Thea a raffle ticket and a safety pin. 'This is your number. You need to pin it on your front. There are two auditions this morning. The under-twelves are in the large rehearsal room. Go straight on in and wait for further instructions. Next!'

Thea inspected the ticket.

'It's thirteen,' she said to Ben. 'That's lucky.'

* * *

The hopeful children were ushered by further volunteers straight to the large rehearsal room, which sounded a great deal grander than it turned out to be. The room smelled of decades of dust and sweat. The furniture looked like it belonged in a skip. The sight of so many worn-out high-backed chairs put Ben in mind of the old people's home where his mother had worked before she got her position in the very swanky retirement place she now managed.

Ben and Thea found themselves a corner and sat down to wait. They didn't know what they were supposed to be doing. There were some old hands there. Children who had definitely done this before. They were warming up with pliés and side bends and practising scales and other voice exercises. Their focus was impressive. Ben felt intimidated and he was a fully grown man. He could only imagine what it was like for Thea.

'Are you sure you want to do this?' he asked, even though he knew he shouldn't question her enthusiasm. Even attending this audition could do her the world of good regarding her confidence. Though it was hard to imagine that any of the other children there would become Thea's friends should she get through. They seemed so . . . well; *competitive* was the only word for it.

'Yes,' Thea nodded. 'I want to do this.' She was kneeling upon her chair and studying the photographs on a pin board behind them. 'Look at this. They did *Cinderella* before. I want a costume like that.'

Ben peered at the photograph. 'I think I went to school with that mouse,' said Ben. The young lad in the picture did look familiar. Ben couldn't immediately think of a name to match but the face gave him an odd sensation of unease.

'Should I be brushing your hair?' Ben asked.

'No, Dad,' Thea shook her head. 'You always pull too hard. I can do it.'

'Well, should *you* be brushing your hair? Everyone else seems to be smartening themselves up.'

'I already did it this morning.'

Ben was astonished to see that some of the other girls of Thea's age were actually putting on make-up. It seemed a bit inappropriate. Or was it just that he was old-fashioned? They were all taking selfies too. Pouting and putting the Hadid sisters to shame. Thea did not yet have a phone of her own. Ben had promised he would think about it for her tenth birthday. 'Who do you have to phone?' was one of his arguments. Probably half her class, he thought, seeing the youngsters busy uploading images to Instagram.

Ben wished the auditions would get going. It had just struck him that he was the only dad in the room and suddenly he didn't know where to look. Should he even be in that rehearsal room at all? Was it supposed to be a woman-only thing? Nobody had said it was.

His thoughts were interrupted by the arrival of the girl with the clipboard and another woman, slightly older, who clapped her hands to gain everyone's attention and introduced herself as Elaine – stage manager and assistant director for the production.

She ran through the programme for the day. To begin with, all the auditionees would be working together. They would be doing warm-ups and playing games to give Elaine an idea of how the children worked as a team. Ben was grateful that, to start with at least, all the children would be singing and dancing together so that if Thea was out of tune or clumsy, it would not be immediately obvious. Everyone would be too busy concentrating on his or her own performance to laugh at anyone else.

Thea was listening intently. Ben gave her shoulders a squeeze for reassurance, though really he felt in need of reassurance himself. He had a sudden flashback to the day Thea was born and how, when he held her in his arms for the very first time, he felt suddenly terrified by the responsibility of being a father. But then he'd stroked her tiny hands and Thea, not even an hour old, had grasped his thumb with astonishing strength. He realised then that she was going to be holding him as much as he was holding her. She was an old soul and she was telling him they were in it together.

As he squeezed Thea's shoulders, she looked back at him and gave him a quick smile and nodded to confirm that even if he wasn't ready for this, she was.

'OK, everybody,' said Elaine. 'Into the centre, please. Let's get warmed up.'

Thea pushed her glasses up her nose and joined the other children in the middle of the room. She looked back at Ben and he gave a covert thumbs-up.

'We're going to start by rolling our heads from side to side,' said Elaine. 'OK. Now let's shrug our shoulders up and down. Swing your arms backwards and forwards. Relax those muscles. Watch out for the people behind you. And now let's make arm circles. Shake out your feet.'

Thea smiled widely. She was keeping up.

'Stand on one leg.'

It was going to get harder now.

But Thea did it. She stood on one leg and, to Ben's surprise, she didn't wobble. She hopped. She skipped. She swayed like the branches of a tree in the wind. She prowled like a cat. She jumped like a monkey. She kept up. She seemed to be enjoying herself. When Elaine suggested a five-minute break during which the children could return to their parents to have a drink, Thea told Ben that she was having a lovely time.

'You were a great monkey,' he said.

'I was a chimp, Dad,' said Thea. 'A chimp is an *ape*.'

Next the children warmed up their voices. Glynis the pianist sat at the piano and played Christmas carols that all the children were bound to know. 'Jingle Bells'. 'Away In The Manger'. 'Little Donkey'. Ben was sure he could hear Thea's voice over the others. She was giving it her best, opening her mouth wide and annunciating just as she'd learned from a YouTube singing class video.

All the time, Elaine circled the room, listening closely to each individual child and making notes on her clipboard. When she came to Thea, she smiled and nodded. 'Very good,' she mouthed. Ben's heart swelled with pride. He hoped she wasn't just saying 'very good' because she already knew she was going to let Thea down and wanted to give her a little encouragement anyway.

At the end of a second rendition of 'Little Donkey', Elaine announced that it was time for another break. In fifteen minutes, she would be back to let the assembled children and parents know who was through to the next round, which would require the children to give individual performances in front of the director himself.

Those fifteen minutes seemed to last for hours. Thea was patient but Ben was on tenterhooks, checking his phone roughly every thirty seconds to distract himself. He'd never been so anxious waiting for news during his own brief foray into theatreland. Then Elaine reappeared with her clipboard. She began with a speech about how hard everyone had worked that morning.

'It's been an absolute pleasure to meet every single one of you. You've all been so professional and so good it's been very hard to decide which of you to ask back. But here it is. This is the list of names of the people we'd like to see again. In alphabetical order . . .' she paused.

Get on with it, Ben thought. He couldn't bear it if Elaine decided to handle this like her own personal version of *Britain's Got Talent*.

'Can't read my own handwriting,' she said by way of an excuse for making them wait. 'Here we go. Arnold, Cherry and Jerry.' The first two to make the cut were rhyming twins. They high-fived one another and punched the air. 'Barnton, Georgie . . .' Little Georgie Barnton stood up and took a bow.

The list seemed endless, though it had just fifteen names on it. In the second rehearsal room, a further fifteen children were being chosen too in the twelve to sixteen age group.

'Teesdale, Althea.'

They'd been waiting to hear Thea's name so long that Ben and Thea almost missed it.

'That's me?' Thea pointed her thumb at her own chest.

'It certainly is, killer,' said Ben.

He really wished he'd brought along some music now.

'If all those children could be back here at eleven o'clock, please. On the dot. The rest of you, I want to thank you again for coming here today and sharing your talent with us. Please keep an eye on the NEWTS' website. There will be more shows in the New Year.'

The stage mother who had snorted at Ben's lack of preparedness stalked Elaine out of the rehearsal room.

Her daughter's name had not been among those read out and she obviously thought there'd been some kind of mistake. Ben tried not to look too interested in what was going on in the corridor.

'Come on,' he said to Thea. 'We better go and find some sandwiches somewhere in case you're here for lunch.'

Chapter Sixteen

When Elaine met with Jon and Kirsty to compare notes from the two group auditions they'd held that morning, she was hopeful they'd be able to pull together a good chorus from the children they'd seen so far. There were several who'd worked with the NEWTS before who were known to be solid performers with reliable parents (that was almost as important as the ability to sing and dance. Getting the children to rehearsals and performances on time was largely the responsibility of the parents after all). They needed fourteen children to cover the seven roles they would be assigned, because there were strict rules in place about how many hours the under-sixteens could be expected to work, even in an amateur production.

Kirsty was very pleased to see the name 'Althea Teesdale' on the list. That had to be Thea – the little girl from the beach and the print shop. She wondered if Thea's good-looking dad had brought her along or whether the woman in the drawing was with her instead.

Jon was less optimistic about the chances of pulling together a good team. While Elaine had been auditioning her group *en masse*, Jon and Kirsty were already onto individual performances with the older children, who were trialling for actual speaking parts. And he was fed-up to the back teeth of 'Somewhere Over the Bloody Rainbow'.

'If only we could afford to rule out anyone who sang it on the grounds of unoriginality,' said Jon.

'It's so easy to massacre,' Elaine agreed. 'But if we did rule it out, we'd have nobody left to audition.'

'It's a terrible song,' said Jon. 'I've never seen the appeal of Judy Garland.'

Kirsty closed her ears to the heresy. 'Somewhere Over the Rainbow' was more than just a song to Kirsty.

Kirsty couldn't remember a time when she hadn't wanted to perform. Her mother told her she could sing before she could talk. Certainly, by the time she was five and a half and she'd seen that first panto, she had her heart set on the stage. Her mother Nicole was fully behind her, paying for ballet lessons, tap lessons, singing . . .

Kirsty attended her first professional audition at the age of seven. It was for an ad. All these years later, Kirsty couldn't recall the product. Maybe something to do with cleaning. She did remember that the audition took place during half term. Nicole told Kirsty's dad Stu that she was taking Kirsty into London to see a relative – her great-aunt. Stu had no idea what was really going on.

Kirsty wasn't nervous as she sang 'Somewhere Over The Rainbow' for the three adults at the advertising agency. Her mother had filled her with such confidence that she wasn't in the least bit surprised when she was offered the part.

The trouble began when they got home. Nicole proudly announced her daughter's success at the dinner table. And Stu exploded. He did not want Kirsty to be on television. He accused Nicole of trying to live vicariously through their daughter's talent. Kirsty was sent upstairs with a bowl of ice cream while her parents 'discussed' the matter in louder and louder voices. Kirsty crept out onto the landing and listened.

'It's *her* dream to be on stage,' Stu told Nicole. 'It's *yours*. You can't live your life through our daughter. You've got to stop thinking about yourself and ask what's going to be important for *her*. Prancing about singing to a bottle of washing-up liquid is not going to help her in the real world.'

Stu put his foot down. He would not give his permission for Kirsty to do the ad. He told Nicole that if she accepted the job on Kirsty's behalf, he would get lawyers involved. All the dancing and singing so far, Stu had only tolerated because he thought it was just a hobby. No daughter of his was going to be pimped out on stage. Being a child actor was no kind of life. Child stars either became unbearable brats or drug addicts.

Almost twenty-five years on, Kirsty still felt the weight of her father's disapproval. When she told him she was leaving her steady office job to work on a cruise ship, he had struggled to hide his horror. He hadn't ever congratulated her on winning a place on the cruise line's prestigious entertainment team. He'd said, 'If you're sure that's what you want, I suppose there's nothing I can do to change your mind. You're a grown woman.'

Perhaps Kirsty shouldn't have been surprised. Her relationship with Stu had often been difficult, especially after he and her mum divorced when Kirsty was eleven.

Then Kirsty's mother died and Kirsty had to move in with Stu and his new wife Linzi. Kirsty didn't blame her father's new love for the end of his marriage to her mother. Even as a teenager, Kirsty was mature enough to know that problems in a relationship are never truly one-sided. All the same, it was hard for her to warm to Linzi. Just as she was sure that Linzi found it equally hard to warm to her. There were only ten years between them and Kirsty was mortified when they were mistaken for sisters when they were out in public together.

Her little half-sister though, was a different matter. When India came along, Kirsty fell instantly in love. If it weren't for India, Kirsty might have stopped bothering with her father altogether. Wanting to be part of India's life was what kept Kirsty going back to endure the painful Sunday lunches where Linzi tried to keep the conversation going while Kirsty's father seemed to simmer with the things he couldn't say.

Kirsty had told herself that one of the things she would do, since she was going to be spending a winter in the UK, was make a serious effort to spend time with her half-sister. So far, she hadn't even called to let them know she was back. But then a telephone works in two directions, doesn't it? Kirsty's father hadn't tried to call her either.

Back at the theatre, Glynis the pianist joined Jon, Elaine and Kirsty in their discussions.

'If I have to play "Somewhere" one more time,' she sighed.

'I know,' said Jon.

Elaine mimed stabbing herself in the stomach at the thought.

Maybe it was because they were being so mean about 'Somewhere' that Kirsty couldn't help wanting to defend it and the best way to defend it would be to tell Elaine (and remind Jon – she was pretty sure Jon knew what the song meant to her, she must have told him) that as well as being the song she herself sang at her first audition, it was also the song her mother had asked her to sing at her funeral. Kirsty was only sixteen when she sang it to wish her mother goodbye.

She decided it wasn't fair. It would certainly bring the conversation to a halt but it would also make Jon, Elaine and Glynis feel bad. She didn't want that.

So instead, Kirsty ate a stick of Twix – hardly even tasting it – as Jon and Elaine went through the candidates so far, working out the order in which they would appear in the next phase. Glynis needed to be finished by four.

'Community service,' she said again. And again they all assumed she meant charity work.

Having a low blood sugar moment, Kirsty finished the first Twix stick. Jon took the other but just kept it next to his clipboard, from where it tortured Kirsty with its chocolatey call.

Chapter Seventeen

At eleven o'clock sharp, Ben and Thea were back at the theatre. This time the remaining children were to wait in the rehearsal room until they were called. There was a lot of psyching out going on, Ben thought. The children didn't interact much with each other but concentrated on the trial ahead. Hair was re-brushed. Make-up touched up. More selfies taken and Instagram updated.

Elaine explained that the children would be called up in alphabetical order which meant that Thea would have quite a wait. The Arnold Twins were called up separately. They wished each other luck and parted with hugs and kisses but Ben wondered what would happen if one twin got a part while the other didn't. How would that work out at home?

Ben decided it would be a good idea to give Thea a little pep talk. He felt sure it was what Jo would have done.

'You know how proud I am of you for wanting to do this audition, don't you?' Ben told her. 'It's very brave to come and do something you've never done before. And it's fantastic that you've made it to the second stage. But you also need to know that if this is as far as you get, it's still an amazing achievement.'

'I know, Dad,' said Thea. 'You don't have to worry about me.'

Ben's heart squeezed. There it was again. Thea was reassuring him.

When Thea spoke to him like that, Ben could hear her mother in every word.

'You don't have to worry about me.' Jo said those exact words in one of their last conversations. 'When I'm gone, I don't want you to waste a second being sad. I want you to carry on having adventures, you and Thea. I want you to be happy every day. And if being happy involves meeting somebody new . . .'

Ben shook his head. He would never meet somebody new.

' . . . if being happy involves meeting someone new, then I know you will make the right choice.'

'Althea Teesdale!'
Thea was on.

Chapter Eighteen

Kirsty, Jon and Elaine sat in the third row of the auditorium while the children filed in and did their party pieces. Glynis the pianist was on stage at her electric organ – the 'electric light organ' as she liked to call it. She was ready to play whatever was set in front of her, with her brilliant sight-reading. Though in truth, she was very rarely presented with a piece she didn't know. If the children weren't singing 'Somewhere Over The Rainbow', they were singing something from *Joseph*, *Cats* or *Les Mis* and Glynis knew all of those musicals by heart.

Indeed, the first two under-tens to take the stage, the Arnold twins, both sang 'Somewhere Over The Rainbow'. The twins were identical in appearance and their mother had chosen to dress them in identical clothes. There was not so much as a button between them. Their performances too, were so very much of a muchness, that when it came to deciding if they should go through, their auditions blurred into one. Elaine said, 'We'd better take both and put them in the same performances. Otherwise we'll land their mother with a logistical nightmare.'

So Cherry and Jerry were nodded through and Ben, waiting upstairs, would not get to find out what happens when you cast just one of a set of identical twins.

Georgie Barnton took the stage next. She was determined to stand out by not choosing 'Over The Rainbow'. She sang 'Close Every Door To Me' from *Joseph* instead and was technically perfect. Plus, as Elaine whispered to Jon, 'Her father's law firm sponsored the programmes for *Separate Tables*.' Georgie Barnton was in.

Georgie was followed by Amelie Carter. In a ridiculous coincidence, Amelie had also chosen to stand out from the crowd by singing *Joseph*'s most turgid lament. But poor Amelie forgot the words halfway through and burst into loud, noisy tears. Kirsty felt terribly sorry for the little girl but Elaine and Jon, who had done this sort of thing before, hardened their hearts. They had to whittle down the shortlist somehow. Amelie Carter's parents were not sponsoring anything. Amelie was let go.

There followed three more little girls who didn't make the grade or didn't have parents in the NEWTS who might bump them up the list by virtue of nepotism.

'A boy next,' said Jon. 'Thank goodness.'

And for the first time in the auditions, a song that Glynis didn't know how to play.

'What are you going to sing?' Kirsty asked Thomas Nuttall.

'Your Feet's Too Big,' Thomas told her.

'Now now,' said Jon. 'No need for insults. She can't help it. It's because she's so tall.'

Kirsty sighed and shook her head. Thomas was confused. 'It's what I'm singing,' he said.

'Is it really an actual song?' Jon asked, suddenly interested in a way that Kirsty found disturbing.

'It's by Fats Waller,' little Thomas confirmed.

'I've got to look the lyrics up on Google,' said Jon. '*Feet's too big*, you say.'

Thomas nodded. Kirsty tucked her own feet a little further beneath her chair.

'If you can't play it,' Thomas told Glynis. 'I can always accompany myself. On the spoons.'

'Get that boy a couple of spoons,' Jon insisted. 'This we have to see.'

Thomas Nuttall sang 'Your Feet's Too Big' to the accompaniment of two filthy old spoons from the props store, which he played against his leg. Jon loved it. Thomas was cast as one of the speaking mice without further ado.

'*Your feet's too big*,' Jon muttered as Thomas left the stage. 'There really is a song for everything.'

'I wonder if there's a song called "*Don't push your luck with your girlfriend with the perfectly average-sized feet for her height*",' thought Kirsty. Out loud.

Chapter Nineteen

'Thea, it's your turn now. Thea's dad, you can watch from the side of the stage if you like,' Elaine told Ben.

They followed Elaine from the rehearsal room down a dusty staircase to the back of the stage. The auditorium was empty but for Elaine, Kirsty – who gave Thea a double thumbs-up when she saw her – and the director.

'Jon Manley.'

Ben didn't need an introduction. All at once, he remembered exactly who the mouse in the photograph in the rehearsal room was. *Jon Manley.* It was a name Ben hadn't heard in a while.

Jon, however, didn't seem to have made the connection between Thea Teesdale – who was standing on stage, answering questions in a loud clear voice – and Ben. Ben admitted to himself that he'd probably changed quite a bit since school. Jon certainly had. He used to have thick brown hair. Now he had hardly any. All the same, Ben was glad to be hidden behind the curtain.

'OK, Thea,' said Elaine. 'Tell us a bit about yourself. How old are you and where do you come from?'

'I'm eight and I'm from here. I'm from Newbay.'

'And what are you going to sing for us today?'

'I'm going to sing "Somewhere Over the Rainbow".'

Jon groaned and slumped in his seat. Ben, who was

out of sight in the wings but able to see Jon quite clearly, frowned and mouthed 'arsehole'.

Thea saw her father from the corner of her eye. 'Language,' she mimed back.

Jon remembered his manners and straightened up.

'"Over The Rainbow". That's great,' he said. 'We haven't heard that one in ages. Glynis, please take it away.'

Thea grasped the microphone with both hands. A spotlight shone upon her. Thea screwed up her eyes while she got used to it. The pianist counted down.

'A-one, a-two, a-three . . .'

The first chord.

Thea took a deep breath and began.

Once she started singing, it was easy. The lights on the stage made it impossible for her to see the three people she thought of as 'the judges' and instead she could imagine she was just performing in the living room at home, for Judy and Ben who thought she was great no matter how well or not she performed. She remembered all the words and nailed the phrasing. The only difference was Thea had to sing more loudly than usual to compete with the electric piano.

She did all the verses. Then she closed her eyes and raised her arms in the air just like she'd seen in a YouTube video as the last chord died away.

When she opened her eyes again, the lights had been changed so that she could see her three judges. The two women were already standing to applaud.

'Thea,' said Kirsty. 'That was amazing.'

'We loved it,' said Elaine. 'You've got a real talent, young lady. You're exactly what we're looking for today.'

Only Jon remained in his seat, leaning back, giving it his best Simon Cowell. Elaine rolled her eyes at his lack of enthusiasm

'Does this mean I've got a part?' Thea asked.

'It does,' said Elaine.

'Absolutely,' Kirsty agreed.

'But it's not just about today,' said Jon. 'You've got to keep up to that standard of performance the whole time or you're out.'

Elaine swatted at Jon with her clipboard. Kirsty scowled.

'Thea, you were marvellous,' said Elaine. 'And we're very, very happy to have you on the team. Assuming you still want to join us, now you've met the grumpy old so-and-so who's going to be directing.' She jerked her thumb towards Jon.

'Yes!' Thea jumped up and down on the spot. 'Yes I do!'

'Excellent. Now, this is just the beginning,' said Elaine. 'It's going to be very, very hard work.'

'I'm so glad you decided to come along today,' said Kirsty. 'I knew you'd be good the moment I met you. You've got star quality, Thea.'

Ben felt a rush of warmth towards Kirsty when she said that.

'Take a bow, Thea Teesdale,' said Elaine.

Thea took thirteen, for luck.

As she scampered off stage, Ben gathered Thea into his arms and swung her around.

'Where did you learn to sing like that?' he asked her.

'I get it from you, Dad,' she told him. 'That's what

Grandma says. She said you were really good on the stage when you were younger. She said you could have been a star.'

'Did she really?' said Ben. 'I think Grandma's exaggerating, but wherever you get your voice from, it's brilliant.'

Later in the lobby, Cinderella herself – Kirsty – joined Ben and Thea as they got ready to go. Ben straightened up a little and self-consciously pulled in his stomach as Kirsty approached.

'It was definitely worth getting the leaflets printed in your shop,' Kirsty said to Ben. 'We got a new recruit into the bargain. Well done, Thea. But how about you, Ben? There are still places in the adult chorus and we're desperately short of men. Auditions start in an hour. Thea can sit in the auditorium with me.'

'Oh, I don't think so,' said Ben. 'I've got two left feet. And I can't sing for toffee.'

'That's not what Grandma says,' said Thea.

'You could always stand at the back and mime,' said Kirsty. 'That's what half the adult chorus does anyway, or so I've heard. You just have to make the ball scenes look busy.'

'I've got, er, other commitments.'

'Ah well,' said Kirsty. 'If you do come across anyone who fancies themselves as a thesp, please let them know. And, Thea, I'll see you at rehearsals.'

Kirsty made a fist for Thea to bump.

'You did it,' Kirsty whispered. 'I knew you would.'

* * *

It was at moments like this that Ben especially missed Jo. He knew that Jo would have been over the moon with Thea's happy news. She would have known all the right questions to ask.

Sitting in the car park, Ben called his mum. Judy asked that Thea be put on the phone right away. Ben handed his mobile over. Thea quickly put it onto speakerphone. For some reason, she preferred to talk into the phone as if she were in one of those excruciating taxi scenes in *The Apprentice* rather than put it to her ear. Still, it meant that Ben could be in on the whole conversation.

'I'm going to be a mouse. It's not a speaking part,' Thea explained. 'But the director said it is still very important. We're Cinderella's helpers and we help get her to the ball. We're going to have eight songs.'

'That's a lot of singing,' said Judy.

'I know. We're going to be doing lots of rehearsals. There are seven mice altogether in my group. There are two groups because of the law . . .'

Knowing that Thea and Judy could be talking for some while, Ben turned the car engine on.

As he drove around the front of the theatre, Kirsty came strolling out. She was with Elaine and they were laughing about something. She had taken her hair out of its ponytail and it was frizzing out around her face like a halo, catching the last of the November sun. Ben loved big hair like that and it suited Kirsty especially well. Then she half-turned in the direction of Ben's car, still smiling at Elaine's joke and Ben felt an echo of a feeling he hadn't felt in a long time. Though Kirsty almost certainly couldn't see him looking at her, Ben blushed.

'And Cinderella is really beautiful,' said Thea to Judy.
Ben silently agreed. She is.

Chapter Twenty

The adult auditions for places in the chorus were dealt with far more quickly than the children's, attended as they were by the usual suspects, whose capabilities were only too well known. There were exactly the right number of applicants for the available roles so even Moira Jones, who couldn't hold a note if you drew it on a piece of paper and stuck it to her hand with sticky tape, got a part. On the strict understanding (at least between Jon and Elaine) that she would be placed at the back of the stage at all times and would definitely not have a microphone.

'And she'll have to dress as a bloke,' Jon added. As Kirsty had told Ben, there was a serious lack of male talent.

Anyway, Jon and Kirsty were back in the flat by six o'clock. While Jon checked his emails for news of employment opportunities from his theatrical agent in London, Kirsty made a phone call to Jane from the bedroom, catching up with her news and filling her in on the day's events in Newbay. When the call was finished, she went back into the living room, where Jon was hard at work scribbling on his copy of the *Cinderella* script.

'What are you doing?' Kirsty asked. 'Isn't it a bit late to be making alterations to the script now everyone's learned their lines? If you're changing Vince's lines, you'll need to give him another fortnight to get used to them.'

Vince had a great memory for dirty jokes, but the script seemed to evade him.

'I'm just changing one of the songs,' said Jon.

'Whose song?'

'One between you and Buttons.'

'Which one? I don't know that Trevor will be too excited at the prospect of having to learn something new at this stage either.'

'He probably won't have to learn anything. He'll know it already. The song is from his era.'

Jon finished typing something into his document. He grinned to himself, as though hearing a private joke.

'Which song?' Kirsty asked again. She was growing suspicious, though she didn't quite know why.

'I know how much you don't like singing "If I Can't Have You" with Trevor.'

That was true. Kirsty wasn't sure that Jon's version of the seventies disco classic, which he had entitled "If You Can't Be Mine" really worked in the context of the panto and she especially disliked the sexy dance that Trevor insisted went along with it. Not because it was sexy so much as because she feared he might break a hip.

'So I've swapped it for something much better.'

'Which is?'

'Remember that little boy at the audition today? The one with the spoons?'

'Thomas Nuttall. Yes.'

'Well, that song he sang was perfect. It's just right for the scene. Buttons is in love with Cinderella but he can't tell her. So, instead of declaring his true passion, he turns it into a joke and sings—'

'"Your Feet's Too Big".' Kirsty filled in the punch-line.

'Exactly!' Jon rocked back in his chair. 'It's absolutely genius. We can get Thomas to come on with his spoons while you and Buttons are singing it.'

'Great.'

Kirsty turned her back on him and went into the kitchen. Jon followed close behind.

'What's the matter? It could be really funny. People will love it.'

'A really good joke,' Kirsty agreed. 'At *my* expense.'

'What do you mean?'

'What do you mean, what do *I* mean? Why are you suddenly always going on about the size of my feet?'

'Darling, I wouldn't joke about them if they really *were* monstrous. It's just a tease.'

'It doesn't feel like that.'

'Look, if your feet really were huge, I wouldn't dare take the mickey. As it is, they're only slightly bigger than average and, as you said, you'd fall over without them.'

'Thank you.'

'Oh, come on,' Jon tried to cuddle her from behind. 'Where's your sense of humour?'

Kirsty pulled out of his embrace and tried to ignore him. She opened the fridge and pulled out a bag of salad. Salad, again. On such a miserable wet and cold evening when all she really wanted was something filling and warming like a nice big shepherd's pie. But it was a fast day – as Jon kept reminding her – and salad was all they were allowed.

She pulled the salad bag open, tipped half the leaves onto her plate and half onto Jon's. Then she garnished it with two slimy-looking pieces of ready-poached salmon that she struggled to get out of their plastic tray. It was a very uninspiring supper. All the time, Jon was dancing around her, trying to make her laugh and smile again. He might have had an easier job were Kirsty not facing another evening listening to her tummy rumble and complain about the short rations. She'd wasted half that day's calories on one stick of Twix.

But then Jon blew it big time. As Kirsty turned from the kitchen counter to slap their plates down on the table, he came towards her with his jazz hands, singing the blasted song.

'Oh. That's it!' Kirsty put the plates down so hard that one of the pieces of salmon leaped off the plate and onto the kitchen floor, where it landed on one of Kirsty's feet.

'Don't say that if my feet were smaller, the salmon would have missed,' she warned him. 'Don't say anything.'

'I wasn't going to—'

'Don't!'

Kirsty abandoned all hope of a successful fast day and made herself some cheese on toast. She let Jon have the remaining piece of salmon.

He looked pained all the time he was eating, as though her outburst had been entirely unprovoked and unreasonable. He did that, Kirsty had noticed recently. If he provoked her and she retaliated, he always somehow managed to make it seem as though *he* was the victim of an unexpected attack. And he was generally so good at appearing hurt that she would end up feeling guilty and, before she knew it, she would be trying to appease him. Doing what she could to make him feel better when she was the one who should be smarting. That was a very special skill.

'You're right,' said Jon later, as they were watching the news. 'I'm going to leave "If I Can't Have You" in that scene. "Feet's Too Big" doesn't have the right tone. And I'm sure Trevor would be disappointed if he didn't get to show off his disco prowess.'

'Thanks,' said Kirsty.

But she was left feeling that she'd been a bad sport and by bedtime she was sure that's exactly what Jon had intended because the only way to feel better about the whole thing would be to agree that he was right after all and give in. Which was exactly what she did the following morning.

'All right,' she said. 'Write the bloody song into the show.'

'I knew you'd come round,' said Jon. He sang it all day long.

By this time, Kirsty and Jon had been in Newbay for two months. Because they were renting the flat through one of Jon's father's friends, they had a fairly flexible arrangement. They'd signed a six-month lease but would be able to leave sooner if and when they got work in another part of the country.

Like Jon, Kirsty had a theatrical agent who was busy looking out for opportunities on Kirsty's behalf. While working on the cruise ship, Kirsty had put together a show reel that had been getting lots of positive feedback from casting agents and producers. Her agent assured her it was a matter of time before she was offered some work.

But Kirsty was not about to take any old job. She had moved back to the UK to be with Jon and thus the last thing she wanted to do was take a part in a musical in Edinburgh while Jon was all the way down south in Newbay. Every time Kirsty's agent suggested something new, Kirsty would weigh it up in terms of what it might mean for her relationship. After all, Jon had told her, when he asked her to come to Newbay, that he couldn't bear the thought of being away from her for any longer than a weekend.

'Now I've got you in my life,' he said. 'It seems impossible that I was ever without you.'

He called her his soul mate. His muse.

The ideal scenario was that they would both find work in London. They didn't have to be in the same show. They just had to be in the same city. London, with its West End and its fringe theatres and its film and television companies was the place where they were also most likely to find opportunities that would suit them both. It was where Kirsty was concentrating her search.

Jon, however, was suddenly thinking further afield.

'Berlin could really work for me,' he announced the night after he'd upset Kirsty with all that *Feet's Too Big* business.

'What do you mean?' Kirsty asked.

'They've got a really vibrant arts scene. Or Prague. Prague could be good too.'

'But what could I do there?' Kirsty asked.

Jon's background was very different from hers. He went to a fancy school and actually spoke German and French and some Italian and probably Japanese for all Kirsty knew. He had studied drama. Ultimately, he wanted to be a 'serious' theatre director doing Shakespeare, Pinter,

Beckett. Kirsty's talents definitely lay elsewhere. Was there room for a cruise singer in Berlin?

The conversation left Kirsty feeling unsettled, even if Jon did promise her that he wasn't about to run off overseas without telling her. They would take all decisions about their next step together. They were a team. Weren't they? And Kirsty's career mattered just as much as his.

Chapter Twenty-One

The children's rehearsals got underway the weekend after the auditions.

There were strict rules regarding the appearance of children in stage productions. The first was that there was a limit to the number of performances they were allowed to take part in. The second and most important rule was that the children were to be chaperoned at all times. When they weren't needed on stage, they were confined to a rehearsal/dressing room under the watchful eye of a responsible adult who'd passed all the necessary CRB checks. When it was time to go down to the auditorium, the chaperone would accompany the children all the way and watch from the wings every minute they were on stage.

The NEWTS took all these rules very seriously indeed. Thankfully, there were those among their number who actually enjoyed wrangling over-excited children on performance nights. There were a couple of older ladies – Gwyneth and Megan – who were always first to volunteer. With their own children and grandchildren long since grown up, the noise and the bad behaviour were a novelty to them. By contrast, most of the parents of the children involved in the NEWTS' shows were mysteriously busy on rehearsal and show nights. After dropping their children off at the stage door, they always had to go back to work to 'finish a project' or dash round to Grandma's to 'help the old dear out'. For them NEWTS was a very cheap baby-sitting service.

Ben was not so lucky.

Though she had met some of the other children who would be performing alongside her at the auditions, Thea said she was nervous about spending time at the theatre without having her father nearby. So Ben had to attend the first rehearsal with her.

Ben thought he would sit at the side of the room with a book. He wasn't going to get away with that. Thea wanted to know that Ben was paying attention.

'Did you see that, Daddy? Did you see that?' she would ask every couple of minutes.

The children chosen to play the mice had a great many songs and dances to learn. Ben had no doubt that Thea would learn the songs very quickly but the dances . . . Well . . .

'Thea,' Elaine called. 'Thea, come closer to the front, sweetheart. You need to watch my steps. Start with the right foot. No, sweetheart, your *other* right . . . That's better. Just watch what I'm doing and do exactly the same thing. Is everybody ready? A-one, a-two, a-three . . .'

The dances seemed a good deal more complicated than the few they'd had to master for the audition. Somehow, Thea always seemed to end up travelling across the room in the opposite direction from everyone else.

'That's all right, sweetheart,' Elaine reassured her. 'We've got plenty of time to practice and I'm sure Daddy's going to help you at home.'

Elaine looked at Ben, who shrugged and pulled a face that said, 'I haven't a clue.'

'In fact,' said Elaine then. 'Everybody in the room should learn this one. Gwyneth? Megan?' Elaine gestured to Ben. 'Thea's daddy?' She didn't know his name yet.

'Ben,' he obliged.

'Ben. Would you mind coming into the middle of the room for this next bit. Then when Thea's practising later, you'll know how the dance is supposed to go. And when you're on stage, boys and girls, you're going to have to dance alongside the adults. This is to give you some practice of getting out of the way of their great big feet. Come on.'

Elaine would accept no excuses. She took Ben by both hands and hauled him out of his chair.

Ben felt like the BFG, standing in the middle of a sea of tiny eight and nine year olds. Gwyneth and Megan were both fairly small and didn't stick out half so much.

'You might actually remember this one, Ben,' Elaine told him.

She pressed a few keys on her laptop and the theme to *Saturday Night Fever* filled the room.

'I'm not that old,' said Ben.

'Oh, I know this,' said Gwyneth, moving straight into the dance everyone knew in the 1970s.

'Excellent. Follow Gwyneth's lead,' Elaine shouted over the music. 'Step, step, step . . .'

Thea's faced was creased with concentration, matching her father's. Ben realised he had to move or be trampled. He did the side-wind across the floor with the best of them. Arm actions too. And, within a couple of minutes, he realised he was rather enjoying it. He didn't sit down for the rest of the rehearsal.

'Are you sure you don't want to join the adult chorus, Ben?' asked Elaine.

Chapter Twenty-Two

While the children (and Ben) learned their song and dance routines, rehearsals continued for the adults too. But as the members of the main cast perfected their performances for the stage, it seemed they had stopped pretending to be anything other than their very worst selves in real life. On the third full Sunday rehearsal, Vince did not arrive with Bernie. She told her castmates that Vince seemed to be fighting off the flu. She hoped he would arrive later in the day. Trevor Fernlea took Bernie at her word and said he hoped Vince made a swift recovery but some of the others were less generous.

'Flu?' Annette snorted. 'More like a hangover. He's sleeping it off.'

The Giggle Twins agreed. 'Tell him to take more water with it,' said George.

'I wonder whose bed Vince is sleeping the flu off in,' said Andrew Giggle.

Bernie stoically ignored them. Kirsty tried to ignore the innuendo too. She wasn't sure she liked the way the gossip was going. Bernie never stooped to gossip herself and Kirsty could tell she was upset.

* * *

'How did you and Vince meet?' Kirsty asked during a tea break, hoping to distract Bernie with small talk. Asking people how they met their beloved usually led to a happy conversation.

'Oh. It's not in the least bit romantic,' said Bernie, though she was already smiling at the memory, just as Kirsty had hoped. 'I broke a tooth. There used to be a French restaurant in the old town. It was called Chez Jacques and it was terribly pretentious. And very expensive. All about seasonal food grown locally. Everything organic. They even produced their own snails.'

'Really?'

'Yes. And ordering those was my mistake. I was on a boring date with a *very* pompous actuary. I think I ordered the snails in a misguided attempt to shock him. Well, one of them had some grit in it. I bit down and cracked a molar. I was in agony. Vince was the only dentist I could find who would see me on a Sunday. And the rest is history, as they say.'

She looked wistful.

'On our first date he took me to an Italian. Spaghetti's altogether less dangerous than snails. You know, we'll have been married for twenty years this December.'

'That's quite an achievement,' said Kirsty.

'Oh, it's been easy,' said Bernie. 'He makes me laugh every day. That's the most important thing in a relationship. The ability to lift each other up. He's always been able to do that for me. And he always brings me a cup of tea first thing.' She smiled at the thought.

Kirsty wondered if Vince even knew how much Bernie loved him.

Just then, George Giggle joined them by the kettle.

'How's Vince's flu?' he asked, making air quotation marks around the word 'flu'.

Bernie frowned.

It was worse when, a little later on, Annette remarked, 'Well, The Cockle Picker will have opened by now. I don't suppose we'll see Vince until tomorrow.'

The Cockle Picker was one of Vince's favourite pubs.

As it happened, Vince did turn up after lunch. It was immediately obvious to everyone in the rehearsal room that he'd had a few 'sharpeners' on his way in though. He was swaying as he walked into the centre of the circle of mismatched chairs for his scene with Cinderella. Kirsty couldn't help recoiling from the strong smell of alcohol on his breath as he spat his lines all over her. He seemed like a different man from the one she'd last seen leading a sing-song in the theatre bar on Friday night, after she and Jon had gone to watch a different set of NEWTS in *Separate Tables*. Then Kirsty had enjoyed duetting with him on that Elvis classic 'Suspicious Minds'.

It wasn't just the smell of alcohol on Vince's breath that was a problem. Vince couldn't remember his lines. At one point, he skipped eight pages of script, leaving Kirsty, Annette and the Giggle Twins baffled. When Jon pointed out that Vince had jumped ahead, Vince swore it was an easy mistake to make. Especially when the script was so bloody repetitive. He seemed to have forgotten that Jon actually wrote the thing.

'Perhaps you'd like to put your suggestions in writing,' said Jon.

'Go for it, Euripides,' said George Giggle.

'Look, everybody. Can we just get on with it?' asked Lauren. 'I've got to be in the TV studio at seven tomorrow morning. I need to get my beauty sleep.'

'Well, if you could ever put your phone down for long enough to notice your cue,' said Jon. 'We could get through everything a whole lot faster.'

'Oh!' Lauren took great offence and retreated to the ladies' room.

'*We know what you're doing. We know what you're do-ing*!' chanted George and Andrew as she left. It was what they did every time one of the cast members went for a 'comfort break'. Apparently, it was the punch-line of their children's act. It was infuriating. But in this case, Lauren would be doing exactly what everyone expected.

As soon as Lauren had left the room, Kirsty opened the Instagram app on her phone and counted the seconds until Lauren posted a selfie. The light in the ladies' room was very flattering and Lauren never failed to take advantage. This time, she went for a moody look and commented beneath: 'Beginning to understand how hard the likes of Suranne Jones and Sarah Lancashire work. *#acting #givingiteverything*.'

George and Annette saw the selfie come up on Annette's iPhone.

'Hashtag *Giving It My All*? Hashtag *My Arse*,' said Annette.

Though of course, when Lauren came back into the room, everyone pretended they didn't know what she'd been up to at all.

During the tea break, Vince was straight outside for a cigarette. Bernie followed him.

'I don't know why she bothers,' said Annette. 'He's a waste of space and he has about as much respect for her as he has for a pair of old slippers.'

Kirsty tried to change the subject but Annette continued. 'Bernie wants to ask herself what Vince is really up to when he says he's at those dental conferences.'

Annette nodded knowingly. Kirsty gave a little shrug.

Annette seemed envious of Bernie. She was always quick to chip in with criticism when Bernie was on stage. She couched her comments in the spirit of, 'I don't want to cause offence but . . .' She was also especially hard on Lauren.

But then Lauren was no angel. Kirsty had heard her talking to Andrew Giggle earlier that afternoon. Lauren complained that, 'It's totally unrealistic that I'm the prince while *she's* Cinderella. She's way older than me for a start . . .'

Kirsty was on a fast day when she heard that, so she couldn't even eat a bloody great cake to console herself.

But Lauren's throwaway comment, so brief but so bitchy, was soon to fade into insignificance.

In the last week of November, the main cast had their costume fittings.

Chapter Twenty-Three

The wardrobe was one of Kirsty's favourite parts of the NEWTS' theatre. It was right at the top of the building, reached via a dark staircase that put Kirsty in mind of the staircase to Sleeping Beauty's tower in the Disney film she'd adored as a child. Climbing up there, you felt as though you were ascending into another realm; one where anything could happen. Where you could become someone else. No matter how long and hard they had been rehearsing, for most of the actors it was putting on a character's clothes that really made the difference. That was when they started to feel as though they could convince an audience. And themselves.

Bernie said the wardrobe reminded her of *Mr Benn*, a children's series from her childhood, in which a mild-mannered city worker would drop into a fancy-dress shop as he wandered home from work. The shopkeeper, who wore a fez to denote his unlikely magical powers, would suggest an outfit. Mr Benn would try it on and suddenly find himself in a whole new world, fighting dragons in a suit of armour, caring for lions in his zookeeper's uniform or floating through space in bubble helmet.

Yes, the wardrobe was a magical kingdom. Even

though it smelled like a particularly unsavoury charity shop.

Unfortunately, the wardrobe was the domain of three witches far worse than anything in *Macbeth*; three indomitable women who had been in charge of the company's costumes for as long as anyone could remember.

When she was summoned, Kirsty knocked and waited to be asked inside. No one was supposed to go into Wardrobe without permission. There were real treasures in there if you knew what to look for. Genuine dresses from the fifties and forties that would fetch a fortune at a vintage store. Likewise, suits and hats and handbags. Rumour had it there was a genuine crocodile Birkin that would be worth several grand on eBay hidden away in one of the many cabinets, which were labelled in a cramped handwriting like medicines in an old-fashioned pharmacy. Kirsty longed to be able to rummage through the accessories cabinet.

'Enter,' said Sally in stentorian tones.

Kirsty stepped inside making sure that the door closed, quietly, behind her.

Sally, Angie and Debbie were sitting at the mending table. Sally was stitching sequins to chiffon. Angie was darning a hole in the elbow of an old sweater. Debbie was working on the crotch of a pair of men's hose. Kirsty wondered if they were the trousers that were the subject of much hilarity on the last night of the company's performance of Romeo and Juliet. Apparently Trevor Fernlea was mid sword-fight when the crotch went. There were rumours of sabotage. Of stitches unpicked.

'So, you're our Cinders,' said Debbie, pushing her

glasses to the end of her nose so that she could look over them to appraise her latest victim.

'I told you,' said Sally. 'Twelve to fourteen.'

'Fourteen,' said Debbie.

'Maybe even sixteen on the bottom half,' Angie chipped in.

'Twelve,' said Kirsty, firmly.

'Hmmm. Last time we did Cinderella, she was an eight to ten,' said Sally. She sucked air in through her teeth. 'This is going to be difficult.'

Debbie put a finger to her lips and tapped them as though she was trying to think of a solution.

'Double Spanx?' she suggested.

'I'm still here,' Kirsty pointed out.

'It makes our job much easier if characters stick to a standard size,' said Debbie.

'Indeed it does,' said Angie.

Sally got up from the table and went to the rails to bring out a costume. 'This might do, if we take the collar off and stick some marabou around the hem. You're tall, aren't you?' she added to Kirsty, as though that too was an issue.

'I intend to lose three inches before the show,' said Kirsty sarcastically. These women were making her itch. Or maybe that was the flea-bitten lamé dress Sally had thrust into her hands. It smelled musty and was distinctly yellow around the armpits. It was a far cry from the costumes she had worn on board *The European Countess* which were all made just for her.

Still Kirsty put it on. The NEWTS didn't have the funds for new costumes for every show. Kirsty understood that. But wearing the silver dress, which had possibly been quite avant garde in the 1980s but was definitely not fashionable now, she certainly didn't feel like the Cinderella of her childhood dreams. Though, ironically, that Cinderella had probably worn something similar, given the era. Puff sleeves as big as her head.

Reluctantly, Kirsty stepped out from behind the changing screen and allowed Sally, Angie and Debbie to make their appraisal. They didn't hold back. It was worse than any audition Kirsty had ever attended. They circled her like a pack of hyenas waiting for their prey to tire and give in to their snapping jaws.

'We'd need to let it out,' said Debbie.

'I'm not sure how much seam allowance we've got to work with,' Angie complained

'Double Spanx and a corset?' said Sally.

'At least.' Debbie concurred.

'I need to be able to breathe,' Kirsty reminded them. 'It's pretty much a requirement for singing.'

Despite the fact that it was obvious the dress would not close, Debbie gave one more tug on the zip anyway, succeeding only in pinching some of Kirsty's skin between the teeth.

'Ow.'

'You've broken the zip,' said Debbie.

'You've broken my skin,' Kirsty retaliated.

'No need to get tetchy. We're only trying to make you look your best,' Angie reminded her.

'It might look better with the shoes,' said Sally. 'Where are they?'

Debbie picked up a pair of silver court shoes – which were in fact white ballroom shoes, sprayed silver – that had been pulled out and put to one side for Kirsty's fitting. Kirsty knew at once there was no chance she would be able to get them on. Hadn't these three witches read any of the details Kirsty had filled out on their fitting form?

'These are a size four,' said Kirsty. 'And I, obviously,

am not. Because if I had size four feet,' she added for what felt like the hundredth time, 'I would fall over.'

'What size are your feet?' Debbie asked.

'They're 41.'

'What's that in English?'

'It's a seven and a half . . . Or an eight.'

'I didn't know ladies' feet went that big,' said Sally. 'Have we got anything to fit her at all?'

Angie consulted the plan on the desk, then scuttled off to the deepest recesses of the attic room. Kirsty could hear her swearing as she pulled out a trunk. She dragged the trunk to where Kirsty stood.

'In 1997 when we did *It Ain't Half Hot, Mum* there was a scene in which all the soldiers dressed up as women to put on a show within the show. Do you remember, ladies?' Angie asked her witchy colleagues.

'I do,' Sally said.

'Oh, it was a good one,' Debbie agreed. 'Trevor Fernlea was brilliant as Bombardier Beaumont.'

'This trunk should have those costumes in. And the shoes.'

Angie got the filthy old trunk open, using a teaspoon as a jemmy. The catch had rusted shut.

'Bingo,' she said.

All four reeled back as the trunk let out a gust of stale and ancient air. It was as if they'd opened the Ark of the Covenant.

Angie pulled out a pair of golden shoes. A mouse had been nesting in the toes of the right foot. She banged the shoe on the table to dislodge the droppings.

'I'll use a pair of my own,' said Kirsty.

* * *

Most of the cast was on a tea break when Kirsty got back downstairs. Bernie was in the rehearsal room, trying to get to grips with her magic wand, which crackled and sparkled when she pressed a little button. It must have been obvious to her from the look on Kirsty's face that the costume fitting had not gone entirely to plan.

'I would rather have my toenails pulled out than go through that again. You should have seen what they tried to put me in. It was the very opposite of the scene where the Fairy Godmother gets Cinders ready for the ball. They made me look like a scarecrow. And feel like one.'

'Don't take any notice of those old bags,' said Bernie. 'Bitching away like they're Lagerfeld, Galliano and Chanel, when they're really just a trio of middle-rate seamstresses who spend their days in a room that smells of mothballs and armpits. No wonder they're sour. It's all the camphor.'

'Thanks,' said Kirsty.

'The wardrobe department is shocking. I've known people get parts just because they've got the right shoes.'

'Talking of shoes,' said Jon, interrupting. 'Did they find you something?'

Kirsty winced as she remembered the men's shoes with the mouse droppings. Maybe in a couple of years, it would make a good anecdote – Cinders, whose feet were so big she had to wear the Ugly Sisters' clogs – but right now she was feeling a little bruised.

'I've got a silver pair back at home,' she said. 'With a few of those stick-on jewels they'll be all right.'

'Didn't they have anything for you at all?' Jon persisted.

'I'm not sure I'm all that keen on the idea of wearing shoes some other Cinders has sweated in.'

She was too embarrassed to tell him the full and awful truth.

He went off whistling 'Your Feet's Too Big' all the same.

Chapter Twenty-Four

So the NEWTS had adult costumes going back decades – the wardrobe was a vintage dealer's dream come true – but when it came to the children, they were much less well equipped. That was because children seemed to be so much harder on the costumes than adults. They were always spilling things and splitting things and leaving things on the back of the bus on the way home from rehearsals. For that reason, when children were involved in a performance, the wardrobe crew did their best to outfit them in costumes that were cheap and easily replaced at the last minute.

The panto mouse costume was a classic of the genre, consisting of a grey leotard over grey tights, accessorised with mouse ears of grey fabric stiffened with cardboard and tails made from thick pieces of string.

When Thea came out of rehearsal with the list of costume requirements, however, Ben didn't have a clue where to start. As Thea had stayed away from dance classes thus far in her little life, he had no idea where to buy a leotard. However, he was determined not to let Judy see another example of his incompetence. In the end, he bought one online and was feeling very proud of himself until it arrived and he discovered that he'd bought the wrong size. A woman's size eight instead of age eight for a child. Judy came to the rescue, explaining that the school outfitter in town carried exactly what he was looking for and grey tights were available just about anywhere.

'Who knew?' said Ben.

The ears were the real challenge. Judy helped out by buying the fabric that was required but it was down to Ben to assemble the headband with its big Minnie-style protuberances. The wardrobe ladies had helpfully given each child an A4 sheet with the ear 'pattern' printed onto it, but the accompanying instructions might as well have been written in Sanskrit for all the sense they made to Ben. As for the actual sewing, Ben calculated that the last time he had picked up a needle to do anything more complicated than stitch a loose button back onto a shirt was twenty-five years earlier at primary school. Ben and the rest of his class were given a crash course in sewing in order to make a purse for Mother's Day. The project got quite complicated, as the children had to stitch their mother's initials onto the front as a finishing touch.

Judy still had the purse Ben made. She kept it in the top drawer of her dressing table and used it to keep spare buttons she thought might come in useful. When Ben told her that he had to sew Thea's mouse ears, Judy got the purse out to remind him that, once upon a time, he'd been pretty nifty with his chain stitch. It was also her way of saying that Ben was on his own.

And how hard could it be?

Ben cut out the pattern and used it to create four grey pieces. But he didn't place the pattern quite right on the fabric, so he only managed to get three and had to buy another piece of the grey material the next day.

Sewing was more difficult than he remembered too. He kept pricking his finger but Judy's thimble was too small. Getting the earpieces stitched together took hours.

And then Ben realised that he should have put the cardboard stiffening into the ears before he closed up the edges, so he had to unstitch them and start again from scratch.

By the time Ben finished, it was three in the morning. Barely able to keep his eyes open, he tiptoed into Thea's room, where she slept with a copy of the *Cinderella* script beneath her pillow, and hung the newly made headdress from the end of her bedframe like a Christmas stocking. Maybe, Ben thought in a moment of fatigue-induced madness, that year he could make Thea a personalised stocking. He'd seen a pattern somewhere. In one of Judy's magazines. Yes. It seemed like a good idea. They needed some new Christmas traditions. A handmade stocking would be a great place to start.

At five past three, Ben flopped into bed with visions of sugarplums running through his head.

Thea wore the mouse ears down to breakfast, which was when Ben discovered that though the ears were the same size and had been made with exactly the same kind of cardboard inner, one of them simply would not stand up. It didn't seem to matter that it had been made in exactly the same way as the other. No matter what Ben did to try to fix the ear upright, it would droop forward over Thea's eyes again.

'There must be loads of mice with droopy ears in real life,' said Ben.

Though he knew as well as Thea did, that just wasn't true. You saw rabbits with droopy ears. You saw dogs with droopy ears. Even the odd cat with a droopy ear. But a mouse? Never. It just didn't seem to happen.

'It'll be all right, Dad,' said Thea. 'Someone at the NEWTS will know how to sort it out. You know, I really like it there. I'm glad I got a part.'

That, at least, made the late-night sewing seem worthwhile.

Chapter Twenty-Five

By this time, rehearsals for the main cast had moved from the rehearsal room to the stage itself, which was free again after the end of a highly successful run of *Separate Tables*. Though the cast of Cinderella had been practising the 'blocking' – how they would move around a scene – for weeks and seemed to have that down pat, everyone knew that to be on the actual stage would be very different. In the rehearsal room, the perimeters of the area the actors had to play with were imaginary. Down on the stage they would have to deal with the curtains – or rather the tabs – all the backdrops, all the scenery, all the props.

Two students from the local art college, who were using the project as part of their degree coursework, were creating the scenery for the production. They'd listened intently as Jon described the look and feel he wanted them to create. They nodded sagely when he referred to his favourite films and artists.

'A cross between the underworld in *Pan's Labyrinth* for the magic and Baz Luhrman's *Moulin Rouge* for the colours,' was the log line it all boiled down to. Looking at the sketches and collage they produced after their first meeting, Jon was confident that the art students would be able to translate his vision to the stage with no problem whatsoever.

But so far, they had only created a backdrop for the ballroom scene that looked about as appealing as a bus station and one for the outdoor scenes that was uncannily similar to the bright-green world of the Telly Tubbies, complete with grinning flowers.

'It will look different when the lighting's been sorted out and it's all covered in glitter,' Kirsty promised when she saw how disappointed Jon was by the realisation of his careful brief.

So. Back to the first rehearsal on stage. It was going pretty well. Kirsty was very pleased to be taking the performance to the boards at last. It suddenly felt much more real. She loved to stand in the actual wings as she waited for her cue. Though she had to try not to get distracted by the graffiti that had been scrawled onto the backs of old scenery panels. Some of it seemed to be in the same hand as the graffiti that had appeared on the cast list.

It was a tight squeeze in the wings, filled as they were with the technical equipment that would create all the magical effects.

'Don't ever press those buttons,' said Trevor Fernlea, as he and Kirsty waited to go on. He pointed to a small control box with two big red buttons marked Pyroflash.

'Why not? What does it do?'

Trevor pressed it.

There was the sound of an explosion and a blinding light. On stage, George and Andrew Giggle, who were in the middle of a complicated dance routine, fell straight onto their stomachs and covered their heads.

'That's what it does,' said Trevor.

'That's the first shot in a war,' said George, shaking his fist as he got back to his feet.

'Actually,' said Trevor, 'it's the last shot in an old battle. That's for cutting a hole in the bottom of my hose on my last night as Mercutio.'

Kirsty liked Trevor more and more.

Once the twins had recovered themselves, insisting all the while that they had nothing to do with Trevor's trousers, and Jon had given the entire cast a lecture about not playing pranks with expensive lighting and sound equipment, the rehearsal continued and all went smoothly until the ballroom scene. The Ugly Sisters and their mother were newly arrived at the palace. They were standing by the imaginary buffet table, knocking back imaginary booze and helping themselves to imaginary canapés.

'*You don't get vol au vents like this in Lidl*,' said George.

'*That's why the Prince is on the lookout for a wife with a good dowry*,' said Andrew.

'*Are those pigs in blankets?*' asked Annette.

'*How dare you be so rude about the Duchess of York and her daughters!*' George shrieked.

Jon read a line that would be given by one of the chorus, announcing the arrival of the prince. Lauren stepped in. She arranged herself at the top of the wobbly staircase to the right of the scene. But instead of her line, she said, 'No. This isn't working for me.'

Everyone looked at her expectantly.

'What's not working?' asked Jon.

'The blocking. I can't do it. I didn't realise how it was going to be when we were in the rehearsal room. I thought the audience was going to be the other way round. But it's in front of me.'

'Eh?' Jon was confused. 'Of course the audience is in front of you.'

'So I want to come on from stage left,' she said.

'What?'

'I'm going to come on from stage left.' She turned to head off-stage again.

'You can't.'

'Why not?'

'You're a goody,' said Jon. 'Panto goodies always enter stage right.'

'Yeah, but if I come on from stage right, then the right side of my face is going to be towards the audience for the whole of my speech, isn't it, and . . . well, that's not my best side. If I come on from stage left, my left profile will be the one the audience sees first.'

'OK,' said Jon. 'I see what you're saying, Lauren, but . . . no.'

'Why not? It doesn't matter, does it? All that has to happen is everyone else turns in a different direction as I enter. You can have a new door cut in the backdrop. The staircase can go there instead of here.'

'No,' said Jon. 'The staircase stays where it is. Goodies always enter stage right.'

'That's just stupid,' said Lauren. 'Who says?'

'It's a panto tradition.'

'Who cares about tradition?'

'You're right,' said Jon. 'Forget tradition.'

Lauren started to smile, assuming she'd won.

'It's a panto *law*,' said Jon.

'And I'm a law-breaker,' Lauren tried.

'And I'm the director,' said Jon. 'My word is gospel.

You'll come on stage right like I'm bloody telling you to.'

'I can't!' Lauren suddenly wailed. 'I never do anything from the right. Never. Look.'

The rest of the cast were transfixed as Lauren pulled her phone out of the back pocket of her tight jeans and opened Instagram. She made Jon watch as she scrolled through her selfies. 'Left side, left side, left side,' she said. 'I do my forecasts from the left side too. It's my *best* side.'

'I can't tell the difference,' said Jon. 'Both sides look perfectly fine to me.'

'No,' said Lauren. 'Look properly, Jon. From the left, my nose is really straight. From the right . . .' She looked visibly pained as she told him. 'My nose is really . . . it's really witchy.'

Well, that had the Giggle Twins intrigued. They flanked Lauren and examined her actual profile themselves.

'How does it look on your side?' George asked Andrew.

'Straight as the hypotenuse of an isosceles triangle.'

'Eh?' said Lauren.

'How is it on your side?' Andrew asked George.

George grimaced. He didn't need to say anything to set Lauren off.

'See! See!' she shrieked. 'He can see it. It *is* witchy!'

'Lauren,' said Bernie. 'You of all people could never look like a witch.'

Lauren took no notice of Bernie. She was too busy using the photo app on her iPhone as a makeshift mirror.

She took a snap of herself from each side and compared them with growing despair. 'My left side is so much better. Please,' she begged Jon. 'If I have to come on from stage right, I'll spend my whole time on stage worrying what the audience are thinking about my nose.'

'I imagine they'll be too transfixed by the fact they can see straight through her head,' said Annette. 'Hashtag *brainless*.'

Bernie shot Annette a warning look.

'Trust me,' Kirsty said to Lauren. 'It will be fine. The audience will never notice that there is an *infinitesimal* difference between your left and right profiles. Some of them might even prefer the side that isn't so straight. Everyone likes a bit of quirky. And being on stage is entirely different from a still photograph. They'll be concentrating on your lines, your dancing, your . . .'

'Yeah. Well, you're happy to come on stage right because that is *your* best side,' Lauren interrupted her. 'You don't have to worry.'

'She's coming on from the right because she's Cinderella!' Jon said with exasperation.

'She's coming on from the right because she's *your* girlfriend and you let her do whatever she likes.'

I wish he did, thought Kirsty. She was on a fast day and Jon was making certain she stuck to it. She knew there was half a Twix in his man-bag. She could hear the damn thing.

'For as long as there have been pantomimes, the left versus right rule has always been in place,' said Jon. If it wasn't actually true, he made it sound convincing. 'It comes from the Latin. In Latin, the left is the *sinister* side. From *sinistra*. *Destra*,' he pointed to the right. '*Sinistra*.' To the left. 'The left side has represented evil from the beginning of time. Why the heck would we change it now?'

'Because it's stupid. And what you don't understand is that people aren't used to seeing me from the right. They'll be expecting to recognise me off the telly and they won't because I'll be standing the wrong way round. People will be paying good money to come and see me act.'

'And what a treat they'll get, seeing that you actually exist in three dimensions and you're not just some cardboard cut-out that's actually blank on the backside.'

'As opposed to entirely blank on the inside,' Andrew muttered.

'Come on,' said Jon. 'We're against the clock here. Let's just carry on with the rehearsal. Lauren, you look great from all sides. So let's take it from the beginning of the ball scene again. Prince Charming enters stage *right*.'

'I will not,' Lauren said.

'Heaven's sake. George and Andy, will you carry her on?'

The Giggle Twins stepped forward to do the director's bidding.

'Don't touch me,' Lauren snarled.

'Look, Lauren,' Jon pleaded. 'If we change the way you enter for every scene you're in, then we'll be changing pretty much everything. The blocking is done. The scenery has been painted. The props are all in place. You come in stage *f-ing* right.'

'I'm calling my agent.'

'Great. Please do. I'm sure he'll be delighted to explain why we're doing this my way.'

'I just don't see why everything has to be so *traditional*,' Lauren shrieked. 'It's weird all the rules you theatre people have. All this don't come on from the left and don't say the last line until the opening night and never, ever, ever say *Macbeth*.'

There was a gasp from Trevor Fernlea in the wings. Lauren might as well have shouted the C-word.

'Who even cares about some old Dickens play anyway?' Lauren continued.

While the others were agog about the Dickens reference, Lauren shouted, 'Macbeth, Macbeth, Macbeth!'

Bernie covered her ears and closed her eyes. The rest of the cast were aghast.

'Macbeth. There. I said it. *Macbeth*!' she yelled it out at the top of her voice. 'And nothing happened, did it? Stupid. It doesn't make a difference at all. Like coming on stage right. It's all from a time when people still thought the earth was round, for heaven's sake.'

'Er . . .' George raised his hand but Lauren was not to be corrected.

'So why can't I go on and off from whichever side I want . . . Like this—'

Lauren stomped off stage left to prove her point.

In doing so, she promptly tripped over the song-sheet easel and, in a desperate attempt not to hit the deck, pulled down and ripped the ballroom scene backdrop in two.

The backdrop fell onto Trevor, which wouldn't have been such a disaster in itself. It was just a big sheet of paper after all. Not heavy enough to give anyone serious concussion. However, it did give Trevor quite a shock and, suddenly blinded by the paper over his head, he stumbled across the boards towards the edge of the stage.

George and Andrew tried to catch him before he tumbled into the orchestra pit but only succeeded in making Trevor totter off stage right.

Where he fell over Cinderella's stool.

And blundered straight into a freestanding spotlight.

And when that toppled over on top of him, it fell onto his head. And the weight of the lamp was more than enough to knock Trevor out cold.

Annette called for an ambulance while Kirsty, Bernie, Jon and the Giggle Twins tried to bring Trevor round. The twins got Trevor into the recovery position. Vince offered a quick sniff from a small bottle of whisky in lieu of smelling salts. Elaine tried to find the first aid kit in the ladies' dressing room. Annette found the first aid kit in the gents'. There was nothing in it except for a tube of Savlon from the days when Savlon tubes were still made of metal and three plasters that had long since lost their stick. Bernie fetched a far superior first aid kit from her car though Trevor had no real use for bandages, sterile dressings and anti-histamines. Kirsty found a pillow for Trevor's head. Meanwhile Lauren shrieked and cried and posted her distress, at length, on Twitter and Facebook.

'Hashtag *f-ing brain-dead*,' muttered Annette.

'And that,' said Bernie, 'is why we never mention the Scottish play . . .'

Chapter Twenty-Six

It was bad news. Trevor was awake and sitting up in the front row of the stalls by the time the ambulance arrived but the paramedics decided that, due to his age – as they estimated it – and the fact he had been unconscious, albeit for less than a minute, it was best they took him straight to the hospital. Bernie and Kirsty followed the ambulance in Bernie's car, stopping off at his house en route to pick up Trevor's wife of fifty years, Cynthia, who was not best pleased to be interrupted in the middle of hosting her monthly bridge club lunch.

'He does this on purpose,' Cynthia said as she put on her coat.

'No,' said Bernie. 'It was definitely an accident.'

'That's what you think,' said Cynthia. 'You don't know that man like I do.'

Poor Trevor, thought Kirsty as Cynthia outlined Trevor's faults at length. No wonder he spent practically every waking hour at the NEWTS.

By the time Kirsty, Bernie and Cynthia arrived at the hospital, Trevor was on the ward. The doctor on duty explained they would like to keep him in overnight for observation. Though Trevor seemed to be quite perky, it was too early to say for certain that he was out of the woods. Head injuries were tricky things. You could bang your head, get up, walk home, then, *whompf*, brain clot and 'goodnight, Vienna'.

'Really?' Cynthia looked a little too interested. 'Does that happen a lot?'

'It's like Natasha Richardson,' Trevor mused. 'Look what happened to her.' Trevor went misty-eyed. 'One of the greatest actresses who ever walked the boards. I saw her in 1993.'

'Oooh. What in?' Bernie asked.

'Actually it was on the Circle Line at Paddington.'

Cynthia tutted. 'And you've gone on about it ever since. You always had a thing for her. Well, if you're not dying, I can't sit here all afternoon,' she said. 'I've left Joyce in charge of the lunch. I don't want her taking all the credit for my canapés.'

'That's all right, dear,' said Trevor. 'You go on home.'

'Coming?' Cynthia said to Bernie. Bernie had forgotten she was Cynthia's driver.

'Oh, yes. OK. But . . . Just a minute. Trevor. Is there anything you need? Toothpaste, pyjamas? Something nice to eat?'

'I'll put his night things in a bag and you can drive them back over later,' said Cynthia.

Bernie followed Cynthia out to the car. Kirsty hesitated for a second. She couldn't believe how brusquely Cynthia had dealt with her husband. Though Kirsty had found him irritating beyond belief at times during rehearsals, she realised as she looked at him in his hospital bed that she had grown rather fond of Trevor Fernlea.

'Would you like me to stay and keep you company for a while?' she asked. 'I hate to think of you all on your own in this ward.'

Just then, a hospital volunteer appeared with a cup of tea and three biscuits.

'You're only supposed to have one,' said the volunteer. 'But seeing as how you're a star of stage and screen and all . . .'

The volunteer placed Trevor's extra biscuits within reach and moved on.

'She saw me in *Romeo and Juliet*,' Trevor explained. 'I've said I'll tell her all about stagecraft when she's finished her rounds.'

Kirsty knew then that Trevor would be well looked after.

'OK.' She squeezed his hand. 'We'll swing by with those pyjamas later. I'd better get back to the theatre.'

'Yes,' said Trevor. 'The show must go on.'

'Indeed. The show must always go on,' Kirsty agreed with him.

Unfortunately, the show would not be going on for Trevor Fernlea. Follow-up tests the day after his accident showed that he had been more badly affected by the knock to his head than was at first suspected. He found it hard to get back on his feet and walk in a straight line. He was slurring some words and altogether forgetting others. He stayed in hospital for a further three days. During that time, several of the NEWTS – including Lauren who claimed on Facebook that she was desperately sad – visited his bedside. Not least because they all wanted to get a peek at his notes, which would finally solve the eternal mystery: how old was Trevor Fernlea anyway?

* * *

After three days, during which no one from the NEWTS managed to get close enough to his notes or wristband to find out his date of birth, Trevor was allowed to go home. Because Cynthia couldn't drive and Trevor *shouldn't* drive while on his medication, Bernie went to fetch him. She returned to the theatre with the news that the doctor had only agreed to allow him to go home on the strict understanding he would continue to take it easy.

'Bed-rest,' was his prescription.

Trevor's need for bed-rest was going to be a big problem for his wife, who relied on him being out of the house so she could host her bridge club without interruption. It wasn't that Cynthia was entertaining any gentlemen bridge players with intent. She simply found it easier to be herself when Trevor wasn't around, wanting to tell everyone about the bloody NEWTS.

However, Cynthia's problem was an even bigger problem for the NEWTS. Trevor's concussion left them a man down. Had Trevor been a member of the chorus, it wouldn't have mattered so much but Trevor was Buttons. He had lines. Hundreds of them. He had songs. He had the actual song-sheet to present. That was, without doubt, one of the most important moments in the whole show.

When Trevor had been out of action for a week, Jon admitted to himself and to Kirsty that he was going to have to recast Trevor's part. It was not going to be easy.

Chapter Twenty-Seven

Jon sat at the kitchen table with a sheet of paper and tried to work out what he was going to do. He asked the NEWTS' pianist and secretary, Glynis, to email him the society's entire membership list so that he could go through it for potential cast members he might have missed. It was a depressing process. Of the seventy or so paid-up members, at least forty-five were women. Of the remaining men, three of the best – Vince and the Giggle Twins – were already playing important parts. Four had moved out of the area. Five were missing, rumoured dead. The others were variously too old or just plain awful.

'Perhaps Vince could play Buttons and you could cast someone else as Baron Hardup?' Kirsty suggested.

'Vince can't be Buttons,' said Jon firmly. 'Can you imagine him interacting with the children on stage for the song-sheet? He'd knock them out with booze fumes. Besides, he can't remember half the lines he's got already. Buttons is a much bigger part than Baron Hardup.'

'Then what if one of the Giggle Twins did it?'

'No. They've got the sisters down pat. It'd be a shame to split them up.'

'Buttons could always be a girl?' Kirsty suggested then.

'We're doing provincial panto, Kirsty. We're not at the

National. It's one thing to have a girl playing Prince Charming but a three-way female love triangle is much more than Newbay can stand.'

Kirsty wasn't sure that was true. She'd heard rumours of a three-way female love triangle in the wardrobe department for a start.

Jon broadened his list of potentials with some names that Kirsty didn't recognise.

'Who are these people?' she asked.

'They're from the other am-dram societies in the region. It's not strictly kosher to ask them and chances are they're already booked up for the season anyway, but you never know.'

Jon put down his pen and sighed.

'This time next year,' he said, 'we could be back in the sun.'

Kirsty nodded. 'Yes. Please. That sounds great. But what about your seasickness?'

'Oh, we're not going back on a ship,' he said.

'Then where will we be getting our Vitamin D?' Kirsty asked.

'I've applied for a job in the UAE.'

'The University of East Anglia?' Kirsty guessed. 'Not much sunshine there.'

'UAE not UEA, my darling fluff-head. In the Middle East. Dubai.'

This was news to Kirsty. Since the night they'd talked about Berlin and Prague, Jon hadn't mentioned working overseas again. 'Doing what?'

'Directing a season of Shakespeare.'

'In the Middle East?'

'It's a great job.'

'You didn't tell me you were going for it.'

'I just put my application in this morning.'

'I thought we were going to talk through all possible job options together.'

'We're talking about it now.'

'You know what I mean. If you get this job, what am I supposed to do?'

'You'd love it out there. All the sunshine you can handle.'

Yes, thought Kirsty. And all the restrictions that went with it. One of the girls who worked on *The European Countess* had done a season at a hotel in Dubai. She'd filled Kirsty in on the reality.

It was especially galling that Jon could even think about dragging her to Dubai without discussing it with her first when she had already followed him back to Newbay. Standing in their decidedly dark kitchen (it was a particularly gloomy day) she couldn't help thinking where she might have been that winter. She hadn't even considered pressing Jon to follow her. And he could have. He could have met her at various stopovers. They could have had a wonderful winter.

Kirsty had valued their relationship too much to risk spending so much time apart and she thought Jon felt the same way, yet that was exactly what Jon was suggesting now. Because there was no way, was there, that Kirsty would really be able to follow him? She could go and visit him for a week or two at a time, she was certain, but to spend any more time with him would mean getting a special visa, surely? And how would she be able to get a visa to stay in a strict Muslim country with a man to whom she wasn't married? Had Jon thought about that? It suddenly crossed Kirsty's mind that not only had Jon thought about the complications, he had embraced them. Perhaps he had chosen to apply for the job precisely because it would be difficult for Kirsty to follow him.

'Show me the job advert,' she said.

Jon turned his laptop so she could look at it.

He had applied to direct an all-male Shakespeare company. All male. Kirsty couldn't even have applied to join the tour as a performer in her own right. Not that she had ever done any Shakespeare. She hadn't picked up one of the Bard's plays since she finished her GCSEs. Kirsty was all about musical theatre. She would never play Juliet.

Kirsty's heart was in her boots. Right then, however, she decided against arguing with him. Jon hadn't got the job yet. He'd just sent a CV off. She told herself he would have discussed it with her had there been more time before the application deadline.

'It looks really good,' she said. 'The money's amazing.'

'And tax free,' said Jon. 'I knew you'd be pleased.'

Maybe Kirsty was a better actor than she thought.

'We could have a really good time out there. I'm sure we can find you a job.' And then he said, 'You've got secretarial experience. There must be loads of options—'

'I'll pretend you didn't say that,' said Kirsty.

'You know what I mean,' said Jon.

'I'm not sure I do.'

Jon pulled her onto his lap and started kissing her neck. 'I just want us to be together.'

On his terms only? said the little voice in Kirsty's head.

Chapter Twenty-Eight

After the Dubai revelation, Trevor's continued ill health was the biggest thing on Kirsty's mind. Someone from the NEWTS spoke to Trevor on a daily basis but though he talked a good game, they knew he wasn't coming back. His short stay in hospital had changed things. He had been discharged in what passed for full health, according to the NHS, but he seemed suddenly much older than the seventy-year-old they thought he might be. The idea they had ever thought he would be able to sustain a fortnight-long run of very physical theatre suddenly seemed quite laughable.

But who was going to play Buttons instead? Jon had a clandestine meeting with a player from another local company, Newbay Arts and Theatre, who was disgruntled with his own crew because he'd been passed over for the part of Scrooge in their version of *A Christmas Carol*. Kirsty was astonished by the cloak and dagger business that accompanied Jon's meeting with this bloke called Craig. They didn't dare be caught together in Newbay, so they agreed to meet in the car park at a service station near Exeter.

Though it was late November, both Jon and Craig wore sunglasses to their rendezvous. They treated the whole thing with the sort of seriousness you could perhaps imagine in Hollywood. Say, if you were Barbara

Broccoli meeting a potential Bond and didn't want the paparazzi to break the news before you had a chance to break it yourself.

'I don't get why you have to be so secretive,' Kirsty said.

'You have no idea of the politics,' said Jon. 'If it gets out that Craig has met with me, his own company could blacklist him for years. He'll never get a lead part again. I don't want to screw things up for him if he isn't right for us.'

Craig wasn't right for the NEWTS. Not because of his acting skills or lack of them. Jon would have snapped Craig up to play Buttons in a heartbeat, but when Craig heard that Annette Sweeting had been cast as the stepmother, he said he would have to decline. Turned out that Annette and Craig had history. Before Annette was a NEWT, she was an NAT (Newbay Arts and Theatre). She and Craig had played opposite one another in a very racy production of *Dangerous Liaisons*. They had succumbed to a 'showmance'. Annette was newly widowed, but Craig had a fiancée. Caught up in the drama of their on-stage/off-stage affair, Craig called off his engagement, only to have Annette dump him as soon as the show run ended. Seven years on, with a wife and small children, he still wouldn't consider being on the same stage as the woman who had 'wrecked his life'.

So that was that.

Craig's tale was not unusual. The amateur-dramatic scene of Newbay was full of similar stories. Showmance was rife.

'Which is why I made sure that your love interests in this panto were played by a girl and a pensioner,' Jon joked to Kirsty.

Then he pulled Kirsty into his arms. He'd been especially

tactile the last couple of days, as if he knew that Kirsty was still smarting from his suggestion that she take a secretarial job in order to be able to follow him abroad again. She was trying hard to take his explanation for that at face value. It wasn't that he didn't think she could have a career on the stage, it was just that he didn't want to be apart from her. Their relationship was more than a showmance.

'Does that mean you're going to find me a totally unlovable Buttons?' she asked him.

'I hope so,' said Jon.

Chapter Twenty-Nine

While all this was going on, the wardrobe witches were doing their worst. Kirsty's heart sank when she went for a second fitting and saw how they had altered the eighties dress. If it was possible, they had made it look even uglier. Bernie, who was in Wardrobe at the same time to be fitted into her Godmother garb, pulled a face that let Kirsty know she felt her pain.

'I can't wear that thing,' Kirsty said as she and Bernie made their way back down the stairs.

'I agree,' said Bernie.

'It makes me look like a turkey wrapped in foil. But what can I do about it? Those old cows are determined to make me look more like a jacket potato than a princess.'

'Leave it with me,' Bernie said. 'I am your fairy godmother after all.'

'Thanks, Bernie,' said Kirsty, though she wasn't sure what Bernie could do. The three witches had dressed Bernie in something that resembled one of those knitted doll covers for a loo roll. If that monstrosity represented Bernie's sway in the wardrobe department, then Kirsty had no hope at all.

* * *

The following evening, however, Bernie texted Kirsty and asked her to come over to the house she shared with Vince around tea-time. Vince wasn't there. He was doing a late night at his dental surgery. A surprising number of people wanted to get their teeth whitened ahead of the party season, Bernie explained.

Bernie and Vince's house was lovely. It felt like a proper home, which was something that was missing from Kirsty and Jon's stark rental flat. Kirsty immediately felt comfortable as Bernie invited her to sit down on their big blue squashy sofa and placed tea and homemade cake on one of the occasional tables.

'Vince made the cake,' Bernie told her.

Kirsty was surprised.

'So you might find he overdid the brandy.'

Kirsty wasn't so surprised about that.

While Bernie ran upstairs to fetch something, Kirsty admired the photographs on the mantelpiece. In a photograph of their wedding day, Bernie and Vince smiled at each other as though they'd both thought they'd won the lottery. Vince was slim and elegant in a dark-blue suit. Bernie looked like a princess in her red velvet dress. She swooned in his arms. There was no doubt they were truly, madly, deeply in love.

Bernie came back into the sitting room, carrying a garment bag and found Kirsty looking at the wedding photo.

'We got married in December. The thirtieth,' she said. 'Mostly because it was cheaper than doing it in the summer. But I'd always wanted a winter wedding. I never fancied being a June bride.'

'I think you were right. You looked stunning in that dress,' said Kirsty.

'And so will you.'

Bernie unzipped the garment bag and jumble of red tulle and velvet suddenly tumbled out.

'Is that it?' Kirsty asked.

Bernie nodded.

'It is. My wedding dress. It should fit you,' she said. 'You might even have to have it taken in a bit to show off your lovely waist.'

She shook out the dress so that Kirsty could see it in all of its glory. It was even more beautiful in life than it looked in the pictures. And it was obviously expensive.

'It's Vivienne Westwood,' Bernie confirmed. 'I absolutely couldn't afford it. I went right up to my credit card limit to buy the silly thing. But you only marry the man of your dreams once, right?'

Kirsty nodded.

'Our wedding day was perfect. I felt so happy and confident wearing this. And Vince's eyes when he saw me at the top of the aisle. I'll never forget how he looked at me. Now it just hangs in the wardrobe in the spare room. It's time it saw the light of day again. Try it on.'

'I couldn't possibly—' said Kirsty.

'You know you could. And if a fairy godmother can't magic up a dress, then what is she good for?'

Kirsty touched the skirt. She was certainly tempted.

'Try it on, you goose,' Bernie persisted. 'There is no way you're wearing that eighties monstrosity the witches want you in.'

Bernie laid the dress across Kirsty's arms and sent her upstairs to the spare room.

* * *

Kirsty knew at once that this was her Cinderella gown. When she was inside it, Bernie joined her to help pull up the laces on the back of the bodice.

'It fits you perfectly. I knew it would. And it suits you.'

Though Bernie and Kirsty could not have been more different in terms of colouring, somehow the red of the dress was just right for them both.

'Oh, this is wonderful,' said Kirsty, smoothing down the skirt and admiring herself in the mirror on the wardrobe door. The dress was cleverly constructed to turn any figure into an hour-glass. Kirsty could hardly believe how tiny her waist looked, while her bosom and hips were suddenly Monroe-esque rather than something to be five-two dieted into oblivion.

'There,' said Bernie. 'That's settled. All we've got to do is find some shoes and a tiara and you will go to the ball.'

'In this dress,' said Kirsty, channelling Cinders, 'I think I could dance all night.'

'Just remember to be back home by midnight.' Bernie winked.

Kirsty could hardly believe Bernie's generosity as she carried the dress back to the flat. There she tried it on again for Jon and was delighted to hear him whistle.

'That's my Cinderella,' he said. 'You'll be fighting the prince off.'

Then Jon wrapped his arms around her and kissed the back of her neck and Kirsty allowed herself to believe that some of the magical love Bernie and Vince had clearly felt for each on their wedding day might be rubbing off on Jon too. They would make it. Even if he did go to Dubai.

But the next rehearsal was difficult thanks to Vince, who once again managed to skip whole pages of script and called the Giggle Twins all manner of vile names for daring to point out his mistake. It was quite astonishing to hear Vince swear like that. It was equally astonishing to see the twins suddenly transformed from mincing dames into growling bare-knuckle boxers. Jon had to step into the middle before Vince had his lights punched out.

'You've got a drinking problem,' George Giggle said.

'The only drinking problem I've got is that I don't have a glass in my hand right now to smash your face with,' Vince replied. And then he and George Giggle were flailing at each other again. The rehearsal was adjourned earlier than planned and everyone – except Vince and Bernie – retired to the bar.

Vince and Bernie were later seen arguing in the car park. They could not have looked more different from the blissful young lovers in the wedding photograph.

Chapter Thirty

The bar was open and busy that evening because the children were practising their songs in the big rehearsal room. Their parents gathered early for a sneaky pint. The prices in the NEWTS' bar were remarkably competitive.

Having arrived half an hour before he needed to, Ben found a table in the corner and nursed half a lager while he checked the news on his phone. The lager was watery and the news was generally bad, as usual, but Ben relished the chance to have half an hour to himself. It wasn't that he couldn't have had more time if he wanted. Judy was always trying to get him to go out with his mates, always offering to babysit. Ben just didn't feel it was right to ask her to give up her night so that he could just sit in a pub on his own, which was all he really wanted to do. That would be too sad.

Half an hour by himself in the NEWTS' bar was different. He had a reason for being there. He secretly hoped Thea's rehearsal might overrun. As it happened, Thea's rehearsal was overrunning but the adult actors soon broke into the peace.

Ben knew Jon Manley was directing the panto, of course, having seen him at Thea's audition. Ben hadn't bothered to renew their acquaintance then and he hadn't had an opportunity since, as Elaine oversaw Thea's rehearsals. But here Jon was and he'd spotted Ben at last.

'Oh, my word! Ben Teesdale!' Jon slapped Ben on the back. 'It is you! I knew it. I recognised the back of your head. Those ears. I haven't seen you in years. How long has it been?'

Ben righted himself after the shock of Jon's overly friendly slap, which had caused him to spill the top inch of his pint. 'Erm . . .' he hesitated.

'Ten years. It's got to be at least ten years,' Jon said. 'Where was it? Probably in The Sailor's Arms. That was the pub we all used to go to,' he explained to Kirsty, who had joined them. 'It was the one place where they didn't ask for ID if you were underage. Everybody went there when we were in the sixth form. We used to go back in the university holidays too. Where was it you went to for uni, Ben?'

'Exeter,' said Ben.

'Keep it in the county, eh? Don't want to go too far.'

'It was the right course,' Ben pointed out.

'Yeah. Ben and I were at the same school,' Jon continued for Kirsty's benefit. 'We didn't really hang out together then. I suppose we got to know each other down the pub once we'd left St Edward's. Sinking pints, playing pool, chatting up the girls.'

Kirsty smiled indulgently.

'Have you met our leading lady?' Jon asked Ben then. 'Cinderella – Kirsty – this is Ben—'

'We've already met,' she said.

'You have?'

'I got the audition flyers printed in Ben's shop.'

'Oh, right. Hey, do you remember Charlie Leyton?' Jon asked Ben. He gave Ben a comedy nudge. 'She was a goer.'

Ben looked oddly uneasy at that particular reminiscence.

'She was my girlfriend,' said Ben.

'Shit,' said Jon. 'You're right. I forgot about that. Sorry. Still, if she'd been worth worrying about, she never would have got off with me, right?' Jon gave a comic grimace. 'Wait. You're going to tell me you're married to her now, aren't you?'

'I'm not,' said Ben.

'Thank goodness for that. She was a slapper.'

'She married my cousin,' was Ben's response.

'But you met someone better, I'm sure.'

'Yes, I did,' said Ben. 'But I lost her three years ago.'

'Careless,' said Jon.

'Cancer,' said Ben.

Kirsty winced.

Jon was momentarily stuck for words. But only momentarily.

'So, mate. What are you doing here anyway?' Jon asked. 'You're the last person I ever thought I'd see at the NEWTS.'

'My daughter is in the panto,' said Ben.

'Really? Which one's your little girl?'

'She's called Thea.'

'Elaine says she's doing really well,' Kirsty told Ben. 'She's got all her dance steps learned. She's one of the mice,' she then explained to Jon.

'Light-brown hair, thick glasses,' said Ben. He didn't want Kirsty to have to give a physical description.

'I know the one,' said Jon. 'A diva in the making. Not that she's a diva, of course.'

'I should hope not,' said Ben.

'She's far from being a diva,' said Kirsty. 'She so sweet and polite. Really a pleasure. Very well brought up.'

Ben knew that she meant it and smiled.

'How funny that you should end up here because of your kid,' said Jon. 'Have you thought about doing anything yourself? You used to love acting. You were in all the school productions.'

'Yeah. But that was ten years ago. A lot has changed since then.'

'Ha! Well, your voice has broken now. That's a start.'

'We were at an all-boys' school. I played a lot of female roles,' Ben said to Kirsty.

'And you loved it,' Jon persisted. 'I mean the stagecraft. Not the dressing up as a woman per se. Though if you want to dress up as a woman, then the NEWTS is definitely the place to be. You did more drama stuff at uni too, didn't you? The thing is, Ben, we're in a bit of trouble, as you may have heard. Trevor Fernlea – remember him? He used to teach geography at St Edward's. Retired in our first year – well, he's a keen NEWT and he was supposed to be our Buttons but he took a bang to the head and there's no way he's going to be well enough to do the season. Which starts in just over a fortnight, as you know, obviously, since Thea is going to perform.'

Ben said nothing.

'Which means we need someone to step in really quickly. Someone who can learn lines fast. Who doesn't need too much hand-holding. Someone with a bit of stage experience. Someone who looks right alongside Kirsty.'

Kirsty put her hands together in mock prayer.

'Someone, in fact, just like you.'

'I don't know,' said Ben. 'I did a few plays as a school kid, Jon. I don't think that counts as stage experience. I can barely remember—'

Jon put his hand on Ben's shoulder. 'You see this man,' he said to Kirsty. 'When we were seventeen, he beat me to the part of the judge in our school's production of *Joan of Arc*. I was furious at the time but when I saw him on the stage, I knew that the right decision had been made. The better man got the part. So, Ben Teesdale, don't tell me that you don't think you've got it in you to play Buttons. You're the man who brought the house down with your Hamlet. You could do Buttons without a single rehearsal.'

But for once Jon's charm wasn't working. Ben wasn't budging.

'It's not my thing any more,' said Ben. 'I don't think it ever really was.'

The juniors came tumbling into the bar then, accompanied by the chaperones.

'OK, mummies and daddies,' chaperone Megan announced. 'Here are your little darlings!'

The chaperones looked exhausted and extremely glad to be handing their charges back to their parents. Ben, on the other hand, was thrilled to see his daughter. Not least because her arrival cut Jon's schmooze-fest short. Thea handed him the carrier bag containing her costume and her floppy mouse hat.

'We've got to go,' said Ben. 'Supper will be on the table. It was nice seeing you again.' He directed that last comment to Kirsty.

'Tell me you'll think about it at least!' Jon called to Ben's retreating back.

Ben gave a wave, which was meant to be dismissive. All the same, he couldn't help being just a little bit pleased at the idea that he 'looked right alongside Kirsty'.

Chapter Thirty-One

'Shit,' said Jon. 'I really thought he'd go for it. He would be perfect.'

'So, you know Ben from school?'

'Yeah. Can't say I really liked him all that much. He took himself so seriously. Never arsed about with the rest of us at lunchtime. He was always in the library with his nose in some book.'

'But he was into drama?'

'The English teacher encouraged him. I think she thought it might break him out of his shell and help him make some new friends. It might have done, had he not been so bloody serious about acting too.'

Jon took a sip of his beer.

Kirsty didn't point out that Jon was pretty serious about theatre himself.

'He hasn't changed,' Jon continued. 'He's still completely up himself. Too grand to do anyone a favour.'

'Hmmm.'

Kirsty wondered if that was the whole story. Something had passed over Ben's usually very friendly face when he first saw Jon. He'd not exactly looked pleased to see him. Rather he looked as though he would have liked to avoid having a conversation. There was something really awkward about that whole exchange, and not just because of the unhappy revelation about Ben's marital status that came halfway through it. Poor man, thought Kirsty. No wonder he'd looked awkward when Thea showed Kirsty that drawing of the three of them in front of the house, while Kirsty was waiting for her printing. It was a dreadful thing to have to keep explaining your loss, she knew. But it was more than that. It was as though part of Ben – and part of Jon – was picking up where they had left off more than a decade earlier.

Though, of course, Kirsty hadn't known Jon during his school days, she thought she had a pretty good idea of what he might have been like back then. When they got together with his school friends, they were full of tales of pranks and hi-jinks and Jon was always at the centre of any story. He was the class clown.

But when she heard about some of the 'jokes' Jon had played on his schoolmates, at times she asked herself if they didn't actually border on bullying. While Jon and his friends howled with laughter at the recollection of putting a dead squirrel in someone's desk, Kirsty thought of how awful it must have been for the recipient to find a deceased rodent squashed between his textbooks. She knew if it had happened to her, she would have been really upset. And where was the fun in setting light to someone's school jacket while shouting, 'It's a blazer! Let it blaze!'

What if it had been made of nylon? It didn't bear thinking about. Many of Jon's favourite schoolboy wheezes seemed to involve near-death experiences for his poor victims.

'I was just a bit boisterous,' Jon claimed.

She imagined Ben, who seemed like a gentle sort of

person, sitting in the library at lunchtimes, and wondered if he didn't go there for some peace. Had Ben found himself the butt of Jon's jokes? After that awful conversation in the bar, in which Jon had referred to Ben's old girlfriend as a slapper, Kirsty could understand why Ben might assume Jon hadn't changed. Why should he want to do Jon a favour now?

'Maybe little Thea will be able to persuade him,' Kirsty said.

'The one with the bug eyes?' said Jon.

'The one with the *glasses*,' Kirsty said. Why did Jon have to be so casually cruel? She'd been noticing it more and more frequently as they rehearsed.

Kirsty heart squeezed as she thought of Thea, knowing now what they had in common beyond a love of 'Somewhere Over The Rainbow'. Kirsty wouldn't have wished losing a mum to cancer on anyone. Especially so young. It made her want to hug Thea – and Ben – close.

Chapter Thirty-Two

Ben wasn't exactly overcome with joy and warmth at the sight of Jon Manley. Of course he remembered him. How could he possibly have forgotten? St Edward's was not a big school, so although Jon and Ben were not in the same class, they had been aware of each other's existence from the very first term of their secondary school career. At eleven years old, Jon Manley was already substantially the person he would grow up to be. Which, in Ben's opinion, was a total arse.

Coming from a tiny primary school with just a couple of hundred pupils, even St Edward's, which had five hundred and fifty students in all, seemed enormous to eleven-year-old Ben. His first week there was awful. Ben – like poor Thea – had a hopeless sense of direction. If he didn't gather himself quickly enough to follow the herd from class to class, he would get lost. He met Jon for the first time when he accidentally gate-crashed 1K's geography lesson. The teacher was kind enough when he realised Ben's mistake, telling Ben where he should be – the history room next door – but Jon, who had quickly established himself as class clown, made a crack about Ben needing a new pair of glasses. Ben blushed from tip to toe. His glasses – just like Thea's – had extremely thick lenses. To make matters worse, they were NHS specs. They didn't suit him. They accentuated

Chrissie Manby

the way his ears stuck out. They made him look like a mole. In fact, thanks to Jon, Moley soon became Ben's nickname.

'Moley Poley.' An added reference to his puppy fat, Ben assumed.

Jon never bullied Ben in any obvious way. There was nothing physical. None of the shoving and punching that some of the kids in Ben's year had to put up with from older, bigger kids. Jon was more subtle than that. He disguised the name-calling as friendly banter. Ben knew that if he dared to object, then Jon would accuse him of lacking a sense of humour – a terrible insult in itself. So Ben tried to shrug the dull jokes off and pretend they didn't affect him. And when he didn't feel he could keep shrugging the jokes off, he hid in the library, which was the last place Jon and his gang would be likely to come looking for fun. He longed for the holidays when whole weeks went by without having to worry about Jon at all. And then, at long last, it was time for them to leave school for good and Ben hoped he would never have to see Jon Manley again.

He was unlucky on that front. There were only a couple of decent pubs in Newbay – as in ones which weren't popular with the tourists and thus hadn't jacked up their prices to the sort of levels you expected in London. Jon and his crowd landed on the same one as Ben and his friends. They still called him Moley, though Ben had saved up and got himself contact lenses as soon as he could. He'd lost the puppy fat too.

Then Jon had become really friendly for a while. He would include Ben in his round when he went to the bar. He asked Ben for tips on what sort of music he should be listening to. Who were the cool new bands, etcetera? After a while, Ben actually started to relax

160

around his former nemesis. Maybe Jon had grown up and grown out of taking the mick. Maybe they were really becoming friends.

Maybe they did. For a short time at least. But all that changed when Ben met Charlie Leyton. They worked together in Sainsbury's during the uni holidays and started hanging out in the evenings too. Ben was quickly head over heels and it seemed that Charlie felt the same way. Ben had kissed a few girls before but Charlie was his first proper 'girlfriend'. She was everything a teenage boy dreams of. She was funny and clever and into the same sort of music. It helped that she was also beautiful in a perfect, ethereal way. When she wasn't in her Sainsbury's uniform, she drifted around in charity shop maxi dresses like a proto-Florence Welch. She was so different from the rest of the girls Ben knew.

As happens when you're eighteen, Ben was convinced he had found the girl with whom he would spend the rest of his life. He wore a ratty piece of wool around his wrist – a friendship bracelet she had made for him – for months.

Then Jon came back from uni too and gave Charlie the full force of his charm. Charlie and Ben were virgins. She said she didn't want to 'do it' until they were both really sure their relationship was serious. They stuck to heavy petting. But while Ben still thought he and Charlie were an item, Jon took Charlie's virginity in the back of his car. Jon went out with Charlie for two months – seeming to turn up with her wherever Ben went to drown his sorrows – before he dumped her and told Ben, in front of a great many people at the pub, 'You can have her back now.'

That really stung. Ben was so cut up about it that it knocked his confidence. He wouldn't go out in Newbay again for years. He gave up acting with his uni drama group. Then he failed an important set of exams. He was lucky that the university let him resit the year.

As an adult, Ben knew that he and Charlie would not have gone the distance. He was able to see how she turned out because she really had married his cousin. The ethereal beauty had grown into a very average woman. Her youthful drama was replaced by bitterness and cynicism. Perhaps it was just because she was married to Ben's boring cousin, who made pomposity an art form, but he suspected it had been there all along.

Jo – the real love of his life – didn't have a cynical bone in her body. Ben felt sure she would not have grown harder with age.

No, in retrospect, Jon Manley had done Ben a favour. If Ben had not been so cut up about Charlie, he'd have finished his degree in the usual three years. Had he not had that fourth year, he might not have met Jo, who was a year behind him. Having been kept back, he joined her tutor group. And without Charlie, he was free to fall in love with her. Every cloud has a silver lining. However, that did not mean that he could look back on that painful moment when Charlie and Jon waltzed off to lose their virginity in the back of his Ford Focus with complete unanimity. Jon had proved himself to be a bad friend. Someone not to be trusted.

Ben was not thrilled that the NEWTS had brought Jon Manley back into his life but Thea was full of enthusiasm and news from the children's rehearsals. She was enjoying herself so much. Ben was delighted to hear her talking about the other kids in such a positive way. His eyes prickled with tears of happy relief when Thea announced, 'So, Georgie has invited me to her birthday party. We're going to watch DVDS and have a sleepover.' Thea had never been invited to a sleepover before. 'And can I have Georgie and Thomas to tea at our house,' she continued.

Ben was pleased to hear her ask. 'Of course.'

Back at home, Ben cooked Thea's favourite Saturday night supper – fish fingers and oven chips. Judy was working that night. They ate in the living room, sitting on the floor with their plates on the coffee table, while *The X Factor* played on the television. Thea gave her own running commentary, explaining to her father that the singers were probably wearing radio mics.

'You don't have to have a really loud voice to be on the stage,' she said.

While Ben washed up, Thea sat at the kitchen table and drew a poster for *Cinderella*. In Thea's version, she had top billing alongside Kirsty. Her representation of herself in a mouse costume was impressive.

'Daddy, I would like you to be Buttons,' said Thea suddenly.

'You would?'

'Yes. The man who was going to be Buttons – Trevor – well, he was very nice but he was much too old. He kept forgetting his words and he was ever so stiff when they danced. And now he's hit his head, he can't dance at all. You would be much better.'

'I'm no good at dancing,' said Ben.

'Yes you are. You were good at my first rehearsal. And I can help you practise,' said Thea. 'Come on.'

She jumped to her feet and pulled Ben away from the

sink and into the centre of the kitchen. Arranging her father's arms into a classical ballroom hold, she gently stepped onto the tops of his feet. She was a little bigger now than she had been when Ben first danced her around the room this way, but he let her carry on.

'Right foot forward,' Thea instructed. 'Left to the side. Right together.'

Ben took his first steps gingerly. Mostly because he felt Thea was slipping off. She rearranged herself and they carried on.

'Left foot forward. Right to the side. Left together. That's no good. Come on. Concentrate.'

They waltzed around the room. Ben soon forgot about the weight of Thea on his insteps as they danced. It took him back to when she was tiny and obsessed with *Strictly Come Dancing*. He remembered how Jo had laughed as she watched them from the sofa. When they finished, she held up an imaginary 'ten'. How he wished that Jo could see them now.

'Please, Daddy,' Thea whispered. 'It would be so nice if we were in the panto together. And I know that Kirsty wants you to be in it too.'

'Does she?' Ben asked.

He was embarrassed to find he wanted to hear more. 'How do you know that?'

'I heard her talking to Elaine. She said they were desperate to find somebody. Elaine said she knew you could dance because she'd seen you at my rehearsals. She didn't know if you could sing though. Kirsty said it didn't matter. That can be . . .' Thea hesitated as she searched for the word. 'Fudged? Someone had to ask you. They both said that you were the best of a bad bunch.'

Ben laughed. Mostly at his own vanity when he realised had been waiting, or rather hoping, to hear some fabulous compliment. But no. He was just the best of a bad bunch. 'Well, in that case,' he said.

'Are you going to do it?' Thea gazed up at him.

Ben wasn't sure he wanted to but there were plenty of reasons why it would make sense. He was going to have to be at the theatre for pretty much every night the show was on in any case. And it would be something for them to look back on – him and Thea. How long would it be before she didn't want him to be around all the time? He'd heard that the teenage years started earlier and earlier these days. She'd probably find him too embarrassing to be seen with by the time she turned ten. He should make the most of this opportunity to spend time with her, making memories that would last for ever.

And perhaps he was slightly motivated by wanting to get to know Kirsty better too.

'If they haven't already found someone else, then I will,' he said.

'Hooray!' Thea cheered. She jumped backwards from his feet onto the floor, landing badly and catching Ben's toe as she did so. She stumbled forward, butting his stomach with her head.

'Ooof,' said Ben. But he couldn't think of a nicer way to end up winded.

Chapter Thirty-Three

Ben had Elaine at the NEWTS' number because of Thea but he didn't call and ask her to pass on the news. He waited until he was dropping Thea off at rehearsal the next day to let Jon know in person that he would be in the panto after all. Jon was in the auditorium with Kirsty. He was directing her in a solo.

Ben and Thea waited in the doorway until Kirsty had finished singing. When she saw her little audience, she beamed.

'Still looking for a Buttons?' Ben asked.

'Are you serious?' said Kirsty.

Ben nodded.

'Thank fuck,' said Jon, emphatically.

'Language!' said Thea.

'We're so pleased,' said Kirsty. 'You've saved the show.'

'You haven't seen me act yet,' said Ben.

'Well, we can remedy that right away,' said Jon. 'The rest of the cast will be here in five. Welcome to the cast, Ben Teesdale.'

Ben deposited Thea at the door of the large rehearsal room where the children were practising a dance routine. She didn't need him to stay by her side any more. He could hardly believe the difference in Thea's confidence from that first afternoon of rehearsals. As soon as Ben opened the rehearsal room door, Thea spotted Georgie and Thomas and shot in under Ben's arm to be with them. She didn't even look back to wish him cheerio. Ben left the lunch-box with Thea's sandwiches and snacks on top of the fridge in the corner of the room.

It was a bittersweet moment. He couldn't remember a time when she hadn't looked back to give him one last wave. And yet he knew that this was much better. He wanted her to grow in confidence and independence every day. It was the way of things that she would grow apart from him at the same time. As Jo had warned him, back when they were talking about a future Jo wouldn't see, he would know that he had been a good parent when Thea went off to college and forgot to call him for weeks on end, just as he had once neglected to telephone Judy.

Leaving Thea with her friends, Ben followed the hand-written signs back to the auditorium. Though from the outside the church building was plain and rectangular, inside it was labyrinthine. Ben found himself out in the theatre lobby again before he made it to join the rest of the cast.

He got a very warm welcome. The entire gang was mightily relieved to see that Trevor had been replaced by such a good candidate. One who had four working limbs, all his teeth and his own hair. And he was under forty! Who cared if he could act or not? He looked the part. He might even fit the costume.

Ben took his seat in the wings – Trevor's old seat – which was a restraint chair left over from a performance of *One Flew Over the Cuckoo's Nest*. Straps still dangled from the sides. Jon handed him Trevor's script, which was heavily annotated.

'You might not want to take any notice of those notes,' Vince suggested. 'If you can even read them.'

Ben remembered Trevor's awful handwriting from when Trevor marked his geography homework.

'Ladies and gentlemen,' Jon clapped his hands. 'Shall we take it from the top?'

Bernie spoke the opening lines. Ben wondered what on earth he was getting into.

'Well,' said Jon, when the read-through was finished and they were all back downstairs in the bar. 'That wasn't awful.'

He patted Ben on the back as though they were mates again.

'You were great,' said Kirsty, making up for Jon's faint praise. 'I can't tell you how relieved I am you agreed to do this. We were looking at having to rewrite the entire script or kidnap some romantic hero from a society in Cornwall. Now the show really will go on.'

'It was Thea who convinced me.'

Kirsty nodded. 'I had a feeling she would.' But when she looked at Ben as she was saying that, Ben couldn't help wondering if Kirsty knew that she'd formed a big part of his motivation too. There was something knowing in her eyes.

Megan the chaperone delivered the children to their parents.

'Was Dad good?' Thea asked Kirsty.

'He was very good. Where did he learn to dance so well?' Kirsty asked.

'I taught him,' said Thea. 'Like this.'

Ben held out his arms to her and Thea jumped onto his feet.

'You'd better not try that with Kirsty,' Jon remarked.

Kirsty rewarded Jon with a tight smile.

Then Lauren – Prince Charming – joined them.

'You were wonderful, darling,' said Jon, wrapping his arm around Lauren's shoulders and kissing her on the top of the head.

Lauren pursed her lips. 'I need to have a conversation with you about the Giggle Twins.'

Jon rolled his eyes skywards as Lauren took hold of his collar and led him off.

There was something about the gesture that seemed familiar to Ben. Then he remembered that it was the face Jon had always pulled when Charlie, the girl he'd stolen away all those years ago, was in a mood with him. There was something of Charlie in Lauren too. Her petite frame, her glossy chestnut hair, her pout. Jon clearly had a type.

'Jon!' Lauren complained. 'Don't roll your eyes at me.'

'Sorry, sweetheart,' Jon said.

Kirsty shook her head as she watched Lauren take Jon into a corner.

'Looks like he's in trouble,' Kirsty observed. Then her attention was drawn to Thea, who wanted to tell Kirsty all about the upcoming Christmas Fayre at her junior school. And then Kirsty was endlessly patient as Thea told a story that involved two boys and a girl who had all-but-identical names. When Thea drew breath, Kirsty turned back to Ben.

'Are you going to be able to make the rehearsal on Tuesday?' she asked. 'I know this is all quite a surprise for you and you've probably got a diary full of things to do in the run up to Christmas.'

'No,' said Ben. 'Except bringing Thea here, there's nothing in my diary except work.'

'Wonderful. I mean. You know what I mean . . . If you do have time,' Kirsty continued. 'If it's not too much of an imposition, maybe you and I could rehearse on our own at some point, to bring you up to speed with what Trevor and I had planned? I could come to the shop one afternoon. While Thea's at school. If you're not too busy?'

Ben said he thought that was a very good idea.

'It's short notice, but how about tomorrow after-noon?'

Ben thought about everything he really had to do. All the paying jobs he needed to get out of the way before the beginning of the Christmas holiday. Then he said, 'That would be great. What time?'

'How about lunchtime? I'll bring some sandwiches.'

'Dad likes ham and cheese best. With pickle,' Thea told her.

Chapter Thirty-Four

The following morning, Ben raced into the shop after dropping Thea off at school. He had enough jobs to keep him busy for months. Most of them were supposed to be sorted out before Christmas. But Ben spent his first two hours in the shop doing anything but paid work. Instead, he tried to make the place look half decent. He wished he had the resources to employ a cleaner. Since he didn't and since he hadn't actually done anything beyond slosh bleach down the loo a couple of times a month since he took the shop over, Ben had his work cut out before Kirsty's arrival. He donned rubber gloves and scrubbed and scrubbed and scrubbed. In two hours, he actually rendered the shop cleaner than when he'd moved in. Who knew the tiles on the tiny bathroom floor were actually pale-blue and not grey?

As a finishing touch, Ben dashed across the road to the corner shop and bought one of the deep-red poinsettias on the flower rack outside. The plants were all fairly shabby specimens that definitely wouldn't last until Christmas but he found one that would probably make it through lunchtime and paid an extra three quid for a chipped ceramic pot decorated with snowflakes to put it in. It gave the place a colourful festive touch. It made it look as though Ben cared.

And Ben did care, he found. He wanted Kirsty to be

impressed. It was a sensation he hadn't felt for a long while.

Kirsty arrived exactly on time. In a bright-blue dress over dark-pink tights, Kirsty was like a wild tropical bird. A walking blast of sunshine. Outside, it had barely got light at all that day and it would be going dark again by four, but having Kirsty in the shop was like being transported into July for a moment. And they had a picnic for that extra touch of summer in December.

'It's lovely to see you,' said Ben.

He had been agonising over how he should greet her. In the end, he went for a luvvie kiss – after all, they were going to be spending the afternoon acting – but he went for the wrong cheek and they ended up bashing noses.

Kirsty stepped backwards, holding her hand to her nose as her eyes began to water. It was not the best of starts.

But it got better. Ben took Kirsty's coat and hung it alongside his in the office at the back of the shop. He pulled out a chair for her to sit on.

'Lunch first?' Kirsty suggested. 'I took Thea's advice on board and made you ham and cheese. I hope they're OK.'

'Anything I don't have to make myself is OK by me,' said Ben.

'I know what you mean.'

Ben put the kettle on while Kirsty unpacked her picnic.

The sandwiches were doorstops. What Ben didn't know was that Kirsty didn't ordinarily make such enormous sarnies but while she was supposed to be on a diet and Jon said she should stick to two sandwiches only at lunch, she was going to make sure they were as big as reasonably possible.

And they were delicious. One of Kirsty's first missions upon arriving in Newbay was to find the best bakery in town. She asked around and was guided towards Motcombs, one of those artisan bakeries where everything is made with the very best ingredients. Motcombs prided themselves on making their bread with 'ancient, naturally low gluten grain'. Which turned out to make loaves of bread that were as heavy and indigestible as breezeblocks. Not to mention the fact they cost nearly a fiver a time. Kirsty bought three during her first three weeks in Newbay and tried to convince herself they were doing her good. They were certainly giving her jaw a workout. But in the end, Kirsty decided that life was too short for joyless artisan baked goods and she asked for directions to the nearest Greggs. It was Greggs' bread they were eating now.

'And these are for afters,' Kirsty said, whipping out a bag containing two huge mince pies. 'I'd have bought yum yums but the first door is open on the advent calendar so I declare it is officially the mince pie season.'

The mince pies were slightly warm and when Kirsty opened the bag, the scent of allspice filled the shop.

'Now, doesn't that smell like Christmas?' she commented as she cut one in half.

Ben agreed. Despite having been in the shop for six months, Ben didn't think the place had ever seemed so warm and cosy.

After lunch, Ben and Kirsty set to work on their lines. Though Cinderella was all about getting to meet the prince, there was no doubt that her scenes with Buttons were the real heartbreakers. Not that you would have known that had you seen Kirsty playing Cinderella opposite Trevor Fernlea in the role as her besotted friend. Coming from a chap who was certainly north of seventy, Buttons' more flirtatious lines seemed cringe-worthy at best. The words took on a very different tone when Kirsty played opposite someone she might feasibly have fallen in love with.

Since agreeing to step into Trevor's shoes, Ben had worked quickly to learn his lines and he and Kirsty soon found an easy rhythm to their exchanges. If Ben was nervous, Kirsty didn't know it, and playing two old friends soon had them acting like old friends too.

But the lines were easy. The dancing was the part of the role with which Ben most wanted to be brought up to speed. Together, he and Kirsty moved everything on the shop floor out to the edges of the room to give them the space they needed. Their first dance together came at the point in the panto when Cinders thinks she is going to the ball, before her Ugly Sisters squash her hopes.

'*But I don't know how to dance!*' Kirsty cried in character.

'*Everyone knows how to dance,*' said Ben as Buttons. '*You just have to follow the rhythm of your heart.*'

He placed his hand on his chest, as the script required, but if Ben had followed the rhythm of his own heart right then, he would have been dancing a jitterbug. Kirsty cast her eyes towards the ground shyly as Ben held out his hand to her. Of course, she was only acting coy but the way she looked up at him from beneath her lashes made him catch his breath. Though she was still dressed in her quirky dress and tights, when Kirsty became

Cinders, even in the unprepossessing surrounding of a computer repair shop, Ben could already see her in a ballgown with the light of a chandelier glittering on sequins and casting stars about her face.

'*How could any prince fail to fall in love with you,*' he said, sticking to the script but suddenly meaning every word.

Kirsty stepped into his arms, '*Oh, Buttons,*' she sighed.

'*Just pretend I'm the prince . . .*'

Kirsty swooned in Ben's embrace. They hovered in that tableau for a moment, then . . .

There was a knock on the shop door.

Laughing, Kirsty stepped away.

'Am I interrupting something?' asked the man in the long brown overcoat. 'Do you clean hard drives?'

Kirsty perched on the counter while Ben attended to his customer, who looked exactly like the sort of person who should be worrying about the state of his hard drive. It seemed to take an age to reassure him that Ben could return his laptop to factory settings. But at last . . .

'*Shall we dance?*'

Ben and Kirsty found each other again in the middle of the shop floor.

It wasn't quite as it had been before the customer interrupted them. They didn't go over the set-up to the scene again but concentrated on the dance steps. A couple of times they danced right into the shop window – the space wasn't large enough – which had them both laughing. Ben was delighted by the sound of Kirsty's giggle.

From time to time, people passing by stopped to watch the dancing. An old couple linked arms and smiled indulgently as they remembered their own dancing days.

'*I could have danced all night*,' said Kirsty, as Cinders getting home from the ball.

Me too, thought Ben. Me too.

Chapter Thirty-Five

After nearly an hour, Ben and Kirsty stopped for a tea break and to eat the last mince pie.

'So, you're a Newbay native,' said Kirsty.

'Yep. Lived here all my life apart from uni and a few years in London after that.'

'It seems like a good place to grow up.'

Ben told Kirsty about his childhood in Newbay and how much had changed – or not – in the thirty-odd years he'd known the town.

'The seafront is exactly the same as it was in the eighties,' he explained. 'The only thing missing is the donkeys. And the donkey mess. When I was five, I tripped over and landed face first in a steaming pile,' Ben admitted.

'I'm sure that's supposed to be lucky,' Kirsty said.

'Didn't feel like it,' said Ben.

Then Ben told Kirsty about her former co-star, Trevor Fernlea, who had taught geography before he retired.

'He was a crack shot with a board rubber,' said Ben. 'Got me on the side of the head for not concentrating a couple of times. I don't think you're allowed to throw things at children any more.'

'Thank goodness,' Kirsty said. 'That sounds brutal. And he seems like such a gentle soul. It's hard to imagine Trevor ever getting into a rage.'

'You can't imagine what a pain in the proverbial it must have been to teach us lot.'

'I don't believe *you* were so bad,' said Kirsty. After all, Jon had told her that Ben was a swot.

'I was irritating in my own way. I was a dreamer,' said Ben. 'Always looking out of the window.'

'Nothing wrong with dreaming,' said Kirsty.

Kirsty told him about her own childhood, growing up in Essex.

'I was always scribbling dresses in rough books. Dresses for my film premiere. Dresses for the BAFTAs. The Oscars . . .'

That made Ben smile.

'I was so sure I'd be a star.'

'And now you are.'

'Thank you.' Kirsty accepted the compliment with grace. 'You know, I always wondered what it would be like to live by the sea all year round. We came on holiday. I didn't think it was possible to grow up here. I don't know who I thought lived in places like Newbay in the off-season. How lovely to be able to go to the beach after school.'

'But you got to go to London at the weekends when you were a teenager,' Ben countered.

'Yeah. I suppose I did have that.'

'When I was a teenager, I wanted to be in your position. I wanted to be in the big city. Newbay seemed so small. It still is.'

'But there's something comforting about that,' said Kirsty. 'I love living in a place where people nod "hello" when you pass them in the street.'

'And where they know all your business. Trust me, at least one of those little old ladies who stopped to watch us will have been on the phone to my mother by now.'

Kirsty laughed. 'Then we should have given them something worth gossiping about. Something like the Argentine tango.'

She pouted at him and did a little dance with her arms. Was she flirting?

'Can you do the tango?' Ben asked.

'I'll show you next time.'

'But how did you end up here?' Ben continued. 'It must be dull being in Newbay after travelling around the world on a cruise ship.'

'Not at all,' said Kirsty. 'I'm making some good friends. Like you.'

There was a pause. Kirsty didn't get round to explaining why she was in Newbay – about Jon – instead she said, 'I was sorry to hear about Thea's mum. It must have been very hard for you. Still is, I bet.'

'It gets easier,' said Ben. Which was different from how he'd felt such a short time ago. He didn't stop to question why.

'Can I ask what happened?'

'It was about three years ago. Breast cancer.'

'Oh.'

'Yeah. It was terrible. One day she was fine. We were planning the rest of our lives together. Next day she found a lump. She had a mastectomy right away but it had already spread. She died about six months after she was diagnosed.'

'That's awful.'

'It still gave us time to talk about a lot of things,' said Ben. 'We said things we might not have said to each other if we thought we had the rest of our lives. Good things. I'm grateful for that.'

Kirsty nodded. 'I think I know what you mean. My mum died of cancer too.'

Ben offered his sympathy.

'It was nothing short of hell to see her dying, but because we knew what was coming, we had so many conversations we might not otherwise have had. We were able to say that we loved each other. And Mum had time to show me how to use the washing machine, boil an egg, write a cheque. Stuff like that.'

Ben gave a sort of laugh.

'Jo made sure I knew how to use a washing machine before she married me. And if I hadn't known how to boil an egg, we'd have both starved. But she left me lots of instructions for Thea. Not just practical stuff. Stuff like make sure she never falls for the Cinderella myth.'

'What's that? That we women have to sit around and wait to be rescued? And if our feet are too big, it'll never happen.'

'Big feet, big heart,' said Ben. 'Not that your feet are anything other than average.'

'Exactly.'

Ben was glad Kirsty knew his joke was meant kindly.

'Anyway, I'm sorry it came out like it did. About Jo. It's not exactly small talk for a theatre bar.'

'You don't need to be sorry,' Kirsty exclaimed. 'What else were you supposed to say when Jon asked? And I know what it's like. You lose someone special then you spend all your time trying not to make other people feel bad by not mentioning it. You don't need that on top of everything else.'

Ben nodded, grateful for the recognition.

'I'd just turned sixteen when we lost Mum, so I was much older than Thea. But if you ever want to talk about what it might be like for her, for Thea, that is, I'd be happy to. I'd be happy to talk to her too.'

Ben had already decided that he would like to keep

talking to Kirsty all day long. And all night. Her kindness only made that feeling stronger.

But all too soon, it was time to pick Thea up from school.

Kirsty kissed Ben lightly on the cheek as they parted. Though they had been dancing almost cheek to cheek, this felt much more intimate. It wasn't a luvvie air kiss. Her perfume was warm and spicy as the mince pies and just as delicious. As Ben stepped back from her, he hoped she couldn't see he was going red.

'I'll see you tomorrow night at the theatre,' she said.

'Can't wait.'

Chapter Thirty-Six

Ben's casting came just in time. At the end of his second rehearsal, on the Wednesday night, the main cast put on their costumes (Ben's would have to be taken in) and assembled on the stage for a quick photo shoot for a poster.

The NEWTS' programmes and posters were always done in house by Bill Woodford, another old-timer who fancied himself a bit of a David Bailey. Prior to retiring, he'd worked as the in-house photographer for the local paper, shooting pictures of everything from local regattas to lost dogs, taking it every bit as seriously as Don McCullin's war photography.

On the Cinderella poster shoot, Bill spent most of the time being baffled by the buttons on his new state-of-the-art digital camera, to the extent that Thea, who'd been photographed with the rest of the mice and was getting bored as she waited for her dad to be ready to take her home, offered to show him how it worked. Then Bill had to spend half an hour on Lauren, who insisted on seeing every shot as he took it. She deleted forty-nine of fifty.

'I've got to protect my brand,' she said. Thankfully, Bill, who had also photographed Lauren at several Alzheimer's support group fundraisers over the years, was used to Lauren's insistence on bad photo veto. And like so many men, he was so enamoured of her, he didn't care.

It was while the photographs were being taken that Ben learned something which somewhat took the shine off his day. He had very much enjoyed another chance to be with Kirsty. In the space of the theatre, they were able to practise their dances properly. Ben hadn't laughed so much in a long time as he did while they whirled around the floor in the scene where Buttons helped Cinders learn her dance steps for the ball.

When Bill Woodford had finally taken a photograph of Lauren that she was happy to see go into print, Bill fired off a few small group shots. Kirsty pulled Ben into the centre of the group arrangement and suggested they pose in a dance hold. Ben could have stayed there all day, with Kirsty in his arms. At one point she swayed backwards in a dip, so that her lovely long neck was exposed to him. Ben felt an overwhelming urge to lean over and kiss her.

But then the photo shoot was finished and the witches of Wardrobe were waiting impatiently for costumes to be taken off and put away properly before anyone managed to tear something/get too sweaty. They were visibly irritated to have to deal with Bernie's Vivienne Westwood frock, which was now officially Cinders' ball-gown.

'If this gets damaged,' said Angie, 'we're not taking responsibility.'

'I wouldn't have expected otherwise,' Kirsty assured them. Bernie rolled her eyes at the witches' silliness.

It was while Ben was in the wings, being released from

his jacket, which was bulldog clipped into shape at the back, that he heard Jon ask Bill if he would take a picture of Jon with Kirsty, before she got out of the gorgeous red dress. Ben watched as Kirsty stepped into Jon's arms for the photo. Then Jon pulled her close and planted a kiss on her lips.

Until that moment, Ben had not realised that Jon and Kirsty were an item.

How had he not guessed? Ben went back over the times he had seen them together. Obviously, Jon wasn't going to be all over her during rehearsals. But they hadn't seemed very connected when they were standing together in the bar either. In fact, Ben would have put money on Lauren being Jon's girlfriend, given the proprietorial way she had grabbed him by the collar and pulled him off into a corner to talk after Ben's first rehearsal as part of the cast.

Still, Ben felt very foolish. Surely someone must have said something about Jon and Kirsty's relationship, but obviously it hadn't sunk in because subconsciously Ben didn't want to believe it. He tried to sound casual as he asked Lauren for confirmation.

'Oh yeah,' said Lauren. 'That's obviously why she got the part. You don't think it was all about talent.'

Actually, Ben had assumed it was all about talent. As far as he was concerned, Kirsty was a proper star. But why hadn't he realised the truth about her relationship with Jon? Why hadn't Kirsty said something when they were together in the shop? They'd talked about pretty much everything else.

Ben felt oddly deflated.

'Thank goodness that's over,' Kirsty said, as she joined Ben in the wings. 'I hate having my photograph taken.'

'I'm sure you'll look great in all of them,' said Ben.

He wondered if Jon would get the photograph of him and Kirsty printed out and put it in a frame. Ben remembered the first time he and Jo were photographed together. It was at a Christmas ball at uni. A proper photographer took shots of all the students as they arrived. Ben had bought their picture and given it to Jo for Christmas. It was a significant gesture, which let her know that he was serious about her. Of course, that was back before digital cameras were widely used, when people didn't waste film on people they weren't in love with.

'I think those shots of you and I doing our dance hold will turn out really well,' Kirsty continued.

But she wouldn't be putting one of those on the mantelpiece, Ben guessed.

The posters were rushed into production. Two days later, they were ready to be distributed all over town. The design was simple. Kirsty and Ben seemed to lean out from the centre, while the other characters smiled beatifically or glowered from the stars around them, depending on whether they were good guys or bad.

Each cast member was given a roll of ten posters to place strategically all over Newbay. And, of course, posters were placed all over the theatre itself. And then Kirsty came to understand Bernie's comment about the Hitler moustache. Less than two hours after the poster went up in the theatre lobby, Kirsty's face had gained a Hitler moustache and several hairy warts. The only consolation was that all the other women on the poster had received the same treatment. Bernie had glasses and a beard. Annette, who had been smiling broadly in her portrait, looked as though she had no teeth. Even Lauren hadn't escaped the poison pen. Her nostrils had been amended to look like deep dark tunnels you definitely didn't want to go into.

'Congratulations,' said Bernie to Kirsty as they admired the vandal's handiwork. 'You got the moustache. That's your last rite of passage done. You are now officially a full-blown NEWT.'

Chapter Thirty-Seven

Talking of fully blown NEWTS, with just a couple of weeks left to go before the opening night, Vince had missed three rehearsals. Kirsty's heart went out to Bernie every time she turned up alone.

'He's got that bug that's been going round,' Bernie said.

Everyone knew it was closer to the truth to say that Vince *was* the bug going around. The Christmas party season had begun and Vince hadn't missed a single shindig so far. There was no party without Vince. The previous evening, the Giggle Twins had seen him staggering out of The Sailor's Arms as they headed for nineties' night at Maestro, Newbay's premier club.

As she lied on her husband's behalf, Bernie's eyes were sad and Kirsty felt the urge to hug her. Kirsty asked Bernie if she was OK, but got no further than, 'Of course.' Kirsty didn't push. She understood that if Bernie didn't want to talk about her husband, it was not Kirsty's place to try to force any revelations out of her. Bernie's marriage was her business. It was hard, though, not to want to give Bernie a pep talk.

However, when it was her turn to be on stage again, Bernie knew how to turn on the sparkle. Unlike her husband, Bernie was determined that she would not let anyone down. Kirsty hoped that acting happy went some way to making Bernie feel happy too.

'Ah well,' said Bernie, when another Saturday rehearsal was finished. 'I'd better get home and play Florence Nightingale.'

That evening, Jon was going to be staying late in the theatre for a meeting with Elaine and the technical crew, so Kirsty decided she would walk into the centre of Newbay and take advantage of the late-night shopping. She wanted to get a head start on her gift buying though there weren't really that many people on her list. Just Jon, Jane and India, her half-sister.

Kirsty still didn't know whether she would actually see her half-sister over the Christmas season. Kirsty hadn't seen her father since the spring, just before she went off to join *The European Countess*, when she had been so disappointed by his lack of enthusiasm for her upcoming adventure.

When she told him she was quitting the cruise line to come back to the UK, he was even less impressed.

'I knew you wouldn't stick it out,' he said.

Kirsty protested that it wasn't a matter of not sticking it out. She was coming back because of Jon. But that didn't impress her father either.

After that exchange, Kirsty decided it was best she and her father agree to disagree about her career and her love life. One sure-fire way to avoid getting into a disagreement was to avoid one another altogether. She still texted, to let him know she was alive and to make sure he was too, but she hadn't visited.

Maybe she should. Stu might not approve of the way Kirsty lived her life, but he was still her dad. She still loved him. And Kirsty very much wanted to see her half-sister. As she walked into Newbay, inspired by the inviting glow of the Christmas lights in the shop windows, she pulled out her phone and sent a text. Not to her father but to her stepmother. She was more likely to get a prompt response that way.

She was delighted when Linzi replied within minutes. 'We'd love to see you!' followed by a string of possible dates. Kirsty plumped on the following Thursday evening. Would it be OK if she brought Jon?

'Of course!!!' was the effusive reply. 'We want to meet him!'

The little text exchange made Kirsty feel warm inside. Her stepmother's enthusiasm convinced her they hadn't been sitting around talking about what a disappointing daughter she was after all. The visit was something to look forward to. It also meant that Kirsty had to step up her Christmas shopping game now that she had less time than she thought to find something for India.

Kirsty headed straight for Topshop. Her little sister was not so little any more. She was well into her teens. There was bound to be something just right for her there.

After half an hour in Topshop, however, Kirsty was losing the will to live. She had hoped she would walk in and find the perfect gift within minutes, but everything looked wrong to Kirsty's eyes. It was all too brash, too cheap and too short. She reminded herself that she was looking at it from the perspective of a woman twice her sister's age. To India, everything in Topshop probably looked just right. It would have looked right to Kirsty once. She loved bright colours. She loved lace and sequins and fluffy feather boas. There wasn't a pair of heels too high or a skirt too short.

These days, she still liked bright colours. She was still drawn to them whenever she walked into a shop, but she no longer grabbed for the brightest, shiniest things and threw them into her basket. She had begun to ask herself if the clothes she liked were 'appropriate'. Did they highlight her best features and disguise the ones she wanted to hide? And, all of a sudden, there seemed to be so many more features that she wanted to hide. Like her feet.

Kirsty was in the shoe department. She picked up a pair of gold sandals with a platform sole. They were exactly the kind of shoes she adored. In fact, she had once owned a pair just like them. She had a feeling they'd been left behind in the back of a taxi when she changed into a pair of foot-saving flat shoes on the way home from a club. Kirsty's heart reached out to the golden shoes but as she was turning them over to see what size they were, the voice in her head chipped in to point out that those platform soles would make her taller than Jon – something he really didn't like – and, of course, they would draw attention to the fact that Kirsty had big feet.

She put the shoes back. She wasn't supposed to be shopping for herself anyway. She needed something for India.

Kirsty watched as three girls who were about India's age went into raptures over a short black playsuit with subtle silver stripes. They all three grabbed one each from the rails and raced to the changing room. When they were gone, Kirsty went to look more closely at what they had been gushing over. If the three of them were that enthusiastic, then maybe India would like the suit too.

'Done,' Kirsty said to herself. She imagined India's delight as she opened her Christmas gift. Kirsty would get major big sister points for scoring something so trendy. She went through the suits on the rack and found the last of the size tens. She took it straight to the counter. The bored-looking assistant searched for the price tag.

'This is a size ten,' she observed. She didn't need to add, 'It won't fit you.'

The assistant tossed the playsuit into a carrier bag. Kirsty thanked her but in her head she was already composing an online review. 'Never have I met a ruder sales assistant than in the Newbay branch of Topshop.' It made her feel better to think of it though she knew she wouldn't post it. She stepped out into the cold December air and focussed on more important things. What would she buy for Jon?

Chapter Thirty-Eight

Kirsty didn't manage to find anything for Jon that evening. Instead, she picked up a couple of calorie-counted ready meals at Marks & Spencer and turned back to the flat. It was as she was heading away from the town centre, past the town's leisure centre and swimming pool, that she saw Vince.

He was weaving down the street ahead of her. From time to time, he tottered dangerously close to the edge of the pavement and the oncoming traffic. Still, he seemed to be making his way somewhere with a certain determination.

So much for Vince being 'ill'. He had obviously spent the day getting bladdered, just as Annette and the Giggle Twins had insinuated. Did Bernie know where he was, Kirsty wondered. Was she at home worrying? She toyed with texting Bernie to let her know that she'd seen him. But what was the point? Vince was an adult. He could go wherever he wanted. Kirsty had no right to treat him like a child by reporting him to his missus. She had no right to humiliate Bernie by exposing her husband's lie.

All the same, she decided to stay close behind Vince for a while – if only to stop him from falling in front of a lorry – and, if he did go into a pub, perhaps she would follow him in there and meet him at the bar in an attempt to persuade him that another night of drunkenness would not help him be at his best for the next day's rehearsal. Vince's tendency to slur his words had not gone unnoticed and while the rest of the gang still laughed at Baron Hardup's prat-falls, Kirsty wasn't sure the laughter was as friendly as it had been. There was an edge to it.

Vince continued on his meandering path. From time to time, he took out his phone to check directions, perhaps, on his maps app. Kirsty tailed him at a discreet distance but she soon realised that Vince wasn't ever looking behind him. He wouldn't have noticed if he was being tailed by three elephants wearing cloaks and Homburg hats.

He was heading away from the centre of town towards the university. Kirsty was surprised when she saw him arrive at what looked like a student accommodation block. He rang a door-bell. He slumped against the doorframe, massaging his forehead with one hand as though to chase away a headache, while he waited for someone to answer.

The entry system can't have been working properly because Vince wasn't buzzed in. Instead, a young woman came to open the door.

Thanks to the light in the building's porch, Kirsty, who was pretending to wait at a bus stop, had a very good view of Vince's new friend. Though she lived in a student building, the woman wasn't very young. She was perhaps in her mid-twenties. But that still meant she was a good two decades younger than Bernie. And she was strikingly pretty. She was tall, with a figure that gave Kirsty a quick prick of envy. No Topshop assistant would have suggested she try a larger size. Her black hair was cut into a sharp bob that framed her heart-shaped face to perfection. Her eyes were beautifully made up and her mouth was bright scarlet with perfectly applied lipstick. She was wearing a tight black knitted dress over bright-pink lacy tights and biker boots. She was obviously quite the hipster. And now she was folding Vince into her arms.

The young woman joined him in leaning against the doorframe for a while, holding him tightly. Then she unwrapped him, just a little, and, taking his hand, led him inside the building.

'Oh, no,' thought Kirsty.

What should she do? Was this what Vince had been doing on all those afternoons when he claimed to have migraines, the flu or a vomiting bug? Not just nursing a hangover but sneaking off to meet another woman, while Bernie made excuses at the theatre? It was so unfair. And what did that girl even see in Vince? She was young and gorgeous. When Kirsty first caught sight of Vince rolling down the road, she thought he was a down and out. But Vince did have his own dental practice. He drove a BMW. The young woman probably thought he was loaded and that made him a catch.

For a moment, Kirsty felt the heat of righteous fury. She should march in there and drag Vince out. At the very least, she should tell Vince she'd seen him with that woman and he was being a fool. If he thought someone like her could really be interested in someone like him for anything but the wrong reasons, he was an idiot.

But by the time she got back to the flat, Kirsty was

already chickening out. It was none of her business. Perhaps Bernie already knew. Kirsty was far more likely to look like a busybody than a heroine if she revealed what she'd seen. All the same, it was hard not to feel differently about Vince now. They arrived at the theatre at the same time the following day and he greeted her with an oddly cheery hello. Kirsty pretended not to have seen him.

Chapter Thirty-Nine

Meanwhile, Jon's CV had been enough to secure him an interview for the Dubai job. Kirsty tried to look pleased though she had been pretending that night when Jon first told her about the position and the ensuing conversation that led to him suggesting she take a secretarial job had never happened.

The interview would take place in London. The businessman who was setting up the company would be in the UK for just a week, staying at Claridge's. He was not about to waste a day of his trip on travelling down to Devon to see Jon at work with the NEWTS. Fortunately, he agreed to see Jon on the one and only day between now and the beginning of the run when Jon would not be needed at the theatre.

Jon did not ask if Kirsty wanted to go to London with him and Kirsty didn't push it. Jon decided against taking the car because he wasn't sure the old banger would make it all the way to London and back. Instead, he would take the train. Even booked in advance, a return ticket from Newbay cost roughly the same as a flight from Exeter to Majorca. It was an indulgence that Kirsty could not afford. She was burning through the savings she'd made while working on the ship. And if Jon went alone, he could sleep on a friend's floor. Together, they would have to get a hotel room. More expense.

Besides, something had come up that would keep Kirsty busy.

One evening, at the end of rehearsals, Kirsty met Ben's mother – Thea's grandmother Judy – in the theatre lobby. Thea, who was with her grandmother at the time, was very excited to be able to introduce the leading lady. Kirsty was pleased to be able to tell Judy how well the little girl was getting on.

'And how about my son?' Judy asked.

Kirsty grinned. 'He's doing pretty well too. He's a natural.'

And they had good stage chemistry. Though Kirsty was very fond of Trevor Fernlea, there was no doubt she looked forward to her scenes with Buttons much more now that Ben was in the part. She enjoyed the moments they shared when they weren't on stage too. She and Ben saw lots of things the same way.

'Gets it from his dad,' Judy said. 'Performing is in the Teesdale genes.'

Judy's words caused Kirsty a brief but painful moment of reflection as she remembered her father Stu telling her she had a tendency to drama on her maternal side. Thankfully, Thea broke Kirsty out of it by asking her to show Judy a photograph of the mice, which Kirsty had snapped on her iPhone.

'We must get home,' Judy announced after a few minutes. 'We've got a hundred mince pies to make.'

'Why so many?' Kirsty asked.

'For the senior citizens' party tomorrow lunchtime,' Judy explained.

Kirsty knew from having spoken to Ben that his mother managed an old people's home on the outskirts of town. 'Thea is going to help me with the baking. And Ben—'

Ben shuffled out of the auditorium, all wrapped up in his coat and scarf.

'Well, Ben is in charge of entertainment.'

'He's going to sing,' Thea explained.

'I'm going to work a karaoke machine,' Ben corrected her.

'But he *should* sing,' said Judy. 'Don't you agree, Kirsty? You know, I've just had an idea. What are you doing tomorrow afternoon? Many of my old ladies and gents were big supporters of NEWTS when they were still able to get out and about. Wouldn't it be lovely if we could take a little piece of the theatre to them? You and Ben have duets in the show, Thea tells me. If you could pop along and perform just those songs, I know everyone would be thrilled.'

Kirsty looked to Ben to try to get a handle on what he wanted her to say. As far as she was concerned, it sounded like a very easy way to spread a little Christmas cheer. Jon was going to be at his interview. Kirsty had nothing planned for the weekend.

'I'm game. I was just going to be at home writing my Christmas cards,' she said.

'Fantastic,' said Judy. 'Though I'm afraid I can only pay you in mince pies.'

'That sounds like a bargain to me,' Kirsty assured her.

* * *

'You're doing *what* while I'm in London?' asked Jon when Kirsty told him the plan.

'I'm going to sing at the old people's home Christmas party.'

'Rather you than me,' said Jon.

'Well, I think it's going to be fun,' said Kirsty. 'And I like the idea of giving something back to the community. Everyone's been really nice to me since I moved here with you.'

'Probably because you moved here *with* me,' said Jon. 'You should sing "Feet's Too Big". They'll know what one.'

'Thanks a lot,' said Kirsty.

'Oh, come here,' said Jon, pulling her towards him. 'You know I love you from your head to your great big massive toes.'

Chapter Forty

But before the weekend and the Christmas party, Kirsty was due to visit her dad. When she first told him about the plan, Jon agreed to accompany Kirsty to her father's house, which was an hour and half's drive from Newbay. They would be staying overnight. On the day itself, Jon was not so keen.

'I can't spare the time,' he said. 'You're asking me to take a whole day out at the most crucial moment in the process. I've got to chase up the set designers, talk to the techs, talk to Wardrobe . . . I've already got to take a day out for that interview.'

Before he could tick off any more reasons, Kirsty said she would go alone.

The drive was an opportunity to listen to the music she liked, at least. She and Jon had very different taste in music and at the flat they generally listened to the music he preferred because, if Kirsty tried to force one of her favourites on him, he would complain so loudly that she couldn't hear it anyway. Without him, it was disco all the way up the A303.

Though Kirsty had never lived in the house her father, stepmother and little sister had moved to five years previously, there was still something about heading there that felt like going home. That's what home is really, Kirsty mused. Not the place but the people inside it. She was really looking forward to seeing them all. Particularly India.

Indeed India, Kirsty's sixteen year old half-sister, was first to the door. She must have heard Kirsty's car because Kirsty didn't even get a chance to knock. While she was still getting things out of the boot, India threw the front door open dramatically, as though she were about to run out rather than let someone in.

'Thank goodness you're here,' she said. 'You can take the pressure off.'

'Hello to you too, little sister.'

India threw her arms around Kirsty. 'I've missed you, Big Sis!'

'So, what's happening? Why so dramatic?' Kirsty asked.

'You'll see. Come on in. Quick. Mum's making chilli.'

'My favourite,' said Kirsty.

In the kitchen, Kirsty's stepmother Linzi was standing at the hob, stirring an enormous pot. It smelled delicious. She turned to give Kirsty a half-hug without breaking off from her cooking.

'I always end up burning it to the bottom if I stop stirring for even a second,' she explained. 'Your dad's just on the phone about work. He'll be down in a second.'

He was literally a second.

'I finished my call as soon as I heard your car.'

Stu folded Kirsty into a big bear hug that left Kirsty

wondering why she had stayed away for so long. There was no trace whatsoever of the tension that sprang up between them when they were last together and Stu criticised Kirsty's choice of vocation. He just seemed pleased to see her.

'You're looking well,' he said.

'Fat,' said Kirsty.

'I said well,' said Stu.

'You're looking *gorgeous*,' said Linzi. 'Where did you get that dress? It's lovely.'

'Thanks,' Kirsty gave a little twirl.

'Looks a bit cold,' said Stu.

'I'm wearing thermals underneath,' Kirsty joked. Her father was always about practicality.

'How was the drive?' he asked.

'Oh. Easy,' said Kirsty. 'Hardly any traffic.'

'Remind me to have a look at your tyres before you set off again tomorrow. It's going to get icy over the weekend. You want to make sure you've got enough grip.'

Kirsty smiled. This was her father's way of showing love, she knew. Making sure that she was safe. He asked when she'd last checked the oil. The windscreen wash? The headlights?

'I'm getting a moped,' India interrupted.

'No you're not,' said Stu.

'But you're always complaining about having to drive me places.'

'I'd rather drive you places than have *you* drive a motorbike into a ditch.'

'It's not my fault anyway,' said India, immediately on the defensive. 'If we didn't live in the middle of nowhere, I could just get on a bus.'

'There's a bus that leaves from the bottom of the lane,' said Linzi. 'That takes you straight into town.'

'Yeah. But it only goes once a day and I've got to come back again at seven o'clock.'

'Late enough for a sixteen year old,' said Stu.

India rolled her eyes. Kirsty winked at her. This was a replay of a discussion she'd once had with Stu herself. Many years before.

'Will you girls lay the table, please?' Linzi asked.

'Come on,' said Kirsty to India. 'You need to show me where everything is.'

When they were alone in the dining room as they laid out the tablemats and cutlery, India pleaded for her sister's support.

'They treat me like I'm a child. Will you just keep backing me up tonight, please? I'm sixteen. I'll be seventeen in eight months. I'm legally allowed to work. I'm legally allowed to ride a motorbike. I think I'm even legally allowed to join the army without asking their permission. When are they going to face the fact I've grown up?'

'I'm not sure parents ever see their children as grown-ups,' said Kirsty.

'Ugh. It's so boring. I wish I could leave home tomorrow.'

'Then you'd have to do your own cooking, your own washing, pay your own bills . . .'

'Yeah. But I'd have my freedom. I am going nuts here, Kirsty. You don't know what it's like.'

'I think I have an inkling,' Kirsty said. 'You and I share a dad, remember.'

'What are you two talking about?' Stu joined them then. 'Would you like a glass of wine, Kirsty?'

'I'll have one,' said India.

'No you will not. You're not eighteen yet.'

'You can drink when you're five if you're drinking at home,' India told him.

'That's not true,' said Stu.

'It is. Look . . .' India fished out her smartphone and Googled 'legal drinking age UK'. She read out loud, 'It is *not* illegal for a child aged five to sixteen to drink alcohol at home.'

'It may not be illegal but it isn't right,' said Stu. 'School term hasn't finished yet. Do you want to be doing homework with a hangover?

'See?' India appealed to Kirsty. 'See what I have to put up with?'

'See what *I* have to put up with?' Stu echoed, as he poured a glass of wine for his elder daughter only.

Chapter Forty-One

Kirsty wasn't overly worried about the way her little sister and father bickered. It was normal, wasn't it? India was pushing against the boundaries. Stu was busy trying to keep them intact. At some point he would give up. Then India would get what she wanted and find out it really wasn't worth all the fuss. She would probably even come to agree that Stu had been right all along. When one day her own children wanted mopeds and wine with their dinner, she too would be suitably outraged. For now, however, Kirsty knew that India's bid for freedom was the most important thing in her life. No amount of telling her that things would be different in a couple of years would persuade her to stop arguing now.

'So what happened to your boyfriend?' Stu asked, ignoring India's bid to convince him she was old enough for a motorbike and Merlot. 'I thought he was coming with you tonight.'

'He's not feeling too good,' Kirsty lied, not sure why she didn't feel like mentioning Jon's upcoming interview. 'There's a bug going round so I told him he'd better stay home rather than come here and make you guys ill as well.'

'That's thoughtful,' said Stu. 'Nothing worse than getting ill at Christmas. It's a shame though. We'd have liked to meet him. Is he still doing the show business thing?'

'Yes,' said Kirsty. 'We both are.'

Linzi brought the chilli to the table. It smelled delicious and Kirsty was secretly glad that Jon hadn't come after all. She could imagine him sitting across the table, putting his hand across his plate to stop Linzi from overloading it, signalling with a look that Kirsty should do the same. But he wasn't there and he couldn't see how much she was going to eat so she decided she would eat as much of Linzi's chilli as she wanted. And she would load it with cheese and sour cream and guacamole. Linzi seemed pleased by the endorsement.

'You'll have to show me how to make this,' Kirsty said, though she knew after one bite that she would never be able to make it for Jon. Way too hot.

'So, tell us what's been going on?' Linzi said. 'How are you liking Newbay? I used to go there on holiday when I was a child. Is the pier still there?'

'They're planning to refurbish it next year.'

'Oh, I loved going on that pier. Me and my brother would be given a pound each to play the slots. He would spend hours on those machines where you try to make the pennies cascade down. I would always spend my money on the fortune-telling machine. It was a glass box with this model of a wizard in it. You stuck ten pence in. The lights would start flashing and the wizard's head would roll around a bit then the machine would spit out your fortune on a little piece of card. I ended up with hundreds of them.'

'Load of rubbish,' said Stu.

'Well, it foretold that one day I would marry a handsome man,' said Linzi, looking at him fondly. Before she added, 'I suppose that must be my second husband.'

'Ha! Good one, Mum,' said India.

'Don't speak with your mouth full,' said Stu.

'That fortune-telling machine still exists,' Kirsty told Linzi. 'But it's in a cafe on the seafront now. They've got a few of the old machines from the pier.'

'Did you try it?' Linzi asked. 'What did it say?'

'Oh, I didn't try it,' Kirsty lied. She didn't want her father to pooh-pooh the message on the piece of card she had been carrying around ever since that glorious afternoon when the autumn sunshine, Jon's good mood and the automatic fortune-teller had convinced her that she was in the right place. *You are where love is.* That feeling was a little fragile now.

'I thought Newbay was the most glamorous place on earth,' said Linzi.

'When you were five,' said Stu.

'It does have a sort of faded beauty still,' said Kirsty, surprised to find she wanted to defend the town that had been home for such a short time. 'And you can't deny it's in a beautiful setting. The beach is wonderful. As the sun goes down, it's really magical. The pink light on all the white buildings. I can see why people used to love it. If the weather weren't always so dodgy, I'm sure people would love it still.'

'Cheaper to go to Spain,' Stu observed.

'But what's going on with you?' Kirsty asked her little sister. 'How are you getting on at school?'

'Good question,' Stu mumbled.

'I got a really good report,' India reminded him.'

'She's on target to do well in her GCSEs,' said Linzi proudly.

'So,' India began. 'I've got to choose my options for A Levels. I've already chosen English Literature and French – I'm definitely going to do them – but I've got to come up with one more. I know what I *want* to do, but—'

'No way. It's a waste of time,' Stu interrupted.

Linzi looked between Stu and India nervously. Kirsty sensed then that this was what India had been getting stick about before she arrived.

'What are the contenders for third subject?' Kirsty asked.

'Well,' India lowered her eyes to the tablecloth. 'Dad is suggesting Economics.'

'That sounds like a good choice. Very sensible,' said Kirsty.

Stu nodded enthusiastically. 'It is. There's always a job for economists.'

'Or Politics,' India continued. 'That's another one.'

'That could be interesting,' Kirsty agreed.

'It's a good thing to know how the world really works,' said Stu.

'But . . .' India took a deep breath. 'What I *really* want to do is A Level Drama and Theatre Studies.' The words tumbled out all at once.

'Drama,' said Kirsty. Her face lit up and she was about to tell India that was the best idea of all when—

'It's a waste of time,' Stu jumped in.

'Kirsty doesn't think that,' said India. 'Do you?'

Kirsty could suddenly see storm clouds gathering. She didn't have a clue what to say that wouldn't kick off a fight. She tried to remain neutral. 'I didn't actually ever study Drama,' she said carefully.

'But if you'd had the chance, you would have, wouldn't you? If Dad hadn't made all your decisions for you, like he's trying to do with me.'

'I'm not making your decisions for you. I'm just guiding you in the right direction.'

'Drama *is* the right direction as far as I'm concerned.'

'You don't know what you're talking about. You're not supposed to be choosing subjects based on your hobbies, you're supposed to be choosing subjects that will help you get a job.'

'I want to get a job as an actress.'

'I don't think Theatre Studies was even an option at my school,' Kirsty tried to bring the temperature of the discussion down.

'But Dad even stopped you doing it outside school,' India reminded her. 'And look how hard it's been for you to catch up from that. You were thirty-two before you finally got to do what you wanted. It isn't fair. You should have been allowed to be an actress and singer when you were a kid. And I should be allowed to choose my own options. I don't want to be an economist. I don't want to be a politician. They're all shits.'

Stu glared at his daughter.

'Well, they are,' said India. 'And I'm not interested in going into the corporate world. I want to be an actress. I know where my talents lie and Dad is trying to stop me from developing them. It isn't fair. It's none of his business. It's *my* life.'

'It is my business while you're living in this house and I'm paying for it,' Stu thundered in reply.

'Then I'll leave home,' said India. 'There's nothing you can do to stop me now I'm sixteen. I'll leave home and get a job and get my own place and study Drama at a sixth form college.'

'You have no idea,' said Stu.

'Kirsty's made it all by herself. I can do it too.'

'Kirsty worked for an accountancy firm.'

'Because she had to. Because you gave her no choice. If she'd been allowed to take those advertising jobs when she was a child, she would have been able to pay her own way through drama school when she was my age. She could have gone straight into the arts.'

Kirsty was surprised that India knew about the advertising jobs Kirsty's mother Nicole had put her forward for. She wondered who had told her. Surely not Stu. Unless he held them up as an example of 'what not to do'.

'You're an idiot, Dad,' India continued, making her mother and sister blanch. 'All you care about is money and stability.' India made little inverted commas with her fingers when she said stability. 'There's more to life than that. What about living in your own way? Being happy? Being authentic?'

'You try being authentic when you've got a mortgage to pay. Life is not school. You don't get to be "authentic".'

Kirsty tried to calm things down by interjecting. 'I'd say that none of the people I've met in show business actually studied Drama at school,' she tried.

Stu and India were taking no notice. Stu was giving his younger daughter both barrels.

'You've got no idea what's waiting for you in the real world. I'm trying to protect you from yourself.'

'I don't need that kind of protection. I want to be me.'

'India,' said Linzi. 'We're supposed to be having a nice family dinner. We don't need to talk about this now.'

'Then when?' India cried. 'When is anybody actually going to listen to me?'

'We listen to you all the time,' said Stu. 'Going on about how you want to be famous. Do you really think you're that special? Do you really think you're going to be the one who makes it big? There are families having discussions like this one all over the country. There are thousands of teenagers just like you who think it's going to be different for them. Well, guess what? It's not. I had to work my arse off to get where I am today and it's going to be far harder for your generation. So I'm not going to let you make mistakes on my watch. You're not doing bloody Theatre Studies. You'll thank me one day.'

'Or maybe I won't. Maybe I'll be like Kirsty, having to wait thirty years to do what I want and hating you all the time.'

'I don't hate . . .' Kirsty tried but India was on a roll.

'She had talent. That was picked up when she was seven years old. Imagine how far she could have gone with your support.'

'She's hardly Helen Mirren,' was Stu's reply.

'Thanks,' said Kirsty, quietly.

'Sorry, Kirsty,' said Stu. 'But you know what I mean.'

'I'm not sure I do . . .'

Linzi quickly grabbed Kirsty's hand and squeezed it. 'Come on,' she said. 'I need you in the kitchen. Now.'

Kirsty gratefully followed Linzi out.

'I am so sorry,' said Linzi. 'I'm so sorry. I'm really embarrassed for your dad. You know he didn't mean it?'

'He's right,' said Kirsty. 'I am no Helen Mirren.'

'I've never rated her anyway!' said Linzi in desperation.

Kirsty managed a smile.

'He's just so worried about India. I've told him to calm down and let her win this battle. She's doing French and English. They're both good, solid subjects. But he's scared she's putting herself out of the job market. It doesn't help that his firm has been talking redundancies.'

'Really?'

'They're going to make an announcement right before

Christmas. He's pretty sure he's for the chop. That phone call he was taking when you arrived . . .' Linzi dabbed at her eyes. 'That's what it was about. His whole team is likely to be made redundant. He's so stressed-out.'

Kirsty knew how much her father's work meant to him.

'He just sees the world as a big bad place and he wants to keep India safe,' Linzi continued. 'And because he's always tried so hard to protect her from life's harsh realities, she doesn't have a clue. She just keeps pushing and pushing until he pushes back and ends up saying something really awful.'

'Like the Helen Mirren thing.'

'He didn't mean it. He's really proud of you. I know he doesn't always show it . . .'

Kirsty shook her head. 'You don't need to say anything. Look, I should go. I've only had one glass of wine. I'll be OK to drive back.'

'What, now? But it's the middle of the night. I've made up the spare room.'

Linzi's eyes were swimming with tears. In that moment, Kirsty couldn't help feeling more sorry for her stepmother than she felt for herself.

'Please stay. Stu will be so upset if you go. I'll be upset too. And India.'

'OK,' said Kirsty. 'I'll stay.'

'Oh, thank you, sweetheart. Thank you. Will you help me carry these dishes in?' she asked. 'Hopefully they'll have stopped arguing.'

'Yes,' said Kirsty.

'This is doing my head in,' said Linzi. 'You know, I really don't remember you ever arguing with your father like this.'

'You've got a short memory,' said Kirsty.

Chapter Forty-Two

Stu and India did seem to have agreed a temporary truce and Stu apologised again about the 'Helen Mirren' crack, but even after Kirsty assured him she hadn't taken offence, the echoes of the argument still hung in the air and made it difficult to choose a new subject to talk about. Kirsty was conscious that talking about the pantomime might cause India to segue onto Drama and Theatre Studies again. Likewise, school in general was out of the question. She now also knew she shouldn't ask her father how his work was going.

Linzi did her best to ride to the rescue by talking about a cookery programme she was keen on. She announced that she wanted to try cooking one of those 'bird within a bird' roasts for Christmas lunch. But that only made India frown and say that she could never eat duck. In fact, she was thinking of becoming a vegetarian. And that prompted Stu to say, 'Another of your faddy ideas.'

'It's not faddy!' India went from nought to furious in less than a second. 'Apart from the fact that farm animals are kept in appalling conditions, there's tons and tons of medical evidence to suggest that eating meat is really bad for you.'

'What are you going to replace meat with?' Stu asked. 'More crisps?'

'Stop it!' Linzi put her hands over her ears. 'Stop it, both of you.' She started to clear away the dessert dishes before anyone had actually finished.

With the table prematurely cleared, Kirsty tried a peace-making mission of her own. 'Come and see what I got you for Christmas,' she said to India. 'You might as well open it now so I've got time to change it if it's wrong.'

India followed Kirsty into the living room. Stu came with them. Kirsty proudly handed India her parcel. Kirsty had gone to great lengths to make the gift look especially pretty. India cooed over the wrapping, which featured a skull and cross-bones in a Santa hat as a recurring motif. 'This is really great. Where did you get it?'

'A little shop in Newbay. They sell all sorts of goth stuff. I thought you'd like it.'

India ripped the paper off. She unfolded the playsuit and held it up.

'Oh wow!' she said. 'Wow. This is amazing.'

'I hope it's the right size.'

India inspected the label. 'It is. It's perfect. I'm going to try it on right now.'

'What is it?' Stu asked. 'Is it pyjamas?'

'It's a playsuit,' said India, not bothering to hide her disdain for her father's lack of fashion savvy.

'A playsuit?'

'Like a jumpsuit with short legs. I'm going to wear this to the end-of-term party.'

'You're going to wear *that* outside the house?' Stu asked.

'Er, yeah,' said India.

'Oh, no,' said Stu. 'You're not wearing that in public. It's too short.'

'It's meant to be short. You wear it over tights.'

'I don't care. Kirsty, you'll have to take it back.'

'I don't want her to take it back. I love it.' India clutched the playsuit to her chest. 'I'm going to put it on.'

'Let Kirsty take it back to the shop. I don't know what she was thinking anyway.' He turned to address Kirsty directly. 'It's hardly appropriate for a sixteen year old. It looks like something one of your showgirl friends would wear.'

'And that means it's not respectable, right, Dad?' asked India.

Kirsty got up from the sofa. 'I'll take it back and get you some vouchers,' she said to India.

'No way.' India quickly ripped the sales tag off, instantly rendering the playsuit impossible to return. 'I'm keeping it.'

Kirsty couldn't help offering India a quick complicit smile.

'Well, you're never wearing it,' Stu roared. 'So that's just a waste of bloody money.'

'It's what everyone's wearing this year,' Kirsty tried. 'They're really not that racy.'

'You could try to back me up,' said Stu. 'You're supposed to be an adult. But I suppose I'm expecting too much from you.'

'Right,' said Kirsty. 'I really am going this time.'

Thank goodness she'd switched to drinking water after the 'Helen Mirren' jibe. She knew that family tensions are never improved with alcohol.

'Kirsty,' Linzi pleaded.

'Look, I'll give you a call at Christmas. I just don't

think it's a good idea for me to stay here a moment longer. I don't want to say anything I might regret and I'm sure you feel the same way, Dad.'

'Nobody listens to me anyway,' he lamented.

'We've listened to far too much of you tonight,' said Linzi, suddenly venting her own pain.

Kirsty gave India a hug.

'I can't believe you're leaving me here on my own,' India sobbed. 'You were supposed to be my ally.'

'I think I'm just making matters worse. I'll see you soon,' Kirsty said. 'Thanks for a lovely dinner, Linzi. Dad . . .'

Stu had his back to her. He actually turned the television on and was flicking through the channels as Linzi and India saw Kirsty to her car.

Kirsty managed to wave quite cheerfully as she set off. It was only when she was a couple of miles down the road that she started to cry. She pulled her car to the kerb and sat there with the hazard lights on for fifteen minutes.

'No Helen Mirren.'

That was one insult it would take her a long time to shake off. And from her dad! All she'd ever wanted to do was make him proud.

He was right, though. She felt it deep inside. She was chasing a dream that would never be hers. He had seen that when she was a child. All those restrictions he'd placed on her were to protect her from finding out too late that she really didn't have it after all.

* * *

When Kirsty got home, Jon complained that she had woken him up.

'I thought you were staying overnight.'

'I decided to drive back and be with you instead. I'd rather wake up here tomorrow morning.'

There wasn't much point telling him about the row. Kirsty told herself she didn't want to talk about it anyway. Least said, soonest mended. She certainly didn't want to say the words 'Helen Mirren' out loud and watch for any hint of agreement on Jon's face. He'd already suggested that she should go back to office work.

She found what she really wanted to do was tell Ben.

Chapter Forty-Three

Jon left early on Saturday morning to catch the train to London. Kirsty didn't have to get up when he did but she decided she would, to show him some support. While he showered and dressed, she padded about the cold kitchen making him a packed lunch. Sandwiches – cheese, ham and pickle. Like she'd made for Ben, only not so thick. She added a packet of crisps and one of the forbidden Penguins she could not allow herself while she still had to fit into Cinders' ballgown/Bernie's wedding dress. She tucked them all inside a Tupperware box with a couple of sheets of kitchen roll in lieu of a napkin. Then, while Jon was still making himself look interview ready, she cut a piece of paper into the shape of a heart and wrote on it: 'Break a leg!' She put that inside the lunchbox too, hoping he would find it later in the day and it would give him a boost to know that she was thinking of him.

Not that she really wanted Jon to get this job. While Jon had been waiting to hear about Dubai, Kirsty had received some work-related news of her own. Her agent in London had arranged for Kirsty to audition for a part in *Les Misérables* at the Jubilee Theatre in nearby Westhampton. It was a provincial theatre but a large and prestigious one and to play there would be a stepping-stone to the West End. A role in such a big show was top of Kirsty's wish list. It would be a dream come true. The audition wasn't until January. If she was successful, the work wouldn't begin for a couple of months after that. But if she did get the part, from March onwards, Kirsty would be very busy indeed and she would still be in Devon. If Jon got the job in Dubai, they wouldn't see each other.

Unless . . . Kirsty didn't take the *Les Mis* job. She hadn't even told Jon about the audition yet, let alone won the part. Jon had so many other things to think about, what with the panto and with preparing for today. She didn't want to burden him with her dilemma. There would be time to discuss it in the weeks to come. If she was even good enough to be cast. And if Jon didn't get the Dubai job, there would be no need to worry at all. He could stay in Newbay with her.

Kirsty sealed the lid on the Tupperware box again just as Jon walked into the kitchen.

'How do I look?' he asked.

He looked great. In his smart suit he was every inch the professional theatre director. At least, every inch the professional theatre director dressed to impress a wealthy client who probably had f-all idea about the filth and clutter of real life back stage.

'You'll knock 'em dead,' said Kirsty.

'I hope so,' said Jon. 'This could be a serious career-changer,' he continued as he looked into the little mirror by the back door and rearranged his hair. 'Not to mention the money. I've got to get it.'

'I'm sure you will,' said Kirsty. 'Look.' She picked up the Tupperware box. 'I made your favourite. Cheese, ham and pickle. There's a Penguin too.'

'I hope you didn't have one yourself at the same time,' Jon said.

'Of course not,' said Kirsty.

'It is a fast day.'

'I know.'

'I'm only saying it for your own good, Kirsty. You asked me to help keep you on the straight and narrow.' Jon glanced at the kitchen clock. 'I'd better get going,' he said. 'This is one appointment I don't want to miss.'

Kirsty went to give him a cuddle but Jon held her at arm's length, telling her he didn't want to get creases in his suit. She tried to kiss him from that arm's-length distance. As she puckered up and moved in on his lips, Jon turned his head so that she hit his cheek instead. It was a subtle reminder that while he was washed and dressed and had spent five minutes cleaning his teeth with his Sonicare toothbrush, Kirsty had on her pyjamas, her hair was in full bed-head style and she still had morning breath. Kirsty tried not to be offended. She stepped back and smiled.

'I hope you have a great time after the interview,' she told him.

'Yeah. It'll be good to catch up with some of the old gang afterwards. You enjoy your day with the cotton-tops.'

Then he put on his coat and left. Leaving the packed lunch on the kitchen table.

'Ah well,' said Kirsty. She waited a couple of minutes to see if Jon would realise he'd forgotten the box and come back to retrieve it. He didn't. So Kirsty put the box in the fridge to have as her own lunch later. Then, remembering how pained Jon had looked when she went to kiss him with her unbrushed hair and teeth, she opened the fridge, opened the box, pulled out the Penguin and had that for breakfast instead of the boiled egg (no soldiers) she had planned.

'F-ing fast days,' she muttered.

Chapter Forty-Four

Because Jon had taken the car to drive to the station, Kirsty needed a lift to the old people's home. Ben turned up a couple of minutes early. Thea was in the back of the car wearing her new party dress. Ben sent her to ring the bell. Thea was delighted, as it gave her the chance to twirl and whirl and get Kirsty's opinion on the froufrou extravaganza Ben had agreed to buy in Debenhams the previous weekend. Ben was surprised when Thea asked for the dress. Something so pink and princessy was not her usual style. But then Thea seemed to be changing in many ways since she had joined the NEWTS children's group. She was blossoming before his eyes. If that meant she was suddenly taking more interest in fashion, then Ben was fine with that.

Kirsty too had made an effort. Ben's mother hadn't mentioned anything about a dress code – she was just over the moon that Kirsty and Ben would be singing – but Ben knew Judy would be pleased to see that Kirsty had dressed up. She was wearing a red wrap dress beneath her puffa coat. The red was very festive. On her feet, she wore a pair of satin heels that matched the dress exactly.

'They're surprisingly comfortable,' she assured him. 'Though I'm very glad to be getting a lift.'

Ben was in a suit. He didn't often wear a suit now

that he worked for himself, but he had to admit he enjoyed putting it on again. And now he'd seen how lovely Kirsty looked, he was glad he'd changed out of his jeans. It would have looked strange had he been dressed so casually when she was so beautiful. Now they would look like a pair.

Not that it mattered. They weren't a pair, full stop.

As Kirsty and Thea chatted happily about the day ahead, Ben hoped Jon Manley knew how lucky he was.

The old people's home – The Bella Vista – was not far from the centre of town. It was set high on a ridge with a fabulous view of the sea. As they drove there, Ben explained to Kirsty that it had once been a very fashionable hotel. During the 1920s, everyone who was anyone wanted to stay there. It stayed popular right through the seventies. But, like many British coastal towns, Newbay had been hammered by the rise of cheap flights and bargain bucket trips to the Med. The English Riviera would never be able to compete with the Costa Del Sol when it came to the weather and, really, who could blame people for wanting guaranteed sunshine on their two precious weeks off a year?

So the Bella Vista struggled to find customers, fell into disrepair and was eventually closed. It was the hotel owner's grandson who reopened the place as an old people's home, finding a rich seam of residents among the people who had stayed there as children and had fond memories of the hotel and the town.

The home still retained some of the grandeur it had in its glorious prime. The lobby was not at all as you might expect – sterile and full of mobility scooters – it was like walking into the 1920s. The reception desk and the staircase had been lovingly restored. You expected to see a glamorous debutante posing against the shiny brass rail.

'Though not many people go up that staircase these days,' said Ben. 'There are lifts down the corridor, there.'

Judy met them in reception.

'You're here! And don't you all look wonderful.'

Thea gave her grandmother a twirl.

'Everybody is waiting for you in the *salle de bal*.'

'That's the ballroom,' said Thea for Kirsty's benefit.

'Oh, how lovely,' Kirsty said. 'Where did you learn to speak French?'

'Grandma told me,' Thea said proudly.

'I've arranged for one of the empty guest rooms on the same floor to be your changing room,' Judy continued. 'In case you want to gather yourself before you go on.'

'Thank you,' said Kirsty. 'But I just need somewhere to hang my coat. I'm not Céline Dion.'

'You wouldn't guess that from the excitement your coming has generated,' Judy assured her. 'I'll go in and tell them you're here.'

Ben and Kirsty had discussed a possible running order by text. They only had a couple of songs in Cinderella. Nowhere near enough to make a proper set. So they decided they would throw a few old favourites into the mix. Fortunately, Kirsty and Ben discovered they liked many of the same old standards. They'd had no time to practice them but Kirsty assured Ben she was certain they would do just fine. Their accompaniment was iTunes on a laptop, after all, not the London Symphony Orchestra. No one would mind if they weren't absolutely perfect.

Ben had printed out the set-list three times. Once for Kirsty, once for himself and once for Judy, who would be in charge of music that day. Having let the residents know that the entertainment had arrived, Judy cued up the first song.

'Are you ready for this?' Ben asked his co-star.

Kirsty nodded and smiled as she tucked her arm through his, reminding him yet again of all that he was missing. Bloody Jon Manley.

'Ladies and gentlemen,' Judy announced. 'Let's have a warm welcome for Kirsty Watson and Ben Teesdale, or, as I prefer to call them, Cinderella and her real Prince Charming . . . Buttons.'

Thea held open the ballroom door and Kirsty and Ben entered to rapturous applause.

They opened their little show with 'Baby, It's Cold Outside', to get everyone into the Christmas mood. The ballroom had been decorated in a manner befitting such a grand space. An enormous tree garlanded in silver and gold tinsel provided a backdrop for the entertainment. The fairy lights, reflected by the tinsel, scattered flattering light all over Kirsty and Ben.

After a slightly shaky start, they soon warmed up. They followed 'Baby, It's Cold Outside' with two of their duets from *Cinderella*. Then Kirsty did a couple of solos. Songs she had sung on board *The European Countess*. After that, they were back on the Christmas theme. 'Oh Little Town of Bethlehem' went down well. They'd wondered about 'A Fairytale of New York', with its swearing, but it went down a storm. In fact, most of the residents seemed to know the words.

Thea joined Ben and Kirsty to sing 'Silent Night', her little voice hitting the perfect spot between them. The whole room joined in for 'O Come All Ye Faithful' before Ben and Kirsty gave a rocking finale of 'Rudolph the Red-Nosed Reindeer'.

The crowd insisted on an encore.

'Do you do requests?' a lady in the front row asked.

'Do we?' Kirsty asked Ben.

'Depends on the request,' said Ben. 'What would you like to hear?'

'All I want For Christmas Is You?' A murmur of approval went around the room.

'We've got it,' Judy confirmed.

'Then we're singing it,' said Kirsty.

There was nothing to do but ham it up to the max. Ben and Kirsty crooned at each other. They gave it everything. They gazed deep into each other's eyes as if there were no one else in the room. When the song finished, they burst into laughter. The audience burst into applause.

'That was brilliant,' said Thea.

Kirsty was still laughing.

'You make a very good Mariah,' said Ben.

The residents were howling for an encore.

'One more time?' Ben suggested.

'Why not?'

Second time around was even better and, as they finished, Ben swung Kirsty backwards in a fancy ballroom dip. She wrapped her arms around his neck and kissed him on the cheek as he lifted her onto her feet again.

'Thank you,' he said to her.

'No. Thank *you*,' said Kirsty. 'I don't think I've ever had more fun.'

She was just saying that. Of course she was just saying that. But Ben couldn't help wishing it were true.

Chapter Forty-Five

When the concert was finally finished, Judy set iTunes to play a medley of festive songs while the Bella Vista residents and their guests availed themselves of the sumptuous Christmas lunch buffet, which included those hundred mince pies baked by Judy and decorated by Thea. In fact, there were just ninety-nine mince pies because Thea had 'accidentally' dropped one that was quickly hoovered up by Buster the dog.

Ben and Kirsty split up to circulate among their audience. Ben had the advantage over Kirsty, having visited the home many times since his mother started work there. Now that he was settled in Newbay again, he was a regular visitor, often running errands for his mum and some of his favourite old ladies. They adored Ben. They were so proud of him for doing his best to parent his daughter without Jo by his side. And, naturally, everyone loved Thea. She could not cross the lobby of the home without having someone press sweets upon her. Judy sometimes joked that Thea had a hundred great-grandmas.

'And if you eat all those sweets they give you, you'll have a hundred fillings to match.'

* * *

One of Ben's favourite residents at the Bella Vista was April. Though she was close to a hundred years old, April had the energy and joie de vivre of someone decades younger. With her youthful enthusiasm she sometimes made Ben feel quite ancient by comparison. April did not agree that getting old meant letting go. She liked to keep up with the times, not spend her days endlessly looking backwards as others were prone to do. She wholeheartedly embraced the digital age and was an avid reader of fashion blogs on her tablet. She dressed in the latest styles and was never seen without red lipstick. She very much approved of Kirsty's dress. She told Ben.

'She is *beautiful*. We're so glad you've got yourself a new young lady, Ben,' said April. 'We've all been so worried about you—'

Ben stopped her. 'I haven't got a new young lady, April. Kirsty and I are just friends. We're appearing in the panto together, that's all.'

'But you looked so in love when you were singing,' April protested.

'It's just acting.'

April tilted her head and gave Ben a sceptical look.

'Hmmm. Well, maybe you should ask her out for real.'

'I can't. She's got a boyfriend.'

'And? I had a fiancé when I met my husband Malcolm. I was supposed to be getting married in less than a month. But I bumped into Malcolm at a bus stop and I knew when I met true love. I didn't hesitate. Malcolm and I eloped to Gretna Green on the day I should have been marrying the other fella in Teignmouth. I never regretted it for one minute. We were married for sixty-three years.'

'Then you made the right decision,' Ben agreed.

'Exactly. I followed my heart and I can see where your heart is right now. So don't go telling me you can't ask her to go out with you because she's got a boyfriend. All's fair in love and war.'

'Thanks, April,' said Ben. 'I'll bear that in mind.'

Clearly it wasn't 'all fair' in love or Jon Manley wouldn't have got the girl. Again.

Ben pressed a kiss to April's powdery cheek. She squeezed his shoulders.

'Go get her.'

On the other side of the *salle de bal*, as Ben's mother insisted on calling it, Kirsty was doing the rounds with a plate of mince pies, making sure that those who couldn't get up easily did not miss out on the food. She chatted happily with the audience members. Ben watched her from across the room. It was easy to see why April thought Kirsty was a good catch. She wasn't just lovely to look at, she was lovely, full stop. He had noticed that the very first time they met, when she was so calm and easy-going about being attacked by Buster.

Ben had been mortified when his mother asked Kirsty to join them at the party that afternoon. Why on earth would she want to? But if Kirsty was doing it out of any sense of duty, it didn't show. She was laughing and having fun. She was so gracious and funny and kind.

Ben wished that April were right. He wished it didn't matter that Kirsty had a boyfriend. But Ben understood from listening to the gossip in the rehearsal room that Kirsty had actually chosen to follow Jon back to Newbay rather than spend the winter on a cruise ship in the

Caribbean. It was hard to imagine she'd made that decision on a whim. She must really love Jon to have given up such a glamorous job for a winter of wet weather and am-dram with the NEWTS, lovely though they were.

And, in any case, Ben had already decided that he was never going to go head to head with Jon Manley over a woman again. Though more than a decade had passed, during which Ben had found and fallen in love with Jo, he could still remember the soul-crushing moment when his old girlfriend Charlie chose Jon over him.

What was it about women and men like Jon Manley? Ben had pondered the mystery of women's taste in romantic partners ever since his first game of kiss chase. The myth of the bad boy getting all the girls was true. But it wasn't just bad boys that seemed to get the love. Not in the old-fashioned 'James Dean on a motorbike' sense. It was the plain arrogant ones.

Was it the challenge? Was that what women wanted in a man? Had Ben always been too easy, in the sense that when he fell in love all he wanted was to shower his beloved with kindness and affection and do whatever he could to make her life brighter and happier? Thank goodness Jo seemed to like being loved the way he wanted to love her. He couldn't imagine ever having made her the butt of a joke or the target of a bad mood.

As Ben watched, Kirsty did a twirl to show one of the old ladies her dress and the whole room seemed to fade into soft focus around her.

'Dad,' Thea interrupted. 'Dad. Hold your plate up. You're dropping mince pie crumbs all over the floor.'

Chapter Forty-Six

It was almost three o'clock. The party was coming to its conclusion. The ladies and gentlemen of the Bella Vista wanted to retire to their rooms and take a nap before coming back down to the lounge for tea and the grand finale of *Strictly*. April explained that she'd placed a tenner on the newsreader to win out over the Olympic rower in the last dance. Kirsty had no idea who she was talking about. The past few Saturdays she had been rehearsing whenever *Strictly* was on. The battered old television in the flat didn't have that catch-up capability. It could barely get three channels. Still, Kirsty feigned interest as April ran through the merits of each contestant's cha-cha-cha.

'You know, Ben looks a bit like that newsreader,' said April. 'He's very good-looking is Ben Teesdale.'

'He is,' Kirsty agreed.

'And he's nice with it. So often you find men that handsome are all a bit up themselves, if you know what I mean?'

'I agree.' Kirsty laughed.

'And he's doing such a good job with little Thea,' April continued. 'It can't be easy for him on his own. Oh, I know he's got his mum around but that's not the same.'

'I suppose not,' said Kirsty.

'A man like Ben does best with a partner. And seeing

how he is as a father, you know that if he finds love again, he'll treat that lucky lady like a goddess.'

'I'm sure he will.'

Kirsty wondered where the conversation was going. It seemed increasingly like a sales pitch. Not that Kirsty needed telling that Ben was a good catch.

'It's a shame you're already taken,' April said then. 'You made a nice pair while you were singing. You had proper chemistry.'

'I suppose that's because we've been doing so much practice for the show,' said Kirsty.

April patted her on the hand. 'I suppose it is.'

Kirsty wondered if April was teasing her. Indeed, April gave her a conspiratorial wink.

'Tell me about your boyfriend. What's he like, dear? Tell me how you met him. Then tell me about your plans.'

Kirsty happily told April how she had come to meet Jon, but when it came to telling her about their plans for the future, that was a different story. She paused and felt a little shiver of sadness as she said, 'He's got an interview today. In London. For a job.'

'Oh dear,' said April. 'London is a long way from Newbay.'

Try Dubai, Kirsty thought. But she decided against telling April the full story. Instead, she ad-libbed about how she too hoped to get a job in the West End.

'I'm sure you will. You're a proper talent. Your voice puts me in mind of Susan Boyle.'

It was a nice comparison, Kirsty decided. She loved Susan Boyle's voice.

'Have a very merry Christmas, April,' she said, getting to her feet again. Squatting beside April in order to be on her level was taking it out on Kirsty's thighs.

'You too, dear. There's some mistletoe hanging over the desk in the lobby if you want to catch Ben on the way out.'

April gave another wink.

'OK. Thank you. I'd better just . . .'

Kirsty seized on the opportunity to help Judy, who was passing by with a pile of plates far higher than seemed safe without a tray to spread the load.

April's comments had left Kirsty feeling a little discombobulated. She *had* enjoyed singing those soppy duets with Ben. She'd enjoyed singing with him far more than she ought to and it had obviously showed. What if Jon had noticed the same dynamic at rehearsals? Was that the real reason why he had seemed so spiky lately? Was that why he hadn't wanted her to go to London?

Kirsty would have to tone it down. Apart from anything else, Cinderella wasn't supposed to have a thing for Buttons. Buttons was just a friend. She should only have eyes for the prince.

Just then, Kirsty realised that she had been gazing in Ben's general direction and now he was looking back at her, an uncertain smile on his lips. Oh, no. He'd spent ages talking to April earlier that afternoon. What had the old lady been saying to him? Had she remarked on their chemistry to Ben too? It was just stage chemistry. Wasn't it?

Kirsty stepped out of the way of another resident who was trying to get by with one of those walking frames. The woman paused and placed her hand on Kirsty's arm to get her attention.

'You were very good, dear. Especially with the duets. We're so glad Ben has found a nice young lady like you.'

'I'm not—' Kirsty began, but the woman was on her way again.

Kirsty told herself it didn't matter. So, a bunch of people she had never met before thought that she and Ben might make a good match. They'd been singing love songs. It was the sort of conclusion she might have jumped to herself had she been in the audience. It made a nice story. Why else would Kirsty have volunteered to spend the last Saturday before Christmas here, when she could be shopping, if it wasn't because Ben was her sweetheart?

All she had to do was make sure that no one back at the NEWTS came to the same conclusion. Especially Jon. And avoid the mistletoe on the way out of the Bella Vista.

But Kirsty was not about to be allowed to go home and get out of the danger zone.

'You've got to come back to our house,' said Thea. 'We're going to do the Christmas tree.'

'I'm sure Kirsty's got something planned for the rest of the afternoon,' said Ben.

'Have you?' Thea asked bluntly. 'Earlier you said you were free all day.'

Children. You can't get much past them. Before Kirsty could come up with an excuse, Judy chipped in.

'You'd be very welcome. We certainly need help finishing off these mince pies.'

Kirsty looked to Ben for confirmation that it was all right with him.

'If you're really sure you want to,' he said, making it sound as though it was some kind of chore.

'She *does* want to,' said Thea. And her smile was so appealing. And Kirsty was growing so fond of her.

'I'd love to,' said Kirsty to the little girl. 'Decorating Christmas trees is one of my favourite things. I'm not promising I'm any good at it, though.'

So they all drove back to Judy and Ben's house – via Kirsty's – so that she could change out of her pretty dress into her jeans.

Kirsty felt a rush of guilt as she stood in front of her wardrobe, choosing between her grey sweatshirt – which was most suitable for tree decorating – and the blue sweater, which brought out the colour in her eyes. Oh, and showed her bust off to its best advantage. She chose the blue. When she got back into the car and Thea commented that she liked the blue, Kirsty's eyes momentarily met Ben's in the rear-view mirror.

She felt a quick stab of guilt. But there was nothing wrong with spending the afternoon with friends, was there?

Chapter Forty-Seven

'What a great tree,' said Kirsty.

Ben and Thea had picked a good one. It was more than six feet in height and beautifully full all over. It was the perfect size for the bay window overlooking Judy's beautiful garden.

Now that she was no longer in her best dress, Kirsty was able to help Ben wrestle the tree into the tub and trim a few stray branches so it fitted neatly into its space. Thea hopped from foot to foot while Ben strung lights from top to bottom. She couldn't wait to start the best bit – hanging up the baubles, of which there seemed to be hundreds.

Kirsty noticed that many of the baubles had place names on them.

'We used to pick one up whenever we went somewhere on holiday,' Judy explained. 'Starting when Ben was small. And Ben's done the same for Thea,' she added.

'We got this one at Disneyland,' said Thea, handing Kirsty a bauble decorated with Minnie Mouse. 'That was our first holiday after Mummy died.'

'Oh,' said Kirsty. Thankfully, Thea kept on talking. She was utterly matter of fact as she talked about the Disney trip and how Jo had actually planned it with them, though she knew she wouldn't be going. And Kirsty knew, from her own experience, that losing someone you loved didn't mean you wanted to stop talking about them. Just as you would talk about good times with an old friend you hadn't seen in a while, why shouldn't you talk about the people you would never see again?

'This was Mummy's favourite bauble,' said Thea, showing one from Barcelona. 'Have you been there?'

'Yes,' said Kirsty. 'When I was working on a cruise ship. I had a couple of days off in Orlando.'

'That sounds like the best job in the world.'

'It's where she met Jon,' said Ben.

'Yes. That's right,' said Kirsty, slightly taken aback by how abruptly he'd brought that up.

'So why aren't you still on the ship?' Thea asked.

'Because Jon gets chronic seasickness.'

Kirsty was sure she heard Ben snort.

It took an hour to put up all the baubles. The size of the tree meant that it was only really possible to see how things were progressing by taking a step back from time to time. Then you would notice the big bare patches. Since Thea was small but very fast with her hanging, the bottom branches of the tree were soon overloaded with those beautiful baubles that really deserved a better setting – not to mention to be hung safely out of the way of Buster's busy tail. Whenever Thea wasn't looking, when she was raking through the box of baubles for a particularly special one, Judy, Ben and Kirsty would do a little redistribution.

As they worked, they listened to Christmas music. Judy put on an album by Pink Martini, which was a little different and hipper than the usual festive fare. She also warmed up a bottle of M & S ready-mixed mulled wine on the hob. The smell of that, sticky and spicy, mixed with the aroma of an orange-scented candle, really helped to set the atmosphere. The music, the smell, the fairy lights reflected in the glittering baubles, turned Judy and Ben's sitting room into a set from a Hollywood movie about the Christmas season. Even Buster got into the spirit of things, allowing Thea to fasten tinsel to his collar.

While Thea, Kirsty and Ben put the finishing touches to the decorations, Judy disappeared into the kitchen to warm some more of the many mince pies left over from that afternoon. When she returned, she was brandishing an envelope.

'Oh, gosh!' Judy said, pulling out the envelope's contents. 'I can't believe I almost forgot. I won the Christmas raffle at my Zumba club last week.'

'Well done,' said Ben. 'What did you get?'

'Well, that's the thing. I got a voucher for dinner for two at an Indian restaurant in town. Bit of a disappointment for me really since I'm not a fan of Indian food. Can't eat anything too spicy any more. Gastric reflux,' she elaborated for Kirsty's benefit. 'And it has to be used by the end of this week. I think the woman who ran the raffle must have been given the voucher months ago and used it as one of the prizes because she doesn't eat curry either.'

'That's a pity,' said Kirsty.

'But you two could still use it. You could go tonight!'

'I thought you were cooking something,' Ben said.

'It will keep until tomorrow lunchtime. Thea and I

can go down to the chip shop on the corner instead. We've all had a busy day. The last thing I really feel like doing is any cooking.'

'Chips!' Thea was delighted at that prospect.

'Go on,' said Judy. 'The voucher is for fifty pounds. It would be a terrible shame if it just went to waste.'

'The restaurant have already got their money,' Ben pointed out. 'They won't care if the voucher's used or not.'

'Oh, Ben,' said Judy. 'You are a spoilsport. Kirsty, do you like Indian food?'

'Love it,' said Kirsty.

'There you go then. Ben, Kirsty would like to use the voucher.'

'If you don't go, Dad, I won't be able to have chips,' said Thea.

That was the clincher.

Chapter Forty-Eight

'I hope you don't mind,' said Ben, as they found themselves on the High Street half an hour later. 'I don't think
Mum is actually trying to set us up, but she is always
trying to make sure I get a night out from time to time.'

'It's very kind of her,' said Kirsty. 'I'm just pleased to
have the chance to eat curry. Jon doesn't like anything spicy.'

Jon. There he was again. Ben was disappointed to
hear his name, but he made an effort to appear interested
in his old rival's gastric preferences.

'How's he getting on in London?' Ben asked.

Kirsty waggled her iPhone as if that might get a text
to come through. 'I have no idea. I haven't heard from
him since this morning. I'm assuming that no news is
good news.'

'He's interviewing for a job in Dubai, right? Elaine
mentioned it the other day.'

'Yes,' said Kirsty. She forced herself to smile. 'It sounds
really exciting. It's a great opportunity. The money is
fantastic. I really hope he gets it.'

Ben was not convinced.

'At least he won't get seasick there,' he said.

'There is that.'

* * *

The restaurant – called The Great India Tandoori – was buzzing. Though it was unprepossessing from the outside, inside it was standing room only. Four people were already at the bar, waiting for a table to become clear. Ben and Kirsty joined them and ordered a couple of pints of lager.

'I shouldn't be having this. I'm supposed to be on a fast day,' said Kirsty, as they chinked their glasses.

'Eh?' Ben – lucky fellow – wasn't familiar with the 5:2.

'It's a diet thing. I can eat what I want all week but on Saturdays and Sundays, I'm only allowed five hundred calories.'

'That sounds miserable.'

'You have no idea how miserable until you've worked out how many Snickers bars add up to five hundred.'

'How many?'

'About one and a half.'

'You're kidding. That is awful. But why are you doing it anyway? You don't need to lose any weight.'

Kirsty sighed. Ben was just being kind, she was sure.

'Thanks for saying that,' she told him.

'I'm not just—'

Kirsty raised a finger that was meant to say 'stop there'.

'If we talk about diets for a second longer, it'll put me off my food. Let's have another toast. To your mum, for letting us have her voucher.'

'To Mum.'

A table became available.

'Most romantic table in the house,' the waiter assured them.

'We're not—' Ben began.

'Lovely,' said Kirsty. 'Thank you.'

They sat down.

'Do you think this is the most romantic table because it puts you in such close proximity with the table next door?' Kirsty whispered as she watched Ben try to find a position where he wouldn't be bumping elbows with the man on the table to his left. 'You'll be sitting in his lap next.'

The waiter returned with menus, which he placed on the table with a flourish.

'How will you know which one of these curries takes you up to five hundred?' Ben asked Kirsty.

'I'm not even going to think about it. I've been having a great day and I don't intend to spoil it now.'

'Excellent,' said Ben. 'What will you have?'

'Hmmm. I think I'll go for a chicken madras.'

Ben nodded his approval.

'Or maybe even a phall.'

'Whoah,' said Ben. 'That's hot.'

'Don't tell me you had me down for a korma kind of girl,' said Kirsty.

'Well, that's what I'm going to have,' said Ben.

'Lightweight,' Kirsty pronounced. 'Still, not as light-weight as Jon. He can't take spicy food at all. So I haven't had a curry since British Curry Night at the twenty-four-hour buffet on ship. Jon stayed in his cabin. There was a force two.'

'Is that a strong wind?' Ben asked.

'Not particularly.' Kirsty struggled to keep a naughty smile off her lips. 'I think the definition of a force two is "rustles the leaves". But, to be fair to Jon, he really was suffering.'

Jon couldn't sail. He couldn't eat curry . . . Ben was

glad the waiter reappeared before Kirsty could carry on.

The restaurant was having a very busy night. The ambient noise level forced everyone to talk more loudly and lean more closely to hear what their dining companions were saying. Ben did his best to keep his eyes on Kirsty's face when she leaned over the table to tell him something about life on a cruise ship.

'Do I look all pink?' she asked, when she'd finished eating her super-hot curry.

'You look lovely,' said Ben.

'What?'

She hadn't heard him.

'You look fine,' he edited.

'I love hot food but it makes me go completely beetroot. Jon tells me I ought to avoid it or risk ending up with bright-red cheeks like a drunk.'

Does Jon ever tell you you're beautiful too? Ben wondered to himself.

Kirsty dabbed at her forehead with her napkin and smiled shyly.

'Sorry,' she said. 'I know I'm being really gross.'

Even being gross, she was lovelier than any other woman in the room, thought Ben.

They moved on to discussing that day's gig at the old people's home.

'I had a great time today,' Kirsty said. 'Thank you for asking me along.'

'Thank you for singing.'

'Oh, it was my pleasure. It's always fun when you've got a responsive audience like that. I hope they enjoyed it.'

'I think so. Mum has already got us pencilled in for next year.'

'We'll have to learn some new songs,' said Kirsty.

Ben was secretly pleased she hadn't said she wouldn't be around then.

'I don't suppose half the audience will remember what we did this time around,' Ben joked.

'I'm not sure about that. April's sharp,' Kirsty commented.

'She doesn't miss a thing,' Ben agreed. 'Not a thing.'

They both suspected they'd had the same speech. They held eye contact over the table, breaking it only when a waiter leaned in to place some dessert menus in front of them.

'Your mum is very proud of you and Thea,' Kirsty observed. 'She's really behind your foray into the theatre. I can't believe you haven't done it before. Especially since you're every bit as good as Jon said you were.'

Ben shrugged. He didn't want to tell her that he wouldn't have gone within a mile of Jon Manley's theatre group if it weren't for her. He definitely didn't want to tell her that Jon Manley was the cause of the twelve-year hiatus since he had last been on stage.

'It's good to have something that Thea and I can do together,' was what he said instead.

'I agree.'

'But what about your family?' Ben asked.

Kirsty had already shown Ben a couple of photographs of India on her iPhone. She was full of pride for her pretty little sister with her quirky style and her youthful enthusiasm. Ben agreed that the teenager had style.

'Will they come to the pantomime? They must be very proud of you.'

Kirsty snorted. 'Not exactly.'

'What do you mean?'

'Dad didn't want me to go into the theatre. He thought it was a mistake to leave my office job.'

'But he must think differently now.'

Kirsty shook her head.

'I don't think so.'

Then she found herself telling Ben all about the awful evening at her dad's house and the argument between Stu and India that had escalated until Stu inadvertently revealed how he really felt about Kirsty's performing career.

'No Helen Mirren.'

As she said the words and let them hang in the air, Ben's face hardened. It was as though he was hearing the words straight from her father's mouth.

'That's what he said. He told me I'm no Helen Mirren.'

This time, Kirsty used her napkin to dab at her eyes.

Chapter Forty-Nine

Ben was surprised to feel so upset on Kirsty's behalf. No Helen Mirren? How could her father have been so unkind?

'I can't believe he said that.'

'He did,' Kirsty assured him.

'But what did he mean by it anyway?'

'He meant I'm never going to be a great actress. And he's right. I'm not. Look at me. I'm just playing Cinderella in an am-dram performance in a little seaside town.'

'For the moment,' said Ben. 'But so what? Everyone at the NEWTS knows you could easily be doing something bigger. And you will. You hold the show together.'

Kirsty shook her head.

'I mean it,' Ben persisted. 'And it's not just the fact that you could sing and act the rest of us right off the stage. You have a way of making the show complete.'

'I just get up on stage and say my lines.'

'Don't be so modest. Some of the lines you have to say are awful.'

Kirsty didn't disagree with that.

'But you make them sound sincere. And when you share a scene with someone, you don't just act your own heart out, you find a way to make them shine too.'

'Do I?' Kirsty asked for reassurance.

'Yes. You do. I know you make my performance better. I feel . . . I feel oddly safe when you and I are on the stage together. It's like I can forget about the audience. It's as if we're just in a room, you and I, having a real conversation. I don't have to feel self-conscious.'

'I hope you still feel like that when the show opens and there actually is an audience,' Kirsty said.

'I'm sure I will. Oh, Kirsty, you even make Lauren look talented. Like her flat delivery is all part of the joke. That's a skill. To raise the whole panto rather than be content to glitter at the centre of a pile of . . . well, of shite, if we're honest.'

Kirsty laughed.

'If your dad came to see you in our show he'd eat his words, I promise you.'

'He's not going to see it.'

'Well that's his loss. He's an idiot.'

'He's my dad.'

'Doesn't mean he's always right. Don't let anyone tell you you're not a good actress, Kirsty. And you're a knockout singer. When you're doing a solo, it sends shivers right through me.'

Ben momentarily closed his eyes, as though he could feel the shivers right then.

'Don't let anyone tell you you're no Helen Mirren. Unless it's to tell you you're a cross between Marilyn Monroe and Judy Garland instead.'

'Am I?'

'Monroe's singing voice and Garland's legs,' Ben joked.

Kirsty snorted. 'I still think that's the nicest thing anyone has ever said to me.'

'It's easy to say nice things to you. All I have to do is say what I see. And what I see when I look at you is a beautiful, talented woman, who combines her great talent with a generosity that touches everyone.'

Kirsty looked down shyly.

'Thea adores you. She was so pleased you agreed to come today. There's no one she was keener to see her party dress.'

'She did look lovely.'

'She said she wanted to look like you.'

'Oh, Ben.'

'You had the Bella Vista gang in the palm of your hand and, believe me, they're no easy crowd. When Cinderella opens, you will be the toast of the town.'

'Stop it!' Kirsty protested half-heartedly. 'You're making my head swell.'

Ben continued, 'The most important thing about you, Kirsty Watson, is that everything you do, you do from the heart.'

Ben put a hand on his own heart as he finished his speech.

Kirsty reached across the table and squeezed his hand. Ben looked at their hands, together on the table.

'Bloody hell,' he said. 'I'm sorry for going off on one like that. You don't need me to flatter you. I'm sure Jon must tell you something similar every day.'

It was on her lips to tell Ben exactly what Jon had said, about her getting a secretarial job if he got the contract in Dubai. Instead, she released Ben's hand and sat back from the table. The invocation of Jon's name had slightly changed the mood.

'I'm stuffed,' Kirsty said then. 'I think I can declare my fast day well and truly blown.'

'I'll drink to that,' said Ben. He downed the last inch of his lager.

They were the only remaining people in the restaurant.

The waiting staff had not been so ungracious as to plonk the bill on the table, but they were clearing their way closer and closer. When one of the waiters put chairs up on the table right next to Kirsty and Ben's, they took the hint. It was almost midnight.

'But I don't want to go home just yet,' said Kirsty. 'I feel like I need a walk after all that curry. Will you come with me?'

'Where do you want to go?'

'Let's go and look at the sea.'

Chapter Fifty

It was a cold night but a clear one. An almost full moon bathed the town in soft blue light. Of course, being Newbay born and bred, Ben knew the fastest way from the curry house to the sea. He led Kirsty through the oldest part of town, down small streets that she had yet to come across herself. Once upon a time, before the Victorians and their mania for sea bathing, Newbay had been a simple fishing village.

The Victorians had known the importance of a good walk. The promenade along the main beach was generous and grand. The city council had wisely retained the old ironwork along the sea wall. Thousands were spent every year in maintenance, but it was worth it. On any given day, even in the depths of winter, the promenade welcomed visitors. But at just past midnight on a Saturday in December, it was as quiet as it ever got. The coach parties had long since gone home.

The white fairy lights, which were strung between the lampposts all year round, had been replaced with strings in more festive colours – red and green, for the holly and the ivy. Each of the lampposts sported an illuminated Christmas decal. A fat-bellied Santa, or a triangular Christmas tree, or a reindeer. Tacky as hell, but somehow perfect at the same time. And Ben and Kirsty had it to themselves.

They walked along the promenade for a while before Kirsty suggested, 'Let's go down onto the sand.'

Ben agreed.

The promenade was quite a bit higher than the beach itself and the steps down seemed to be a long way off, so Ben climbed over the iron railings and jumped.

'You're nuts!' Kirsty shouted down at him.

'It's not that far,' he said. 'And I'll catch you.'

'If this goes wrong I'll *flatten* you,' said Kirsty as she prepared to follow him down to the sand.

Ben made a comical show of bracing himself. In the end, he didn't need to, because Kirsty made a far more careful descent to the sand than he had. She sat down on the sea wall first and lowered herself as though getting into a freezing cold swimming pool. Ben merely had to steady her when her feet touched the beach. She did need a fair bit of steadying though, after three pints at the Indian.

'Thank you,' she said, brushing sand off her hands. She noticed how slowly Ben took his hands away once she found her balance.

The beach was deserted. The moon glittered on the ink-black sea and on the wet sand, spreading stars at their feet as they walked. The tide was high but the sea was calm. The waves made hardly a sound as they inched their way onto the shore and slipped away again with barely a whisper.

'I love it out here,' said Kirsty.

'Me too. It really puts things into perspective, doesn't it, standing by the edge of the sea? It reminds us how small we are.'

'I like that feeling,' said Kirsty. 'That sense of wonder.'

'Yes. It's comforting somehow, to think that the moon and the sea have always been here and will still be here long after we've gone,' said Ben.

'Deep,' said Kirsty. It came out strangely. Like half a hiccup.

Ben couldn't help laughing. It was a hiccup. Kirsty had polished off at least one more beer than she could manage.

'Are you taking the mickey out of me?' Kirsty asked.

She gave him a playful shove then ran off away from him. Ben gave chase along the water's edge. Kirsty ran as far as the pier before she had to stop. It wasn't the distance but the difficulty of running in the sand that did for her. She doubled over and rested her hands on her knees as she caught her breath. Then she straightened up and leaned against one of the pier's painted wooden struts. Her chest heaved as she recovered from the exertion. And she was still hiccupping.

Ben was a little way behind her, having somehow managed an embarrassing trip in the sand along the way, but eventually he caught up with her and, to Kirsty's astonishment, leaned against her as he found his own breath.

After a moment or two, Ben righted himself. But he was still standing very close. Their faces were inches apart. Ben reached for Kirsty's hands. Kirsty let him take them. His fingers were warm. The way they were standing reminded her of the last scene of the pantomime, when Prince Charming takes Cinderella's hands before he falls to his knees and proposes to her, having realised she is his beloved princess. It was wrong and yet Kirsty couldn't remember when something last seemed quite so right.

Kirsty felt her heart rate beginning to rise up again as they just stood there, looking into each other's faces, silently questioning each other on the wisdom of what they both felt sure they were about to do.

Chapter Fifty-One

'Sad!'

From the shadows beneath the pier came the sound of laughter and Kirsty and Ben suddenly realised they were not alone on the beach after all. A trio of teenagers were hiding out there, swigging cider straight from a two-litre bottle.

'Get a room!' shouted one of the witty youngsters.

That moment of exquisite beautiful tension in which Kirsty and Ben had been held as if in a dream was abruptly broken. They moved apart again. Out of kissing distance. Out of danger.

'That's told us,' said Ben.

'Come on. Let's get out of here,' said Kirsty.

Ben continued to hold Kirsty's hand as they waded their way back through the dry sand to the steps but it wasn't the same. In the shadow of the pier, something magical had almost happened. Now they were back in the real world and Ben was just trying to make sure Kirsty didn't fall flat on her face.

When they got to the sea wall, Ben let Kirsty go ahead of him up the steps.

'It's later than I thought,' he said when he joined her on the promenade. 'I should get back so that Mum can go to bed.'

Kirsty agreed.

'Let's find a taxi.'

They didn't join hands again. They walked in silence to the taxi rank outside Chillings, the department store that had once been the glamorous place to be seen shopping but which was now just rather old-fashioned. Most people drove to the big John Lewis in the development just out of town. The dummies in the window at Chillings hadn't been changed since the eighties. They had stiff plastic hairdos and thick painted make-up. They provided a spooky audience as Ben and Kirsty waited for a taxi to come.

Though it was a Saturday night, there were no cars to be seen for what felt like ages. Coming out of the Indian restaurant, high on lager and flirtatious conversation, Kirsty had not felt the cold but now she pulled her coat more tightly around her. Ben, who was wearing just a jacket, stamped his feet and blew on his fingers. If things had been different, they could have huddled together for warmth. That was out of the question now.

They didn't say much while they waited. Kirsty kept forming sentences in her mind but never letting them get as far as her lips. Ben must know as well as she did that this was a crucial moment. They way they handled it would set the tone for everything that followed. Should Kirsty admit that she'd been excited when she thought that Ben might kiss her? Should she laugh it off? Pretend it never happened? They couldn't pretend it hadn't happened.

'Ben, I'm . . . On the beach. Just then.' Why couldn't she get the words out?

Ben looked at her, as if willing her to finish her sentence the right way. His eyes were soft.

'I shouldn't have . . . It's Jon . . . I'm in a relationship and the show . . . I . . .'

A quick smile flickered on Ben's face. The sort of smile you give when someone tells you that you weren't lucky this time. Your numbers didn't come up.

A taxi came.

'Thank goodness,' said Ben and Kirsty, wracked with guilt, was sure he meant that thank goodness they would not have to be together much longer. Then he added, 'It's getting really cold.'

'It is,' Kirsty agreed.

Settling into the back seat, she rubbed her hands together to bring the feeling back to her fingers. Ben looked out of his window. She looked out of hers.

Ben had the taxi driver drop Kirsty off first, though it would have made sense to do things the other way round.

'Tell your mum thank you for the restaurant voucher,' said Kirsty.

'I will.'

'And I'll see you at the theatre in a couple of days.'

'Yes,' said Ben. 'Sleep well.'

'I think I will after all that food.'

'Me too.'

They were back to pretending it had never happened. That nearly kiss. It was for the best.

Kirsty waved him off then went inside.

It was the first time Kirsty had spent a night in the Newbay flat by herself. She had never before let herself in to find the place so quiet and dark. So lonely. As she moved from the hallway to the kitchen, she turned on all the lights to cheer herself up. She checked her phone. Still nothing from Jon, but she sent him a message, feeling guilty as she did so.

'Hope you've had a lovely day. Can't wait to see you tomorrow! Have been missing you!'

The exclamation marks made it seem more true.

Because it is true, Kirsty told herself. I'm missing Jon. Of course I am. I can't wait for him to come back to Newbay. But . . .

In the bathroom mirror, she saw that her face was flushed. She'd had too much to drink. Since meeting Jon, she'd been much more careful when it came to drinking alcohol. Not because he didn't like to see her drunk but because – as he never failed to remind to – drinking wine was like drinking pure sugar. It was because she had been so good recently that three pints of lager had left her pretty much smashed. Ben had been tipsy too. That was why that silly moment under the bridge occurred. Just alcohol. Drink talking. It was the beer and the moonlight. Thank goodness they'd been interrupted. If they'd kissed . . . If Jon had found out . . . What might have happened to the show?

While Kirsty was brushing her teeth, her phone pinged to let her know she had a message. By the time she got to it, she had two. The first one was from Ben.

'Thank you for making the party go with a swing today. Everyone had a wonderful time.'

The second text was from Jon. 'Great interview. Think I've got it. Still out celebrating with Des. Will be getting later train back tomorrow.'

Kirsty re-read both texts but responded only to Jon's.

Chapter Fifty-Two

The following day – Sunday – Kirsty woke with a throbbing headache. She had only herself to blame. All that beer! Kirsty was glad Jon wasn't there to see her first thing. If he thought she was borderline disgusting on a normal morning, then goodness knows what he would have made of her in this state with her boozy curry breath.

That said, Kirsty guessed Jon was waking up with a sore head too. She wished she could picture where. She didn't know the friends he had stayed with overnight. They were people he knew from university. She had yet to meet them, though Jon was always promising she would.

Kirsty was not only feeling ill, she was feeling guilty. As she replayed the previous day's events, Kirsty found plenty of moments to make her groan with embarrassment. Not just the moment under the pier. Everything that had gone on before then. The way she and Ben had gazed into each other's eyes while singing 'All I Want For Christmas'. Her conversation with April, who had suggested the chemistry was obvious. The fact that Ben had obviously had the same lecture. The confidences they had shared. It made Kirsty cringe.

Kirsty made herself some tea and sat down at the kitchen table with her head in her hands. What was Ben doing right then? Was he nursing the mother of all headaches as well? What might have happened if those teenagers hadn't been hanging out under the pier?

Kirsty decided she mustn't think about it. She was in a relationship with Jon. A serious relationship. The only reason she was in Newbay at all was because she wanted to be with Jon Manley. She shouldn't even have thought about flirting with Ben. If things hadn't been quite so wonderful with Jon lately, it was only because he was stressed about the pantomime. The pantomime she had put into jeopardy by even thinking about kissing her co-star.

A text from Jon at around eleven o'clock confirmed that he too had started the day slowly and in need in several aspirin. There was no way he could make the train he had planned to catch but he hoped he would make the one which left Paddington just after four, putting him back in Newbay by seven-thirty or so.

It was later than she had expected or hoped, but Kirsty resolved to make the most of the time she had left to herself by making amends. Having completely wrecked what was supposed to be a fast day on Saturday, she would kick things off by being really strict with herself on the food front. No breakfast for a start. Not that she actually felt like eating anything.

The bedroom was a tip. She had upended half the drawers and emptied the wardrobe when changing from her dress into something suitable for Christmas tree decorating. She had made yet more mess undressing when she got in from her midnight walk on the beach. Kirsty put everything back where it was supposed to be.

Then she got out the vacuum cleaner and removed all evidence of sand from the carpets. Jon would be especially unimpressed to see that Kirsty had walked sand into almost every room in the flat. When they first moved in, the landlord had impressed upon them that the carpets were brand new and he expected them to be in exactly the same condition at the end of the lease. For that reason, Jon had imposed a strict 'shoes off at the front door' rule, which also applied to any visitors.

Kirsty's heart sank as she tried and failed to get a particularly stubborn mark out of the bedroom carpet. She ended up moving the rug to cover it, hoping that Jon wouldn't notice.

As Kirsty wasn't intending to allow herself any lunch, there was no need to stop for it. Instead, to distract herself from her increasing hangover, Kirsty went down to the city centre. It was probably guilt that made her spend more money than she could afford on Jon's Christmas presents. She braved Chillings to get a bottle of his favourite aftershave and a real cashmere jumper. Not one of the cheap ones you get in most department stores at Christmas time, which are really more long-haired rabbit than cashmere. She bought Jon a proper Scottish cashmere sweater, for almost two hundred pounds. The kind that's meant to last a lifetime. Like love.

It made her feel better to think of Jon opening the parcel on Christmas Day and wrapping himself in the embodiment of her feelings. Though she had a brief slump again as she considered the fact that if he had nailed the Dubai job, he wouldn't need a sweater, come mid-January. In his text, he'd said that the interview went well.

'Cheer up, love. It'll never happen,' said the man who was manning the pop-up Christmas tree stall.

'Thanks,' said Kirsty, not meaning it. She hated people who told people to 'cheer up'. How did they know that the 'it' they claimed would 'never happen' hadn't actually happened already?

'Have you got your Christmas tree yet?' the tree stall man continued. 'I can do you a special offer to make you smile. How about this one?'

He indicated a scraggly thing, not quite three feet tall. 'Yours for a tenner.'

'I don't think so,' said Kirsty.

'Five quid.'

He obviously didn't think this particular tree would hang on to its needles until Christmas Eve.

Kirsty shook her head.

'Aw,' said the tree man. 'Come on. This little thing is going to be all on its own in the yard come Christmas Eve. Crying its pine-scented tears. Chopped down in its prime and for what? To languish in a yard for the whole of December and end up in a chipper come January without ever seeing so much as a string of tinsel?'

Kirsty couldn't help smiling at that. And, to her embarrassment and dismay, she couldn't help feeling sorry for the little tree either. Oh, it was ridiculous. Feeling sorry for a tree. Anthropomorphising a farm-grown pine sapling. Of course it didn't care if no one took it home to decorate their house. Kirsty's hangover and the fact it was a fast day were messing with her brain.

'I can't carry it,' she said, in an attempt to end the debate.

'We'll drop it off,' said the tree man. 'Just think how happy it will be. I can tell you'll give little Twiggy here a really good home.'

'Oh, for heaven's sake.'

So Kirsty parted with a fiver and the tree man was true to his word. By six o'clock, he was at the door to Kirsty's flat with her unwanted mini pine. He carried it into the living room and put it down carefully on the towel Kirsty had laid out to protect the carpet.

'There. Place looks more festive already,' he said.

Because she and Jon had not been planning to decorate, Kirsty had no decorations. But now that tree had found its way into her heart and her living room, Kirsty resigned herself to going the whole hog. It being Sunday, she was too late to get decorations from the shops in the town centre, but the mini-market at the junction with Beach Road would still be open. Kirsty had noticed they were stocking Christmas baubles. She spent a tenner on twenty plastic baubles each, some tinsel and a string of lights that would almost certainly not work.

But they did work. In fact, they were rather pretty. They had several settings too. Kirsty chose 'twinkle'. It amazed her that a string of lights so cheap could have actual settings, but she wasn't complaining. Kirsty set to work with an album of carols from Canterbury Cathedral playing in the background. The music made a very welcome change from the *Cinderella* soundtrack that never seemed to leave her head.

It took Kirsty less than half an hour to decorate the tree. It wasn't a *Homes and Gardens*-style affair. The baubles were mismatched and tacky. Yet somehow it all came together. Kirsty was very pleased with the finished look. She couldn't wait for Jon to come home and see it. She toyed with sending him a picture via text but decided against it. The surprise would be much more effective if the first he saw of the tree was when he walked in.

'It's beginning to look a lot like Christmas,' Kirsty told herself.

Chapter Fifty-Three

With the tree decorated, Kirsty had momentarily run out of distractions, and distractions were all that was keeping her from ruining another fast day. She decided to phone Jane. Once upon a time, Jane and Kirsty would not have gone a day without communicating in some form or another, but since Jane had found Rob, her free time was pretty much spoken for.

Kirsty was delighted when Jane picked up the phone and said that, yes, she had plenty of time for a chat.

'We just got back from Bath,' Jane told her. 'Rob took me there for a surprise mini-break. It was so Christmassy, Kirsty. You would have loved it. The town is so pretty all decorated for the holidays and our hotel was really special. Rob booked the best suite in the place. We had our own living room with a proper fire in the fireplace.'

Kirsty was full of envy as she listened to the details of Jane's weekend. It sounded like the perfect way to kick off the Christmas festivities.

'How about you, Kirsty? How was your weekend?'

Kirsty's groan said it all.

Jane was immediately concerned. 'Are you OK? What happened?'

Jane was less concerned when Kirsty told her she was still hungover after her big Saturday night.

'Jon was away so you got drunk with Ben?' was what

Jane pulled out of Kirsty's long description of her night out. 'Did something happen?'

Kirsty had stopped short of telling Jane what went on by the pier.

'No,' said Kirsty, a little too forcefully. 'Of course not.'

'You're lying,' said Jane. She had known her friend for the best part of twenty years, after all.

'Nothing happened,' Kirsty insisted.

'But secretly you wish it had, right?'

'No!' Kirsty denied Jane's insinuation. Jane just laughed.

'You went for a walk on the beach in the dark. Funny place to practise your lines.'

'It was just a walk. Ben's just a friend. I wanted to see the sea!'

'You can fool yourself but you can't fool me.'

'Give me a break.'

Kirsty changed the subject to Jon's interview. She made it sound exciting. An opportunity to be grabbed with both hands.

'It'd be a step in the right direction for Jon, for sure.'

'But what will happen if he gets the job in Dubai?' Jane asked. 'You can't go with him. Or can he get you a job in the Shakespeare troupe too?'

'It's all men but . . .' At last Kirsty dared to tell Jane what Jon had said. It had been on the tip of her tongue when she and Jane had spoken since that night when Jon first suggested Kirsty fall back on her admin skills.

'I don't have to work in the theatre.'

Now she realised that she hadn't previously mentioned it because she knew Jane would be unimpressed. Jane would reflect back to Kirsty how she really felt about Jon's idea. She would take it as an insult.

She did. Twenty minutes later, Jane was still stuck on the point.

'Wait. Jon said you could get a secretarial job?'

'He didn't mean it in a bad way.'

Jane wasn't so sure. 'Kirsty, he's basically telling you that his career is more important than yours. You worked in an office for fifteen years. You were incredibly brave to step away from that world. You can't go back to it now. You've been getting just as many auditions as Jon has. One of them is bound to come off. You'll just have to be long distance for a while.'

'But what if nothing comes off? What if no one wants to give me another job on stage?'

'Kirsty,' said Jane. 'I can't believe we're having this conversation. When I saw you earlier this year, between training in Los Angeles and going to join *The European Countess*, you were full of enthusiasm and confidence. And you were great. You must have been. You were offered a second season. The cruise line isn't in the business of offering work to people who don't deserve it. Don't give up on your dreams to follow Jon halfway round the world again without any reason to believe he would do the same for you.' She paused. 'I worry he doesn't appreciate you.'

'Don't you like him?' Kirsty asked her best friend.

'I like Jon just fine,' said Jane. 'But I love you like a sister. You mean the world to me. And you of all people should never let yourself be relegated to someone else's support act.'

When her conversation with Jane ended, Kirsty felt worse than she had done when she woke up with a headache. Jane's indignation rang in her head. And Jane had very rarely been wrong about the men in Kirsty's life.

Jon was not home by eleven. Kirsty, knowing that the next day she had rehearsals, simply had to go to bed. She left the tree lights on, to welcome Jon back, and climbed under the covers. She would have to wait until morning to hear what he thought of it. She was fast asleep when he finally let himself in at one o'clock the following morning.

Chapter Fifty-Four

'What did you waste money on a tree for?' Jon asked Kirsty almost as soon as her eyes were open on Monday. 'We're not going to be here to look at it. And you got a real one. With the way the landlord is about the carpet? I really hope you're ready for all the vacuuming.'

'I'll do it,' said Kirsty. 'I just thought it would be nice. Make this place feel a bit more like home.'

'Yeah. Well. As long as you're going to do the extra housework.'

'Of course,' said Kirsty.

'I don't have the time . . .'

Kirsty told herself that Jon was only being so sharp with her because of how the weekend had gone. Perhaps the interview had not been the roaring success he led her to think it was. He didn't give her much more information over breakfast. She decided not to push for any appreciation for the tree. She just hoped that as Christmas got closer, Jon would be pleased she had gone to the bother of decorating. They would be waking up in the flat on Christmas morning, after all. It would have been too grim if the flat looked like it did the rest of the year. A boring rental with magnolia walls furnished top to toe by Ikea.

Kirsty's guilt went a long way towards her decision to be patient with Jon. She was glad he didn't even ask her what she had done that weekend while he was in

London. He knew about the lunchtime concert at the old people's home, of course, but she was relieved she didn't have to tell him about Ben and the curry and the walk on the beach afterwards. It didn't strike her for a while that maybe he didn't ask because he didn't to want to know. As though he didn't expect her to have done anything interesting anyway.

There was a rehearsal on Monday night.

As it was raining, Jon declared that for once they shouldn't worry about how many steps they'd done that day. They would go to the theatre in the car. They pulled into the car park just as Ben was arriving. Kirsty raised her hand to wave to him. He didn't acknowledge her. She hoped it was just because he hadn't noticed.

Later, she began to think differently.

It's strange how, even when you're holding someone in your arms, it can feel as though they are a million miles away. The change was so subtle. Kirsty was sure that the other cast members who were watching wouldn't have noticed any difference. But she did. When the time came for Buttons and Cinders to stop dancing, Ben definitely let his hand drop from her waist more quickly than usual. And he'd avoided talking to her before they needed to be on stage together. He claimed he needed to check some work emails on his phone but Kirsty wasn't convinced.

As they stood on stage, Jon stepped in to show Ben how he'd like to see the dance between Cinders and Buttons end.

'I don't understand what's happened with you two,' Jon told him. 'I thought you had this bit sorted. Last week you were like Torvill and Dean.'

'They were ice-skaters,' said Ben.

'You know what I mean. Ben, watch this. Come here, Kirsty.'

Jon's body language when he took Kirsty in his arms was entirely different to Ben's. He pressed Kirsty to his chest. He was very much there.

When she first met Jon, they had danced together at a crew social on board ship. He had held her tightly then and she had loved it. He'd made her feel as though she was gossamer light. He took command but she felt that there was respect in the way he touched her. But now it suddenly felt like ownership. And control. Had he sensed the atmosphere between her and Ben too? Was he making some kind of point?

'Like this. You say your line: *wishes always work better when you make them for someone else*, then—'

Jon whirled Kirsty around so that she was facing Ben. For just a second, she saw an unguarded expression on his face. An expression of sadness. When he saw that she was looking at him, he quickly plastered on a smile. And so did she. And then she stepped on Jon's toes.

'Ow!' Jon complained. 'Like being stepped on by a bloody horse.'

He made a theatrical show of it, hopping on one foot while clutching at the one Kirsty had trodden on. 'Actually, Ben,' came the punch-line. 'Maybe I can see why you don't want to get so close to her after all. I think she might have broken a toe.'

Kirsty gamely laughed along.

So did Ben.

* * *

While the rehearsal continued, Kirsty made a plan to catch up with Ben straight afterwards and tell him face-to-face that she was sorry about what had happened on Saturday night and her clumsy explanation as they waited for a taxi. They had to remain friends for the sake of the show. She hadn't intended to lead him on. She hoped he knew that. It was just the alcohol.

And the fact that Ben was so easy to talk to. And his kindness. And his warmth. And the way he had of making her feel like she was the only girl in the world.

But Kirsty's plan to talk to Ben was scuppered by Lauren. As soon as Jon announced that he was happy with that evening's work, Lauren grabbed Kirsty by the arm and dragged her into the ladies'.

By the time Lauren had finished talking to her, Ben had already gone home.

Chapter Fifty-Five

It was not long at all until the pantomime opened now. The poster defacer had upped his or her game. Every time a new fresh poster was put up, the vandal would get busy with the Sharpies. The insults had a festive tinge now. Lauren got a big red reindeer nose. Bernie had Santa's Elf ears. Kirsty still had her Hitler moustache. Only in green glitter pen, which was a nice touch.

Who did all this defacing was still a mystery. Annette suggested a bag search at the beginning of every rehearsal to see who was carrying pens. They all were.

But there were other things to worry about. The technical rehearsal was one of them. For the first time, the whole cast would be rehearsing with lights, music and special effects. Technical rehearsals could take hours. They were deathly dull for just about everyone involved, but they were also terrifically important.

'Never *ever* insult the lighting tech,' Bernie advised Kirsty as they waited on stage in suspended animation while the lighting tech tried to make Bernie's dress glitter with a strobe. Bernie continued at a whisper. 'Annette once upset a lighting tech. When she stripped off in *Calendar Girls*, he lit her so that her arse looked like the surface of the moon and twice as large.'

'Ouch,' said Kirsty.

The power in any theatre really did lie behind the scenes, Kirsty mused.

Talking of behind the scenes, the three witches of Wardrobe were there on technical day, of course. Many of the show's big moments would rely on super-fast costume changes. Kirsty had several throughout the course of the show.

The wardrobe witches insisted on practising the quick change so Kirsty dutifully donned double Spanx and endured the run-throughs stoically, trying her best to block out the commentary. They were still upset that Kirsty and Bernie had overruled them regarding Cinders' ballgown. They made an endless fuss about how difficult it was to lace up the Vivienne Westwood frock at speed. And how Kirsty fitted into it.

'She's at the top end of her weight,' said Angie. 'If she puts on an ounce, this side zip will break, mark my words.'

'I can hear you,' Kirsty reminded her.

Then Angie yanked the zip up, unnecessarily fast, Kirsty thought, and pinched Kirsty's flesh in the process. Again.

Still, at least she didn't have to wear the silver lamé dress the witches had produced at her first fitting. And when the three of finally them stood around Kirsty to admire their handiwork at the dress rehearsal – they insisted on sourcing the tiara at least – they almost looked pleased with the results.

* * *

On the day of the technical rehearsal, Lauren had warned her colleagues that she would be a little late because she had to go to the beauty salon. Though he had told everyone the technical rehearsal was compulsory and everyone needed to be available all day long, Jon didn't bother to argue with her. Until the pantomime run actually began, Lauren was still doing the day job. She was reading the weather on the morning news and that meant she had to keep up the incredibly complicated regime of grooming required to make sure that she was ready for her close-up at all times.

Kirsty had been treated to a run through of the maintenance required. It was exhausting, involving a baffling number of steps and treatments. Lauren even admitted to having Botox twice a year.

'But you're twenty-eight,' said Kirsty.

'That's the best time to start. Before the wrinkles have a chance to take hold.'

'But what about being able to use your face when you're acting?'

'I can still totally move my forehead,' said Lauren, trying and failing to do exactly that. It explained a great deal, thought Kirsty. Thank goodness the part of the Prince didn't really require much dramatic range.

So, Lauren got permission to come in late for the technical rehearsal and while the rest of the cast were rocking up to the theatre, she checked in on Facebook to say that she had reached Pink Me Up, Newbay's premier hair and beauty salon, and was ready for her manicure.

The Giggle Twins kept the others informed of Lauren's progress.

'The manicure is done. She's posted a picture. Nice colour. If you like that sort of thing. And now she's having her eyebrows threaded,' George Giggle told anyone who would listen.

'You men don't know you're born,' said Bernie. 'The stuff we have to go through. The pain.'

'And we don't?' protested Andrew Giggle. 'Sweetheart, don't talk to me about the pain of beauty maintenance until you've had a *back, sack and crack*.'

'I'm surprised you need the "sack" bit,' was Bernie's reply.

'Ladies, please,' Ben winced. He was sitting on the other side of the rehearsal room. Kirsty threw him a quick smile to show she felt the same way about the Giggle Twins' grooming habits, but Ben didn't seem to see her.

While she wasn't needed on stage, Kirsty checked her own Instagram account. Lauren's photographs dominated the photo feed that morning. Kirsty clicked the little heart beneath all of them out of habit, though she thought the polish colour actually made it look as though Lauren had trapped her fingers in a door and her nails had reached that blackened stage which comes just before they drop off altogether.

'She's out of the tanning booth,' George Giggle announced.

Moments later, Lauren posted one of those strange selfies of her legs from thigh crease to knee. They looked like those weird mahogany-coloured sausages you can only get in chip shops. Perhaps that was just the filter Lauren had used. Lauren loved to use an Instagram filter. This one must have been 'Instant Kardashian'. Heavy on the orange.

Having posted that pic, she was on her way to the theatre. She said so in the photo caption. 'On way to theatre. #Cinderella #PrinceCharming #methodacting #livingformyart'.

'Hashtag *method acting*?' Annette mused. 'What does she mean by that?'

'I'm sure she hasn't the faintest,' said George. 'Unless she actually thinks she's playing a chipolata.'

But they were all glad she was on her way in. Several of them were waiting to do scenes with Lauren. Everybody wanted to go home.

Especially Kirsty. Was Ben going to avoid her when they weren't actually on stage together for the whole of the pantomime's run?

Chapter Fifty-Six

Though she said on Instagram that she was on her way to the theatre, the ten-minute journey from Pink Me Up took Lauren another hour and a half. Via Topshop. She posted from the changing room. That sent Annette into a proper rant.

'Doesn't she think the rest of us have got better things to do? It's selfish, is what it is. I don't think I've ever had to work with such a bunch of amateurs. What with Lauren's selfies and Vince's sickies . . .'

'I'm right here, Annette,' said Vince. He'd made it in for once. Though he'd been like a bear with a sore head for the whole rehearsal.

Ben was keeping out of it. He continued to read news on his iPhone. Kirsty wished she could talk to him. She missed sharing a joke. When he laughed at something he was reading, Kirsty saw her chance.

'Something funny?' she asked.

But then Jon walked in.

'Where the hell is Prince Charming?'

'Bloody hell,' Vince muttered as the door to the rehearsal room, where everyone was having lunch, finally swung open.

Kirsty and Ben turned to see what had attracted his attention. George Giggle's mouth sagged open in shock. He was halfway through eating a sandwich.

'What is it?' Andrew had his back to door but, seeing his brother's face, he turned round too.

Lauren had just walked in.

Perhaps it was just an unfortunate choice of outfit – a pair of white jeans and a cream coloured jumper – that made the contrast seem so stark. Kirsty certainly hoped so. Lauren hung her new pink fake fur coat – the last-minute Topshop purchase – on one of the pegs by the rehearsal room door, then she turned to face the others full on.

'What?' she asked, when she saw that they were all staring at her. 'What's the matter? What are you all looking at me like that for?'

Nobody present was going to tell her. Nobody, that is, except Jon, who returned at that moment from the gents'. He went to kiss Lauren 'hello' but as he got close, he too did a double-take and exclaimed. 'What have you done to yourself? We're doing *Cinderella* not *Charlie and the Chocolate Factory*!'

'What do you mean?' Lauren asked. 'What are you getting at? What's going on?'

Jon meant that something had gone horribly wrong with Lauren's fake tan. More wrong than usual. The Instagram photo of her Kardashian coloured legs had actually been misleadingly flattering. That day she was exactly the same colour as the Oompa Loompas in the classic Gene Wilder film version of Roald Dahl's beloved tale.

Jon rubbed it in. 'What on earth happened? We'll have to call you *L'Orange* instead of Lauren.'

Jon was pleased with that. One of the Giggle Twins sniggered.

'Jon,' Kirsty warned him. But he wasn't ready to stop.

'L'Orange, please tell me that it's going to wash off and reveal some natural, actual human-coloured skin underneath.'

Lauren's bottom lip wobbled. 'I don't know what you're talking about.'

'You look like a blinking satsuma!' Jon laid it on the line.

'It's for the TV cameras,' Lauren explained. 'If I don't go a shade darker than normal I look washed out.'

'You can't do the panto like that.'

'I can't do my *job* without it.'

Jon threw up his hands. 'There's still a couple of days. I suppose it might fade. We can't waste any more time on this now. We've been waiting ages for you to come back from the salon as it is. Where do you go? What do they use to get that finish? Do they do car bodywork too?'

Lauren looked fit to explode.

'Come on, everybody.'

The cast trooped back down to the auditorium.

Jon gave them their instructions.

'Let's pick up where we left off. Cinders has arrived at the ball. She is announced to the room. The prince – *L'Orange*, that's you – turns and notices her.'

Lauren let him get away with it the first time. And the second time. And the third time. But when Jon called her *L'Orange* for a sixth time, she finally flipped.

'That's it!' she said, flinging her copy of the script to the floor. She was the only one who still needed to see her lines in print. 'I don't have to put up with this a moment longer. It's bullying, that's what it is. You're a bully, Jon Manley!'

George Giggle gave her a slow clap.

'Come on, Lauren,' said Bernie. 'Jon was only joking but he knows he's gone too far. Don't you, Jon? I think you should apologise.'

'Yes, I'm sorry *L'Orange* . . . I mean, Lauren.'

'Oh! That's it! I'm going.'

Lauren made for the stage door. She tried to grab her coat as she left but it was stuck on the peg and she ripped it in her attempts to pull it loose. That made things even worse. Kirsty ran after her. She shook her head at Jon as she passed him. There was no need for him to get involved.

'Lauren,' said Kirsty. 'Please come back inside. Jon will behave now, I promise. I bet Bernie is giving him a proper earful in there.'

'I'm not orange,' said Lauren. 'I'm not.'

Kirsty hesitated to respond.

'Am I?'

'Well, maybe the colour you went for today is a little stronger than your usual tone,' said Kirsty. 'But I'm sure it will look completely different after a couple of showers. And I know what you mean about the cameras. They do wash you out. People don't understand that looking natural on screen or stage, for that matter, takes an awful lot of make-up.'

'Exactly,' said Lauren.

She had taken out her phone and was using the photo app as a moving mirror again. She examined herself from all sides then took a couple of steps left to see if that changed the light for the better. Satisfied, she took a snap.

'See?' she showed Kirsty. 'It looks perfectly natural on a screen.'

All the same, Lauren subjected the raw photo to three filters before she uploaded it to Instagram with the hashtag *#hatersgonnahate*.

It took a while for Kirsty to persuade Lauren to come back inside and the rest of the technical rehearsal was fractious. Though Jon did not call Lauren L'Orange again, he continued to draw attention to her salon mistake by asking the lighting tech to do something to bring down those 'yellow tones' whenever Lauren was on stage.

There was one more excruciating moment for Kirsty. When she and Ben did their dance scene. For some reason, the lighting tech couldn't seem to decide how to light them to best effect, so he had them standing there in the middle of the stage, in a dance hold for what seemed like for ever.

'Are you ready for Christmas?' Kirsty asked, desperate to break the silence.

'Ready as I'll ever be,' said Ben.

'Thea must be excited.'

'She is.'

They stood slightly apart. Kirsty looked at the floor between them. At her shoes, which looked incredibly cheap and tacky in the weird light that wasn't quite working.

'Will you be staying in Newbay?' Ben asked.

'Yes. We're going to Jon's family.'

Kirsty was surprised to find herself blushing when she said that. She didn't know why. It was no secret. She'd have told any other friend. And that's what she and Ben were. Just friends.

With the spotlight upon them, it was difficult to see anything but each other and their immediate surroundings on the stage. It gave them an odd sense of isolation.

'I'm still really glad you agreed to play Buttons,' Kirsty tried again.

Ben glanced at her for a second. A sad smile flashed across his face. The music began again and they danced out of the moment. The music ended and they let each other go.

Why did Kirsty feel so much regret?

Chapter Fifty-Seven

Thea was incredibly excited to take part in the final dress rehearsal. She was especially delighted to see her father in his costume. To Thea's eyes, Ben was the real prince of the production.

The children of the chorus gave an impressive performance in this first full proper run through. It was touching to see how hard they had all worked and how seriously they took their part in the whole. There was not one moment when Elaine needed to raise her voice to them. When they weren't on stage, they waited in the wings with the chaperones, perfectly silent and perfectly attentive. Ben was full of pride for his little girl.

Joining the NEWTS had been transformative for Thea, just as Ben and Judy had hoped it would be. The day after the technical rehearsal was the end of term. When Ben went to meet Thea from school, Mrs Griffiths confirmed that Thea seemed to be having a much better time.

'She's more outgoing. She gets more involved in things. She's becoming a very popular member of the class.'

It was the best Christmas present Ben could imagine, knowing that his daughter was happier. Indeed, he had to wait quite a while for Thea to be ready to go home that afternoon as she was busy saying goodbye to a whole group of friends Ben hadn't heard about before.

'They all want to have my autograph,' she informed him. 'Because of the show. They think I'm going to be famous.'

'Do they want my autograph too?' Ben asked.

Thea considered the question for a moment. 'I don't think so.'

'Do you want to see Father Christmas this evening?' Ben asked as they drove home. 'I think Chillings is open until eight tonight. We could go to the grotto there.'

There was a moment's silence.

'Dad,' said Thea. 'I've got something to tell you.'

Ben looked at his daughter curiously.

'Father Christmas isn't real.'

'Oh.' Ben was disappointed. 'What makes you say that?'

'I've known for two years. Ever since I saw you putting the presents at the end of my bed.'

Two years. Ben recalled that Christmas only too well. It was their first Christmas without Jo. He thought he was doing well but on Christmas Eve, when both Thea and Judy were in bed, he was struck by a huge wave of sadness. He tried to drink his way through it with the result that by the time he decided Thea must be deep enough in sleep for him to risk setting out her stocking, he was so unsteady on his feet that he crashed into a small table on the landing on his way to her room. He must have woken her up.

'I pretended I didn't know because I didn't want to upset you,' said Thea.

'Well, thank you. But there's no need to pretend anything because you're worried you might upset me. I want you to know that. Whatever you think is important to me. All of it.'

'I'm really glad we're doing Cinderella together, Dad.'

'Me too.'

But the truth was, Ben was looking forward to the end of the run. Since that night on the beach, acting alongside Kirsty had become excruciating. Perhaps he was imagining it, but Jon seemed to be much more physical with Kirsty than before. Kissing her as she came off stage. Absent-mindedly stroking her arm when he came out in front of the tabs to give Kirsty and Ben instructions. Ben couldn't wait until he didn't have to see those PDAs any more.

If it weren't for the show, Ben wouldn't have to be around Kirsty Watson at all. There were moments, however, when he still suspected that if it weren't for the show, Kirsty wouldn't have to be around Jon. He couldn't help thinking back to that night, after the curry. Standing at the taxi rank, she'd reminded him she was in a relationship but she had also mentioned the show. Was that what was holding her back?

Wishful thinking, Ben told himself. And the sodding show had to go on.

Chapter Fifty-Eight

As was traditional, the first full performance of *Cinderella* was to be a combination of press night and charity fundraiser. The audience was handpicked: a mixture of local journalists and dignitaries, with the rest of the seats filled by family members of all the NEWTS who would be performing or working behind stage.

The theatre lobby was decorated for the season. Kirsty loved the smell of pine sap that tickled her nose as she walked through on her way to the dressing room. Trevor Fernlea and the committee always made sure that the NEWTS' annual budget contained a generous allowance for a seriously big tree, even if they were still using some decorations that had been bought for the inaugural performance in the theatre back in the 1980s. The fairy lights would definitely not have passed a health and safety inspection.

Fresh posters had been stuck up on the morning of the charity show, but the secret graffiti artist had already struck. Kirsty tutted to herself when she saw her new red glitter moustache. She hoped Lauren hadn't noticed that the artist had been at her face with an orange pen.

When Kirsty got to the ladies' dressing room, Lauren, Bernie and Annette were already in place, putting on their costumes and applying their make-up. Kirsty was pleased to see that Annette and Lauren looked like the best of buddies for once. Despite having bitched about her trashy look at just about every rehearsal, Annette was actually letting Lauren do her make-up.

'I want it to be a bit Kardashian,' Annette explained. 'Take the skin-tone right on up to full on freshly varnished decking. You know, how you like it.'

Ah well. Maybe Annette hadn't changed her mind about Lauren's make-up skills after all.

Kirsty did her own make-up. During her time on the cruise ship, she had learned plenty of tips from the on-board hair and make-up team. She knew how to dress her features so that even the people at the very back of the theatre could read her expressions with ease. She applied false eyelashes in a matter of seconds. She helped Bernie with her eyelashes too.

'I hope Vince isn't having a "sharpener" in the gents' dressing room,' Bernie admitted as Kirsty did her eyes.

Kirsty knew that Jon had asked the male members of the cast to keep a close watch on Vince.

'It's going to be fine,' said Kirsty. 'What's the worst that can happen?'

'You have no idea,' Annette told her when Bernie was out of earshot.

Upstairs, the children were being dressed and made up in the larger of the two rehearsal rooms under the watchful eyes of the two chaperones. There would be no deviating from the rules now that the show run had started. Wherever there was a child, there was a responsible adult.

Judy had volunteered to help out whenever Thea was needed at the theatre. She was pleased to be seeing so much of her granddaughter over Christmas. Since Ben had to be on stage every night, Thea would be staying home with Judy on those evenings when she wasn't performing.

Judy helped Thea into her costume. Thea's pale-grey tights would be grubby long before she managed to get on stage, Judy was sure, but for a few minutes, Thea looked perfect. Judy applied the base layer of face paint that would anchor Thea's mouse make-up. She did this for several of the children. One of the mums, who worked on a beauty counter at Chillings, was putting the finishing touches on, drawing in black noses and whiskers with an eyeliner pencil.

'Do I look like a mouse?' Thea asked, as she tried to persuade her floppy ear to stay vertical.

'Oh yes,' said Judy, observing with a smile that Thea had already managed to get a streak of greasepaint down those pristine tights.

Downstairs in the auditorium, a bell was rung to tell the audience it was time to take their seats. Behind the scenes, Elaine and her helpers went from room to room telling the cast that they had ten minutes until the curtain went up. Everyone always felt a rush of adrenaline when they heard, 'Beginners, please!'

'OK, ladies and gentlemen,' said Elaine to her child chorus in the big rehearsal room. 'This is it. This is our opening night! Let's go out there and show everyone what we're made of. Whatever happens, if you miss a step or you forget the words to any of the songs, don't worry. Just pick up where you left off and remember to smile, smile, smile.'

Elaine grinned widely to remind them exactly what she meant. They duly grinned right back at her. Thomas Nuttall had lost a front tooth overnight.

The mice were encouraged to have a quick group hug and there was plenty of fist bumping as they got into line in preparation for their big entrance. Elaine did a head count. As she got to Thea, she gave her a special wink.

'I'm relying on you to sing out loud and clear and get everybody else going,' she said.

Thea felt her little heart swell with the delicious responsibility.

'Everybody ready?' Elaine called out. 'Then let's get backstage. Please stay in formation. No talking. Absolutely, definitely no talking tonight. Let's go, my favourite little rodents. Break a leg!'

This time, Thea was very pleased to hear it.

On stage, Cinderella came to the end of her first solo song. She sighed the hefty sigh that was the signal the mice were all waiting for. There was a drum roll and Thea was the first mouse out of the wings. She skipped into position, flung open her arms, and hit the first note.

This was it. This was showbiz. She was going to be a star.

Chapter Fifty-Nine

What the audience at the NEWTS' theatre didn't ever seem to realise was that the actors could hear them whispering. Especially if they were sitting in the front row and had dodgy hearing aids, which caused them to misjudge what a whisper actually was. That night was no exception.

Two old dears in the front row had been chatting away from the opening number, as if they were in front of the telly back in the nursing home instead of in a theatre. They ignored the anguished 'ssshing' of the people around them as they discussed each actor in turn.

'Isn't he that one from *Guys and Dolls?*'

'We saw her take her clothes off in *Calendar Girls.*'

'Oh yes. She had an arse like the moon.'

Kirsty particularly admired Annette's professionalism as she acted her way through that one. But then Lauren came on stage for her first scene. She came on to cheers. She was a bona fide local celebrity after all. She waved and smiled. Big white teeth flashing glamour and health. Tan, er, glowing. But as Lauren started to deliver her first line, one of the old dears spoke.

''Ere, Mary. Is there something wrong with my glasses or is Prince Charming a funny colour?'

Lauren fluffed her first sentence.

'*A single man in possession of a castle with rising damp must be in want of . . .*'

' . . . a very funny colour.'

'Wife,' Glynis hissed from the wings. '*A wife.*'

But Lauren was miles away.

'Pass me your glasses,' Mary in the front row said. 'No,' she concluded. 'There's nothing wrong with them. The prince looks like she's covered in Cuprinol.'

Lauren needed three prompts to get through the scene.

'Those old bags in the front row need to be removed from the theatre,' she announced the moment she was in the wings.

She still had her radio microphone on.

The audience laughed far more heartily than they had done when Lauren was on stage.

And those old bags were the mayor's mother and his aunt.

Jon tried to smooth things over in the interval.

'Lauren meant that we needed to do a baggage check in the front row,' he explained to the mayor. 'It's a health and safety hazard, you see, if people put their big old handbags on the floor in front of them . . . If there's a fire alarm, people might trip and fall in their haste to get out.'

The mayor was unconvinced.

Jon kept smiling as the mayor muttered something about the theatre's licence, but he lost his cool in the ladies' dressing room.

'When you're coming off-stage, don't say anything until you've got your bloody mic switched off.'

'It's not my fault,' said Lauren. 'I don't know how I'm supposed to act in these conditions.'

'Act?' Jon responded. 'Since when have you ever bothered acting?'

'Oh!' Lauren gasped. 'That's it.'

She started to take her wig off.

'Don't you dare,' said Bernie, holding Lauren's wig in place from behind. 'We're halfway through a show. You're going back out there.'

'I can't take it,' said Lauren. 'I work so hard for my art. I don't need this sort of nastiness. I don't look like I've been dipped in Cuprinol. I don't.'

'You're right, the shade is definitely more Ronseal,' said Andrew Giggle.

'I don't think you're being very helpful,' said Ben to Andrew.

Kirsty was pleased to see Ben sticking up for Lauren. She added her own encouragement to her cast-mate.

'You've just got to tune them out, Lauren. That's what I do.'

Which wasn't entirely true. Part way through her scene with Ben, when they'd danced to 'Your Feet's Too Big', Kirsty had heard one of the old dears say, 'They really are and all. Doesn't she remind you of Max Wall when she's dancing?' Ben must have heard it too. She didn't ask him. He took himself off to the gents' changing room before she could.

Then Elaine interrupted to say that the second half was about to begin. She'd been eavesdropping in the bar and assured everyone that the general reception was positive.

'I heard loads of compliments about your song, Lauren,' she lied. 'People really loved it. And the comments about how you're looking in those lederhosen.'

Elaine blew on the tips of her fingers to imply the consensus was 'hot'.

Thank goodness it was enough to get Lauren back in her wig. And, fortunately, the two old dears in the front row slept through the second half.

Chapter Sixty

At least the children were having a good performance. The applause of a real audience was more amazing than Thea had ever imagined. Her little chest swelled with pride. She could have taken curtain call after curtain call. She wanted to. It was only Elaine, yelling, 'Come on, mice, that's quite enough for one night,' that persuaded the little ones to leave the stage. But there could be no turning back now. Thea was instantly addicted to the deafeningly loud feedback of raucous applause.

As Ben helped her to take off the mouse make-up in the bathroom back home, Thea gave him a rerun of every glorious second from the moment the overture struck up to the minute the tabs came down as though he hadn't been there taking part himself.

It was midnight before Ben could persuade Thea to get into bed. For once, she didn't insist on a story because she still had so many of her own. At fifteen minutes past twelve, Ben said he was going to turn in for the night even if she wasn't. He left Thea with the nightlight on, flicking through the programme to see her name. When Ben woke his daughter the following morning, he found she had slept with the programme beneath her pillow.

'Do you think we'll get good reviews?' Thea asked over breakfast.

'Of course.'

She insisted that Ben log onto Facebook to see the photographs Judy had posted and read the comments people had left beneath.

'Everyone agrees that the mice were especially talented,' Ben ad-libbed.

'And what about you, Dad?' Thea asked. 'What did they say about Buttons.'

'Lots of people liked my hair,' he joked.

'You've hardly got any,' Thea reminded him. 'And Kirsty? And Lauren? And the Ugly Sisters? What is everyone saying about them?'

Ben had moved onto Twitter, where he was following both Lauren and the Giggle Twins. He got the impression pretty quickly that all was not entirely well regarding feedback on the previous evening.

'What are people tweeting, Dad?' Thea wanted to know.

Ben showed her a tweet which said, 'Really enjoyed last night's Cinderella at the NEWTS.' He didn't show her the one which said, 'Funniest bit in NEWTS' dreadful *Cinderella* was Prince Charming's orange face.' Or the one which said, '@RealLaurenWhitwell standing out in an otherwise mediocre production. For all the wrong reasons.' To which was appended a photograph in which Lauren looked particularly well bronzed.

'Anyway,' said Ben. 'What does Twitter matter? Those people don't really know about theatre. We want to see what the local paper says.'

When it came out around lunchtime, the local paper – the *Newbay Star* – said, 'Audience members hoping local weather girl Lauren Whitwell would bring some sunshine to the production were not disappointed, but perhaps she should spend a little more time learning her lines and less on a sunbed.'

At least the paper was kind about the mice.

On the other side of town, in Kirsty and Jon's flat, Jon read the same review and started raging.

'It didn't help that you and Ben are suddenly doing your scenes like they're something out of Harold Pinter. What's gone wrong with you two? Has something happened between you that I don't know about?'

Kirsty shook her head. 'Opening night nerves?' she replied.

Chapter Sixty-One

The day after the charity rehearsal, the main cast were supposed to meet to debrief and to discuss what could be improved upon in the shows yet to come.

Nobody expected Vince to turn up. Jon said he would rely on Bernie to pass on his thoughts on Vince's performance – which were scathing. But everyone was surprised when Lauren didn't show. Except for Jon, that is. He had texted her that morning and received a note in response which said 'not feeling well'.

'You've all been on Twitter, I take it,' Jon said to those cast members who had come along. The tweets Ben had read that morning were the tip of the iceberg. By lunchtime, Lauren's disastrous fake tan was actually trending.

'I should drop round and see how she is,' Kirsty said. She didn't want to get into a discussion about the trolling. She preferred to think even Lauren was above being upset by that. 'She lives on her own, doesn't she? She might not have anything to eat in the house. Or any Lemsip.'

'I'm sure she's perfectly fine,' said Jon. 'She's probably spent the afternoon shopping for new clothes to go with her orange face.'

Kirsty ignored Jon's comment. 'If this meeting's finished, I'll see you later.'

* * *

Kirsty was worried about Lauren. During the debrief at the theatre, she had texted her co-star asking for an update on her illness. Lauren did not reply. Kirsty thought that was odd. When Lauren wasn't actually in the middle of a scene, she was always glued to her phone. She was addicted to checking her texts and emails, Facebook, Instagram and Twitter. She couldn't blink if it wasn't being recorded in a selfie. When Jon called her out on it, Lauren reminded him that it was essential for her work as a presenter to keep abreast of what was going on in the news and also to make sure that she responded to her fans quickly. As she had explained to Kirsty, 'You've got to keep on top of it all the time. If someone sends you a tweet saying how much they enjoyed your forecast and you don't at least "like" it within a couple of hours, the next thing you know, they're telling everyone what a stuck-up cow you are.'

'It all seems too much like hard work to me,' said Kirsty, grateful for a moment that she didn't have Lauren's public profile. Would she ever, she wondered. She'd received a couple of fan letters from people who had seen her perform on the cruise ship. It was lovely to get them. It was hard to imagine a day when getting messages of support and praise would seem too much.

As she followed Google Maps in the direction of Lauren's little house, Kirsty thought about the previous evening's Twitter nastiness. Maybe Lauren hadn't seen the worst of it. At the same time, Kirsty knew it was unlikely that Lauren wasn't aware of every single horrible comment. Every clever joke at her expense.

Kirsty texted one more time as she stood at the top of the street, to give Lauren the opportunity to tell her she shouldn't come over. Maybe she was just holed up with a boyfriend. Not that Lauren had ever mentioned someone special. She was always alone in her Instagram photos.

'I'm popping round to yours now,' she wrote. 'Be with you in two minutes unless you tell me otherwise.'

Kirsty waited for two minutes, perched on the street sign at the end of the cul-de-sac where Lauren lived. No response. She was going to have to knock on the door. Kirsty carried with her a ragged poinsettia she had picked up from a garage en route. She knew that flowers always cheered her up. She hoped they would do the same for Lauren.

There had been moments during rehearsals when Kirsty had felt distinctly chilly towards Lauren. After the time she overheard Lauren complaining to the Giggle Twins that it was ridiculous that someone as old as Kirsty should be playing Cinders while she, with her princess hair, was reduced to playing a man, Kirsty would have been within her rights not to bother talking to Lauren ever again. But Kirsty recognised vulnerability when she saw it. Even beneath all those layers of make-up and fake tan. She knew Lauren wasn't as hard as she thought she had to be. And then there was her charity work. Her position as a minor celeb doubtless meant Lauren had to do something, but Kirsty had been learning from her fellow cast members that Lauren went beyond the call of duty. Just that week, she'd put ten more handbags on eBay in aid of Alzheimer's research.

Kirsty rang the doorbell of Lauren's house. Nothing. She rang it again. Nothing.

Maybe Lauren wasn't in. Maybe she had decided to go to her parents' house for the day. Kirsty knew that Lauren's family all lived nearby. But Lauren's car was on the driveway. Surely she would have driven if she went out. Kirsty rang one more time. As she did so, she felt a weird shiver down her spine, as if she already knew at some subconscious level than something was terribly wrong. Just at that moment, her phone began to ring. It was Lauren. Kirsty picked up the call.

'I'm right outside your house,' Kirsty began to explain. 'Thought you might need someone to fetch some Lemsip or something.'

'Help . . . me . . .' Lauren croaked. 'I need help . . .'

Kirsty grabbed for the door handle and tried to get in. It was firmly locked. 'Where are you?' she asked over the phone. 'Are you in the house?' Lauren didn't answer. She just groaned.

Kirsty dropped the poinsettia and looked for another way in. There was a side gate. Kirsty tried it. That too was locked. But she couldn't give up. Not if Lauren was in there, scared and alone. Kirsty climbed up onto the fence. She got to the top of the gate. That was easy enough. It was getting down the other side that would be tough. But she had to do it. Lauren needed her.

Kirsty landed with a painful 'oomph' in Lauren's back garden. She knew at once she had done something awful to her ankle, but there was no time to stop and look at the damage. She needed to get into Lauren's house. The back door, like the front door, was locked. But there was a window, slightly ajar, which let onto a downstairs bathroom. Kirsty opened it as wide as it would go. Which wasn't very far at all. She would have to try to get through it though. Which way was best? Head or feet first?

Just before she attempted the window, she dialled 999. She explained to the man who took the call. 'I *think* I need an ambulance. I think there's a medical emergency.' She gave the details. The controller said help was on its way.

'Try to get inside and keep her talking,' the controller instructed.

Could Kirsty get inside?

She decided it was probably best to go in through the window feet first. She used an old metal dustbin to give her the leg-up she needed. She got one leg over the sill. Then the other. And then she got stuck. Halfway in, halfway out.

'Don't worry, Lauren!' she shouted. 'Help is coming!'

She hoped she was right for her sake as much as for her friend's.

Chapter Sixty-Two

Thank heavens the emergency services controller was true to his word. Kirsty had been stuck for a matter of seconds – though, of course, it felt much longer – when she heard the sound of sirens outside the front of Lauren's house. The cavalry had arrived. She heard the men shouting as they banged on the front door. She called out 'help' from her place halfway through the window. She heard the sound of the garden gate being broken down.

'Oh, thank goodness,' she said when she saw the first police officer.

'What on earth's going on? Are you breaking and entering?'

'Ha ha. My friend Lauren's in here,' she explained. 'I think.'

'You all right there, love?' a second officer asked.

'Yep,' said Kirsty. 'I'm fine. Save my friend first. And just promise you won't take any photos before you get me unstuck.'

Kirsty was right. Lauren was in the house. She was in her bedroom, with the curtains tightly drawn. She was in bed, with a bottle of tablets by her side. She was fast asleep, mouth open, dribbling onto her pillow.

Newly released from the window, courtesy of two police officers, Kirsty watched from the door as a paramedic lifted Lauren into a seated position and tried to wake her up. His colleague examined the tablets. They were sleeping pills.

'Lauren. Lauren. Wake up, Lauren. We need you to talk to us. We need to know how many tablets you took. Come on, Lauren. Wake up.'

Her eyelids fluttered open and she started crying like a little girl.

Kirsty exhaled with relief to see Lauren was still alive. 'Lauren . . .'

The other paramedic had tipped out the remains of the pills in the bottle onto the dressing table and was counting them. He said to his colleague, 'Unless she's got another empty bottle somewhere, I'd say she's taken three.'

Three it was. It transpired that Lauren had taken just one more tablet than the recommended dose, so, while it made it very difficult to stay awake, there was little danger that it would have killed her. There was no need to pump her stomach, the doctor in A and E decided. She would just be groggy for a few more hours. But because she had attempted suicide, Lauren was not going to be allowed to go home until she had seen a psychiatrist to talk about the reasons behind her unhappiness and assess any further risk. Kirsty volunteered to sit with her until that meeting could take place.

While they waited, Lauren opened up to her cast-mate.

'I wanted to take an overdose,' said Lauren. 'After all the horrible things people were saying about me on Twitter. But I even managed to mess that up.'

'Oh, Lauren,' said Kirsty. 'I'm so glad you did mess up. I don't know what we would have done if you'd succeeded. Any of us. We all love you so much. Even Jon.'

Jon had yet to respond to Kirsty's call. Later he would say he didn't think he needed to, since Lauren wasn't actually dying.

'I can't stand it,' said Lauren. 'People think that I'm vain and obsessed with my looks but I just wanted to show them.'

'Who?'

'The people who bullied me at school. When I was growing up, I was really weird-looking. My ears stuck out like a pair of satellite dishes. I had to wear these really thick glasses that made me look like I had frog eyes and because I sucked my thumb when I was little, when my big teeth came through, they were practically horizontal. Nobody called me Lauren at school. They called me Frog-face or Jug-head or Bugs.'

'Bugs?'

'For Bugs Bunny.'

'Oh. Of course.'

'It was horrible. I hated school. My gran used to have to drag me there. She helped Dad look after me when Mum left. She's in a home now. She's got Alzheimer's.'

That explained Lauren's charity.

'I was so embarrassed. I just wanted to stay home where no one could see me and laugh at how I looked and what my family was like. It went on until I was sixteen. Every time I set foot in the classroom, someone would say something nasty. Then my other grandma died and I used the money she left me to get myself sorted out. I had my ears pinned back and got those invisible braces to sort my teeth out. I swapped my glasses for contact lenses. I got my hair straightened.'

'The ugly duckling became the swan,' said Kirsty.

'Yeah. That's what I was hoping. But I'm still the ugly duckling inside, aren't I? That's the thing. So, when everyone on Twitter started going on about how strange I look with my fake tan, I just couldn't rise above it. I couldn't just toss my hair extensions and carry on because the ugly duckling inside me was reading every word and knowing that what they said was true.'

'Oh, Lauren,' said Kirsty. 'It's not true.'

'I've changed everything except who I am on the inside. There's not enough money in the world to make me into the kind of person who really doesn't give a flying toss.'

'But is that necessarily a bad thing?' Kirsty asked her. 'If you hadn't been through that bullying when you were younger, maybe you wouldn't be the person you are in lots of good ways as well as the bad. You bring a lot of happiness to the lives of other people. You do your charity work. And what about all those tweeters who say that having you deliver the forecast makes even the bad weather bearable?'

'Yeah,' said Lauren. 'I suppose there's that.'

'And hundreds of people have bought tickets to see the pantomime for the simple reason that you're going to be in it. That is so important. You bring in the ticket sales that enable the NEWTS to carry on. And NEWTS is a lifeline for so many people.'

'It's a lifeline for me,' Lauren admitted. 'You're all so nice. You and Bernie and Ben.'

'Ben?'

Kirsty couldn't help wanting to know more.

'He rang me this morning. I didn't pick up. He left a really nice message about how his daughter sees me as a role model and how haters are always going to hate but I've got to keep on following my dream and being an inspiration.'

Kirsty felt a small stab of something when she heard that. Was it envy?

'And now knowing that you were worried enough about me to actually come round to my house and find out what was going on. I never expected that. But you proved to me that I do have a friend. You are my friend, aren't you? Really?'

'Of course I am, silly.'

'I'm sorry for all the things I said about how I should have been Cinderella, not you.'

'Forget about it,' said Kirsty.

'You've got real talent,' said Lauren. 'You're an inspiration to me.'

'That's the nicest thing I've heard in a long time,' Kirsty said, still thinking about Ben and his message. 'See, Lauren? You've brought some sunshine into my life.'

The psychiatrist arrived.

'So, you're to get some rest over the next two days,' Kirsty reminded Lauren as she dropped her off at her dad's house later that evening. 'And I'll see you at the theatre on Boxing Day. Don't let me down. What's Cinderella without her prince?'

'I'll be there,' Lauren promised. 'Have a really lovely Christmas, Kirsty. You deserve it. What are you doing over the holidays, anyway?'

'We're having lunch with Jon's family,' Kirsty told her.

'That should be nice.'

'I hope so.'

Outside the hospital ward at last, Kirsty checked her phone. There was nothing from Jon but Ben had texted.

'Just wanted to know how Lauren's getting on,' he'd written. 'If there's anything I can do to help.'

It was the first text he had sent her since that night on the beach. He hadn't blocked her number after all.

'She's fine but I expect she'd like to hear from you,' Kirsty texted back. Then she added, 'Happy Christmas'. And a kiss. She had no right to be churlish just because he'd told Lauren all those lovely things in his voice message to her. Then Kirsty went home to Jon.

Jon was watching TV when Kirsty got in. He didn't take his eyes off the screen as she walked in, took her coat off and settled down on the sofa next to him.

'Has the drama finished for today?' he asked.

'I think so.'

'Thank goodness for that.'

Kirsty leaned into Jon's side and waited for him to put her arm around her. It took a little while for Jon to get the hint. While he watched the television, Kirsty watched the lights on the Christmas tree going through their little routine. Here they were. They were going to be spending Christmas together, just as Jon had promised when they were back on board *The European Countess*. Why was it nothing like the picture-perfect scene straight from a greetings card that Jon had described?

Chapter Sixty-Three

On Christmas Day, Kirsty was first to wake. She got out of bed as quietly as she could, making sure not to wake Jon too. He'd grumbled his way to bed on Christmas Eve. The show and the bad reviews had really taken it out of him.

Though Jon had been unimpressed by Kirsty's tree, she was glad she had gone to the bother of getting it. Where else would she have piled all those lovingly chosen gifts? Kirsty had thought carefully about what Jon might like for Christmas. Switching on the lights on Christmas morning, Kirsty was very pleased with how her efforts looked wrapped with love and care.

In the kitchen, she prepared a special festive breakfast. Freshly squeezed orange juice with a dash of prosecco to make Buck's Fizz. Fresh blueberries (out of season), yogurt and muesli. But, because it was Christmas, there would be salmon and scrambled eggs as well. Kirsty was just cracking the first of the eggs into the pan when Jon appeared at the kitchen door, rubbing the sleep from his eyes.

'What are you burning?' he asked.

'I'm not *burning* anything,' she said.

'Are you making eggs? I don't want eggs.'

'OK,' said Kirsty. 'I'll just make some for me. Merry Christmas!'

'What?' said Jon. 'Oh yeah. Merry Christmas.'

He gave her a peck on the cheek.

Kirsty had planned to lay the table properly for breakfast but Jon tucked into his yogurt and muesli leaning against the washing machine. He swigged his Buck's Fizz.

'This orange juice tastes funny,' he said.

'It's got prosecco in it.'

'What would you do that for?'

'To celebrate. It is Christmas.' She raised her glass to him.

'Everyone makes such a fuss,' said Jon. 'It's just another day.'

'Well, I like being Christmassy,' said Kirsty. 'Now you're up. I'm putting some music on.'

The sound of a choir singing 'Ding Dong Merrily On High' soon filled the flat.

Jon rolled his eyes and shuffled off to get dressed.

It would be better when he had woken up properly, Kirsty told herself. Jon was never at his best first thing.

When Jon was dressed and ready, Kirsty invited him into the sitting room to open gifts. She kneeled down on the floor beside the tree, taking care not to exclaim when she got a pine needle in her kneecap. After all, the 'stupid tree' with its real needles had been her idea. Jon sat on the sofa and flicked through messages on his phone as Kirsty tried to interest him in the carefully wrapped parcels. He barely looked at the bottle of aftershave and the book he'd noticed in the review section of *The Times*. He set the smart black leather wallet Kirsty had bought down on the coffee table without even looking inside.

Jon opened the cashmere jumper.

'Is this wool?' he asked. 'It feels itchy.'

He looked at the label.

'Do you like it?'

'Of course,' he said. 'Thank you.'

Once more with feeling, Kirsty thought.

When all of Jon's gifts were opened, there were two parcels left beneath the tree. This was Kirsty's haul.

'I didn't get you much because I don't know what you'd like. I didn't want to waste money getting something that wasn't right,' said Jon as he handed her the two flat rectangular parcels. One was light. It turned out to be a box of chocolates, which was odd, considering Jon was supposed to be helping her control her weight. The other was a book about a famous Hollywood director, who interested Jon far more than he interested Kirsty. Sure enough, right after Kirsty unwrapped it, it was Jon who started to read the biography.

'Maybe we can get you something else in the sales,' Jon told her, perhaps sensing her disappointment, though she was trying so hard to hide it.

'Oh, no need,' said Kirsty. 'It's only stuff.'

'Great. Well, thanks for all this.' Jon left the room with arms piled high. 'We'd better get ready to go to Mum and Dad's.'

Though they lived in Newbay, Kirsty had not met Jon's family yet. Of all the days to meet your other half's family for the first time, Christmas Day is probably not ideal, but Jon had accepted the invitation on both their behalves at the beginning of December and there was no backing out.

The importance of the meeting sent Kirsty into a panic when it came to dressing for the occasion. Jon was no help whatsoever when she tried to ask him whether or not his family made a big effort at Christmas. Were they the sort of family that wore their 'Sunday best' for the big day or were they more like her family – hanging out in their pyjamas until the last possible moment before changing into comfy old jeans and Christmas jumpers?

Kirsty had no choice but to assume the former. It's far better to be overdressed than under, she reasoned. But when Kirsty emerged from the bedroom, Jon said to her. 'There's no need for you to dress up like a Christmas tree. Mum and Dad have already got one. And you certainly don't need those . . .'

Kirsty took off her Christmas tree earrings. The earrings she had worn every Christmas since she'd bought them in Claire's Accessories the day before her first works do, aged seventeen.

Perhaps, knowing how scathing Jon could be about the dress sense of some of the women at NEWTS, who tended towards the over-embellished, Kirsty should have guessed that his family weren't the type to wear novelty jumpers. Unlike hers. She wondered if her dad was wearing his novelty jumper that day – he had one with a picture of Rudolph on it. The nose used to light up until the battery ran out.

Kirsty hadn't spoken to him since the Helen Mirren night. She had texted India first thing, however, to wish her a merry Christmas and asked her to pass on her love.

India had texted back, 'All I want for Christmas is to be treated like a grown-up.'

Rather than get into another row, Kirsty sent India an emoticon of a smiley face poking his tongue out.

She also texted Jane, who was spending that Christmas with her family. And Rob.

'Having the best day ever,' Jane replied. 'Hope Jon got you some fabulous presents!'

Kirsty snorted at that.

She sent a few more texts on the drive to the Manley family house. Bernie and Vince were having a quiet time at home. Annette was celebrating with her sister at a swanky spa hotel. The Giggle Twins were recovering from Christmas Eve spent partying. Lauren was with her family, being well taken care of. Ben . . .

Ben's response was brief.

'Have a great day.'

No kisses.

I don't care there are no kisses, Kirsty told herself. I don't care. Why should I?

Chapter Sixty-Four

The Manley family house was a 1930s detached number a few miles outside the town. Jon had grown up there with his two siblings, both sisters. He was the youngest. When Jon and Kirsty arrived, his sisters Katy and Anna rushed out of the house to greet them. Or rather Jon. They swept him away from her into the hallway, leaving Kirsty following with the bags full of gifts she had ordered online on Jon's behalf.

Kirsty stood with those gifts, feeling like a total muppet, while Jon was fussed over like the prodigal son. When, eventually, Jon's father asked if he could help Kirsty with her coat, she was ready to cry with relief.

Jon's father, Fred, was generous with the champagne as they waited for lunch to be ready but Kirsty was careful not to drink too much.

She thought of the Christmas before, which she had spent with Jane. It could have been a difficult Christmas, given all that Jane had been through twelve months earlier. She certainly wasn't looking forward to Christmas Eve, which would mark the anniversary of Greg's death. But Kirsty had held Jane's hand – literally – through the worst of it. She had accompanied her to the crematorium, where Greg had his official plaque, if not his actual resting place, on Christmas morning. There were tears, of course. From Kirsty as well as Jane. She had been very fond of Greg, considering him almost a brother in the time he and Jane were together. But after that, Jane was determined to make Christmas Day a happy one and Kirsty was delighted to help her. They'd cooked a chicken for lunch – it was plenty for the two of them – and Kirsty made her famous tiramisu for dessert (neither of them really like Christmas pud). They stuffed themselves silly and spent the afternoon in front of the telly, watching a boxed set of Miranda and eating their way through a family-sized tub of Roses.

It was how Christmas should be, as far as Kirsty was concerned. A day for memories but also for a bit of self-indulgence. Warm and relaxed.

Kirsty found it hard to relax at the Manley's house.

Lunch was served at one o'clock promptly. Kirsty was seated next to Jon's father. On a stool. There weren't enough chairs to go round and somehow Kirsty ended up on the stool that usually lived in the kitchen. At least it meant she couldn't slouch. Jon's mother and sisters were not the slouching kind.

Jon's mother was a perfectionist and she was feminine perfection herself. She produced a magnificent meal without getting all red-faced and sweaty in the kitchen. Kirsty spent not much more than quarter of an hour helping her to transfer the food to serving dishes, yet her make-up ended up sliding down her face as though she were a wax doll left too long in front of the fire.

When the obligatory photographs were taken and Jon showed Kirsty one on his phone, she cringed to see herself looking so rosy-cheeked. Like Vince after a whole day on the sauce. Jon refused to delete it. The photograph captured him at his handsome best. But then he hadn't stepped into the kitchen since they arrived at the house. Instead, he joined his father and siblings in the sitting room, where they sipped gin and tonics and talked about how great it was that Jon was back for the winter and how they couldn't wait to see his pantomime and how he must surely be a shoo-in for that Shakespeare job in Dubai.

'You must be excited about that,' said Jon's older sister Katy.

'Yes,' said Kirsty. 'Of course.'

Though they must have guessed that Kirsty wasn't going to be able to follow him out there, unless she was willing to give up any theatre dreams of her own.

'He's such a star,' Katy breathed. 'He was always the centre of attention, even when we were children.'

By the end of lunch, Kirsty noticed she had been asked barely a single question about her life and ambitions at all. The only questions she'd been asked at all were regarding her view of Jon's brilliance. Jon hadn't tried to bring her into the conversation or steer it in her direction. But neither had his siblings had much of a look in either. It was all about Jon. He really was the golden boy. It made an awful lot of things suddenly quite clear. Of course he didn't think her career was as important as his. Of course she was the support act.

'They liked you,' said Jon when they got back into the car later that evening.

For a moment, Kirsty was surprised to find she didn't care. She didn't say that, of course. Instead she said, 'Oh, good.'

Chapter Sixty-Five

They were back in the flat by nine o'clock but Kirsty felt as though they had been out all night. She was so tired she couldn't even be bothered to switch the Christmas tree lights back on. She checked her phone, which had run out of battery while they were out. There were more messages from India.

'Hope your Christmas Day better than mine.'

'Dad is driving me insane!'

'I've had enough. I'm getting out of here.'

Kirsty texted back, 'Everything will look better in the morning.'

She found she meant it as much as a reminder to herself as to India. She was feeling low after a day that hadn't lived up to her Christmassy expectations. Perhaps she should have gone to her dad's. At least she and India could have cheered each other up.

She could hear Jon in the bathroom cleaning his teeth. Jon wasn't just disciplined around food. He certainly never neglected his dental care routine. Kirsty was coming to be able to set her watch by it. Jon would take exactly twenty-five minutes in the bathroom, morning and night. Sometimes Kirsty could be in and out in less than five, lazily removing her make-up with a baby wipe. No wonder Jon thought she was sloppy.

While he washed, she flicked through the biography

he had given her but found it hard to get interested in the war movie director's early days. Then she very carefully opened the chocolates. She hoped she would be able to sneak one chocolate out then reseal the box so that Jon didn't notice she'd started without him, but the chocolates inside weren't the kind you could rearrange to conceal the fact that one was missing.

Kirsty ate one anyway. If you can't eat chocolate on Christmas Day . . . She thought about Jon's mother and sisters, all refusing the chocolate mints after lunch. All patting their non-existent bellies. Making her wish she'd refused chocolate as well.

Discipline, Kirsty. Discipline.

It was hard to be disciplined when you were feeling so grumpy.

Kirsty knew there were people who thought that Christmas was a big deal and there were people who didn't. There were people who thought gifts were important and there were those who showed their love in other ways. Jon was not the kind of person who would ever be good at gifts, Kirsty reminded herself. For her birthday, he had bought her a model of the cruise ship they were working on. But that didn't mean he didn't care for her. For Jon, showing he cared was about making sure Kirsty ate properly. It was about making sure she gave her all every time she stepped onto the stage. Jon wanted to give her something that would endure far longer than sexy lingerie or some silver knick-knack from Tiffany.

But a silver knick-knack from Tiffany would have been nice.

Jon came out of the bathroom.

'I nearly forgot!' he said. 'There's one more present.'

Kirsty's heart fluttered to the top of her rib cage. One

more present. She knew Jon wouldn't really have got her such an unromantic bunch of rubbish as her Christmas gift. He'd been stringing her along all day. Now for the romantic part. Of course he wasn't just going to give her a box of chocolates and a book.

He looked very pleased with himself as he returned to the living room with another flat package. Kirsty's mind raced through the possibilities. It was the right shape for a box containing a necklace, perhaps. Had Jon secretly taken note when she admired those pretty necklaces in the window of Chillings?

She knew as soon as she took the package into her hands that he hadn't. It was obvious that it contained not a box but a paperback from the weight and the way it was slightly bendy. But there was still a chance that the content of the book would make everything all right. Maybe it was a script from a play that meant something to them both. Maybe it was poetry. Maybe it was a travel guide with two tickets somewhere sunny tucked inside.

'Oh. It's the 5:2 cookbook!'

'Yeah. I don't know about you but I'm getting fed-up with eating salmon and salad all the time. I thought we could take it in turns to do new recipes from this.'

Take it in turns?

Well, at least he wasn't proposing that the kitchen was entirely her domain.

'Thanks,' she said. 'This will be useful.'

The day really couldn't get any better, Kirsty thought. Thank goodness it was time for bed.

Chapter Sixty-Six

While Kirsty was with the Manleys, Ben, Thea and Judy spent their Christmas Day at home. Jo's parents lived in Australia and would be coming to visit the UK in late January, when flights were cheaper. They gave their Christmas greetings via Skype first thing in the morning, which was already evening in Melbourne.

Ben was secretly glad that he only had to deal with his little family on Christmas Day. Jo's parents were wonderful, but having anyone other than Judy and Thea meant that Ben would have to be on his best behaviour and there were moments when that still felt like a strain.

The day started with gifts. Thea had bought a gift for Buster from her own pocket money and insisted the dog open that gift first. Buster was delighted with his new toy. The rest of the family were slightly less excited about the squeaky rubber squirrel, whose squeak-box seemed to take much longer to break than usual. Buster generally had such things silenced within five minutes but the squirrel's squeak lasted all sodding morning. In fact, Ben solved the problem by distracting Buster with a piece of turkey before whisking the squirrel straight into the cupboard beneath the kitchen sink.

Thea herself had produced a short but very specific Christmas list. At the top was a pair of roller skates, which Ben rashly promised to help her use straight after lunch. He was certain that an afternoon of grazed knees lay ahead but, to his surprise, Thea took to them quite quickly. He wondered if it was the dancing she'd been doing with the NEWTS that had improved her coordination.

The other gift she'd asked for was a CD by the latest boy band. Hearing that for the third time, Ben and Judy were surprised to discover that there was something even more annoying than the *squee* and *eek* of a rubberised squirrel.

Meanwhile, Ben gave Judy a cashmere scarf and matching gloves. It was what she asked for year in year out. She liked to wrap up in the colour of the season. That year was a dusty pink. In return Judy gave Ben two tickets to see a·play in London in February.

'You'll come with me, of course,' he said.

'No,' said Judy. 'I shall be here looking after Thea. I am giving you these tickets on the strict condition that you go to the theatre with somebody else.'

'Somebody else?'

'Yes. You can choose. Though if you want suggestions . . .'

Ben rolled his eyes at that. 'Yes, Mum.'

'The tree looks really lovely,' Judy continued in what seemed like a non-sequitur but definitely wasn't. 'Kirsty certainly has an artistic touch. Where is she spending Christmas anyway? She doesn't have family in Newbay, does she? You should have asked her to come here.'

'She's spending Christmas with her boyfriend, Mum. Jon? The one who's directing the panto.'

'Him?' Judy scoffed. 'He's nothing serious.'

'She had a job in the Caribbean lined up for this winter but she followed Jon back to Newbay. You don't get much more serious than that.'

'Or stupid,' said Judy. 'But at least it brought her to Newbay.'

'Where she's living with her boyfriend,' Ben reiterated for his mum.

Judy knew when to shut up. For the moment.

Once Thea had grown tired of her new roller skates, she joined Ben, Judy and Buster in front of the television for sandwiches made from the turkey leftovers from lunch. Judy had cleaned up the wishbone and saved it for her granddaughter, who loved the tradition of breaking it and making a wish (no matter whether she got the bigger piece or not). That afternoon, she did get the bigger piece. Her eyes sparkled as she anticipated her reward – the chance to wish for whatever she wanted. But what did she want?

'You've got your roller skates already,' said Judy. 'And your boy band album.'

'Oh, I'm not going to waste this wish on anything like that,' said Thea, looking vaguely insulted that her grandmother would think her so shallow. 'Like Daddy says when he's doing Buttons, wishes always work better if you make them for someone else.'

It was Thea's favourite line from the show. It had been Ben's too, when it heralded a slow waltz with Kirsty back in the days when they flirted.

'So who are you going to make a wish for?' Ben asked.

'For you, Daddy.'

She didn't need to say 'of course'.

'And what are you going to wish for me?'

'Will it still come true if I say it out loud?' Thea asked her grandmother, who was the font of all wisdom when it came to superstition and magic.

'It will,' said Judy, who naturally didn't really believe in any of it.

'Then I wish for Daddy to be happy again . . . And to find a new girlfriend.'

The lump that had been forming in Ben's throat was gone in an instant.

'Are you and Grandma in this together?' he asked.

Chapter Sixty-Seven

When the cast reassembled ahead of the Boxing Day performance, everybody was determined to make sure the local paper's critic was proven wrong. As Lauren walked into the rehearsal room, her colleagues gave her a standing ovation. Annette enfolded her into a hug.

'Oh, my sweet girl,' she said. 'How beastly we've all been. I feel one hundred per cent *hashtag* ashamed. Will you forgive me?'

When she heard that, Lauren was almost overcome with emotion. Especially when George and Andrew Giggle revealed that while Lauren was recuperating from her sleeping tablet horror, they'd been to Chillings to buy her a bottle of her favourite perfume.

'We know we went too far with teasing you,' said George. 'We're sorry. We should have been more sensitive.'

'Oh, that's OK. I know some of what I did made me well worth teasing,' Lauren responded graciously. 'Hashtag *really irritating*.'

'We hope you'll like the perfume,' said Andrew. 'But we got you these as well.'

Andrew flourished a bouquet of flowers.

'Oh, they're lovely!' Lauren exclaimed.

'And they smell really good,' said George. 'Have a sniff.'

Lauren leaned in. Whereupon she got a squirt of water in the face. Andrew had hidden a fake flower attached to a plastic bulb full of water among the real blooms.

'Good job I'm not wearing my make-up yet,' said Lauren, taking the bouquet and using it to whack George and Andrew around the shoulders. Playfully. Sort of.

Once everyone was together and Lauren had dried her face, Jon had a few suggestions to make the show even better.

His notes for Lauren were gentle.

'Ignore any old bags in the first four rows. I'll have them ejected in the interval.'

His notes for Vince were—

'Where's Vince?'

'He's promised he'll be here,' said Bernie. And indeed he would be. With just five minutes to go before he was meant to be on stage.

'Bernie,' Jon continued. 'You were great. Just keep sparkling. Ugly Sisters, try not to look so utterly bored when you don't have any lines.'

George and Andrew feigned dismay at that. Then went back to looking utterly bored while Jon finished his speech.

'Annette, we need more evil. At the moment you're just too . . . too hot.'

'I'll take that,' Annette smouldered.

'And, Ben, I don't know what happened in your big scene with Kirsty last week but it didn't seem to have the same energy as in rehearsals. You were too far apart. You've got to be closer together. Buttons' unrequited love for Cinderella is by far the most important sub-plot. He's the classic clown. All laughs on the surface but underneath there's melancholy. We want to see that yearning. We want the audience to wonder if Cinders should really be with Prince Charming after all. We want to keep them guessing until the last minute as to whether Cinderella is going to say "yes" when the shoe fits.'

Kirsty tried not to look at Ben while Jon was talking.

'OK,' said Ben. 'Stand closer. I've got it.'

'Show me now,' said Jon, putting a hand on the small of Kirsty's back and practically pushing her into Ben's arms.

There was something in Jon's eyes as he did it. Something challenging.

But then Elaine announced that everyone had just forty-five minutes to get dressed and made up.

Kirsty watched Ben go over to Lauren as the cast drifted off to their respective dressing rooms.

'I'm glad you're back,' he told her. 'You were great the other night. I thought you looked beautiful. You look even more beautiful now I can actually see you properly.'

'Without all my make-up, you mean?' Lauren asked.

'Well . . . Yeah,' said Ben.

'Coming from you, I'm going to take that as a compliment.'

And because she wasn't covered in slap, Kirsty could see Lauren going slightly red and her gaze was soft upon Ben's face, suggesting that suddenly she could see Ben properly too.

According to Twitter, the Boxing Day performance was *hashtag* great.

Chapter Sixty-Eight

Of course, as soon as Jane heard that Kirsty was going to be in the panto, she made arrangements to come and see her perform. Jane was the very first person to buy tickets for the production, getting two for 28th December. She would be bringing Rob. Kirsty suggested they stay with her and Jon in the flat, but Jane insisted they would stay in a hotel to save any trouble, and when the day came around Kirsty secretly was glad Jane had made that decision. Jon was not in the mood to entertain anyone while they were in the middle of the run.

Kirsty and Jon were supposed to join Jane and Rob for supper after the show. In the event, only Kirsty went along. Jon turned up to meet Kirsty's friends briefly, in the bar, but he looked so stressed-out they didn't argue with him when he said that he needed to get home and have an early night. He hoped they would understand and wouldn't think he was being rude.

Kirsty thought he was being rude but she didn't say so.

'Have a great time at the bistro,' said Jon. 'It's one of the best places in town.'

'Thanks,' said Jane.

'Just don't go too mad on the bread. It's addictive.'

'It really is,' said Kirsty.

'Fast day,' Jon whispered in her ear as he kissed her goodbye.

In the restaurant, as Jane and Rob recounted the details of their first Christmas together, Kirsty couldn't help but feel envious. It wasn't just that her Christmas had been rubbish by comparison. They were so in tune with one another. They finished each other's sentences. They were a proper double act. Kirsty knew she wasn't like that with Jon. She never finished his sentences because there was no way he would allow anyone to interrupt when he was in full flow. He was the master of the monologue. Their relationship was no duet. She was beginning to wonder if it ever had been.

'And look what I found under the tree.'

Jane held out her left hand towards Kirsty. Kirsty didn't have to look to know what Jane was showing her. It was a ring, of course. A beautiful, perfect ring. A platinum band set with a diamond in the shape of a heart. Until that moment, Jane had hidden the ring under her fingerless gloves.

'Apart from our parents, you're the first person to hear the news,' Jane said. 'I'm sorry I didn't tell you over the phone. I just thought it would be more fun to tell you when we were together, face to face.'

'Oh, Jane,' said Kirsty. 'Oh, Rob. This is wonderful.'

'I'm glad you think so,' said Rob. 'Jane did tell me that her "yes" was conditional on your approval.'

'As if I wouldn't approve of my best friend marrying someone as lovely as you.' Kirsty reached across the table to grab Jane and Rob's hands. 'You've made my

Christmas,' she said. 'Seeing Jane so happy is the best present in the world.'

Kirsty meant it. She wanted nothing but happiness for Jane. No one deserved it more. Still, tears prickled Kirsty's eyes and she wasn't entirely sure they were 'happy tears'. She felt something welling up inside her that threatened to spoil the moment in a horrible, snorting, sobbing way.

'Act,' she said to herself. 'Act happy, for god's sake.'

She pressed her napkin to her eyes.

'I'm getting all emotional,' she said. 'I'm just so pleased for you both.'

Fortunately, Jane and Rob were so wrapped up in their blissful newly engaged state, they didn't question Kirsty's reaction.

'Oh, you silly goose,' said Jane. 'Will you stop crying if I ask you to be my bridesmaid?'

'No!' said Kirsty from behind her napkin. 'That's going to make me cry even more!' She managed a manic laugh at the same time to show that she was joking. She allowed the napkin to peel away from her face just a little and saw that it was streaked with the remains of the make-up she'd been wearing on stage.

'I must look like a panda,' she said. 'I'm going to sort my face out.'

She fled for the ladies'. She stayed there for as long as she thought reasonable. She would tell Jane and Rob there had been a queue.

She just wanted to be purely and simply happy for her friend. Tonight wasn't about her. Her and Jon. In many ways, it was better that Jon hadn't been with them when Jane flashed her ring. Kirsty would have lost it properly then. Because she knew now that they could never be as happy as Rob and Jane were.

Chapter Sixty-Nine

When Kirsty emerged from the ladies', Jane and Rob were still holding hands across the table and gazing into each other's eyes as though they were the only two people in the world. Kirsty felt her heart squeeze but she plastered on a big smile as she walked towards them and further deflected attention from how she was feeling by getting out her phone to snap a picture of the lovebirds.

'Jane's like a sister to me so that makes you my new brother,' she said.

'I knew you'd be pleased,' said Jane. 'I'm so glad. Your opinion is more important to me than anyone's.'

'Likewise. I would never marry a man you hadn't expressly approved of.'

An odd look passed across Jane's face.

'Oh look! There's Buttons!' she said suddenly.

Kirsty swivelled in her seat to see where Jane was pointing. She was right. There was Ben at the bar. With Lauren.

'Call him over,' said Jane.

'No,' said Kirsty. 'He's with Lauren. They might be on a date.'

She was surprised by how uncomfortable that made her feel.

It was already too late. Lauren had spotted Jane gesturing towards them and nudged Ben to let him know

Kirsty was in the restaurant. Ben turned towards her and smiled. Jane beckoned them over.

'Come and join us,' she called.

Kirsty shrivelled inside, but if Lauren was disappointed that she would no longer have Ben to herself, she didn't show it. She quickly sat in the empty chair that should have been Jon's. Ben fetched a fifth chair from another table.

'We're celebrating our engagement,' said Jane. She flashed her fingers at her new friends.

'Oh! Fab ring,' said Lauren.

'Very pretty,' Ben agreed.

'Rob's just ordered some champagne. Will you both have a glass? Save us getting hammered if we have to finish the lot.'

'I think I can do that,' said Lauren.

'Count me in,' said Ben. 'Thea's with Mum tonight,' he added, for Kirsty's benefit she thought.

'Are you sure you want to join us?' said Kirsty. 'We don't want to interrupt if the two of you were planning to have dinner. Alone.'

'Oh, we were just coming in for a drink,' said Lauren. 'Besides, I want to toast you for having saved my life.'

'Hardly,' said Kirsty.

'Noooo!' said Lauren. 'You did.' She turned to Jane. 'Do you know what Kirsty did when I didn't show up for rehearsal?'

Lauren repeated the story for Jane. Thankfully, she still had no idea that Kirsty got stuck halfway through the window so that bit didn't come out.

'It's just like Kirsty to care for people like that,' Lauren concluded.

'It is,' said Jane. 'She's been my best friend for more than fifteen years. I'll never forget how she cared for me.'

Jane held Rob's hand as she told Ben and Lauren about the cruise that should have been her honeymoon.

'Oh, Kirsty,' said Lauren, who was slightly tipsy by now. 'You're so lovely. You're beautiful and you're kind and you're always thinking of others and—'

'Jon is a very lucky man,' said Ben.

As soon as she was able, Kirsty dragged Jane into the ladies'.

'They're on a date,' she hissed.

'They are not on a date.'

'They are and so now I'm sitting at the table like the biggest gooseberry in history with you lovebirds on one side and those wannabe lovebirds on the other.'

'Well, what does it matter? Unless . . .'

Kirsty knew what Jane was insinuating.

'I just feel awkward, that's all. I'm sure the last thing Lauren really wants is to be sitting with us.'

'She seems fine with it to me. She's having a great time talking to Rob about weather forecasting techniques. She's hardly glanced at Ben. He, on the other hand . . . But it's not Lauren he's looking at—'

'Stop it.'

'Have you really not noticed how he looks at you? On stage too. It makes your big scene with Prince Charming seem rather hollow. No chemistry there.'

'Of course I don't have any chemistry with Prince Charming. He's being played by a woman. By Lauren.'

'But you and Buttons . . . He's completely besotted. And he's such a nice bloke. So polite and attentive. And good-looking. I can see why you followed him down to the beach.'

'That was just two friends going for a walk . . .'

'If I wasn't totally in love with Rob . . .'

'You've had too much to drink,' said Kirsty. 'And so have I. I need to get back to the flat. Jon will be wondering where I've got to. He might be worrying.'

She checked her phone. If Jon was worrying, there was no sign of it. No texts. No missed calls.

'See,' said Jane, looking at Kirsty's phone over her shoulder. 'Jon isn't bothered.'

The words stung. Though Jane hadn't said anything explicitly negative about Jon since the phone conversation in which Kirsty had admitted Jon didn't seem to value her career, Jane hadn't been exactly gushing about him either. 'You can stay out as late as you like,' Jane concluded. 'With us and lovely Ben.'

They closed the restaurant. Just as on that night in the Indian, the waiters had to start the clear-up around them.

'I'll make sure Kirsty and Lauren get home,' Ben told Jane. 'We're all going the same way.'

'If you're sure you'll take proper care of them.'

'I don't need taking care of,' Kirsty protested.

'Oh yes she does,' said Jane, giving herself the giggles as she appreciated the pantomime nature of her line.

'Oh no she doesn't,' Kirsty said flatly in response.

'Ben, it's been so nice to meet you,' said Jane, hanging on his arm as they wobbled towards the doors.

'You too.'

'You will come to our engagement party, won't you? We're going to have one at the beginning of February. January's no fun when everyone is off the booze.'

'I'm definitely coming,' slurred Lauren. 'You two have made me believe in real love.'

'Real love is easy,' said Jane. She looked straight at Kirsty. 'You just have to let it happen.'

The taxi dropped Lauren off first.

Kirsty wished she could have a little time between leaving Ben in the taxi and letting herself into the flat but Ben, ever the gentleman, insisted that he and the cabbie would not move from the kerb until they were sure she was safely inside. So Kirsty had to let herself in and wave to let them know she was fine then try to carve out that necessary moment of solitude just inside the door. She didn't manage long before Jon called from the bedroom, 'Kirsty? Is that you?'

'No,' she said. 'It's a burglar.'

'Ha ha, very funny,' said Jon, in a voice that made it clear he didn't find it funny at all. 'What time is it? I waited up for ages.'

Kirsty glanced at her watch. It was half past one.

'Sorry,' she said. 'Jane and I had lots to catch up on. I didn't notice the time.'

'Right,' he said.

She wondered why she didn't want to tell him the engagement news or that Lauren and Ben had joined them to help celebrate. He would find out the following day that Ben and Lauren had been in the same restaurant. One of them was bound to mention it.

Kirsty hung her coat on the peg in the hallway, took off her shoes so as not to spoil the carpet and padded into the bedroom. It was dark. She tried not to swear when she caught her shin on the corner of the bed. She'd have a big bruise the following morning. She wished she hadn't had that last glass of fizz.

'Ugh, garlic,' said Jon when Kirsty leaned over him to give him a kiss.

'Sorry,' she said.

Jon mumbled and rolled over, burying his face in the pillow as though to defend himself from her stinky breath.

Kirsty dutifully went to the bathroom and cleaned her teeth, giving herself a critical onceover in the mirror as she did so. She'd done a bad job of repairing her make-up after Jane announced the engagement and she burst into tears. If Ben had really spent half the night looking at her, it was probably only because her smudged eyeliner and mascara made her a dead ringer for Heath Ledger as The Joker in *Batman*. When she'd finished her teeth, she went to work on her face. The make-up remover wipe left long stripes where she swiped it.

She looked sad and tired. She drank a glass of water in the hope that it would stave off a hangover that already seemed to be setting in.

When her face was clean, Kirsty climbed into bed. She needed a cuddle but Jon was making it clear, by turning away from her and pretending to sleep – she knew he was pretending because he was so comically still – that he wasn't going to give her the comfort she wanted. She could, she supposed, move closer to him and put her arm around his waist but that would not be the same. It struck Kirsty then that was the way it had always been in their relationship. Other women – women like Jane – could rely on the man in their life to make them feel protected and treasured through the simple medium of a bear hug. Jon never spontaneously hugged Kirsty. If he touched her affectionately these days, what began as affection often seemed to morph into a way of reminding her that she had strayed off the bloody 5:2. A squeeze became a way of measuring her. He might as well be using those callipers that measure BMI.

Kirsty lay on her side of the bed. She was just a few centimetres from Jon yet she felt as though she was a million miles away. All those years of being single, and yet she had never felt so alone as she did right then with the man she had followed halfway round the world.

Chapter Seventy

The following morning, Jon was a good deal more chirpy than Kirsty felt. He had little sympathy for her and her hangover.

'You were supposed to be on a fast day.'

'I can't fast over Christmas,' she said. 'Or during a show run. How would I have the energy to get through it?'

'I'm managing,' said Jon.

Of course. Jon and his discipline. Jon who could eat half a Twix.

'Jane and Rob got engaged,' said Kirsty to change the subject.

'Oh.' Jon looked up from his phone.

'They're really happy.'

'That's nice.' He looked back down.

'It was so good to see them both making plans for the future. Plans which include each other.'

'Mmm-hmmm,' Jon responded. Kirsty realised he wasn't really listening to her. He confirmed it when he tapped out a text on his phone and announced.

'Apparently Vince isn't doing too well this morning. Bernie doesn't know if he's going to make it to the show tonight.'

'Seriously?'

'I don't know what's going on with him,' Jon

complained. 'If I'd known he would be this bad, I never would have cast him.'

It was on the tip of her tongue for Kirsty to tell Jon what she knew. So far she had told nobody about seeing Vince embracing a woman other than his wife, but it seemed to explain so much. She wondered if Bernie was OK. It was Vince and Bernie's wedding anniversary tomorrow, if she remembered correctly.

'I supposed this means I'd better start cramming his lines,' said Jon.

But, as before, Vince arrived with five minutes to go. He pushed past Bernie on his way to the dressing room. He didn't seem to want to tell anyone where he had been. Everyone was sure they could smell booze.

'It doesn't matter,' said Jon. 'So long as he gets through the performance.'

Elaine called 'Beginners, please.'

The show must go on.

Chapter Seventy-One

Having got through four performances without making any terrible mistakes, Ben was beginning to feel confident in his role. On the night of the twenty-ninth he got to the scene where the invitation to the ball is delivered to the Hardup House.

He unravelled the scroll and gawped. Someone had replaced his lines – the only passage he wasn't a hundred per cent sure of because he didn't think he needed to be – with a print-out of a picture of a busty woman in – or more accurately half out of – a Santa suit. It wasn't a particularly shocking photograph, but the surprise of finding Mrs Christmas instead of his lines inside the scroll definitely put Ben off his stride.

At once Ben was sure he knew who had made the switch. Andrew and George Giggle regarded him passively, blinking their big, false Ugly Sister eyelashes.

'What is it, Buttons?' George asked. 'Cat got your tongue?'

Ben struggled to remember his line and, in the end, he had to look to Glynis, who was just off-stage, for a prompt. Except that she was busy cleaning her glasses and hadn't noticed that he needed one.

Ben turned in the opposite direction and there was Thea, waiting with her fellow mice.

'It's an invitation,' she mouthed at her father. 'To the

prince's castle. For a ball to celebrate his twenty-fifth birthday.'

Ben smiled at her gratefully.

'It's an invitation,' he repeated. And somehow the rest came back easily after that.

'You utter gits,' Ben swore at the Giggle Twins as he finally came off stage and found them in the wings.

'What?' asked George.

'You know,' said Ben.

'We don't,' said Andrew.

'Yeah, right. I open my scroll and find this and you don't know what I'm talking about?'

He brandished the scroll in their direction.

George and Andrew both took a step back as though Ben were showing them a gruesome photo taken at a murder scene.

'Ewww,' said George. 'No wonder you forgot your lines.'

'We didn't do it,' Andrew insisted. 'I don't know how you even find photographs like that.'

They seemed so genuinely affronted by the picture that Ben began to doubt that he was right about the perpetrator of the prank after all.

If it was the Giggle Twins, it didn't really matter. The prank was harmless in the grand scheme of things. But that was because Ben had his part pretty much nailed down. He could make it through a prank like that without too much trouble. Vince was another matter.

Though he had been on board with the production from the very beginning, Vince had only made it to half as many rehearsals as Ben, who'd joined at a much later stage. Vince had never really managed to learn his lines, and thus Elaine had gone to great lengths to make sure that Vince never really had to remember more than a few words at a time. She took every possible opportunity to provide Vince with a prompt. She wrote his lines on the back of all sorts of props. So long as Vince was standing where he was supposed to be and remembered to pick up the right item, he would find his next line written on the back. For example, he would pick up a bottle of wine from the kitchen table, while the stepmother and ugly sisters discussed the ball, and find his lines written on the label.

He had whole paragraphs inserted into the copy of *What Carriage* magazine that he held for most of his big scene with Cinders. His big emotional speech at the end of the play, in which he apologised to Cinders for having failed to stand up for her against her stepmother's cruelty was written in huge letters on the back of the song-sheet easel, which had to be placed in the wings so that it was exactly in Vince's eye-line as he appeared to be gazing out of the kitchen window, full of emotion at the news that his daughter was to be a princess.

It was inevitable that something should go wrong. Or rather, be made to go wrong.

The prankster had been busy that night. There were lines written on the back of the song-sheet but they weren't the right ones. Not by any stretch of the imagination. Someone had switched out Vince's heartfelt speech for the lyrics to 'Your Feet's Too Big'. Which meant that Kirsty immediately suspected Jon.

'I would not do that!' Jon insisted when she tackled him. 'You know I would not do that. During an actual performance? I'm trying to make my name as a director. Why on earth would I want any of my actors to screw up?'

Kirsty understood and believed all that. 'But "Feet's Too Big"? That's some coincidence.'

'It is. Just a coincidence.'

Meanwhile, Vince was raging.

Despite Trevor Fernlea's assurances that no one in the audience had noticed (Trevor was sitting in row five that night) or if they had noticed, they found it amusing, the whole cast was shaken by that night's pranks. Everyone was suspicious of everyone else. The atmosphere in the dressing rooms as the cast changed back into their street clothes was tense.

Vince would not talk to anybody. He tossed his cloak and hose in Angie's general direction. She missed them and was horrified to see them fall onto the dusty floor.

'Well, I never!' she exclaimed. 'Did you see how he did that? It's not my fault. I've never experienced such rudeness.'

Kirsty found that hard to imagine, since Angie the wardrobe witch was such an expert at dishing it out.

Kirsty decided that she would go after Vince and try to reassure him that their big scene hadn't really gone so badly. She also wanted to reassure him that she wasn't responsible for the switch. He had glared at her as he left the stage, as though she had pulled the prank, when she had just as much to lose from their big emotional moment going awry.

Kirsty tracked Vince down to the stairwell that led to the back of the stage but she couldn't confront him immediately. He was talking into his phone, his voice urgent and low. He definitely didn't want to be over-heard. But Kirsty, to her shame, was all ears.

'I've had enough,' Vince said. 'I need to see you right now. Where can you meet me? No, I don't think I can hang on to the end of the run. I'm living a lie and I want to end it now. Bernie needs to know what's been going on. They all do. They've all been laughing at my expense. I want them to know how it really is.'

Vince fell silent as his correspondent talked back to him for a while. When they had finished, Vince said, 'I don't know what I would do without you. I don't know what I did to deserve to have an angel like you come into my life. Seeing you is the only thing that keeps me going. I can't keep waking up every morning to see the disappointment on Bernie's face. I've got to break out of this. Promise you'll be there for me when I do.'

Kirsty was pretty sure she knew exactly to whom Vince was talking.

As Vince came back down the stairs, Kirsty flattened herself against the wall, in the shadow of an old pair of tabs, and he didn't seem to notice her at all. She decided not to bother following him. The last thing Vince deserved was for her to try to make him feel better about being such a bad actor when in real life he had been keeping up such a big pretence.

Chapter Seventy-Two

As Kirsty correctly remembered, 30th December was Vince and Bernie's wedding anniversary and Bernie had asked the cast to join them in celebrating with a drink at the theatre bar after the performance. Though Vince wasn't everybody's favourite, they were all fond of Bernie and promised to be there to help eat the cake she had so lovingly made to celebrate almost twenty years with her husband.

The performance, thank goodness, was free from the pranks that had made the previous night so traumatic. Everyone got changed quickly and made their way downstairs.

'But where's Vince?' Jon asked.

'Must be still taking his make-up off,' said Ben.

'He wasn't in the gents' changing room when I was in there,' said Andrew Giggle.

'I haven't seen him,' said George.

Bernie put on a brave smile. 'Ah well. Perhaps he's nipped out for a cigarette. I'm sure he'll be here in a minute.'

Kirsty didn't need a cigarette after the performance but she did need some fresh air. She headed out to the car park and that is where she saw him. Vince was sitting in the passenger seat of a little red Mini. Kirsty knew where she had seen that red Mini before – parked outside the student flats on the road down to Duckpool Bay. Kirsty slunk into shadows so that she could watch for a moment without being seen. The driver of the car reached up to put the ceiling light on and, once she was illuminated, Kirsty's worst fears were confirmed. The car's owner was the young woman she had seen with Vince earlier in the month. As Kirsty watched in guilty horror, the young woman smiled tenderly at Vince and cupped his cheek with her hand.

This was awful. Inside the theatre, Bernie was oblivious, keeping up the small talk with the rest of the NEWTS while she waited for her husband to arrive and eat his cake. And here he was in the car park, already having it!

Kirsty felt like going up and hammering on the roof of the car and telling Vince exactly what she thought of him. Instead, she decided she should let Bernie know what was going on, in as discreet a way as possible, so that she could see for herself what her husband was up to. In the theatre car park. He couldn't have been more blatant.

But when Kirsty got back inside, Bernie was deep in conversation with Trevor Fernlea, who had watched the performance that night too. She didn't want to interrupt but she had to. She tugged on Bernie's sleeve.

'Could I have a minute?' she said.

Bernie smiled broadly. 'Yes, sweetheart, what is it?'

Kirsty guided Bernie a little closer to the door. What

was she going to say? She certainly didn't want anyone else to hear.

'It's . . . I've just been outside. You might want to . . . Vince . . .'

She knew she was making no sense. Rather, given the look of anguish on Bernie's face, she was making matters even more complicated.

'What's happened? Is Vince hurt?' Bernie immediately assumed the worst.

'No. He . . .'

Just as Kirsty was about to spill the beans, Vince walked into the theatre, looking, thought Kirsty, as cocky as you like. She glared at him. He seemed confused. As if he didn't know what he'd just been doing.

'Vince,' said Bernie. 'Everybody's waiting for you. Where have you been?'

Before Vince could answer that question, the door swung open again and the young woman who drove the red Mini entered. This was awful. Were they going to pretend that they hadn't been sitting in the car park canoodling just moments before?

'Bernie,' said Vince. 'I want you to meet Candy.'

'Candy!' Kirsty spluttered.

'Yes,' said the girl, looking mildly offended. 'It's short for Candice.'

Candy held her hand towards Bernie. Bernie accepted the greeting then she looked to Vince for an explanation as to who the young woman might be. It came quickly and, when it did, it was totally not what Kirsty – or Bernie for that matter – had been expecting.

'Candy is my mentor at AA.'

'What?'

'Bernie,' said Vince. 'I know I've disappointed you. I've not been the best husband I could be and to see how unhappy I've made you over the years fills me with nothing but shame. I want to change,' he continued. 'I want to be a better man for you. On Christmas Eve, when I didn't tell you where I was going, it wasn't because I was going out to get drunk. I was going to an AA meeting, my love. I was ashamed and I didn't want to get your hopes up. And when I came out of that meeting, all I could think of was how much I needed another drink. So I had another drink. I had ten. I fell at the first hurdle, my love. I let you down.'

'Oh, Vince.' Bernie shook her head.

'But I'm going to keep trying. I went to another meeting this lunchtime. I want to go for it, Bernie. I want to get off the booze, once and for all. One day at a time. But I want to do it with you by my side.'

After such a revelation, Bernie told Vince she understood if he didn't feel like having an anniversary party after all. Vince insisted instead that he talk to the whole room and tell everyone in the NEWTS what he had just told his wife. In the brightly lit bar, Vince tapped a spoon against an empty glass to attract everyone's attention.

'I want to thank you for hanging around after the show tonight to celebrate our wedding anniversary. I know you're not really here for my sake. You've not got much reason to celebrate me. I know you're really here for Bernie.'

Bernie shook her head in protest.

'No, you're here for Bernie because she is a kind, warm and generous woman and a very good friend to you all. I am a miserable old git, who can't be relied upon to turn up for rehearsals half-sober or remember his lines. You couldn't care less about me. You wouldn't cross the street to wish me Merry Christmas. You're all here to show solidarity with my wife.

'I know that you all know I drink too much. As a result, I've made this production difficult for all of you and for that I'm truly sorry. But I've been drinking too much for a very long time. Now I'm taking steps to change my life for the better. This young lady here – I'm sure you must all be wondering who she is – her name is Candy and she's my mentor at AA. She's helping me to stay on the wagon. From now on, things are going to be different. I want you all to help me keep account-able.'

Not quite knowing if it was appropriate in the light of what they had heard, the NEWTS raised a toast to Vince. Then Vince, with a glass full of Diet Coke for the first time in NEWTS' history, raised a toast to Bernie.

'To my long-suffering, wonderful, beautiful wife. And my very best friend.'

Kirsty found it hard to keep back tears. She looked for Jon but couldn't find him in the crowd in the bar.

'There is nothing more important in this life than love,' Vince continued. 'And I knew I loved this woman the first moment I ever saw her.'

That was when Kirsty, still looking for Jon, found she was locking eyes with Ben.

'Three cheers for Vince and Bernie,' Ben proposed.

'He'll never do it,' said Jon as he and Kirsty were driving home later. It was too cold to walk. 'I guarantee he'll be drunk when he turns up to the theatre tomorrow afternoon.'

'Jon,' Kirsty complained. 'Don't be so negative. He's doing his best. The man's got a huge struggle ahead of him.'

'Yes. And he won't make it. I've seen it all before. Bernie should cut her losses. She's only going to end up nursing him through a liver transplant. But I do hope he at least keeps it up for long enough for us to get this panto run done.'

Kirsty didn't bother to respond. She was upset by Jon's cynicism. She understood that Vince had a serious battle ahead of him, but she wanted to believe that he could succeed. He was a good bloke under his hard-bitten exterior and he clearly loved Bernie with all his heart. Just as she loved him in return. From the very first moment . . .

Often, Kirsty had observed, Jon didn't much seem to like the people he was working with. He treated them all as though they were hopeless cases and the panto would only come together because of his hard work. He didn't have a kind word for any of them. Jon felt he was above this little pantomime in Newbay, that he should be in the West End or on Broadway. He should be working with Tony Award nominees. He should be directing Shakespeare in Dubai.

Kirsty wondered if he'd had any news. Maybe he had and it wasn't good. Perhaps that was why he was being so nasty.

'Ben's performance was a bit better tonight,' Jon observed out of the blue. 'Maybe he got laid or something. What do you think?'

Kirsty looked out of the car window and pretended she hadn't heard him.

Chapter Seventy-Three

On New Year's Eve there was to be only one performance: a matinee. Years of experience had taught the NEWTS that scheduling a performance for New Year's Eve itself was not generally a good idea. There were too many other temptations for the audience on the last night of the year. Almost everyone had a party to go to and if you didn't have a party to go to then the telly was pretty good. Way too much competition for a panto. And that was before you took into account the fact that, particularly when you were dealing with an amateur cast, New Year's Eve was the night when people were most likely to call in 'sick'. It was far easier to save everyone the bother of bad excuses by giving them New Year's Eve off and doing a matinee instead.

'How will you be celebrating New Year's Eve?' Kirsty asked Vince as they met in the lobby after the afternoon's performance. She immediately wished she hadn't. New Year's Eve was the night when even people who didn't touch a drop the rest of the year would have a glass or five.

'A quiet night in,' said Vince. 'A roast dinner and a round of Diet Coke. We're going to do a New Year's ritual,' he elaborated. 'We're going to light a proper fire in the fireplace, write down all our wishes for the next twelve months and send them up the chimney to the universe.'

'That's a nice idea. What are you going to wish for?' Kirsty asked.

'For the strength to carry on the fight,' said Vince. 'And for Bernie to be by my side while I do it.'

'I'm not going anywhere,' Bernie assured him as she joined them. 'We're in this together.'

Vince looked at Kirsty curiously. 'Are you all right?' he asked her.

'Oh, I've got something in my eye,' said Kirsty.

New Year's Wishes. Kirsty had a few.

Kirsty was dejected as she walked from the theatre to the flat. Jon had gone on ahead earlier, saying he needed to send a few emails. Kirsty didn't ask him to wait for her to get changed after the matinee. She wanted some time to think.

What did she want for the New Year?

Right then it was chocolate.

She got her purse out of her bag to see if she had enough money to buy a Twix on the way back to the flat. As she did so, the cardboard strip from the fortune-telling machine fluttered to the floor.

'You are where love is,' it told her once again.

'Yeah, right,' she said. It didn't feel like it right then. Still, she picked it up and tucked it back into its hiding place. When the panto run was over, Jon would be less stressed. When the panto run was over, Kirsty would be able to think clearly again.

Chapter Seventy-Four

There was no question as to where everyone but Vince and Bernie would be going that New Year's Eve. Annette was throwing a party at her big house on the hill. It was not to be missed. Pretty much the entire population of Newbay was always angling to get a look inside Annette's mansion. Her fellow Cinderella cast members were among the lucky few to be admitted to the house that year.

Annette knew how to throw a good party and she had been planning her New Year's bash for at least six months. As far back as August, she'd bagged the town's best catering team to do the food and drinks. Her twenty-year-old nephew, an aspiring DJ, would be taking care of entertainment. She left the decoration to her cleaner, who was training to be an interior designer and had a wonderful eye. She'd transformed the house into something worthy of a magazine spread. All Annette asked was that people dressed up – really dressed up – to come and celebrate. The invitations – she had gone to the bother of having proper stiff cardboard invites printed – specified 'no jeans'. Jon was quite fed-up at that.

'Who does she think she is? I don't want to have to dress up in my downtime.'

'I think it's nice when people make an effort,' said Kirsty. 'It sounds as though Annette is going to be making an effort for her part. Besides, you look lovely in a suit,' Kirsty added, in an attempt to sweeten Jon up.

'Hmmm,' he said.

Jon grudgingly put on the suit he had worn for his interview with the entrepreneur from Dubai. Meanwhile, Kirsty pulled out a dress she felt was made for New Year's Eve. It was a floor-length column dress covered in sequins. She'd bought it when she joined the team of Countess Cruises, feeling sure that her life would be all black tie events from then on.

When they arrived at Great Oaks, Kirsty understood at once why Annette's house was the envy of half the county. The house had been built for a local merchant at the end of the eighteenth century. When his family fell on hard times, they sold the house to the local council. During the Second World War, it had housed evacuees. Then it had been a small private school, which went bust during the recession of the 1970s. It was Annette's second husband who restored it to its original residential splendour. Annette had since added a double garage for her soft-top Porsche. The double garage had a gym upstairs, which was apparently how Annette managed to stay in such good shape.

They were greeted at the door by an actual butler. Albeit one hired for the night. Standing right behind him was a young woman holding a tray of drinks. The butler took their coats. The woman offered glasses of champagne which Kirsty and Jon accepted greedily.

'*Veuve Clicquot*. Very appropriate for the merry widow. She's done all right,' Jon observed. 'And she doesn't have to put up with any of the husbands who funded it.'

'Ssssh,' said Kirsty. 'Here she comes.'

Annette was every inch the glamorous chatelaine that evening. She was wearing a full-length evening gown in inky-blue satin. Her ears glittered with diamond hoops from which dangled pearl drops as big as gobstoppers. There was no doubt that the jewels were genuine. Kirsty was glad she had gone heavy on the bling, though hers were not real, of course.

'I'm so glad you could make it. Kirsty, that's a lovely dress. Jon, you look very dashing.'

'See,' Kirsty teased Jon as they followed Annette into the main room. 'You know you look great in a suit.'

The whole cast had turned up. And the crew. And many other members of the NEWTS who weren't in the pantomime but who had worked with Annette through the years. Even Trevor Fernlea was there, looking much better for having brushed up for the occasion. His concussion was long forgotten. His wife was with him. Clearly an invitation to the biggest house in Newbay trumped a night with the bridge club even if it did mean extra time with her husband. Cynthia was dressed in gaudy pink chiffon and sported a ring on every finger.

'This one,' she said, showing Kirsty a sparkler the size of an ice cube. 'This one is new. Trevor bought it to thank me for being his rock during his recent incapacitation.'

Poor Trevor, thought Kirsty. If that was the price he had to pay to get a little attention.

* * *

Trevor said he even felt well enough to dance and Kirsty agreed to take to the floor with him, when Annette's nephew played something that anyone over the age of twenty-five might actually recognise. In the end, they got up to 'My Heart Will Go On'. It wasn't exactly a dance floor barnstormer, but it was just right for someone with a pacemaker and dodgy knee.

As they danced, Trevor talked about his years with the NEWTS. He'd first performed with them in 1958.

'As a member of the juniors?' Kirsty asked.

'On no,' said Trevor. 'I was already a student teacher.'

Kirsty tried to do the maths. Assuming he left school at eighteen and spent three years at university, it had to mean he was at least seventy-eight. That certainly put his disco moves into perspective.

'We're very glad you came to Newbay, Kirsty. You're the best leading lady I've ever had the pleasure to work with. Though you mustn't tell Annette that. We did *West Side Story* together in 1982.'

Kirsty was flattered, though she was very happy to relinquish her place as Trevor's partner to Lauren when the next song turned out to be 'You Sexy Thing' by Hot Chocolate. Lauren knew how to keep Trevor at a safe distance even when she was twerking.

Jon declined the opportunity to dance, claiming that the music wasn't right. He wasn't wrong about that. Annette's nephew had eclectic taste. But still, everyone did their best to get into the party spirit, following little Thea and the other child players' lead regarding some of the latest dances.

Yes, Ben was there. He had nodded in acknowledgment when Kirsty first caught his eye across the room but they hadn't yet spoken. Like Jon he looked great in a suit, Kirsty observed. He hung back by the drinks table on his own but by the time Kirsty quit the dancing to make a determined effort to speak to him, he was deep in conversation with Lauren, who was reacting to what Ben said with much hair-twirling and other coquettish moves. It was not a conversation to be interrupted. Kirsty spoke to Thea and her little friends Thomas and Georgie instead.

'I like that dress even better than your Cinderella one,' Thea told her. 'You've made me want to be an actress when I grow up. If I'm not an engineer.'

Kirsty smiled. 'You could be both.' When she glanced at Ben again, she thought perhaps he had one ear on their conversation, even though Lauren was still preening in front of him. He was smiling too.

Chapter Seventy-Five

It was about eleven forty-five when Jon tapped the side of his glass with a teaspoon to attract everyone's attention.

'Ladies and gentlemen,' he said. 'Not that I can see any gentlemen in this room.'

Everyone laughed politely.

'Could I have your attention, please?'

The guests all turned to look at him.

'I just wanted to raise a toast to you all. I know the run isn't quite over yet. We've still got one more performance to go and, heaven knows, anything could happen. Especially with you lot. But I wanted to say how proud I am of the NEWTS as I stand here this evening. We've had a great run. I think this production will go down in NEWTS' history. For all the right reasons. Not just the usual spectacle of Trevor Fernlea's trousers.'

'Hear, hear,' the crowd mumbled.

'So, let's raise a glass to that. To the NEWTS and, specifically, to the cast and crew of *Cinderella*. You've all worked so hard. Three cheers to us. Hip hip . . .'

'Hooray!' the others responded.

'What was that?' asked Jon, stepping into panto mode. 'I can't hear you. Let's do that again, shall we? Only this time let's make it *louder*. Hip hip . . .'

'Hooray!' the others shouted gamely.

'That's better. And one more time for luck.'

'Hip hip!'

'Hooray!'

Little Thea shouted loudest. She was throwing herself into the spirit of the event. This was the first time she had been allowed to stay up to welcome in the New Year and she was determined to make the most of it.

'Thank you.' Jon chinked his glass against those of the people standing nearest. 'Thank you. It has been the greatest pleasure to work with you all. Even you two.' He tipped his glass towards the Giggle Twins.

Kirsty allowed herself a small smile as she thought of the bitching Jon had done about pretty much every single person in the room. It was all forgotten now.

'I almost wish that I could stay around to join you all again on *Chitty Chitty Bang Bang.*' That was the show the NEWTS had planned for the spring. Trevor Fernlea had already expressed his interest in playing the Dick Van Dyke part – Caractacus Potts. Jon continued, 'But tonight I've some good news of my own to share.'

Kirsty perked up at that. Good news? What was Jon about to announce and why didn't she know already?

'As some of you know,' Jon continued. 'I recently went to London to interview for an important new job. Well, the good news is, I got it. From the middle of January, I will be directing the Dubai Shakespeare Society in a touring production of *Richard III.*'

There was a murmur of astonishment. Not least from Kirsty. Why hadn't he told her? And why was he telling her now, in front of everybody, when he must know that this news had all sorts of implications for both of them? Surely she should have been told first?

It was too late. Led by Annette, the rest of the party raised a toast to Jon. There was another round of cheers, even louder than before. And then he was swallowed up by all the people who wanted to give him their congratulations and find out more about the job and, more importantly, whether there might be space for a couple of NEWTS on the cast. The idea of a winter in the sun was very appealing in the depths of a Newbay winter.

'Congratulations,' said Ben. Lauren had left his side to add her voice to the choir of people singing for the promise of a cheap holiday.

'To me?' Kirsty pointed at her chest.

'Yes. You'll be getting out of Newbay for the worst of the winter. Soaking up the sun.'

'I'm not sure that I will actually,' said Kirsty. She found that she was trying not to cry. 'Sorry, Ben. I've got to go. Too much champagne.'

She made as if she was going to the bathroom but, as soon as she was out of Ben's sight, she ran out into the garden, like Cinderella fleeing before her dress turns back to rags.

'It's not such a big deal,' said Jon when she caught up with him. 'You actually found out pretty much as soon as I did. I got a text around ten o'clock.'

'Ten o'clock on New Year's Eve?'

'Yes. I don't know why it came through so late. Maybe it was sent earlier. You know how rubbish the signal is here in Newbay.'

That was true. There was more mobile signal in the middle of the Kalahari than there was in some parts of Devon.

'But why didn't you just take me into a corner and tell me first? Privately.'

'Maybe I would have done if you weren't too busy talking to Buttons.'

Kirsty opened her mouth to protest. She had shared just a couple of words with Ben, after Jon made the announcement. Jon was talking rubbish. On the contrary, she had barely said a word to Jon all evening because it seemed to her that every time she got near him, he was deep in conversation with someone else.

'Oh, it doesn't matter,' Jon said dramatically. 'Why should I expect you to be happy for me and want to toast my success like everyone else here tonight? You're only my girlfriend. Why should I expect you to be supportive?'

There it was. Somehow, Jon had managed to make it Kirsty who was at fault for not jumping up and down with glee.

'You know this affects both of us,' she said quietly. 'I gave up a season in the Caribbean to come here. Because I thought we were making plans for the future together.'

'I am taking this job for our future.'

'Expecting me to get another secretarial job so I can follow you? What kind of partnership is it we've got, Jon?'

But Kirsty didn't have a chance to continue with her argument because all of a sudden, though the night seemed to have been inching past, it was midnight. Annette had turned on the enormous wide-screen television above the fireplace so that they could all count down with Big Ben.

'Come on, everybody!' Annette opened the French windows from her sitting room and called out to Jon and Kirsty in particular. 'Make sure you've got something in your glasses. It's time to wish the old year goodbye! And good riddance, eh?'

Jon took Kirsty by the hand and practically pulled her back inside.

Kirsty slipped out into the garden again while everyone was still greeting the New Year with kisses and toasts. Reflexively, she checked her phone and was astonished to see three missed calls from her dad. And a text.

'India missing,' was what the text said. 'Is she with you?'

Kirsty immediately called her father.

'Dad. What's happening?'

'India isn't with you?'

'No. Of course not. What's going on?'

'She walked out of the house this morning. She's taken a bag but she left her phone. We've been looking for her everywhere. She isn't with any of her friends.'

'Have you talked to the police?'

'Of course. But she's sixteen. She's nearly an adult. They just advised us to wait.'

'That's ridiculous. What can I do to help?'

'We've been going from house to house in the village. We're heading into town to do the same. If you could just keep an eye out for her at your end and let us know if you hear anything.'

'Of course I will.'

'I just hope she's on her way to you. She might be. She thinks the world of you, you know.'

The words pricked Kirsty's heart.

'She'll be all right, Dad. I know she will.'

Kirsty went back into the party and told Jon she needed to leave at once.

Chapter Seventy-Six

Jon told his fellow NEWTS what was going on, of course. He didn't want anyone to think that he and Kirsty were leaving the party because they were having a domestic about Dubai.

'It's her little sister,' he said to Annette and Trevor Fernlea. 'They're very close so she might be on her way here.'

'What does she look like?' Trevor asked. 'In case one of us comes across her?'

Jon had no idea so he bluffed. 'A bit like Kirsty, I suppose.'

Only Ben knew otherwise. Kirsty had shown him photographs of India on her iPhone and thus he knew that the sisters did not resemble each other in the least. They both took after their mothers. While Kirsty was tall, statuesque and blonde, India was a willowy brunette like her mum, Linzi. While Kirsty loved to dress in bright colours, India favoured all black, accessorised with skulls.

And Kirsty loved her. The news that India had gone missing was not just an inconvenience for Kirsty, Ben knew. She must be going out of her mind with worry. Sure, as Jon said, India was probably just being dramatic. She was a teenager. She'd almost certainly be found at a friend's house eventually. But Ben knew that Kirsty's thoughts would be racing towards the worst possible scenario.

Ben followed Jon and the others out to the driveway of Annette's house where a taxi was waiting. Kirsty was already getting inside.

'Let us know when she turns up,' Annette called. 'And if there's anything we can do . . .'

Ben wrapped his arms around Thea. The news that a teenager was missing was both exciting and frightening to her.

'Will Kirsty's sister be OK?' Thea asked her dad.

'Of course she will,' said Ben.

He prayed that would be the case.

With Jon and Kirsty gone in the taxi, the rest of the partygoers drifted back inside. There wasn't a lot they could do other than wait for news. India and her parents lived more than an hour away from Newbay. There wasn't much point starting a house-to-house search on Annette's street. Why would India have headed there? So Annette's hired butler refilled the glasses and her remaining guests set to gossiping about the missing teen, about Kirsty and about Jon.

'So he's really going to Dubai?'

'Kirsty didn't look too happy about it,' said Andrew Giggle.

'I suppose it's going to be make or break for those two,' Annette observed. And then she cast a sidelong look at Ben.

* * *

Ben didn't want to hang around to listen to any specu-
lation on whether Kirsty would follow Jon to the Middle
East. Besides, Thea was flagging. It was way past her
usual bedtime. If Ben didn't take her home now, she
would be grumpy from tiredness in the morning. So Ben
and Thea said their 'thank-yous' to Annette and set out
for home.

They were going to walk. Annette's house was just
ten minutes from Ben and Thea's and it was downhill
all the way on the return leg. Ben was glad of the fresh
air and he hoped a little exercise would help Thea to
sleep better. She was completely wired after her night
out. She and her little friends had been on the dance
floor from the moment the party started.

'Is it far, Daddy?' Thea asked before they even got to
the end of Annette's street.

'It's just past the theatre,' Ben said.

In fact, the NEWTS theatre marked the halfway point.
A huge banner announcing 'Cinderella' hung from the
car park fence, which was strung with festive fairy lights
as every year.

'Dad,' said Thea as they drew close. 'Do you think
we'd see the ghost if we went in the theatre now?'

'There's no such thing as ghosts,' said Ben.

'Glynis the piano lady said there is. She saw it. It's a
choir boy dressed in a long red tunic with a frilly white
collar.'

'Well, I'm pretty sure Methodist choirboys don't dress
like that,' said Ben. 'Glynis was pulling your leg.'

'But, Dad . . .Wait!'

Suddenly, Thea froze. She was staring to the side of
the theatre, towards the door which had once led to the
church's vestry but now led straight backstage.

'It's there!'

'What?'

'The ghost!'

Ben held Thea's hand tightly as he too saw a flash of red disappearing round the back of the building.

Chapter Seventy-Seven

Ben felt his heart beat quicken. He wasn't sure what he had seen. Maybe it was something spooky. He wasn't about to tell Thea that though.

'I don't think it's a ghost, Thea. It's probably teenagers messing around,' he said.

'Daddy, it was the ghost.'

'There's really no such thing.'

'But Glynis said—'

'Glynis was having a joke. Come on.'

Thea didn't want to keep walking. She was staring into the gloom. Just then, Trevor Fernlea and Cynthia pulled up to the kerb behind them. Trevor wound down his window.

'You sure we can't drop you two off on our way home, Ben? It's bloody cold out tonight.'

'That's very kind of you but . . . Actually, Trevor. Can I have a word?'

Ben asked Trevor if Thea could sit in the car with Cynthia while Trevor joined him to make sure that no one had broken into the theatre.

'We saw a ghost,' Thea told Cynthia.

'We saw no such thing,' said Ben firmly.

'Whatever you saw, I'm ready,' said Trevor. He got a large torch out of the car glove compartment. 'No one's vandalising the NEWTS' theatre on my watch, I can tell you.'

'Be careful, Trevor. For goodness' sake,' said Cynthia. 'I've got the bridge club coming over for our New Year lunch tomorrow. The last thing I want is to have you hanging around the house because you broke your leg chasing a burglar.'

'I was in the army,' Trevor reminded her.

'You did National Service,' Cynthia corrected him. Ben made a mental note to remember that. The NEWTS were still trying to work out Trevor's age. National Service had to place him in his eighties!

'We're not going to get into any trouble,' Ben promised Cynthia. 'If someone has broken in, we're not going to follow them. We'll call the police right away. We just need to check the place is secure.'

'But if it's a ghost?' Thea persisted.

'It's not a ghost,' said Ben.

'It might be,' said Cynthia. Unhelpfully. 'Glynis told me she saw the spirit of a choirboy in a long red cloak and it sounds as if he was heading towards the vestry.'

Ben nodded. 'Thanks, Cynth. That's great.'

Together with Trevor, who seemed unduly excited at the prospect of catching an intruder, Ben set off towards the back of the theatre. Though he knew it well, it looked very different on a night like this, all shut up and lonely and dark. It was easy to see why someone might think it was haunted. It loomed over them. The buttresses cast deep shadows where anything might hide.

'I'm not sure this is a good idea . . .' Ben began.

'Sssh!'

As they got closer to the spot where Ben had seen the flash of red, Trevor put his finger to his lips. Ben was more inclined to be noisy, to give the trespassers a chance to bugger off without the need for confrontation. He was beginning to wish he hadn't got Trevor involved but had just called the police and let them deal with everything instead. Was he really going to tackle a burglar with no back-up but a geriatric geography teacher?

To make things worse, the battery in Trevor's torch was running low. And then it ran out altogether. Once they got around the back of the building, away from the street lights, they could hardly see a thing.

'Trevor, take care,' Ben whispered. It was a deliberately loud whisper.

Too late.

'What the?'

Trevor went flying.

Ben had no idea what Trevor had fallen over but he landed softly.

On top of the intruder. Or a ghost.

'Get thee behind me, Satan!' Trevor yelled.

Ben started yelling too. As Trevor scrambled to get upright and Ben lit the scene with his iPhone, he was confronted by a grinning skull.

'Get off me!' the death's head protested.

Trevor panicked and kept falling back down. Ben grabbed Trevor round the waist and heaved him upwards. Meanwhile the hooded skeleton scrambled upright and flattened itself against the wall.

'I warn you,' said Trevor, adopting a karate stance. 'I'm army trained.'

'Our Father, who art in heaven,' Ben started muttering. What had they found?

'I'm just a kid,' the intruder bleated.

The trespasser was no burglar. It was a teenage girl. She was wearing a hoodie with a skull painted onto the back of the hood. They could see that clearly now she turned towards them. Her own face was small and pale and no more frightening than a baby bird.

'India?' Ben asked.

'It's OK, Trevor. You can let her go. It's Kirsty's little sister.'

'How do you know who I am?' India asked.

'She told me all about you.'

'But what are you doing here, young lady?' Trevor asked. 'Half of Devon is on the lookout for you tonight.'

Trevor's impression of someone being stern was about as good as his impression of a twenty-something when he played Mercutio – which was why, when working as a teacher, he'd often had to resort to throwing board rubbers at his pupils – but India still burst into tears.

'Hey. Come on,' said Ben, taking off his coat and wrapping it around her shoulders. Her skull-painted hoodie was more decorative than useful. 'It's not that bad. You're safe now. And we're going to take you to your sister. I'm Ben, by the way,' he added.

'You're Buttons,' India said, as her face broke into a smile. 'Kirsty told me all about you.'

*   *   *

Ben and Trevor walked India back to Trevor's car. Thea pressed her nose against the car window, eager to see her ghost. If she was disappointed to see that the ghost was just an ordinary girl, she was thrilled to discover it was Kirsty's sister. A real live teenager was almost as exotic as a ghost to little Thea.

'You ran away from home!' Thea breathed in awe.

'And you've caused everybody a great deal of worry,' said Cynthia, as if she wasn't secretly thrilled that the whole affair would make a very good anecdote for her bridge club.

Ben dialled Kirsty's number and handed the phone over to India before Kirsty could pick up.

'Ben?' he heard Kirsty answer.

'It's India. Ben found me. He's bringing me over to yours.'

Kirsty was waiting by the door when Ben brought her little sister home.

'Oh, you silly thing!' Kirsty exclaimed as she wrapped India in her arms. 'Everyone has been going crazy.'

'Have you called Dad?'

'Of course I have.'

Ben hovered on the doorstep. Trevor, Cynthia and Thea were in the car, craning to see what was going on.

'Thank you, Ben,' said Kirsty.

'It was Trevor who tripped over her bag,' Ben said. 'And Thea who spotted her sneaking round the back of the theatre in the first place. I would have walked straight past.'

'But Ben was really kind to me,' said India. She shrugged off his coat and handed it back to him.

It was so like Ben to try to pass on the credit for his good deeds to others, Kirsty thought.

'So you found her?'

Jon appeared in the hallway. He put his hand on Kirsty's shoulder. He was marking his territory. Ben gestured towards the door.

'I should be going.'

'Yes,' said Jon. He flashed a joyless smile that took Ben right back. He could almost see Charlie, standing between them, making her choice. But Kirsty was too wrapped up in her sister to notice what was happening between Jon and Ben.

Chapter Seventy-Eight

When everyone was gone, Kirsty and India curled up on the sofa together.

'What were you doing at the theatre?' Kirsty asked.

'I didn't know how else to find you. I didn't have your address. I was in such a hurry I left my phone behind.'

'I know,' said Kirsty. 'Dad was going out of his mind.'

'Why? He doesn't care about me.'

'Oh, India. That's absolutely not true.' Kirsty took off her scarf and wrapped it around her little sister's neck. 'You're still freezing. Have you had anything to eat?'

'I had a sausage roll when I got off the train at Exeter.'

'And how did you get here from there?'

'I hitched.'

Kirsty felt nauseous at the very thought.

'I got a lift with three really nice students from Exeter Uni. But they were only going as far as Westcombe so I had to walk the rest of it.'

'That's five miles! In the cold and the wet. On New Year's Eve.'

'I know,' said India. 'And my feet hurt.'

'Come on, let's get you into some pyjamas. I'll phone Dad to let him know you're in one piece.'

'I'm not going back,' India insisted. 'He doesn't understand me, Kirsty. He doesn't care what I want out of life.'

'He cares very much,' said Kirsty. 'I'm sure he does.'

'Don't let him come and pick me up yet. Let me stay for a couple of days.'

Kirsty looked at Jon, who was standing in the doorway with a mug of cocoa. Jon shrugged. It seemed like an agreement. 'Thanks,' she mouthed.

At least it meant they wouldn't have to talk about Dubai just yet.

Jon soon went to bed, leaving the sisters alone.

'After you left, it just got worse,' India explained. 'I can't open my mouth without Dad jumping down my throat about something. It's like everything I do is wrong. Like he thinks I want to go into the theatre just to spite him. He doesn't get that it's my passion. He doesn't believe in passion. He just thinks I should go and work in an office until I die, regretting all the things I didn't do. I'm not going to live like that.'

'He wants to protect you,' Kirsty told India again. 'He worries that by choosing to study drama, you'll be closing down avenues that could save your bacon later on. You're chasing a career in an incredibly competitive field. God knows, it's bad enough at amateur level. I've experienced some surprisingly crushing moments here with the NEWTS and I'm not even getting paid for the pleasure. Dad doesn't want you to face the pain of rejection, the insecurity and instability. All those things are as big a part of working in the theatre as the glamour and the applause.'

'I know that,' said India. 'I know. I'm not stupid. I just think I've got something and if I don't go for it now, I'll regret it for ever. Who knows what you could have been if Dad had supported you when you were younger.'

'The next Helen Mirren?' Kirsty smiled.

Her dad had agreed with Kirsty that India could stay with her for a couple of days. It would do them good, he admitted, to have some time away from each other after such a fraught few weeks. Give them both a chance to cool down. Though Kirsty wondered what would happen when that time was up. Would her father stick to his position? Would India stick to hers? Kirsty had so much sympathy for her little sister. She almost felt guilty that she hadn't done more to pave the way for India. If she had been more successful, would that have made Stu more likely to let India have her way?

Kirsty knew she wasn't exactly a poster girl for theatrical success. What would the New Year hold for her, if she didn't get that part in *Les Mis*? More auditions? How long could she keep going before she admitted to herself that she needed to get a job? Any job? Just as Jon suggested. Would she be able to get one as well paid as the position she'd given up to follow her dream? Would she be able to get a job as good as the one she had given up to be with him?

When Kirsty climbed into bed, Jon was still awake.

'Ben Teesdale's got a crush on you,' he said. 'The way

he was looking at you tonight, when he dropped India off. It was embarrassing.'

'That's crazy,' Kirsty said. 'You're mixing him up with his part.'

'Ben's always been a very average actor,' said Jon.

Chapter Seventy-Nine

On New Year's Day, the NEWTS had the day off. The very last performance of *Cinderella* was to take place on 2nd January. But the year started badly. When Jon and Kirsty arrived at the theatre for the final show, Elaine was in the big rehearsal room where the children waited until they were on stage, pacing frantically as she stabbed text messages into her phone.

'Disaster,' she said. 'Two of my mice have gone sick with the vomiting bug.'

'You're joking,' said Jon. 'Which ones?'

'Lead mice. Thomas Nuttall and Georgie Barnton. Thomas has got lines.'

'Fuck's sake,' said Jon.

Elaine glared at him on behalf of the other children, who were milling around close by, pretending not to be listening. Of course they were all ears. Big mouse ears.

'I mean, for goodness's sake,' Jon corrected himself. 'What can we do?'

'Cut the lines?' Elaine suggested.

'But I know them!' piped up Thea.

The adults all turned towards her.

'I really do.'

'Thea?' Elaine gave the little girl her 'serious' look, the one she adopted when the children in the chorus were playing up. 'Do you really, really know them?'

'I know all the lines in the play,' Thea assured her. 'Every single one.'

'Can you show us? Could you do the lead mouse part now? With me being Cinderella?' Kirsty asked. 'Shall we start with the scene in the kitchen?'

Thea nodded. She mimed pinging a pair of imaginary braces. The lead mouse wore red braces. That's how you could tell him apart from the common or garden mice.

Kirsty got into character too. She gestured that Thea should join her in the centre of the room. She swished an imaginary skirt of rags and clasped her hands to her heart.

'Ready, Thea?'

Thea doffed an imaginary cap.

'*Oh my,*' Kirsty sighed. '*How will I ever get all this work done before my step-sisters come home?*'

'*Don't worry, Cinders,*' said Thea. '*We can help you! Just pass me that brush.*'

Kirsty mimed handing the brush over.

'*And give me that pan.*'

She mimed handing over the dustpan.

'*Come on, everybody.*'

Thea whistled for her 'brothers and sisters'. She had a good loud whistle for one so small. The three remaining mice who didn't have the vomiting bug came squeaking on her command.

'*Ready, gang?*' Thea asked them.

'*We're ready,*' the others shouted.

'*Oooooooh!*' Thea sang the first note of the song that would follow. Her pitch was spot on. The others chimed in. The four mice, with Thea as their new leader, joined hands and encircled their temporary Cinders. They did not put a foot wrong.

Kirsty couldn't help grinning.

'Perfect. She knows the part,' said Elaine.

Jon agreed. 'It'll do. Someone put her in the costume.'

'Will it fit?'

'It'll have to. Give those old bags in Wardrobe something to do.'

'Am I really doing it?' Thea asked. 'Am I going to be lead mouse?'

'Thea Teesdale,' said Elaine. 'You're on. Let's get you in that outfit.'

Thea gave an ecstatic fist-pump.

'I've got lines,' she said to anyone who would listen. 'I've got a speaking part! I've got to tell Dad.'

'Come on,' said Gwyneth, one of that night's chaperones. 'Don't get over-excited just now. You've got the whole night to get through.'

Taking Gwyneth's hand, Thea danced all the way up to Wardrobe.

Meanwhile, India was quickly recruited to swell the numbers of the adult chorus, which had also been hit by the norovirus. She was thrilled to have a chance to show off her skills. She picked up one of the spare scores and set to work learning the songs.

'You could just mime,' said Annette.

'There's no way I'm going to mime. I want to do this properly.'

'Trust me, nobody else will.'

'Come on, Annette,' said Vince. 'That's not entirely true. Everyone has been making such an effort. Even I know all my lines now.'

'Fair enough,' said Annette.

So, the mouse problem was sorted and the chorus had been swelled by one. But worse was to come. The pantomime could easily go ahead without minor players but, with just an hour to go, Jon got the call they had all been dreading. Lauren had been struck down with the vomiting bug too.

'You're kidding me,' said Jon.

'I wish I was. I can't leave the bathroom,' she told him. 'I'm actually calling you from the loo.'

'Too much information,' said Jon, holding the phone away from his ear as though the bug could travel through the airwaves.

'I'm sorry, Jon. I don't want to let you and the others down. Especially not on the last night. But I just can't do it. Every time I think I'm starting to feel better I—'

Jon heard a clatter as Lauren dropped her phone onto the bathroom tiles so that she could hurriedly reposition herself to puke. What followed were sound effects worthy of a horror movie. The rest of the cast watched as Jon went pale and looked as though he might be about to throw up himself.

'Right.' Jon hung up on Lauren and texted her instead, 'Don't come in. Stay home.'

'Get well.' He sent a second text as an afterthought. Then he turned to the others and shouted, 'Shit, shit, shit, shit, shit!'

'Is Lauren not coming in?' Andrew Giggle asked, as though they hadn't guessed.

'But what can we do?' asked Annette. 'We've got no understudy.'

'Don't you think I know that?' Jon sighed.

'There's no one in the chorus who can do the Prince Charming part at such short notice. We'll have to cancel,' said Vince.

'No way,' said Jon. 'Tonight is a sell-out. The show must go on.'

'But who?' Bernie asked.

'Is Trevor available?' Vince suggested.

Kirsty's mouth dropped open.

'There's no way he can do the dances,' said Bernie. 'I spoke to him just this morning. He hurt his hip when he fell over on New Year's Eve.'

India looked at her feet, a little shame-faced.

'Me,' said Jon decisively. 'It'll have to be me.'

'What?' said Kirsty.

'I can play Prince Charming. I know the part as well as anybody here.'

'But you're a bloke,' said George Giggle. 'I thought you wanted this panto to be traditional. Prince Charming's got to be a girl.'

'Just think of it like Shakespeare in the original,' said Jon. 'I will be a man, playing a woman, playing a man. Like the first-ever actor to play Viola.'

'What's playing a viola got to do with it?' Andrew Giggle asked.

'Viola in *Twelfth Night*?' said Jon.

The cast looked back at him. Blankly.

'Oh, for crying out loud. Look, I'm playing Prince Charming and that's it. We can't disappoint the audience. Any more than usual . . .' he added with a hiss. 'Now go and get ready, everybody! The show *must* go on.'

Chapter Eighty

The hour before any performance was always chaotic, but that day the excitement backstage soon reached fever pitch. The last-minute cast substitutes required all sorts of changes. Fearful of breaching any law on the subject, unwritten or otherwise, mousey Glynis, who was acting committee chairperson while Trevor was still officially incapacitated, insisted that they produce inserts announcing the change of cast to go into all the programmes. Unfortunately, the office printer was broken, so the amendments had to be made by hand. Which gave Kirsty a chance to see that Glynis's handwriting was remarkably like the handwriting used to deface the original cast list. She never would have guessed. That was something that would have to be discussed when the chaos was over.

Meanwhile, Jon had an emergency costume fitting. There was nothing in Wardrobe that came close to being suitable. Fortunately, another quick call to Trevor Fernlea revealed that he did indeed have his own Prince Charming costume at home. He and Cynthia were coming to the last night, of course. They wouldn't have missed it for the world. They would come early and bring Jon's new costume with them.

Jon was effusively grateful until the costume actually arrived.

'I had this made in 1976,' said Trevor.

Indeed, the trousers suggested as much. Prince Charming in flares? But it was the smell that was worse.

'It was a bit musty, being in the cupboard all that time, so I gave it a squirt with some Old Spice,' Trevor admitted.

A squirt? It smelled like it had been marinated in a vat of the stuff. Jon's eyes watered from the fumes when he put the jacket on. Kirsty's eyes watered when she got near him.

'Whoah,' she said. 'That is quite something.'

Ben, who had been downstairs in the lobby, helping the volunteers on the front desk to fix a problem with the printer they used for ticketing, finally arrived in the wings. He had not known until then that Lauren wouldn't be playing the Prince that night. When he saw Jon all dressed up and ready to go, Ben struggled to hide his surprise and disappointment.

'That's right,' said Jon. 'Tonight, dear Buttons, your rival for Cinder's heart is me. Ready to lose the girl? Again?'

Ben said nothing.

Annette, squeezing by Jon to get into position, screwed up her face in horror at the copious aftershave.

'Is that Old Spice?' Annette asked him.

'Needs must,' said Jon. 'The show . . .'

'Must go on!' everyone within earshot chorused.

And it went OK. The audience seemed understanding when Jon was a little rusty on his cues. The old dears in the front row were pleased to see him.

'Wasn't he in *The Night Manager*?' asked the mayor's mother, who was back for another go.

'Tom Hiddleston in Newbay?' her friend replied. 'Are you sure you haven't got dementia?'

Jon rose above it. He was secretly thrilled to have been mistaken for one of his idols.

Until the mayor's mother said. 'I don't mean Tom Hiddleston. I meant the short one. The one who was the vicar.'

'Of Dibley? You mean Dawn French? But Prince Charming's a man tonight. Isn't he?'

And then, thank goodness, it was time for the interval. Jon graciously accepted his colleagues' congratulations as they gathered behind the tabs.

'You should have been Prince Charming all along,' said Annette. 'Don't you think so, Kirsty?'

Kirsty agreed. 'Of course.'

Ben excused himself to catch up with Thea.

Chapter Eighty-One

During the interval, Kirsty and the other women in the cast would always retire to their dressing room for a much-needed drink – water or tea only – and to touch up their make-up. Kirsty was re-gluing an errant fake eyelash when Elaine knocked on the door and said, 'Kirsty. There's someone here would like your autograph.'

Kirsty scribbled her name on the front of one of the pile of a hundred photographs she had prepared for just such an eventuality. So far she had needed just three. She passed one to Elaine.

'I think he needs a more personal response than that,' said Elaine.

Kirsty was just about to groan when Elaine stepped aside and Kirsty's father appeared in the doorframe.

'Dad?'

'All right, love?'

Kirsty immediately stepped out into the corridor to join him. She could hardly invite him into the dressing room where Bernie was helping Annette readjust her Spanx.

'Dad. You're here. I thought you weren't coming to get India until tomorrow.'

'But it's the last night of your show tonight.'

'I didn't know you were coming.'

'I wouldn't have missed it for the world.'

Kirsty tipped her head to one side.

Stu looked at his feet. 'I know you didn't ask me to be here.'

'I didn't think it was worth it.'

'And that makes me ashamed. If you don't want me to be here, Kirsty, I quite understand. I said some unforgivable things when you came to dinner. You'd be quite right not to want me around. I'll get out of your hair.'

'No. Dad, I'm glad you're here.' Kirsty gave him a hug. 'What do you think of the show so far?'

'I thought you were amazing,' he said.

Kirsty smiled to prompt more.

'I can't get over how you walked out there and made that stage your own. When you opened your mouth to sing, you really raised the rafters. I couldn't believe it. I had to turn to the woman in the seat next to me and tell her, that's my daughter. That's my little girl. I was so proud of you.'

'Oh, Dad.' Kirsty felt tears springing to her eyes.

'But I don't have any right to be proud of you, do I? India says it like it is. I never supported you in this. I can't claim any credit. Your mum knew what was what. You've got talent, Kirsty, and she spotted it when you were just a little girl. She was right to encourage you and I was wrong. I stood in the way of your dream.'

'Dad.' Kirsty squeezed her father's hand.

'When I saw you today, all I could keep thinking was that you should have been on stage your whole life. Because of me, you ended up giving up your dancing and your singing and working in an office. All because I didn't tell you to go for it when I should have.'

'You did what you thought was best, Dad. You did what any sensible person would have done. For every little girl who follows her dream of being on stage and actually achieves it, there are thousands – maybe even hundreds of thousands – more who don't get there and find that striving to succeed has cost them all sorts of ordinary happiness. Who knows what might have happened if I'd gone ahead and done that advert when I was seven. You're right, I might have been the next Denise van Outen, like I wanted to back then. But I would probably have got fed-up with all the hours of practice I'd need to put in while my friends were all out having fun with boys. Or I'd have had more early success that petered out when I hit puberty, leaving me feeling rejected. Or I'd have turned into a proper prima donna and ended up with a fantastic career but no friends.'

'You'd never have ended up with no friends,' said Stu. 'That's one certain thing about you, Kirsty. I've seen that all your life. You know how to treat other people right. Everybody knows how warm you are. They all fall in love with you. No, I did you a great disservice back when you were a kid. I was frightened and I didn't trust you to have the strength it takes to be a performer. I misjudged you. The stars were there within touching distance for you, my love, and I moved them further away. I should have listened to your mother. I made so many mistakes.'

'Dad,' said Kirsty. 'It doesn't matter.'

'I robbed you of your dream.'

'I'm living my dream right now, aren't I, and however I got here, it was the right way. I'm glad I didn't have everything fall into place when I was still a kid. And I know that everything you've done for me, Dad, has come from the right place. From love.'

'Will you forgive me?'

'There's nothing to forgive.'

And Kirsty was surprised to find, as she said those words, that she absolutely meant them. 'Everything has turned out just right.'

Elaine rang the bell.

'Five minutes,' she warned the players.

'You'd better get back to your seat,' said Kirsty to her father. 'But I'll see you afterwards, won't I? You're not going to grab India and rush straight off without saying goodbye?'

'Of course not. Linzi's here too. She wants to congratulate you. By the way, which one is your boyfriend?'

'The one in the flares.'

'The prince?'

'That's him.'

'Oh, Linzi was sure it would be the other one.'

'Which other one?'

'Buttons.'

'What?'

The bell rang again.

'I'll see you later. Break a leg.'

Watching her father navigate his way through a crowd of mice to get back to the auditorium, Kirsty knew that the second act was going to be her best yet.

Chapter Eighty-Two

Thea was on stage in a great many scenes that evening. She had clearly watched Thomas Nuttall very closely. She did not miss a cue. Not a beat. She whirled and twirled as the fairy godmother turned her into a footman. She squeaked with authentic fright and squirmed and wriggled as the clock struck midnight and her transformation back to rodent began.

Watching from the wings whenever he was able, Ben was full of pride and love for his darling little girl. But best of all was when they were on stage together.

As lead mouse, Thea was now one of only two mice who were on stage when Ben presented the song-sheet. Her job was to sing along and encourage the children plucked from the audience. To make them feel comfortable in what might otherwise be an intimidating situation.

Thea grinned at her father as he went through his spiel. A flash from the stalls told them Judy was capturing the moment for ever on her digital camera.

When the song-sheet was over and the audience members were back in their seats, Ben lifted Thea off her feet and twirled her round. The audience had applauded the brave children who got up to sing. Now Ben asked them to cheer the mice, especially his daughter who'd stepped in at the last moment that night to take a speaking part.

Thea gave a bow. And another and another.
'Come on, floppy ear!'
Ben had to carry her off-stage.

Chapter Eighty-Three

The final scenes went brilliantly. The Ugly Sisters got even bigger laughs than usual. They were demob happy and brought out all their dirtiest jokes, not caring who might be offended. Least of all, Jon. His horrified expression as the sisters squeezed him in the middle of a fake boob sandwich was priceless.

'Is that a Christmas tree you've got in your pocket, Euripides?' George Giggle asked their erstwhile director.

Jon could only pretend he hadn't heard.

Then at last it was Cinderella's biggest scene.

The hunt for the owner of the glass slipper was over. Prince Charming knelt before her by the humble hearth. The Ugly Sisters and their stepmother looked on in trepidation. Baron Hardup prayed for a fast solution to all his money woes. Buttons bowed his head for the moment when his queen would become someone else's princess.

'*Cinderella*,' asked Jon in the guise of Prince Charming. '*Will you marry me?*'

Kirsty had already mentally moved on to the next line and was clasping her hands to her heart in readiness to say '*Yes, oh yes, oh yes,*' as per the script, when she looked down and noticed that Jon was not holding the big comedy engagement ring, large enough to be seen from the upper circle, that usually appeared at this moment. Instead, he was holding what appeared to be a real ring in a small dark-blue velvet box.

'*Huh?*' she gasped.

Jon nodded to confirm Kirsty's suspicions, then he got up from one knee, smoothed down his borrowed flares, and turned to address the audience.

'Ladies and Gentlemen,' he said. 'I hope you won't mind me taking this evening's performance in a slightly different direction from that you're all anticipating. I want to let you all in on a secret. Kirsty, that is to say Cinderella here, is my real-life princess and I'm using this moment to ask her to marry me for real.'

The audience broke into excited applause. Jon got back down on one knee again, smiling his matinee idol smile. The smile which had seduced Kirsty in the canteen at Countess Cruises all those months ago. Kirsty stared at the ring, which was bouncing the light in a way that the crystal prop ring never did. It was a real diamond for a very real proposal.

'Let's start again, shall we?' asked Jon. 'Kirsty Marie Watson, I have loved you from the moment I first saw you.'

That was news to her. He'd previously told her that it took him three months to be certain.

'Since we got together, I've felt able to achieve more and reach greater milestones than ever before. Thanks to you, I've been able to direct this pantomime and at the same time gather the energy and power to win my new job in Dubai. I was always going places but I realise now how much better it is to go to those places with someone by my side, supporting me all the while.

Kirsty, you are the moon around my sun. Will you be my wife?'

There was silence for a beat as Kirsty prepared her answer. What could she say in front of so many people but—

'Noooo!'

The shout came from the wings. From Thea. Her floppy mouse ear jiggled with indignation as she jumped to her feet. 'You can't marry Prince Charming!' Thea told her. 'Buttons is the one who really loves you.'

'Yeah!' the other little mice agreed.

Kirsty whipped her focus to Ben, who was standing right behind her. But Ben was frozen. He was gripping his pill-box hat as he stared back at her, immobilised as if by the fairy godmother's spell.

'For God's sake!' Bernie gave Ben a dig in the ribs. 'Ben? Buttons? Say something!'

'I . . . I . . .' Ben managed at last. 'I . . .'

Nope. That was it.

The audience laughed.

Jon shook his head in a pitying sort of way and continued. 'Kirsty, say you'll join me on the adventure of a lifetime in Dubai. With you by my side, I can achieve miracles. I'll achieve my true potential.'

'Hmmm,' said the woman sitting next to Judy in row H. 'But what about her potential, eh? What does *she* want?'

It was a good question. Judy watched anxiously as the scene played out.

Jon continued, 'Stand behind me, my love, and there's no knowing what we'll . . .'

'Stand behind him?' Judy's new friend spluttered. 'What kind of offer is that?'

'Don't marry Prince Charming,' came a shout from

the stalls. It was April from the Bella Vista. Her grandson had brought her along.

'Yeah! Prince Charming wears flares. Marry Buttons!' yelled someone else.

'Buttons is much nicer-looking,' shouted Judy's friend.

'Buttons has loved you all along!'

'*But-tons! But-tons!*' the chant went up. April from the Bella Vista started it.

'*But-tons! But-tons! But-tons!*' the children on the stage joined in.

And then so did Bernie. And the Giggle Twins. And Vince. And Annette. And the orchestra. Even Glynis when she finally looked up from her paperback and realised the cast had gone wildly off-script.

Jon got to his feet. He glared at Kirsty.

'Well?' he asked her.

'Jon, I . . . I can't hear myself think,' was what she told him.

'For crying out loud,' said Jon. He stalked off stage right, looking almost as evil as Baron Hardup.

'*Buttons! Buttons! Buttons!*' the crowd continued to roar.

'Jon,' Kirsty called after him. 'Jon, wait!'

But Bernie grabbed her by the elbow before she could follow Jon off.

'Just bow,' said Bernie. 'Bow. The audience think it's all part of the show.'

Off-stage, in a desperate attempt to stop the chaos, Elaine was busy trying to bring the curtains down. Meanwhile, Glynis pressed the Pyroflash, sending the first five rows ducking beneath their chairs. It might not have been entirely accidental.

The tabs closed abruptly, then whooshed back up. The other main characters joined Kirsty and Bernie at the front of the stage and bowed for all they were worth before the curtains swished shut again. After three calls, Kirsty shook her hands free of Bernie and Ben's and made for the exit as fast as she could in pursuit of Jon. How on earth was she going to sort this mess out?

'Where did he go?' she asked Elaine.

Elaine pointed Kirsty towards the dressing rooms.

Meanwhile Ben exited stage left, feeling every bit the baddie.

Chapter Eighty-Four

It was mayhem. Backstage, everyone was racing about, trying to find out what was going on. Where was Jon? Where was Kirsty? Can you believe what he asked her? In front of everybody? What was she going to say?

'She's not going to marry him,' said Vince, firmly. 'She'd have said yes right away if she was.'

'But he surprised her. She wasn't expecting it,' said Annette. 'She gave up a job on a cruise ship to be with him. Of course she wants to get married.'

'I'm not so sure,' said George Giggle. 'We've all seen the way she is around . . .' George tipped his head in the direction of Ben.

Ben was in the wings frantically undoing the buttons on his jacket. One of the wardrobe witches was fussing around him.

'Careful!' said Angie. 'This costume's got to be Caractacus Potts in *Chitty Chitty Bang Bang*.'

'I don't care,' said Ben, pulling off his frilly collar. 'I just want to be out of it and out of here.'

'But it's the last night,' said Angie. 'Everyone's going to be in the bar. And maybe we'll have something really big to celebrate if Kirsty tells Jon what I think she will.'

Ben just gave Angie a look.

* * *

Bernie rescued him. She tucked her arm through Ben's and marched him into the small rehearsal room for a pep talk.

'She's not going to say "yes", Ben. I'm sure of it. Don't worry.'

'Why would I worry?'

'Because the way you feel about her is as plain as the nose on my face.'

'Was it so obvious?'

'There are some things even the best actors can't disguise. And I would bet my house on her feeling the same way about you.'

Ben's eyes watered at the idea.

'Bloody greasepaint,' he said.

Bernie nodded kindly.

'Bloody greasepaint,' she echoed. 'Don't rush off, Ben. Not yet. This could be your moment.'

Or it could just be a replay of that awful night all those years ago when Charlie chose Jon, thought Ben. He was always destined to lose out to Jon Manley.

'Your mum is looking after Thea,' Bernie continued. 'At least come and have a drink with the rest of the cast downstairs? Just one. Give the dust time to settle.'

Reluctantly, Ben agreed.

Chapter Eighty-Five

Jon had not gone to the dressing rooms. Instead, Kirsty found him in the props room, in the semi-darkness, leaning on a cardboard Doric column as he considered a plastic skull. When he heard her come in, he turned towards Kirsty with venom in his gaze.

'What do you want?' he hissed at her.

'Jon,' she said. 'I'm so sorry. I wasn't expecting . . . I'm so sorry,' she blundered on. She put her hand on his arm in a placating gesture. He shook her off. 'I'm just so sorry.'

'Is that all you can say? I've never been so humiliated in my life. Buttons!' He spat the word out. 'They think you should be with Buttons rather than me.'

'No they don't,' Kirsty insisted. 'Not really. It's just the story . . . The audience wouldn't have said that if they knew us in real life. They were caught up in the fairytale.'

'And the cast?'

'It was just excitement of the play—'

'*My* play,' Jon reminded her. 'And I didn't write you falling in love with someone else into it. Least of all *Buttons*.'

He didn't seem able to say 'Ben'.

'I—' The words caught in Kirsty's throat. She shook her head.

'Have you fallen in love with him?' Jon asked.

Kirsty just shook her head again. What else could she do? She didn't think he really wanted an answer. Her heart was breaking. She had never seen Jon look so unhappy. So vulnerable and small. And in *his* own theatre. After *his* own show. When he should have been in the bar with the rest of the cast revelling in triumph at the end of a wonderful run. She had ruined it for him. In that moment, Kirsty would have done anything to see him smile. Said anything. Even if it would mean a whole lot of trouble later on.

'You just took me by surprise,' she told him again. 'I was confused by all the lights and the shouting. I didn't know what to do. What to say.'

'How about yes? Or no? Just some kind of bloody answer would have been useful.'

'In front of all those people? If I'd had any inkling that you were going to propose, I would never have let you do it in such a public way.'

'So it was the way that I did it?' Jon asked.

'Yes. I mean, no. Not just . . . But it's not a question I would ever have wanted to answer on a stage, for heaven's sake. You must understand that. Some things are private. We should have talked about it, just the two of us first.'

'I wanted to surprise you.'

'You certainly did that.'

'Oh, Kirsty. You're my princess. My leading lady. Can't you see how much I love you?'

He certainly seemed to love her right then but there were so many other things going on in Kirsty's heart. When she looked at Jon, she could see both the love-struck suitor who had asked her to marry him in such an ostentatious way and the selfish boyfriend who assumed his dreams trumped hers all at once.

Suddenly Jon put down the skull and grabbed Kirsty around the waist. He pulled her against him,

'Seeing you on stage night after night in that wedding dress of Bernie's, looking so lovely, what was I supposed to do? I had to make you mine. And I wanted everyone to know that I'd chosen you for my wife. Everyone. So what if I asked you on stage? I'd have asked you on the TV news if I could have. We can make this work,' he said. 'I know we can.'

Then he took her face in his hands and kissed her hard on the lips. Like a mongoose hypnotised by a snake, Kirsty sank into the embrace.

Which was the point at which Annette opened, then swiftly closed, the props room door, having seen all she needed to draw her conclusions.

The news reached Ben even as the props room door was still creaking shut on the happy couple. Ben bid the rest of the cast 'goodnight' and left the theatre for what he was sure would be the very last time.

Chapter Eighty-Six

As down in the bar the remaining cast members clubbed together for a bottle of champagne to toast their newly engaged director and his Cinderella, the passionate clinch that had convinced Annette the deal was done was over as quickly as it started.

Kirsty pushed Jon away. She wiped her mouth.

'I can't do it,' she said.

'What?'

'I can't marry you.'

Jon looked at her as though she was speaking Mandarin. When he realised she was serious, however, his upper lip curled in disgust and he immediately rushed to make it *his* decision.

'You don't want to marry me? Forget about it. You can consider my offer withdrawn.'

He went from loving fiancé to vengeful ex within seconds.

'I don't know what I was thinking,' he said.

For a moment, she was lost for words. But then she said, 'I don't know what you were thinking either. We hadn't talked about marriage at all until you proposed to me.'

'But I'd been considering it,' said Jon.

'Like I said, isn't it something we both should have

been considering? Together? Like your going to Dubai?'

'You're still going on about that. I proposed to you precisely so you could come with me.'

'I'm supposed to be your partner, not an employee. That means talking about everything. As a couple.'

'I thought it would be romantic.'

'I'm sure it would have been. If it had been right. But it hasn't been right for a while now, has it?'

'What?'

Kirsty looked at her feet, still in their Cinderella slippers.

'Since I've been with you in Newbay, Jon, I've discovered I've got flaws I never imagined prior to your pointing them out. My feet are too big. My arse is too wide. My fingers are stubby. My face is too coarse. I dress too brightly and I laugh too loudly. I like the wrong kind of music. I've got the wrong kind of friends. The only question I have is why you would want to marry someone so very imperfect at all?'

'Because I love you?'

'You don't love me, Jon. Not really. You only properly show an interest in me when somebody else does. You asked me to marry you because of Ben.'

Jon snorted but Kirsty knew she'd hit the mark.

'You guessed that he liked me and you just had to show him who's boss. Well, I'm glad you're withdrawing your offer of marriage because I should have said "no" when we were on stage. For heaven's sake, even your proposal was all about you!'

Jon opened his mouth to protest.

'I'm not your Cinderella, Jon. And you're not my Prince Charming. I should never have followed you back to Newbay. I would have left you at the beginning of December if it wasn't for the stupid show.'

Jon tried again to interrupt her. Kirsty put a finger on his lips.

'Jon, what we had wasn't love. It was a showmance.'

Needless to say, Kirsty and Jon did not join the rest of the cast in the bar that night. They left the theatre separately. Jon in his car. Kirsty with her dad, half-sister and stepmum, who, once informed of what was really going on, waited by the vestry door like getaway drivers.

Jon went to his parents' house. Kirsty imagined his mother was very pleased to see him and probably even more pleased to hear that Kirsty had turned the proposal down. Perhaps he wouldn't even tell his family that he'd asked.

Kirsty had Stu, Linzi and India drop her off at the flat.

'Are you sure you want to be on your own?' Stu asked.

'More than anything,' Kirsty told them.

Still, the flat was horribly empty without Jon. The Christmas tree looked as sad as Kirsty felt, with half its needles already in the carpet. Jon would not have been pleased about that. With a heavy heart, Kirsty found a cardboard box and put all the baubles away. Without a care for the clothes she was wearing, she then carried the pathetic little tree outside and left it alongside the wheelie bins for the council's one-off Christmas tree pick-up.

She made herself scarce for the next few days, staying with Jane to give Jon time to collect his stuff. She did not see him again before he left for Dubai.

Chapter Eighty-Seven

About two weeks after the break-up, Kirsty went for Sunday lunch at her dad's. This time when India opened the door, she didn't seem ready to run straight out of it.

'Excellent. You're here,' she said.

Her dad cooked this time. Linzi was sitting at the kitchen table, flicking through the Sunday papers while Stu basted a roast chicken. The atmosphere was very much lighter than it had been before Christmas. India even offered to help her dad with the lunch.

'Guess what? I'm going to do Drama and Theatre Studies,' she said, when they were all sitting down at the table.

'On the condition that she takes it seriously,' said Stu.

'Thank you, Kirsty, for helping me to convince him.'

'You did that,' said Kirsty. 'With your excellent last-minute performance in the chorus. Next year, you could be the lead.'

'You're the best big sister in the world.'

'What's happening with Jon?' Linzi asked. It was a natural sequitur from talking about the show.

'He's in Dubai,' said Kirsty. 'I heard it through Elaine. I bumped into her in town and she said she'd got a text message.'

'Are you going to stay in Newbay?' asked Stu.

'For the time being. I've got to give three months' notice on the rent on the flat. After that . . . Well, I had an audition.'

She told them all about *Les Mis*.

'Wow,' said India. 'My big sister in a proper theatre.'

'I've got to get the part first.'

'They wouldn't dare give it to anyone else,' said Stu.

As it happened, Kirsty did not get the part in *Les Mis*, but the producer who saw her audition instead suggested she put herself forward for a production of *The Lion King*, which would play in Exeter for six months. That suited Kirsty. And it meant she still wouldn't have to move out of Newbay. She could commute.

The thing was, Kirsty had come to realise that she loved Newbay far more than she had ever loved Jon. She would never have believed that she could come to be so fond of a run-down seaside town, but there it was. A warm glow in her heart when she thought of the place. She wanted to stay by the sea. Though she would probably have to work a little more on expanding her social life.

Kirsty had been to the NEWTS just a couple of times since the last night of *Cinderella*. She was relieved that everyone who had worked with her on the production was still friendly. She had worried that their sympathies would lay with poor, humiliated Jon. Instead, the gang seemed glad to see her. Lauren even invited Kirsty to join her on a girls' night out with her friends from the television station. That resulted in a dozen selfies to remember.

It was great to see Bernie and Vince, in particular. Vince was still attending AA meetings every day and though he had only been off the sauce for a month, he was physically transformed. His face was no longer red and puffy. He'd lost some weight around the middle. And his mood was very different too. He was no longer the cynical old git she had come to know so well. He was gentler and softer. More likely to laugh at himself than at others. And he was endlessly solicitous to Bernie. Kirsty could almost see why Bernie had fallen for Vince in the first place now.

Since the last performance of *Cinderella*, two big NEWTS' mysteries had been solved. The phantom graffiti artist who defaced all the posters had been unmasked. It was Glynis. Glynis, of all people! Turned out that the 'community service' she kept dashing off to do, really was *community service* and not, as everyone had assumed, charity work. Unknown to the NEWTS, she had received a community service order as punishment for defacing a picture of the Queen which hung in the council offices where she worked by day. She'd also sprayed a swear word on the side of the police station. Graffiti was a compulsion for Glynis. When they found out, the NEWTS committee invited her to design their posters rather than deface them, in the hope of channelling her compulsion there.

Leading the move for leniency was Trevor Fernlea.

'You understand the need for forgiveness when you get to my age,' he said.

'Which is?' Glynis was finally bold enough to ask.

'Eighty-three,' he told her quite simply. Annette, who had put money on eighty-three in a NEWTS sweepstake, bought everyone a drink with her winnings. Out of Trevor's earshot, the committee resolved to present him with a 'long service' award at the next NEWTS' 'Oscar Night' party.

So the NEWTS swam along. For Kirsty it was odd to be at the theatre with two notable absences. Not just Jon. Kirsty had not seen Ben since that last night of the run. She had not seen him since she turned and fled the stage, dropping his hand at the end of the curtain call as though it were burning hot.

'We haven't seen anything of him since that night,' said Annette.

'Haven't even had a text,' said Lauren.

'I think he might have taken Thea to join the NATS instead,' said Bernie.

It seemed obvious why.

No, Kirsty told herself. That was such a self-absorbed conclusion to draw.

At the last performance, Ben had looked horrified when the audience chanted for Cinderella to say 'yes' to Buttons instead of her prince. He had only been acting his tender feelings for her. The connection they'd had was as unreal as the fairy godmother's magic. It only worked under the spotlights. It was just that old showmance thing again.

She thought about texting him, but decided against it. He hadn't rushed to contact her.

At the end of January, Kirsty got an email from Jon.

'I wanted you to hear this from me instead of on the grapevine. I've met somebody new and I've fallen in love.'

So quickly? Kirsty found herself smiling. All the anguish she had felt over whether she might have feelings for Ben when all along Jon can't really have been sure about their relationship either. She responded at once.

'Thank you for letting me know.' Then she added a couple of kisses.

Having received Jon's email definitely made Kirsty feel lighter. It immediately absolved her of the guilt she had been feeling since she told him they couldn't be married. Despite the drama of the broken engagement, Jon's life hadn't been ruined. He was carrying on very happily indeed. Kirsty also realised that for pretty much the whole of her relationship with Jon she had been holding her breath. Always waiting for the next barbed comment disguised as helpful advice. She didn't miss him at all. She could breathe freely. Breathe the fresh sea air . . .

Chapter Eighty-Eight

Early on a Sunday morning at the beginning of February, the beach was deserted. The tourists would not be back for months. Even the locals were staying indoors. Except for the odd crazy swimmer. There was always someone in the sea, convinced that the ice-cold water was doing them the world of good. Kirsty shivered just thinking about it. If she was going swimming, then it had to be so hot that she would sizzle when she got out of the water to dry off.

Instead, Kirsty got her exercise by walking backwards and forwards across Duckpool Bay. She had done five circuits by the time she noticed the little girl.

It was Thea, running after her grandmother's small Border Terrier who, in turn, was running after a ball. The ball rolled close to Kirsty's feet. She scooped it up. Judy's terrier pogoed around Kirsty's legs, yapping that she should throw the ball again at once.

Kirsty dutifully hurled the ball back towards Thea. To Thea's astonishment and delight, she managed to pluck the ball out of mid-air, like an England cricket team fielder.

'Great catch!' Kirsty shouted.

'Cinderella!' Thea shouted back. 'It's you!'

Ben was on his way down the steps.

'Hey,' he said when he got to them.

'Hey,' said Kirsty.

'How are you?'

'Oh, you know. And you?'

'The same.'

'I can't believe how nice it is today. It's almost like spring.'

Kirsty pushed ahead with the small talk when what she really wanted to say was, 'Where have you been, Ben? Why have you been avoiding me?'

'Supposed to rain tomorrow,' Ben said.

'Buster!' Thea suddenly shouted. 'That way's quicksand.'

It was too late.

Kirsty and Ben ran after the dog. Then Kirsty stumbled backwards and planted her right boot in exactly the wrong spot. Before she knew it, the sand was up to her shin.

'Help!' she shouted.

Ben and Thea were quickly to the rescue. Thea stood back while Ben held out both his hands to Kirsty and tugged to get her free. Thea wrapped her arms around his waist to add her own effort. It wasn't long before Kirsty was back on the safe dry sand. Her wellington boot, alas, was not so lucky.

Kirsty stood on one leg. Thea helped her to stay steady.

'I'm going to have to hop all the way home!' she wailed.

'Was it a very expensive boot?' Ben asked.

'Stupidly,' said Kirsty. 'For a welly.'

'Well, it's gone now,' said Ben.

The sand had closed over the top of it.

'But wellies aren't expensive,' said Thea.

'They are if you've got feet as big as mine and you don't want to wear a big pair of men's boots. What am I going to do?'

'Did you walk here?' Ben asked. 'To the beach?'

'Yes,' said Kirsty. 'The car's back at the flat.'

'We can give you a lift,' said Thea.

'You've got to get to our car first,' said Ben. 'I can carry you.'

'Don't be ridiculous.'

'I've carried you before,' he pointed out, reminding Kirsty of a night on another beach.

'If I can lean on you, then I can probably hop.'

Ben stuck a stick in the sand.

'I don't know how long that will stay there but I'm going to ring the council and let them know this bit of the beach needs some warning signs,' he said.

'Would I have gone in up to my neck if you hadn't pulled me out?' Kirsty asked.

'Probably,' said Ben.

Thea's mouth fell open.

'No, you'd have been OK. Until the tide came in.'

Thea and Buster went on ahead with two pound coins and instructions to buy Kirsty a coffee from the kiosk to keep her warm while she sat on the sea wall and waited for Ben to return with the car.

'If the NEWTS ever do *Treasure Island*,' said Ben. 'You should audition for Long John Silver. You're pretty good at this hopping lark.'

'Very funny,' said Kirsty.

Kirsty wrapped her arm around Ben's neck. As she did so, she caught a whiff of the aftershave she had come to like so much when they were on stage together. And then Ben put his arm around her waist.

'Just for extra support.'

* * *

'You're still in the same flat,' Ben observed when they got to Kirsty's home.

'Yeah,' said Kirsty. 'I just extended the lease. I'm working in Exeter.'

'I didn't realise you were still in Newbay. Maybe I'll see you around.'

'At the NEWTS?'

'I think my Buttons was a one-off,' Ben told her. 'I'm not really cut out for the stage. I'm sure Jon would agree.'

'I don't know what he would say. We're not together any more.'

Kirsty thought for just a second that a look of pleasant surprise passed over Ben's face but if it did, it disappeared quickly.

'I'm sorry,' was all he said. 'I didn't know. I haven't seen anyone from the NEWTS since the night—'

'I said no.'

Another smile flickered on Ben's lips.

Kirsty wondered if she should invite them in – Ben, Thea and Buster – but before she could do so, Ben told her that they had to be getting back. Judy was expecting them. And that was that. Kirsty waved them off.

Chapter Eighty-Nine

Back at the house, Thea was eager to tell Judy all about the quicksand adventure. The way she told it, Kirsty had been right up to her neck in the treacherous mud before Ben pulled her out. It was a miracle she hadn't lost more than a welly. But Judy wasn't really interested in the old rubber boot. She said to her son, 'So, she's still in Newbay. And Jon Manley is in Dubai. Without her?'

'Yes, Mum,' said Ben.

'How come you've just found out?'

Ben was too embarrassed to tell his mother that after he rushed from the theatre after the last night, he'd blocked every single NEWTS number in his phone so that nobody could tell him what was happening if they wanted to. The last thing he wanted was to be invited to Jon and Kirsty's engagement party.

'And you've still got two tickets to the theatre in February and nobody to take along with you.'

'I'll think of somebody.'

'Seems to me that the person you should be asking is obvious.'

Ben shrugged the huge hint off.

'It doesn't have to be romantic,' his mother pointed out. 'You can go to the theatre as friends. Though I always thought she liked you just as much as you liked her.'

Ben pretended not to hear. He all but said 'la la la . . .'

The rest of the day passed quietly. Thea was absorbed in drawing. Judy was reading a cookery book. Ben was trying to get some work done. But at four in the afternoon, Ben suddenly asked, 'Mum, would you mind keeping an eye on Thea for a couple of hours. There's something I've got to do before it gets too dark.'

'Of course,' said Judy. 'But what—'

'I'll tell you when I've done it,' said Ben.

Judy grinned and gave him the thumbs-up. No one knew Ben Teesdale like his mum did.

Chapter Ninety

Back at home and feeling much warmer, having changed out of her soggy jeans, Kirsty called Jane to catch up on her news. Jane was full of excitement about her wedding plans, which were beginning to come together already. A date had been set for June. Kirsty had agreed to be matron of honour, though on the strict understanding that she would get to choose her own outfit.

'No lilac. No empire-line.'

Jane asked how Kirsty was getting on. Kirsty had yet to tell her about the email she'd received from Jon, telling her he had already moved on and was in a relationship with someone new. She told her now.

'Well,' said Jane. 'Good luck to her. But what else is going on? Have you see Buttons?'

'You mean Ben?'

'That's the one. Have you seen him?'

'I saw him today actually. On the beach.'

'The scene of the crime.' Jane referred back to the curry night and the 'near kiss'.

'Not that beach.'

Kirsty recounted the embarrassing encounter, which had ended in her missing a boot.

'He came to your rescue!'

'But he didn't ask to see me again.'

'Did you ask him?'

'Of course not.'

'Kirsty!' Jane sighed.

'If he was interested, I would know by now, wouldn't I?'

'Did he know you'd split up with Jon before today?'

Then the door-bell rang. It wasn't late but Kirsty wasn't expecting anybody. She asked Jane to stay on the line while she went to the door and checked that her caller wasn't bringing bad news. Jane agreed. Since Greg died, they both had a dread horror of unexpected callers after dark. Even if it was still relatively early. Jane promised she would not come off the line until she knew all was well.

'I'm ready to drive over if you need me,' she said as Kirsty walked to the door with the phone still at her ear.

'It's probably for one of the neighbours,' said Kirsty. 'People forget which flat their friends live in so they ring my bell instead because it's number one.'

Kirsty picked up the intercom. She could see no one on the grainy screen.

'Who is it?' she asked.

A male figure stepped into view. She couldn't see his face.

'Not today, thanks,' she said.

Then the man moved so that she could see him more clearly.

'I'll call you back,' she told Jane.

'What! Wait! Don't you dare go without telling me what's going on. What's happening?'

'You're never going to believe this.'

'Tell me.'

'It's Ben.'

Kirsty buzzed him in.

Chapter Ninety-One

Ben looked nervous when he finally got to Kirsty's front door.

'It's already dark,' he said. 'If it's too late and you're doing something or you just don't want any visitors, I can turn around and go right away.'

'I'm not doing anything than can't be interrupted,' she said. 'Come on in. It's cold outside. Baby,' she added, reminding Ben of their singsong at the Bella Vista.

Ben stepped into the flat. Kirsty was reminded of how shyly he had waited on the doorstep when bringing India home in the early hours of New Year's Day. She saw him make a surreptitious inventory of the hallway. She wondered if he was checking for any sign of Jon. There was none, Kirsty knew that. Jon was thousands of miles away. Both physically and psychologically for Kirsty now.

'To what do I owe this pleasure?' Kirsty asked.

'I . . .' Ben had something behind his back. Kirsty felt her cheeks growing warmer as she wondered what he was hiding. Had he bought her flowers? Kirsty cocked her head. Her smile softened. If he had bought her flowers, if this visit was for the reason she hoped, then she wanted Ben to know that it was OK. He could say what he wanted to say. She was happy to see him. She was ready to say 'yes' to whatever he wanted to ask. There was a long moment of silence before Ben said,

'*I've come in search of the woman to whom this beautiful slipper belongs.*'

'What?'

And he suddenly flourished Kirsty's missing wellington boot.

'You found it!' She laughed.

It was clean and shining. Kirsty hadn't seen the boot look so good since the day she first saw it in the shoe department at Chillings.

'Did you really go back to the beach and pull it out of the mud?'

Ben nodded. 'It was easy,' he lied.

'And then you cleaned it?'

Ben nodded again.

'I can't believe you'd do that. But I'm very glad you did. Thank you.'

Kirsty reached for the boot but Ben suddenly fell to one knee, still holding the wellie as though it were every bit as precious as Cinders' missing slipper.

'*Madam,*' he continued, paraphrasing the *Cinderella* script. '*Are you the fair maiden with whom I danced on the beach in the moonlight? With whom I stood beneath the pier, listening to the sound of my racing heart drowning out the crashing waves? Are you the beautiful woman in the yellow mackintosh I should have kissed when I had the chance?*'

Kirsty grinned from ear to ear.

'*That I am, dear prince,*' she said. '*That I am.*'

'Well, I'm afraid you'll have to prove it by putting this wellington boot on.'

It was a struggle. Getting wellies on was always a struggle for Kirsty. But she did it. And when she did it, Ben lifted her to her feet, so that her face was level with his.

Eye to eye.

Nose to nose.

Mouth to mouth.

'You *are* my real princess,' said Ben.

And then he kissed her.

The fortune-teller had been right all along. Kirsty was where love is.

And they both lived happily ever after.

Acknowledgements:

Being a writer is a wonderful job for many reasons but possibly the best is that it gives you an excuse to peek behind the curtains at other people's lives. Or should I say 'peek behind the tabs', Ben Tisdall?

When I asked Ben to tell me a little about his experiences in the amateur dramatic world, I had no idea how generously he and his fellow 'toads' would respond to my request. The TOADS Theatre Company, who perform at The Little Theatre in Torquay, are a fantastically talented bunch. In particular, I would like to thank Roger Heath, who very kindly gave me a tour of the theatre itself. Meanwhile, Lydia Dockray, Jessica Hunter, Jon Manley, Craig Northway, Anna Reynolds and Jolyon Tuck had me in stitches for hours with their stories from behind the scenes. Thank you all. Names have been changed. Except for Jon's.

In London, I was lucky enough to be able to pick the brain of actor Stephen Carlile, who played Scar in the European musical adaption of Disney's *The Lion King*. Thank you, Stephen, for being so kind in answering all my questions.

I met Stephen through Bernie Strachan, fellow novelist and dear friend. I am fortunate to have a great bunch of literary girlfriends. Bernie, Victoria Routledge, Michele Gorman, Alex Potter, Fiona Walker and Lauren

Henderson – brilliant writers all – I don't know what I would do without you. Thank you too, dear Bia Nasr, for your friendship. I am working on that Tuscan guest suite!

A Fairy Tale For Christmas is my twenty-first Chris /Chrissie Manby novel for Hodder. As I reach this literary coming of age (getting older but, I suspect, not maturing), I am grateful for being in the care of a wonderful editor. Emily Kitchin, for your wise insights and your gentle notes, I salute you. Thank you also to Eleni Lawrence, Lucy Upton, Louise Swannell and Richard Peters for getting my books into readers' hands. Thank you, Nicky Lovick, for your expert copy-editing. The beautiful cover is the work of Joy Laforme.

My agent Laetitia Rutherford at Watson, Little has been another valuable early reader. Thank you, Laetitia, for your kindness and patience and careful suggestions too.

As ever, I'd like to thank my family: Mum, Dad and my sister Kate, who have always been there for me. Also my nephews, Harrison and Lukas, who never fail to make me laugh. Even if it is by asking Siri 'Is Auntie Chris a rubbish writer?'

Don't answer that, Siri.

Finally, thank you, Mark, for everything. But especially for the tea.

Do you wish this wasn't the end?

Join us at www.hodder.co.uk, or follow us on
Twitter @hodderbooks to be a part of our community
of people who love the very best in books and reading.

Whether you want to discover more about a book
or an author, watch trailers and interviews, have the
chance to win early limited editions, or simply browse
our expert readers' selection of the very best books,
we think you'll find what you're looking for.

And if you don't,
that's the place to tell us what's missing.

We love what we do, and we'd love you to be part of it.

www.hodder.co.uk

@hodderbooks

HodderBooks

HodderBooks